The Carmelite

BOOKS BY
ELGIN GROSECLOSE

Fiction

THE PERSIAN JOURNEY OF THE REVEREND ASHLEY
WISHARD AND HIS SERVANT FATHI

ARARAT

THE FIREDRAKE

Political Economy

MONEY: THE HUMAN CONFLICT

INTRODUCTION TO IRAN

The Carmelite

A Novel

by

ELGIN GROSECLOSE

New York · 1955

THE MACMILLAN COMPANY

IN HIS PRAISE

and to

My Friends of the Persia Missions

Author's Note

The stanza from the hymn by St. Theoctistus, given on page 102, is from the edited translation by John Mason Neale; the verse from the *Masnavi* on page 147 is from the translation by E. H. Whinfield.

Contents

The Carmelite friar, Juan Thaddeus, whom the Pope sends on a quasi-diplomatic mission to the court of the legendary Abbas the Great, Shah of Persia, is a man of great courage and determination. He has to be, for his mission is both dangerous and delicate: to win freedom from persecution for the Christians in that heathen land and to spread the glory of the Gospel. His chances of success hinge on the unpredictable personality and disposition of the Shah himself, an intelligent and imaginative ruler but a barbarian at heart, subject to violent fits of jealous rage and capable then of monstrous cruelty.

Abbas is strongly attracted to the lovely Princess Shamala, his niece, who resists his advances and becomes Fray Juan's first convert. A desperate struggle is personified in Shamala — a struggle between the demands of the body and the desiring of the soul, between the material power of an earthly king and the spiritual power of the King of Heaven.

Prologue

The mother church of the monastic order of Our Lady of Carmel, Reformed, better known as the Discalced, or Barefooted, Carmelites, is the church of Santa Maria della Scala in Rome. Santa Maria della Scala is situated in the Trastevere district, across the Tiber from the ancient city of the seven hills, but is not to be confused with the imposing, beautifully adorned, sixth century church of Santa Maria in Trastevere, the object of much pilgrim and tourist visitation, from which it is distant not five minutes' walk. The Carmelite church, while large, and gracefully proportioned, and marked by a magnificent altar, by some interesting murals, and by several charming chapels, gives the general impression of neglect, of indifference either to tourists or to communicants, and of self-wrapped solitude. This may be in the spirit of the Discalced Carmelites, or rather of that division within the order that has insisted that its monastic function is contemplation, solitude, and retreat, as opposed to those who hold that its proper function, in the spirit of its founder Teresa of Ávila, is the conversion of the nations through preaching and the teaching of the Gospel. At the time that the church was given to the order by the Pope, in 1597, the former opinion held sway; and it still exercises a strong influence among the membership.

For even monastic orders, disciplined to obedience and austerity and subjection of the will, are sometimes riven with dissension born of strongly held convictions as to the divine purpose in human affairs.

Adjoining the church, and reached by a staircase leading from the vestibule through an ancient apothecary's shop, is the convent. Along the gloomy main corridor of the house hang the portraits of the Fathers General and other dignitaries of the order of the seventeenth and eighteenth centuries. The order was then largely Spanish in membership, and one may note Spanish characteristics in the faces that look down upon the sandaled friars flitting by in the crepuscular light: the piety of a Philip II, the fanaticism of a Torquemada, the mysticism of an El Greco, the bold adventuresomeness of a Cortez or a Pizarro—and sometimes the gentleness of a Murillo, or the humor of a Cervantes.

Among the portraits is that of Father John Thaddeus of St. Elisaeus, first Bishop of Isfahan, and in the half-light of the corridor it is not possible to resolve the meaning which the artist has caught in his expression. One may observe something of the strong practicality of a Charles V and something also of the mysterious two-edged penetration into life that characterizes the insight of the Carmelite poet Fray Juan de la Cruz. The eyes of the bishop seem bent through the gloom toward the sanctuary of the church where rears the altar and where rest the remains of the historic dead. His lips seem about to speak—and, knowing his story, one may imagine him recalling the saying of Jesus which was, in a sense, the legend of his life:

No man, having put his hand to the plough, and looking back, is fit for the kingdom of God.

Set into the floor of the church, gleaming pallidly in the candlelight, is a marble gravestone almost as old as the church, worn and polished by three centuries of passing feet. The inscription, faint but still legible, is to Sir Robert Sherley, English nobleman, and to *Theresia Sampsonia Amazonitis, Sampsuffi Circassiae Principis filia,* "who, fortified by piety, transported her husband's body from Persia to Rome." Sir Robert is he whose journeyings and embassies in behalf of the Persian Shah in the early years of the seventeenth century effected a Persian mode in European dress and manners of the period. He died in Kasvin, Persia, in 1628. His wife, as the inscription indicates, managed, with great difficulty, to bring his body to Rome for burial. Subsequently she took a house nearby and lived in retirement as a tertiary of the Carmelite order until her death, at the age of seventy-nine, in the year 1668.

How an English nobleman whose house was attached to the cause of Elizabeth and the Protestant Reformation, and a Circassian princess, born into the Eastern Orthodox faith, should find final resting places in a Carmelite church in the city of Rome is a question to tantalize the curious. That a lady whose beauty and charm and vivacity were remarkable in an age of remarkable women, who had spent a lifetime in court and society, should suddenly abandon these glittering scenes for the withdrawn and dedicated routine of a lay sister is also a question not without interest to the devout and the romantic.

A partial explanation may be suggested by the first of her names—Teresa. It is common knowledge in the histories of the times that this name—that of the founder of the Carmelite Reform, the Spanish nun Teresa of Ávila—was given her when she was baptized into the Catholic Church. What is not so commonly known is that both her baptism and the solemnization of her marriage to Sir Robert Sherley were at the hand of the Carmelite friar John Thaddeus of St. Elisaeus, the same who was afterward consecrated Bishop of Isfahan, he whose eyes in the portrait seem to be fixed upon some mystery of his meditation. . . .

Sir Robert Sherley is not to be confused with his elder brother Sir Anthony Sherley, who died in penury and disgrace in Spain and who also served the Persian Shah as ambassador on one occasion. It was this elder brother who in a way started the whole chain of circumstance linking the histories of these various personages. Anthony was a gentleman of fortune as Robert was a gentleman of honor; as Robert pursued duty, devotion, and rectitude, Anthony pursued the main chance. On a stage filled with illustrious figures—among them Elizabeth of England, Henry of Bourbon, Philip II of Spain, Boris Godunov of Russia, Akbar of India, and Shah Abbas of Persia—Anthony moved with ease and assurance, serving several of these monarchs in turn, and making them all serve his own ambitious ends. In the year 1599 he took his brother Robert with him on adventure to the East, where a rising star in that firmament—Abbas Safi Safavid, Shahinshah of Iran—engaged his services to promote a daring scheme of world diplomacy. This was no less than an alliance of the powers of Christendom with that of Persia in war against that of the restless and expanding Ottoman Empire.

Anthony's embassy was not a great success so far as its main objects were concerned, and it was not until he reached Rome, in 1601, that his proposals met with encouragement. Pope Clement VIII, a pontiff whose astuteness was matched only by his piety, saw advantages in what the Shah's ambassador offered, and entered into correspondence with the Shah—a correspondence which subsequently involved the Order of Our Lady of Carmel.

So much is history. This much may be read in the chronicles or discovered in the archives. But beyond the fenced in kingdom of recorded fact lies a mysterious region of speculation which is beyond the province of history. Upon the horizon of fact, tempting the imagination to adventure, flash the Northern lights of mood and motive, and in their play and interplay, their soar and subsidence, are formed the images of a tale—of figures moving in the mingled hues of enthusiasm and despair, of cloud-borne castles of probity and the assaulting flames of envy, of snow-rimmed heights of aspiration and the muted caverns of meditation, of salt-encrusted wastes of desire, and the gushing rivulets of charity. . . .

Insubstantial, these images? As insubstantial as the hunger that drives the beggar wailing through the bazaar or the fisherman to his nets or the pilgrim toward the gilded shrine of the Imam. Yes, as insubstantial as the nothingness between the cords of the net by which the fisher snares the fish that feeds his hunger. And as the cord without the nothingness is not a net, so it is that with the net of fiction we pursue the elusive truth of experience.

This, then, is the adventure ahead. This is the realm into which, leaving behind the kingdom of fact, we now enter . . .

PART ONE

Papal Diplomacy

I

It was afternoon of the third day since his departure from Naples that Fray Juan of St. Elisaeus arrived on the outskirts of Rome, coming by the ancient Via Appia. There, on the heights above the catacombs of San Sebastian—now being extensively explored, at the Pope's direction, by the scholar Antonio Bosio—were a wayside shrine, Della Grazia with a fountain nearby, at which carters were watering their mules, and some stalls of fruiterers and greengrocers. From the elevation one could see the walls, the spires, and the domes of the city, shimmering in the coral and amber haze of the summer afternoon.

The friar allowed his eyes for a moment to rove in wonder over the view—the imposing Sant' Urbano tomb to his right, the San Sebastian basilica ahead, and in the distance, resplendent through the haze, dominating the scene, the majestic cupola of the still unfinished San Pietro—and then, the Angelus bell having rung, he crossed himself and, dismissing these monuments of the external world, retired to the shrine to recite the office and the litany to the Virgin.

The image before whom the friar knelt was one of the more lovely Italian conceptions. In contrast to the austere Spanish Virgin of the monastery, it was a thing of blue and compassionate eyes, a figure gowned in azure and slightly inclined as though to hear better the whispered petitions lifted to her in prayer, a face of delicate purity framed in an oval by an enclosing wimple of white, the lips formed into a tender and beatific smile. The friar gazed into the face of the image, his hands clasped, his cowl thrown back revealing his tonsured head, his strong Spanish face with its bony forehead and its large dark eyes glowing with such rapture that one would have said a special communication passed between the two.

Kneeling nearby, a woman of the class recently expelled from Rome, with her head modestly covered by a scarf but with the cut of her dress indiscreetly revealing her throat to the cleft of her breasts, was drawn from her devotions by the presence of the friar, and allowed her eyes to rest upon him in curious appraisal. Her momentary glance must have discovered something in him which even his frayed, patched, and dust-covered habit could not conceal, and which the most rigorous asceticism had not entirely destroyed, and for all his emaciation her eyes continued to stray in his direction while her lips moved in the recitation of the litany.

The friar, finishing the office, became aware of the lady's attention, and, quickly drawing his cowl over his head, stood up and stepped into the open. Erect, his height was impressive, and he moved with the angular grace of a man of great purpose and directness who has, however, deliberately confined himself in bonds for the attainment of his purpose. It was a quality of personality all the more appealing to the lady, something fresh in her experience, and being touched by it she returned to her devotions with new contrition and urgency.

About the fountain, the carters were exchanging the news of the day while their mules drank. It was strange news. In the seven years since Fray Juan had left the world much had happened, and new events and new personalities dominated the world's attention. There was still talk of the campaign in the Lowlands, and the defiance that the heretics were making against the Spanish throne, but it appeared that this war, which had been going on since Fray Juan was a child, was nearing its end. There was talk also of the revolt in Russia; but, most of all, talk turned upon the revival of Turkish power, in eclipse since the destruction of the Turkish navy at Lepanto, but now once more threatening the Empire and the heart of Europe, and making the eastern Mediterranean unsafe.

A coach of state, drawn by four horses at a gallop, swayed on its thorough braces as it thundered by on the Via Appia toward Rome. The rolling wheels, swerving toward the curbing, threw up a cloud of dust that veiled the fountain and settled in a film upon the fruits and vegetables in the nearby stalls. As the dust subsided, the coach could be seen, swaying from side to side, against the outline in the distance of the ancient and unimposing little church of Domine Quo Vadis, that marked the spot where St. Peter, fleeing from the persecution of Nero, was met by Christ in a vision, and turned back to Rome and to martyrdom.

One of the carters, a man from Lombardy, of fair complexion and intelligent gray eyes, followed the coach with an admiring look.

"Cardinal Alferri," he announced. "I saw the crest on the door. He's bound for the Quirinal. Another meeting of the Council. Something's in the wind."

"I'll wager it's about the Sherley embassy," said another. "May it cause the Turk to knock his head toward Mecca in trembling and fear."

"Have done with prayers and embassies," another said vehemently. "A Crusade, I say, or the Turks will be at the gates of Rome." He was a swarthy man, a Neapolitan in his middle fifties, with a long scar upon his cheek, a retired condottiere who had fought with the Venetians against the Turks.

"My boy, but now come from Marseilles," he continued, "tells me that they sighted a Turkish man o' war in the Corsican Straits, and but for the arrival of a Genoese carrack would have been overhauled. I say it's a high pass of affairs when the Turks can show themselves in these waters. A Crusade, I say, a Crusade."

"Mayhap the Holy Father's diplomacy may make another war unnecessary," said the Lombard. "They say he cogitates an alliance that will frighten the Grand Signore from his ottoman. My advice is, trust his Holiness. He's a clever man, and knows the difference between 'soldiers' and 'solidi.' "

"Why, what mean you?"

"This: that money is the price of all things. Buy peace. One sequin is worth twenty men-at-arms. Peter's pence are not gathered for nothing, and the coffers of the Treasury are now begging for work to do. What better work than buying peace?"

The mules had finished drinking, and were tossing the water in their mouths. Fray Juan came over to the fountain to wet his parched lips and drink of the water.

The carters moved aside with perfunctory reverence. Asceticism was not in vogue. In Rome there were many friars about in carriages, embroidered cassocks, and with jeweled crucifixes and pendants hung by golden chains about their necks. When the friar had drunk, he spoke to the carter. "Can you direct me to the church of Santa Maria della Scala?" he asked.

He had a strong, resonant voice, but he spoke in almost a whisper, like one unused to conversation, and in a melodic monotone that made one think at once of plainsong chanted in chorus.

"Santa Maria della Scala?" repeated the Lombard, with a puzzled expression.

"Do any of you know the church?" he asked turning to the others.

"Isn't that across the Tiber, in Trastevere?" the Neapolitan asked. "Given by his Holiness to some new order six or seven years ago?"

"Not a new order," spoke up Fray Juan, his eyes flashing with subdued pride. "The oldest order of all. The Carmelites."

The Neapolitan looked at the friar with skepticism.

"You, a Carmelite?" he exclaimed. "I've seen them in Spain. They don't go about like you. They ride in carriages and live like princes. You're a Spaniard, are you not?" he asked abruptly, at the look of protest in the friar's face. "You have a Spanish accent."

"Yes."

"Then do I not speak the truth?"

Fray Juan began to explain the reformation that had occurred some twenty-five years earlier, through the efforts of Teresa of Ávila and Fray Juan de la Cruz, that led to the establishment of a separate Congregation, but he broke off and contented himself with saying only, "I am of the Discalced."

The Neapolitan, with a curl of his lips, clucked to his mules and drove off. The others went about their various affairs.

Only the Lombard was left, held by an attraction for the friar which he did not understand and which left him rather abashed.

"You look fagged, Father," he said. "Have you come from far?"

"From Naples."

"Afoot?"

"Yes."

"Well," said the Lombard, "you're welcome to a lift. Hop up."
The friar shook his head.

"I can go on foot," he said, and as the mules set out he kept pace
with a long and easy stride.

"Father," asked the Lombard, "if you don't mind, tell me why you
insist on walking—and barefooted too? Is it penance you're doing?"

"I'm not quite barefooted," responded Fray Juan, "though we call
ourselves the Barefooted. I wear sandals, as you see."

"Well, it's all the same. You get sand and dirt under your soles,
and it's like walking on hot nails. Your feet are bruised. Why?"

Again the friar avoided a direct answer.

"Our Lord had nowhere to lay His head," he responded. "Should
I, who seek to follow in His steps, ask for more?"

"Why not? People don't have to live in tents because the patriarchs
did. Everybody has a house. Money makes the world go round—now
that we know it does go round. You go barefooted, and make no
custom for the shoemaker, and so he goes hungry. You eat lentils, and
the butchers starve for want of trade. Where'd we be if it weren't
for people eating and drinking, and making houses for themselves?
Where'd I be? I've a family to support."

"It is an individual question," said the friar, "a matter of personal
calling. Some are called to tread the high way, others the low. Some
are called to feast, others to fast. Some are called to rejoice, others
to mourn. Some sit in solitude, in prayer and in meditation, and
others preach—"

He broke off, caught in his own personal dilemma. He had felt a
calling to preach. The words of the Gospel again filled his ears: *I have
chosen you, and ordained you, that ye should go and bring forth
fruit, and that your fruit should remain.* But preaching was out of the
question for him. To go abroad to proclaim the Gospel was forbidden
him by the requirements of the contemplative and confined existence
to which he had surrendered himself in taking orders. Or was it? That
was the great, disturbing question which would be resolved when he
reached Rome. Until then he must keep silence. He must not even
discuss the matter with this chance acquaintance.

The Lombard, sensing some deep distress within the friar, did not
pursue his questioning. They went on in silence until they came to
the Via di Porta San Sebastiano, followed it past the ruins of the

Circus Maximus, and along the banks of the Tiber until they arrived at the Ponte Sisto. Here the Lombard, after pointing the way, doffed his cap, and took his leave of the friar.

II

The following morning, after a night spent in prayer and with little sleep, Fray Juan was received by the Father General.

Father Peter was a patriarch in the order, a friar who had reached the age of sixty-five and who had been a member since its establishment as a separate Congregation in 1581. By nature kindly and simple-hearted, he had acquired certain dogmatic tendencies as a result of having lived through the dissension in the parent Carmelite order, when Fray Juan de la Cruz joined with Teresa of Ávila to urge a reform and a return to the primitive austerities and rule.

Father Peter received the young friar in the antechamber of the convent—the only room in the house in which conversation was permitted. It was, like the rest of the establishment, almost bare. A crucifix hung on the wall. In one corner a single ruby lamp glowed before an image of Our Lady. On a walnut-topped table were an ink horn and a sand flask, a marble holder for quill pens, a sheaf of paper, a missal, and a breviary. There were two chairs. An aqueous light of early dawn came through a window high in the wall. Faintly, from the street, came the sounds of early-morning traffic.

Father Peter took one of the chairs and with a nod of his head indicated that Fray Juan should take the other. Fray Juan remained standing.

"Do sit, my son," said Father Peter pointedly, "for I have much to say to you."

Thus bidden, Fray Juan sat down, clasping his hands within the folds of his habit.

"It is now three years since I spoke to you in our house in Naples," began Father Peter, "administering our paternal rebuke for expressing certain opinions among the brethren."

"Yes, reverend Father."

"They were not heretical opinions, of course; they were merely inappropriate for a Carmelite."

"Yes, reverend Father."

Father Peter regarded the young man benignly.

"Are you still of these same opinions?" he asked gently.

The young friar bowed his head.

"Yes, reverend Father," he almost whispered.

"Well, well, but you are of a firm mind," commented the General with a slight shake of his head that expressed both puzzlement and admiration. "Then you must have thought a great deal upon these matters in the interval, and can express your convictions somewhat more clearly than before. Would you please state them again for me."

The friar, taking heart from his superior's manner, looked up and spoke.

"I have thought much about them, as you have said, but as I also at the time took a vow of silence on the subject, my words to express them remain awkward."

"Well, do the best you can, for I would like to hear them from you again." He added, somewhat to the bewilderment of the friar, "It does me good to hear strong language of conviction and enthusiasm from the lips of youth."

"You give me permission then to speak?"

Father Peter made the sign of the cross over the friar.

"I hereby release you from your vow."

Fray Juan bowed his head in acknowledgment.

"When the Baron di Cacurri offered to endow a house for our order in the Holy Land, I thought we should accept the opportunity to become missionaries among the heathen."

"You meant, did you not, that we should not simply found a house on Mount Carmel, reoccupying the ancient site of our foundation, but that the friars should go among the people and preach?"

"Yes, reverend Father, as Our Lord has commanded us, that we go and teach all nations. How can we carry out this expressed will of Our Lord if we stay confined in convents?"

Fray Juan's face had suddenly begun to glow in the ardor of his convictions. The General, noting this, sighed heavily.

"Well, well, but you are of a set mind," he commented again, this time with more admiration than puzzlement. "But I like it, I do like it, for all that you have brought our order to a sorry pass."

"How is that, reverend Father?" exclaimed Fray Juan, his enthusiasm turning now to equally ardent anxiety.

"You would take this tender, shade-grown growth, and set it out of doors, expose it to the burning blasts of all the corrupt and wicked influences of the world. We are not ready for that, my son; we must save our souls, we must preserve this remnant from the Babylonian captivity of this licentious age."

Fray Juan regarded the older man questioningly, eager to speak, yet afraid to overstep his privileges. Father Peter nodded.

"Should we not rather advance upon the sea," Fray Juan asked, "trusting, as did Moses and the hosts of Israel, that the waters of opposition will part and yield us passage to the Promised Land?"

"Ah, you know your Scriptures," commented the General, "but you know not the world. You know not how it was when the ancient rule was mitigated, and the friars thought themselves strong enough to face the world and its temptations. 'Let us go and behold,' they said in their conceit. And so, abandoning their fasts and prayers and their confinement within the walls, they went abroad. They would, they said, minister to the needy. But how subtly the Tempter works! For the rich are in need also, being greatly in need of spiritual nourishment. But in the houses of the rich came invitations to stay and break bread. How could a poor friar refuse? From breaking bread it went to quaffing the cup in fellowship, and then another in greater fellowship, and then to rolling under the table. Such is the progress to the swill troughs of abomination. I need not recount for you the depths to which the monastic orders fell during those days, the abuses and the corruptions which infected the conventual houses. From our own order the scandal of that dissolute genius of the Carmelites, the painter Fra Filippo Lippi, has run throughout Europe. But for such laxities our holy faith might not now be plagued with the Protestant heresy."

Father Peter shook his head as he spoke.

"Such," he continued, "was the condition that led our Mother Teresa, founder of our Discalced Reform, to lift her voice in protest, and to guide the way back to the primitive rule. But only after ordeal was the work accomplished, for the tentacles of the Evil One grip deep. There were those within the order who resisted the reform. With Fray Juan de la Cruz I was taken, and we were beaten like common criminals. My son, you do not recall those terrible times.

But God was with us, and the reformation carried through, and the Congregation of the Barefooted was established."

Father Peter's eyes shone with the remembrance of the victory.

"And now," he concluded, "you would break up and destroy this reform by your ideas of evangelism. Well, be it God's will," he added with a sigh.

The morning light was gathering, and fell upon his bald head so that it glowed roseately, like a nimbus, and Fray Juan felt a warmth of understanding and affection for the old man. He wanted to speak, to assure the General that he was content to abide as he had, to accept the wisdom of his superiors, and to continue in the vocation of a contemplative. This he was willing to do, in the spirit of obedience to those in authority, as to God, as was his bounden duty. But Father Peter had begun speaking again.

"After the administration of our paternal rebuke," he said, "I became troubled in spirit by the strength of your convictions, and considered whether God might not be speaking to our Congregation through you. I appointed a commission to examine into the writings of Mother Teresa, as to whether she considered missionary work an appropriate pursuit for the Congregation. The report made by Father John, to whom I confided the presidency of the committee, was startling to me. Sufficiently so that shortly thereafter I had an audience with his Holiness, with several of the senior fathers of the order, and offered the services of the Discalced for such missionary work as he might desire to send us on."

The young friar gasped in his astonishment, and an exclamation escaped his lips: "Praise God!"

The General turned his head sharply, and asked, "You would be willing to go wherever his Holiness directed in such an enterprise?"

"Oh, yes," exclaimed the friar. Then, catching himself, he added earnestly: "In any case, I am under the Church's discipline to go or to remain as my superiors direct. I have no desire to leave our holy order or its rule."

The old man nodded approvingly.

"I am pleased, for you shall have ample opportunity to test the vigor of your intentions."

The young friar's eyes widened with something between amazement and sudden anxiety.

"Indeed!"

"The Holy Father, I may tell you, was greatly pleased with our offer. Know you the land of Persia?"

"Persia?"

"Aye, the land whose ruler, whom some call Shah and others the Great Sophy, recently sent to his Holiness an Englishman as ambassador."

"I am not acquainted with those matters, reverend Father, but is not Persia the same land whose monarch, Holy Scripture relates, released the Children of Israel from bondage?"

"The same. The Holy Father has asked for several religious of our order to go to this land. Do you accept the call?"

Fray Juan half rose from his chair.

"Aye, with all my heart. When do I leave?"

"Well, well," exclaimed the General, "but you are fixed in your way. Be not so hasty. You know nothing as yet of this venture."

"What is there to know beyond the fact that there lies the infidel, and that God has given into my hand the sharp sword of the faith?"

"You must be patient. This is a matter of high diplomacy. The Persian Shah, I fancy, will not take kindly to ambassadors so impetuous as all this. You must go gently. There is much with which you must be acquainted first."

Suddenly Fray Juan's enthusiasm was checked. The words "diplomacy" and "ambassadors" seemed to startle him, and he murmured, "I do not understand." And in a moment he added: "What need have we friars of dealings with the Shah? Such belong to his Holiness and his Holiness's cardinals and princes of the Church."

"His Persian Majesty has requested envoys from his Holiness, and the opening of diplomatic relations between the two powers," explained the General. "In his wisdom his Holiness has concluded that this request will best be met by sending to the Persian court several members of our Barefooted Order."

Fray Juan's thoughts swam in confusion. What devious wisdom was this in the Holy Father that he should send mendicant friars to represent his Apostolic dignity before an Oriental monarch? Fray Juan had the sensation of one who, playing in the surf, has stepped off a shelf and finds himself floundering in the depths. A feeling of shame, of unworthiness for his calling, overcame him. He bowed his head, as the General regarded him sternly.

"As I do not question the reasons of high policy and divine inspiration that prompted his Holiness to this judgment of the matter, neither do you, I pray you," said the General firmly. "Does this satisfy you?" he asked. "Are you prepared to accept these conditions?"

In a moment the friar recovered himself, and said humbly:

"Forgive me, reverend Father, for having lifted my thoughts to objects too high for me. I have no gifts with which to appear before kings. I am of unlettered speech, knowing only the Scriptures and the commentaries and devotions. Though my father, as you know, was hidalgo, yet our family is of the simpler sort, and I have no familiarity nor understanding with the ways and manners of courts."

" 'Twill serve, 'twill serve," broke in the General. "There will be others with you who have understanding of such things. You are of stout heart, and for that I think well of your going. 'Twill not be easy. Neither the journey—for indeed, as to that I have not the slightest idea how one may journey to the land of Persia without traversing the unfriendly country of the Turks, or the Muscovites, or the long reaches of the African coasts—nor the trials of temptation you may endure in the luxury and intrigue of an Oriental court. You will need to tell your beads often, I dare say. But again, are you prepared to this venture? Do you accept this mission?"

Fray Juan lifted his eyes and gazed into those of his superior.

"Aye, reverend Father," he said passionately, "and may God make me worthy of this trust!"

III

It was in the first week of July that the Carmelites were summoned to a papal audience to receive their letters of credence and to hear from his Holiness Clement VIII his personal instructions for the management of their mission. The audience took place in the newly built Quirinal Palace which the Popes now used for their summer residence. After mounting the broad staircase with its magnificent fresco of "Christ in Glory" by da Forlì, the friars were ushered into a high-ceilinged and spacious chamber where the air was as cool as the air of the plaza was stifling. The floor was carpeted with several over-size rugs of Persian weave, and the high windows were curtained so heavily with velvet and damask that candelabra were necessary for illumination. On a dais at one end was a marble throne chair with crimson seat and arm padding. To protect its occupant from drafts in cold weather it was canopied and heavily curtained.

Father Peter, who accompanied the friars, thought of the contrast between the elegance of these quarters and the narrowness of the cells in the monastery in Trastevere, and it occurred to him that this was symbolic of the new life and career that reared before his charges, in contrast to the old, and the thought filled him with sadness and apprehension.

His Holiness was delayed in coming. He was, the papal attendant whispered, attending a meeting of the Council, over which he was presiding, that was considering the controversy between the Domin-icans and the Jesuits on a moot question of dogma: that of grace. "You must be patient," he added, "for if you know the stubbornness of the Dominicans and the argumentativeness of the Jesuits, you will know that this question will not be readily resolved."

While the friars awaited in silence the Pope's coming, they read their breviaries and told their beads; but the old General's thoughts continued to wander away and to dwell upon the embassy on which his friars were entering and how they were being sent forth—as it seemed to him—like shorn sheep to the hillsides. He had suffered much himself during the dissension and the reform, and he valued the peace that he had found in the return to the ancient discipline of solitude and separation from the world, in absorption in prayer and meditation. He thought the friars were offering a great sacrifice to the Church in forsaking the sanctuary of their cells.

There were five of them awaiting audience. There was, first of all, Father Paul of Jesus Mary, whom the General had designated as head of the mission. Father Paul was the son of a Genoese nobleman; be-fore entering the Carmelite order he had sat in the councils with his father, and in consequence he had some familiarity with court protocol and the structure of diplomacy. He had a fine aristocratic dignity that would bear up well in the most elaborate court. On the other hand, he was extremely ascetic, very strict with himself, and of dogmatic tendencies, strongly attached to his meditations and devotions. He was somewhat frail in health. For these reasons the General had had some misgivings about the matter of sending Father Paul of Jesus Mary, though in the end he had concluded to do so.

The second friar was Father Vincent of St. Francis, who had been a cavalry officer in the Spanish army before he was reformed, dedicated himself to the Church, and took orders. His knowledge of horses and of things military had commended him to the General as having qualifications that would be useful in treating with the Shah. They would persuade the Shah that the Pope's emissaries, for all that they were friars, were not entirely ignorant of affairs. Father Vincent was a foil to Father Paul; he was a man of robust health, with a large and powerful frame, and his manner was as jovial, as effervescent, as that of Father Paul was solemn and contained. He was thirty years of age.

On the third member, Father John Thaddeus of St. Elisaeus, the General had not been able to make up his mind. For all his admiration and even affection for the friar, it seemed to him that he was wanting something in maturity, judgment, and discipline—that he was unstable and inclined to allow his impulsiveness to run away with him. Mostly, however, he questioned Fray Juan's aptitude for what the young man considered his true vocation, that of preaching. It seemed to him that the friar was much too diffident in the presence of company to make a good discourse, that he lacked the charm, the ease of manner, the self-assurance and the facility of speech either for the functions of preaching and evangelizing or for representing the Pope's dignity in court. But he had such enthusiasm for missionary work, he had such stubborn convictions as to his calling, that the aging General could not well deny him. And he was of strong and hearty constitution. At the thought of his interview with the friar, the old man sighed deeply. . . .

Besides these three, there were two lay brothers who would accompany the fathers on their journey to Persia. One of them, Francisco Riodolid de Peralta, was also a former soldier and had served for many years with the Spanish forces in the Netherlands. Invalided with a pension, he had offered his services to the Church, and had been accepted as a lay brother in the Carmelite order. The idea in sending him, as it had been in the case of Father Vincent, was that his knowledge of military matters might be of some use in treating with the

Shah. The other lay brother, John of the Assumption, was an Italian from Umbria, a kindly little fellow with small learning but much devotion, whose services would be to carry the slender purse allotted for the journey, and to attend to the necessities of the party.

After long waiting, his Holiness finally appeared. There was a stirring in the outer chamber, and the Pope entered attended by a chamberlain and a secretary. He moved rapidly—in a waddling gait, for he was very large—to the marble throne chair and, drawing his garments about him like a man with a chill, sat down. He was still in the high ecclesiastical garb in which he had presided over the Council, and, in the folded splendor of his dress that concealed all but his head and two white hands, he looked like a draper buried in the bolts of cloth he has spread out for a customer's selection. His manner was preoccupied, and he appeared irritable; the Council must have been a turbulent one. An air of effeteness and dilettantism was conveyed by the thin, sensitive nose and the sensual lips, hedged about by a silky beard.

Father Peter was inclined to wonder whether this Persian embassy were really as significant in the papal statecraft as he had been led to believe, but he was too experienced to be misled by outward appearances. Pope Clement VIII was a prelate to be reckoned with—one of the most extraordinary personages to wear the Fisherman's Ring in generations, a figure produced by the times and the mysterious power of the Church to bring forth leaders in moments of crisis. Appearance to the contrary, he was notably pious, an austere ascetic who confessed daily and wore a hair shirt beneath his pontifical robes. His reign had been dedicated equally to restoring the moral and spiritual authority of the Church and the political influence of the Roman See, both badly shattered by the corruption of the hierarchy and the spread of the Lutheran heresy. The Protestants now controlled all northern Europe, to the great loss of papal influence and papal revenue, and even in those lands where the populations still held allegiance to the Catholic faith the authority of the Holy See was ignored in matters of politics. Even that staunch Catholic of Spain, Philip II, who had spent a lifetime in war against the heretics, maintained a running quarrel with Rome and for a time ceased to forward contributions to the papal treasury.

Such were the conditions which Clement VIII faced on ascending the pontifical throne, and Father Peter had followed with admiration the boldness with which he drove toward his administrative, political, ecclesiastical, and spiritual objectives. The range of his interest was unlimited. Along with expelling from Rome the hordes of prostitutes that had made the city the scandal of Europe, with enforcing the celibacy of the priesthood, with discouraging simony and encouraging the revival of asceticism in the monastic orders, with revising the Vulgate and the breviary, Clement had conciliated the Spanish king, he had reconciled Henry of Bourbon to the Church and thereby had assured Catholic supremacy in France, he had mediated at Vervins the peace between France and Spain, and on the death of the Duke of Este he had annexed Ferrara to the Papal States.

And now, like Alexander sighing for new worlds to conquer, his restless zeal and policy were reaching beyond the seas and into the dominions of the Persian Shah. . . .

The chamberlain nodded, and the Carmelites, in their habits of brown goats' wool and with their white woolen cowls thrown back to show their cropped heads and their emaciated faces, advanced to the throne. Prostrating themselves, they kissed the pontiff's foot, which he thrust out, in a red slipper, from beneath the embroidered fringes of his cassock. The prelate muttered an *In Nomine Patris*, the friars stood, and then the Pope began to address them, drawing upon a sheaf of notes in his hand to refresh his memory.

He talked at some length. He began by explaining the origin of the business upon which he was sending them—how the English nobleman and gentleman of fortune Sir Anthony Sherley had gone to Persia with several companions and had there persuaded the Shah of the value of an alliance between the powers of Christendom and that of Persia to combat the expanding power of the Ottomans. The Shah had responded by dispatching Sherley to Europe as his ambassador to treat with all the Christian princes on the subject. Regretfully, the Pope added, the Christian princes were all so embroiled in their own quarrels that nothing had come of the scheme beyond some courteous correspondence between the Shah and the Pope.

The prelate seemed to believe that an alliance might still be worked out, and he had undertaken to use his good offices to this end. In return for this interest the Shah had invited the Pope to enter into diplomatic relations with Persia.

"This," the Pope said, "I have concluded to do, but not according to the usual fashion of such things. In order that this heathen prince may understand that our power is spiritual rather than temporal, and that we have no military forces at our disposal, and that he may understand that our chief object is the spread of Christ's spiritual kingdom, I am sending to his court not ambassadors but envoys, and not ecclesiastics but religious—friars dedicated, as I understand you to be, to prayers, preaching, and good works."

He now dwelt upon the great opportunity for propagating the Gospel, and outlined the situation among the Armenians.

"The Persian Shah," he said, "has offered us suzerainty over the Armenians in matters ecclesiastical in exchange for an alliance, but I doubt the sincerity of his offer. You must, on no occasion, assert or claim any such suzerainty, for such matters are not determined by fiat, but by the free consent of the believers." He added: "This is the principal reason why I have chosen you of the monastic order to undertake this mission, rather than members of the hierarchy. The Shah must, under no condition, believe that we have designs of such character.

"The objects of your diplomacy," he continued, "are threefold: the first is to gain from the Shah an edict which would secure the Armenians, and the other Christian sects in his empire, freedom from persecution and the right to worship God according to their convictions; the second object is to obtain a similar edict granting your order the right to establish a convent, to maintain a regular observance, and to proselytize. This also the Shah has promised by his letters. The third object of your mission is to extend, by your presence and testimony and good works, the Christian faith and the Holy Catholic Church."

Ending abruptly, and without asking the disposition of the Carmelites toward these matters, or whether they had questions regarding what he had said, the Pope exclaimed:

"Fathers, are you ready to go to Persia? Are you ready to undertake this enterprise?"

The friars bowed their heads in assent.

"You please me, Fathers. You have become noted for your devotion to your ascetic rule, for the discipline of your order. You shall now have opportunity to practice your discipline in other directions. You know something of the hazards of travel?"

Again the heads bowed.

"Then you will be prepared for hazards ten times multiplied. You must go by way of the Muscovite realm, for the direct route is blocked by the Turk, and the route around Africa is long and tedious. The Muscovite is unpredictable. While he avows the Christian faith, it is of another branch, by which we are regarded as heretics. You may or may not find hospitality in Russia. In any event you will be discreet."

"We shall endeavor to be as wise as serpents and as harmless as doves," said Father Paul, speaking for all.

"Very good. Now, as to the expense of your journey—that, I understand, has been provided for."

At this, the General, Father Peter, spoke up.

"We have a small endowment for the purpose—some five hundred scudi."

He rather expected the Pope to enlarge upon this subject, and hoped that his Holiness would forget his usual parsimony in view of the difficulty and the nature of the mission.

"'Tis not a great deal," assented the prelate, "but 'twill serve. Indeed, it must serve. The papal revenues are much straitened. In any case, you must trust in God's providence."

This statement was disappointing to the General, whose heart ached anew at the thought of these five young men, taken from the quiet and seclusion of a monastery and set on a road of such uncertainty and hazard. He recalled that the Pope had dismissed Sir Anthony Sherley with presents of gold cups and gold chains for each member of the embassy and, in addition, two thousand ducats in money. He wished his Holiness could at least give the friars a few words of encouragement, and make them feel that the power and majesty of the Roman Catholic Church were behind them, supporting them materially as well as spiritually.

"It could delay their embassy, your Holiness, and their arrival at the Persian court," he ventured, "if upon the route they find their expenses greater than their means and they be compelled to wait upon the alms box."

"Are you not a mendicant order?" asked the Pope sharply. "Why, say you, have I accepted your offices in this instance? I would not have the Shah think I am the Great Moghul. But have faith in God, as I have faith, and God will provide for your necessities."

The General thought that the Pope had not understood the constitution of the order, which forbade the soliciting of alms in the ordinary way; after all, the number of monastic orders was legion, and a prelate could not be expected to have acquaintance with all. He was on the point of making the distinction clear when Father Paul spoke up.

"We shall endeavor so to trust," the friar said, bowing his head humbly.

The Pope gave an approving nod.

"That is proper speech. Now, as you are a mendicant order, you will continue as such, in strict obedience to your rule, except as it may be mitigated by superior authority. Further, in addition to the general vows you have sworn as Carmelites, of obedience, of chastity, and of poverty, I require you to take the further vows of obedience to competent authority, of embracing death valiantly for the faith, and finally, of receiving no gifts and of keeping no gold, silver, precious stones nor the like except in extreme need, and then only as certified by your proper superior. Do you swear?"

The friars swore the oath.

The Pope now seemed to consider the audience concluded, and bent forward to give the triple blessing; but, taken by an afterthought, he straightened up, and added:

"You must keep ever at the Shah's side, as the envoys that you are, obedient to his wishes and consulting his desires; and you will report to me fully but succinctly all that he may confide to you."

He seemed again about to dismiss them, but fell into meditation, while he kept the Carmelites waiting. After a time he addressed them again, in his peculiarly sharp-timbred, almost nasal voice.

"You will remember also that our blessed Lord, when He founded His Holy Church, did not so upon a book and a candle, nor upon an altar and a relic—nay, not even upon the Holy Cup of His Passion— but upon a man; that what He sent into the world to conquer in His name was neither a doctrine nor a liturgy, nor a season of fast nor a creed to recite, neither a rule nor an ethic—but a man. As God sent His Son into the world in the likeness of sinful flesh, so it is supremely by sinful but redeemed men that the Word must be carried to the heathen. I counsel you therefore to be ever mindful of your vocation, and to understand that in your manhood rather than in your garb, in your order, or in your rule, exists that which will draw men to the salvation which is in Christ."

He now bestowed the triple blessing, and the audience was ended.

Within an hour the three friars and the two lay brothers, riding mules, were on the Via Flaminia bound toward Urbino and Venice. A sumpter mule carried their few belongings—a change of garments, vestments, and sacred vessels. Their general appearance in the gathering dusk suggested no more than a group of religious returning from Rome to their convent in some nearby place. Father Peter had gone with them as far as the Porta del Popolo, and there he stood, with bent shoulders, while his aching eyes traveled with them as the road wound upward into the hills, between the walls of the gardens, until they were lost in the gathering dusk.

PART TWO

---·•·---

In Persia

I

The Princess Shamala, finding the *takhtirivan* unbearable, called for her horse.

It wasn't really the takhtirivan that was unbearable, but the thoughts that kept traveling through her mind when she was within the curtained seclusion of her travel litter. The takhtirivan, borne by two camels tandem, was, for all its up-and-down motion that gave one nausea at first, like a sea ship, a marvelously comfortable means of getting about, and it was one reason the Shah would have no carriages in his realm. Another, of course, was the Shah's notion about the value of the horse in war. "Let the women and the infirm take to litters, but for men, horses, from which they can fight," Abbas was fond of saying. Abbas did very well with his mounted troops, Shamala thought, but he should give more heed to the Englishman Sherley, and his ideas about the value of artillery.

Abbas and Sherley. These were the subject of Shamala's thoughts and the horns of Shamala's dilemma that made the takhtirivan suffocating. But mostly her thoughts were on Abbas.

Fardoush, her eunuch escort, recognized her preoccupation as she parted the silken curtains of the litter and dismounted. The entire caravan, strung along the floor of the plain like a disjointed serpent, had halted for the transfer. Hostlers, tent strikers, overseers, and serv-

ants, and her escort, the troop of the Shah's Qizilbashies, or Red
Heads, strained necks for a glimpse of Nur Mahal, or Light of the
Palace, as the Princess Shamala, daughter of the Shah's feudatory,
Sampsov Khan, Prince of Circassia, was known within the Haram.

"Tell the caravan to move on," commanded the princess, "and let
us ride for a while across the plain."

"Why not?" acquiesced the eunuch. "You will observe how the
land has been devastated by the Ottomans in their ignominious retreat,
and how already the burned orchard is putting forth shoots under the
mild and beneficent sun of his Majesty's rule."

They were journeying through Nestoria, the bitterly contested
ground of the recently concluded three-year war between the Persians
and the Turks, and they were returning from Circassia, where the
princess had spent the summer with her parents.

"His Majesty will be interested in his darling's observations," continued the eunuch in his peculiarly ingratiating way. He was ever the
Shah's advocate before the princess, whom Abbas had forever tempted
but never won. "You will recall how he dismissed the governor of
Baluchistan because of your comment on the condition of his stables."

They had mounted—the princess upon her favorite Lurish stallion,
the eunuch upon a white mule. The captain of the troop, in his jacket
of mail, his scarlet turban and cloak, respectfully waited for the princess to lead off. The princess indicated that one armed horseman was
enough, and that he should stay somewhat to the rear. She wanted
to talk to Fardoush.

"Do you think his Majesty has missed me, that in my absence he
has not taken up with some other favorite?" she asked the eunuch
when they had ridden a little way.

"Bismillah! In the Name of God!" exclaimed the eunuch in a tone
of horror. "My lady must know that she won his Majesty's heart from
the moment her father sent her to abide under his Majesty's shadow
as an earnest of her father's loyalty. How long has that been? You are
now eighteen. Twelve years it has been."

It was true, and Fardoush's reminder caused the princess to reflect
upon her condition. In Isfahan she lived within the vast, high-walled
enclosure of the royal Haram, but she was neither a begum nor a
concubine nor a slave. Nominally she was a political hostage, but she
enjoyed more liberty than any hostage and more influence with the

Shah than any begum or concubine. This was the result of the Shah's
infatuation for her. But how deeply that infatuation went Shamala
could not divine. It was, she knew, something of the captivation of a
boy by a Chinese puzzle, for Shamala's mood was various and never
certain, and she never fully revealed herself to Abbas. But it was also
other things of which she did not allow herself to think. She exercised
upon him the spell an untamed mare among the crags exercises upon
a nomad, a panther moving through the brake upon a hunter, the
heights of Demavend upon a Sufi contemplative.

"Then why will not his Majesty take me as wife?" Shamala demanded petulantly.

"And why will you not accept his Majesty's offer of marriage by
the left hand?" retorted Fardoush. "You know that his Majesty has
already the allotted number of begums permitted by the Holy Koran."

Shamala knew that very well. Four was the lawful number. Her
own aunt, the Begum Tamara, her father's sister, mother of the Shah's
heir apparent, was the chief of these. But Shamala knew also, and she
knew that Abbas knew, that she would never yield to the Shah's embrace except as a wife—a begum—that she would die rather than
accept concubinage. It was beneath her both as a princess and as a
Christian.

For Christian she was—Christian by circumstance of birth—though
of Christian tenets she was greatly ignorant. She was a Circassian of
Kartli. In her veins flowed the blood of her Amazon ancestry—of
Hippolyte and Circe and Medea. She had in fullest measure those
qualities of form and personality that made the women of Colchis
the prize for which shahs and sultans bribed, stole, betrayed, fought
battles, waged war. But with Shamala it was well known that whatever
battles might be fought for her favor, the guerdon of victory was hers
alone to bestow. Her independence and self-will were as well known
as her beauty.

"Why does not his Majesty divorce one of them?" she demanded.
"Then this tug of war would be ended."

Fardoush did not answer, nor had he need. Reasons of state were
the excuse. Wives were the knots by which the great alliances were
tied. Concubines served for the lesser. If she asked her heart, moreover, Shamala was not sure she wanted the tug of war ended. Her
thoughts turned to the Englishman, Sir Robert Sherley. Handsome

he was, and she had been betrothed to him when she was yet a child, for some unexplainable reason of policy; but of that betrothal nothing had been heard since her adolescence. Officially, however, it was still in effect, and from time to time, when Abbas vexed her unbearably, she thought of what marriage to the blond nobleman from Firenghistan would be. The trouble was Sir Robert's indifference. He was perfectly chaste, it was said, and this was believable, for he was utterly indifferent to women—indifferent to everything, it seemed, except duty. He enjoyed great distinction in the realm as one of the Shah's chief officers. There might be advantages in marrying him —if Abbas continued stubborn.

Baffled by her dilemma, Shamala dismissed it and for sport gave her mount the bit. The Luristan sprang to a gallop, leaving the eunuch and his mule swallowed in a cloud of dust. The Qizilbashie kept pace, riding at a great interval to her right. It was sterile country they were in—a vast and somber plain ringed by gaunt, forbidding ranges that made her recall the verdancy of Isfahan, where the plain was green with lucerne, the gardens were without number, and where the bulbul sang in the branches all night long. It was November and a chill was in the air. It was now late afternoon, and the landscape was swathed in a colorless twilight. Shamala skirted a rise in the land, and found herself riding toward the ruins of a devastated and deserted village—one of the many left by the war. Rising above a heap of rubble to strike the eye of the traveler was the stump of a minaret, still encrusted with its faience, and nearby was the debris of an almost destroyed caravanserai—still habitable, apparently, for a donkey was tethered in what had been the courtyard, and smoke from a campfire curled in the evening air.

On the mound, silhouetted against the evening sky, moved a figure in a belted gaberdine with a white cowl thrown back upon his shoulders. He appeared to be gathering brushwood among the sparse growth of the hillside, and as Shamala reined up she could hear him singing as he worked—something in a strange tongue, neither Persian nor Turki nor Cherkess nor Italian, with which the princess had some acquaintance. Curious, Shamala drew nearer. The man looked up. He was tall, she observed, with a clean-shaven face that was lean, almost cadaverous. He had close-cropped hair, a bony forehead, and brooding dark eyes. He passed his hands before his eyes in a gesture of wonder, an exclamation crossed his lips, and then, clasping his hands before him within the sleeves of his gaberdine, he remained respectfully silent.

Shamala considered the effect she had made upon the man. In the brief look he had given her she was sure he had taken in every detail of her appearance. She was appareled in her own indifferent, independent fashion. Upon her head she wore her Circassian coronet of felt edged with ermine, covered with a veil that fell down behind to enclose her mahogany-colored hair. Another veil was caught at her temples and fell around her chin and upon her bosom, framing her face like a wimple. Her jacket was of red felt heavily embroidered in gold. Beneath it was a chemise of fine silk and over it a military cloak of blue woolen lined with crimson satin. She had donned baggy trousers of white woolen for riding, a cummerbund of cashmere in which she had thrust, by way of contrast, her *ginjil* with its jeweled hilt and a rose that she had plucked that morning in the governor's garden. At her saddle pommel hung her bow and her arrow case.

"Who are you?" she asked in a tone intended to be courteous, but edged with the imperiousness of one used to having her own way.

"I am a Christian friar from the land of Rome," replied the other in halting Persian. *Darvish* was the Persian word he used to indicate his calling. It confirmed the princess's suspicions and caused her delicate nose to wrinkle, her famous green eyes to narrow.

"And what is your business in the realm of my lord the Shah?" she asked.

"We bear messages from our sovereign the Pope to his Majesty," responded the man modestly.

Shamala remembered now, and her interest heightened with a kind of dismay. "Ah, then you must be the ambassadors whom the Shahinshah has been expecting these many years. You have much offended his Majesty."

The friar looked surprised, and then smiled, showing a set of strong white teeth.

"How can that be?" he asked, "seeing that we have not met his Majesty."

"Are you not darvishes?" remarked Shamala with asperity. "And his Majesty has only contempt for darvishes, whom he regards as charlatans and leeches. Why does the Christian caliph insult his Majesty in this fashion? And why have you delayed so long in coming? It has been three years since couriers came telling of your departure. Meanwhile, his Majesty has been compelled to make war against the Ottoman without the aid of the Christian princes which he was promised."

The friar opened his mouth to speak, apparently in protest, then closed it firmly, but changed his mind again.

"We had difficulties in passing through Muscovy," he explained. "We were kept at the border for a year. That was on orders of Tsar Boris Godunov, who was at enmity with the Poles and hated all Christians of the Catholic faith. Afterward, when Dmitri came to the throne, we were allowed to enter; but then he was assassinated and in the anarchy that followed we were held under arrest for another year." He added, "We left two of our brethren behind, victims of the Russian winter."

"I am familiar with that," exclaimed the princess, momentarily touched. "It was all because of her whom they call the 'Polish slut'— Marina Georgina, with whom Dmitri became enamored, and whom he insisted on marrying despite the opposition of the boyars. And so he was slain on his marriage couch. News of these events reached us in Isfahan. But the grand duchess escaped, I understand, and married another Dmitri, and with Polish aid and arms has put him on the throne. Tell me, did you find her fascinating?"

"I did not meet the lady," responded the friar drily, "and so cannot tell you."

The princess regarded the friar again through narrowed eyes.

"The mention of women seems to annoy you," she remarked. "Where are your wives?"

"Men of my order do not take wives," responded the friar.

Shamala mused, considering the man. Something about him captured her fancy; she could not say what. Fortunately, Fardoush had ridden up, and he would take the man's measure and explain to her later.

"Strange darvishes you are," she remarked. "Not like the darvishes of Iran, nor even like the Christian priests of the Kafkas, who marry, grow fat, and wear beards that gush like silver torrents upon their pectorals. Then you are, like me, a virgin?" she added.

The question went home. The Christian darvish looked startled,

but, recovering, nodded embarrassedly. Shamala thought him even
more charming. She fell into a teasing mood.

"But if you met someone who stirred your blood, would you not
take yourself a wife?"

"That would be contrary to my oath."

"Perhaps," nodded Shamala knowingly, "when you reach Isfahan
we can find someone for you who will make you forget your oath."

From Fardoush, who was the guardian of Shamala's soul as well as
body, came a grumbling protest against this line of conversation.
Shamala turned upon him in wrath. "Be quiet, you sexless shrew!" she
snapped. "What do you know of such things!" Fardoush subsided
into silence.

Shamala turned again to the friar. A possibility had been turning
over in her thoughts while she was talking.

"Do you speak Italian?" she asked.

The friar responded in that tongue. Shamala sighed in relief and
reined her mount nearer.

"I too am under oath," she confided mysteriously. She examined the
friar again, and it struck her that he was one whom she could trust.
The thought warmed her toward him.

"What is your name?" she asked.

"You may call me Fray Juan."

The friar said this so simply and so directly that Shamala was more
than ever certain that she could expose her strategy to him.

"Well, Fray Juan," she said, "perhaps I can help you to your object
with his Majesty, and in turn you can help me to mine with him."

The look in the friar's face quietly hardened.

"Our affairs are God's," he rebuked, "and not to be made the subject of bargains."

Shamala's heart turned cold within her in incipient wrath. Yet she
did not want to be wroth with the Firenghi darvish, and fortunately
his expression relaxed.

"But if I can help you in any way appropriate to my priestly calling,
I am at your service," he said. "Meanwhile, may I inquire whom I
address?"

Shamala gave him her name, and then said in a wheedling tone,
"Now, if you win favor with his Majesty, will you intercede for me?"

The Christian darvish asked to what purpose.

"Persuade his Majesty that an alliance with the Christian caliph is more to his advantage than his existing alliance with the Great Moghul."

The princess's Italian was as faulty as the friar's Persian, but gradually they came to understand each other.

"That is something I could hope to demonstrate," the friar responded. "And what, may I ask, is your interest in this?"

Shamala glanced furtively toward the eunuch, who was sitting his mule sullenly nursing his reprimand. He would get over that in time; what Shamala feared at the moment was that he might possess some talisman by which he could understand what she was saying in Italian. She bent toward the foreign darvish.

"Then his Majesty will be able to divorce the Bibi Hanim, who is the Great Moghul's niece, and marry me," Shamala announced in a whisper.

The expression of the Christian darvish grew thoughtful, then hostile, and he seemed about to say something unfortunate. But he gained control of himself, his expression relaxed, becoming tender.

"How can you wish such a thing?" he asked. "For if you are a Circassian, as you say, were you not baptized in the Christian faith, and were you not instructed in its rich treasures of wisdom and morality?"

Shamala thought the stranger was taking liberties to counsel her so.

"And what is wrong with desiring to be a wife instead of a concubine?" she demanded.

The darvish held his ground.

"You are not aware of the Christian law that keeps one man faithful to one wife, and the wife faithful to one husband?" he inquired.

Shamala was aware of the custom among her father's people, but she assumed it was because of poverty or convenience, for the Circassians did not hesitate to marry off their daughters to the princes and khans of their Moslem neighbors.

"Were you a Christian at heart, my child," continued the friar, "then would you yield your chastity to no man but a Christian, and then but in the lawful bonds of Christian wedlock. Oh, that I might instruct you in true Christian doctrine!"

The effect of this earnest speech upon Shamala was explosive.

"So!" she exclaimed in the sudden and furious wrath of which she was capable. "You would instruct me in celibacy, have me contemn his Majesty's yearnings toward me—simply because he is a Moslem! You would have me spurn his ardent love-making! Instead you would have me pine and moon for some Circassian shepherd!" She looked down upon the friar from her horse in magnificent contempt, but caught by the firmness of his look, and coming for a moment under the spell of his large dark eyes, she added: "Or perhaps you dream of having me pine for your embrace? How vilely you would insult his Majesty—you crawling vermin of a darvish!"

With a sudden movement she had her bow in her hand and an arrow fitted to the string, and murderous was her impulse. Fortunately for Fray Juan the eunuch's jealous watch had anticipated the movement: he let out a squeal and spurred his mule between the friar and his peril, almost knocking down Fray Juan as he did so.

Shamala's horse reared in fright, and by the time she had brought him under control her own mood had subsided. She contented herself with giving Fardoush a tongue lashing, and then, to the friar, "I would not waste an arrow on such a lowly breed."

A lizard crawled across a rock upon which it had been warming itself. Upon it she fixed her aim, and let fly. The arrow found its mark, and as the reptile quivered in its death pangs the princess's anger dissolved and was succeeded by a mood of contrition.

"I have forgotten you are ambassador to his Majesty," she said quite humbly. "I pray you forgive my forwardness."

The friar was silent for a moment, and then he lifted his hand and made the sign of the cross over the princess.

"May God's Holy Spirit stir you to return to the ancient faith of your people," he said.

Shamala felt abashed, and would have liked to speak further, but Fardoush had begun to protest again, and she wheeled her horse.

But before she rode off, an impulse led her to pluck the rose from her cummerbund and toss it to the friar. It fell to the earth before him. Glancing back after she had ridden the distance of two hundred paces, she saw him still standing, gazing after her, but the distance was too great for her to read his expression or interpret his attitude.

II

In Ardebil the Princess Shamala learned that the Shah had just ended a successful campaign against the Uzbegs of the eastern frontier, had seized another province, and was returning in triumph with twenty thousand heads in the haversacks of his troops. She at once abandoned the caravan and, taking her mounted escort and putting Jafar the eunuch on a horse, set out at full speed to join her monarch.

Shamala found Abbas in Khorasan, where he was holding military durbar for his troops. She interrupted these grave proceedings by riding at a gallop through the shouting sentries to the assembly before the imperial tent. Leaping from her horse and tossing the reins to the nearest Qizilbashie, she pushed her way unceremoniously through the *ilkhans*, the *ostandars*, and the *kalentars* to the open space under the canopy where Abbas sat alone on a carpet save for the scribe Mirza Mustafa Ali at his elbow.

"Hail, Majesty," she cried, throwing herself before the Shah in exaggerated obeisance, "I bring you in all speed greetings from the princes of the north, and felicitations and congratulations on your victories."

She lifted her head and gave the Shah a curious look, halfway between devotion and impertinence. Handsome he was, almost as handsome as the Georgians—his mother, indeed, had been a Georgian—with wheat-colored skin, long narrow mustaches, and brilliant brown eyes; but beyond mere looks was his obvious air of majesty. It was this that charmed Shamala. The imperiousness in his look and gesture, his impatience at delay, his furious temper—these she doted on, adored. Having herself a temper to be reckoned with, she was challenged by it in another; she could not abide meekness, humility, the qualities of the Christian darvish she had met on the Ardebil plain. Recollection of the man, suddenly returning to her, spurred her on.

Abbas's temper was inflamed now by the interruption.

"You she-cub, you panther whelp, you unripe pomegranate! What do you mean by breaking into a durbar?" he demanded hotly, though controlling his voice. "Shall I have you bastinadoed?"

Shamala was delighted.

"Cut off my head, rather, Majesty, for the eagerness of its eyes to behold your glory, the straining of its ears to hear your voice, the impatience of its tongue to speak your praise."

This was the flattery of supplicants, but the tone was not supplicating; it was sarcastic rather, and impudently challenging.

But Abbas was in no mood today for impudence from a favorite, and Shamala, sensing this, became more humble.

"Let his Majesty but allow me to gaze upon him, like his cat, from a corner of his chamber, and I will contain the news I bear him until he have ears for listening."

Abbas grumbled and gave her permission to remain under the canopy, in the background, and the durbar continued.

The durbar, or "sitting at the gate," was a practice Abbas had revived from the ancient days, when kings presented themselves to their subjects in open court, under a canopy or on a covered terrace, and all were free to approach and plead their causes. Abbas had been hearing petitions all morning; it was not these that had vexed his humor, for he enjoyed sitting in judgment; it was something else that plagued him, the nature of which he could not himself define.

Below the royal tent the great army encamped along the *rud* made an imposing display that at other times would have filled his soul to satisfaction. The black tents, clustered by tribes, with corrals and exercise fields between, exhibited the numerous nations that gave allegiance to the Shah; among them, Lurs and Bakhtiaris and Kashgais, Kurds and Baluchis and Memmassanis, Kajars, and Tadjiks and Turkomans, Shahsevans and Shamlus and Ustajlus, and lesser tribes. They were Turkish-speaking and Persian-speaking and Arabic-speaking, and some had their own unrelated tongues. Diverse in garb and custom they were, jealous and contentious among themselves, but all acknowledged the suzerainty of Abbas, all were united in allegiance to the throne, and all shouted *"Zendeh bad Shah"*—Long live the Shah—when he appeared among them.

Abbas's thoughts, as he listened to the blaring of the long horn and the roll of the kettle drums that marked the opening of the durbar, had dwelt in wonder, as they so often did, upon the remarkable fortune that had brought him from a fugitive third son of a disinherited prince to the throne of Jamshyd and Kai Kobad—from plain Abbas, ward of the Shamlu chief Ali Quli Khan, to Abbas Safi Safavid, Shahinshah of Iran, Favored of God, monarch absolute.

By what inscrutable kismet, written on his forehead, had this come to pass? By what decree of God had he been elevated to so great dominion? What an empire this was of which he was the acknowledged and absolute sovereign! All the mountains and plains from Herat to the Zagros, and from the snowy Caucasus to the flaming Gulf; within this expanse, tribesmen without number, and great and populous cities, with tributary provinces as large as kingdoms, the nearest, ten caravan days apart—Hamadan and Kermanshah and Shiraz, city of gardens and poets, Kasvin, his former capital, and Isfahan, his new capital, upon which he was now lavishing the revenues of the empire.

Nevertheless, for all his majesty, Abbas could not command the rain to fall upon the *kavir*, nor the wind to cease to blow in Seistan, and there were other things also which he could not control. His tendency to deep, despairing moods, for one, and remembrances of certain broken promises, such as the one to the ancient, purblind priest who had sheltered him as a youth when he was in flight from the Ustajlus.

Abbas's glance turned upon Shamala, and his thoughts lingered upon her. She was another of the things that he had not been able to bend to his will. But in this case he was not disappointed. It had become a zestful game to do so, and he had hope of carrying off the prize in the end. He turned his attention to his duties of magistrate. . . .

At the close of the durbar Abbas retired to his tent and called for the Circassian to have coffee with him. The sight of her refreshed his soul. At the same time his annoyance returned at how he had given her pretext to deny herself to him. This was because of his foolishness in having betrothed her to the Englishman. Eight years ago, when in a burst of generosity he had bestowed her upon Sherley Khan, she had been a slim-legged, green-eyed hoyden whose only interests were her horse and her bow. In the interval she had grown up; she had become an almond tree in blossom, a Khorasan peach, a melon from the gardens of Ajampur, a cypress by the waters of Bend Ameer.

"You have come to me at a bad time," Abbas remarked as he sipped his coffee and allowed his eyes to travel over Shamala's loveliness. "How is your father and how are your brothers?"

"Well, well," responded the princess. "They will support you against the Ottoman—yes, even against the Muscovites, except that the Muscovites are at war among themselves over some Dmitri who claims to be the son of Ivan."

"Well, let them war till the last man drowns in his own blood," muttered Abbas.

"Are you not glad to see me?" asked Shamala petulantly, noting the Shah's preoccupation.

"Don't expect me to quote you Hafiz and Rumi today," protested Abbas. "Did you see the Englishman as you passed through Kasvin?"

"Sherley Khan, you mean?" asked Shamala with an innocent manner.

"Who else, who else?"

"My lord, I neither stayed nor rested until I reached your side. Do you think I should have loitered on Sherley Khan's account?"

"He is a good man, if stupid. I need good men about me. I need advisers and counselors. Where in this realm will you find honest men?" he demanded with sudden passion. "About me are none but thieves and liars and absconders. You recall Hussein Beg?"

"Your favorite vizier," commented Shamala.

"No more. Hussein Beg himself is no more. He tried to make off with half the imperial treasury. Mishevelli caught up with him, and his head rolled. But Sherley is a good counselor, for all that his brother was a scoundrel. Think well of him."

Shamala was put out at the turn the conversation was taking.

"And what is this news that you bring me?" Abbas asked.

Shamala toyed with her bangles before replying.

"Upon my way hither I came upon the envoys which the Christian caliph is sending to your court."

Abbas sat up, his attention aroused.

"Good, good. I shall give you a purse of gold for your welcome news. Now we shall forge a chain against the Sultan which he shall never crack, and slowly strangle him."

A smile of amusement flitted across Shamala's face.

"And how do they come?" asked Abbas eagerly. "With what retinue, and how many baggage camels?" His eyes were glittering; he loved presents. "Did you speak with the envoys?"

"I spoke with one of them," said Shamala slowly, weighing her words. "He is a handsome man, and very tall, from the land of Spain."

Abbas frowned. He cared neither for Spaniards, who vexed his commerce in the Persian Gulf, nor for tall, handsome men whom Shamala might admire. He was under average height himself.

"But not so handsome as the Persians, the Georgians, or the English," added Shamala mischievously. "Rather gaunt, I should say, but in the eye a look of challenge and command."

"But the retinue? The retinue?"

"They came unattended, your Majesty."

"How? Unattended?" Abbas mused. "But possibly the retinue follows. What else?"

"My lord, the men are darvishes."

The effect of this statement was an explosion.

"Darvishes! You joke!"

"Nay, my lord. Darvishes in rags and patches."

"Darvishes! What is the meaning of this? Has the Pope no sense at all of my dignity, of the weight of my arms? Darvishes!"

"I told him as much, but he seemed undisturbed. However, my lord, content yourself, for you may find these men quite different from the darvishes of this realm, and if not bishops in disguise at least a match for your shrewdest viziers."

"Bishops in disguise?" The idea intrigued the Shah. "That must be it. The Pope is playing a game that I enjoy." He clapped his hands and summoned his scribe. When Mustafa Ali appeared, the Shah said: "Dispatch this letter to all my governors on the route: Receive these envoys as ambassadors, and disbelieve their rags; treat them as princes; load them with gifts; ply them with hospitality; gorge them with wine and food; offer them dancing girls and the hunt; and send them at length in state to Isfahan."

When Mustafa Ali had gone the Shah turned and gazed fondly at the princess.

"Shamala, you frozen snowdrop of Demavend, you are as beguiling in your brilliance as in your other parts. Only, some day, will you melt a little?"

Teasingly, Shamala smiled.

III

In time the Carmelites came to more prosperous countryside, with villages swathed in green at the foot of the ranges and watered fields upon the desert floor, and towns with crenelated walls and domes and turrets that sparkled in the autumn sunlight. Within the towns were winding, covered streets where carpets and silks and silverwork were on display, and barley and rice and honey were in abundance and where the air was filled with the fragrance of spices and sandalwood and rose oil. The walls of the towns, however, were usually in decay, for, as the friars learned, the Shah had great contempt for fortifications and trusted rather to lancers and bowmen for the security of his realm.

But if the road was now easier, other difficulties arose. At every city the friars were received like princes and encumbered so with invitations that they could scarcely continue their journey. It became a vexing problem to the friars to have to explain again and again to the officials that they did not mount horses, that they ate meat but rarely, that they cared not for boar hunts, that they were celibate and could not without great sin look upon exhibitions of dancing girls, much less accept their favors for the night.

Father Paul, to whom asceticism was the heart of his service to God, found all this an exceeding trial, and began to suspect that it was a calculated offense to their dignity on the part of the Persian Shah. Even more determined to keep to the monastic rule, he imposed upon himself and the others ever stricter denials, and refused even to use the mules which were provided. The friars now avoided the larger towns and instead slept in smelly village caravanserais, eating little more than goat's-milk cheese, raisins, and the flat bread of the countryside. This regimen told upon the prior, and he began to show signs of exhaustion.

By the time the Carmelites reached Kasvin, residence of the Shah's viceroy of the north, Father Paul was seriously ill with dysentery and had to be put to bed. They lodged for a week in a caravanserai on the outskirts of the city while the other friars prayed over him and fed him meat stock to restore his strength. Resuming their journey, they arrived on the outskirts of Isfahan early in December. Their coming had been noted. At the city gate they were met by the imperial minister of court, Habibullah Agha, with horses and an escort of the scarlet-turbaned imperial troopers.

"Welcome, thrice welcome to the city of abode of his imperial Majesty the Shahinshah," the minister exclaimed with profound respect. Habibullah Agha was a little, shrunken man of great age, surmounted by a turban as large and yellow as a melon. He was a holdover from the days of the Shah's uncle who had managed to stay in office by his ability to keep to the lee of adverse winds—though it was well known that Abbas detested him. He had dismounted to greet the envoys, and now he indicated horses with empty saddles for the friars to ride.

"I must thank you for your thoughtfulness of our comfort and our dignity," said Father Paul, "but as it is contrary to our custom to ride horses, we shall walk."

The minister looked crestfallen, but acquiesced, and so, mincing along on his spindly legs, accompanied the friars on foot into Isfahan.

The city indeed justified the saying, "Isfahan is half the world," but Father Paul was too intent upon meeting the Shah to pay attention to the minister as he pointed out the sights and identified the various imposing buildings and plazas. Habibullah Agha did not tell the friars that the Shah had no intention of receiving them in audience—at least not at once. When Father Paul finally put the question directly, the Agha explained that his Majesty was not in Isfahan but at Serishabad, with his army. Father Paul offered to go there, not knowing that Serishabad was only an hour or so distant by horse. It would have made no difference to the friar had it been at the farther end of the empire.

Habibullah Agha made excuses. The ambassadors were travel-weary and the journey was arduous. That was disposed of by Father Paul. His Majesty was not well; besides, he was treating just now with the Moghul's envoy, and was absorbed in delicate negotiations. Soon, soon, an audience would be arranged. Meanwhile, the minister hoped that the Pope's ambassadors would acquaint themselves with the wonders of Isfahan and the productions of the countryside, that they might properly report to their sovereign the prosperity and majesty of the Persian realm.

Father Paul resigned himself to waiting, but intimated to the minister that it would be pleasing to the friars if they could be conducted to some small house where they might lodge undisturbed. He was pathetically eager to return to the observance of the conventual rule and order, so long interrupted by travel. To sleep on a board, to dine on lentils, to spend hours on his knees before the altar, to arise in the middle of the night for the recitation of Lauds—the anticipation of all this seemed to fill him with more strength than meat and milk.

But the minister affected not to understand, and escorted the Carmelites to an imposing gateway and through it past a garden to a palace with a glittering façade of faience.

Father Paul's patience now succumbed.

"We want only a hovel," he exclaimed, "where we may erect a cross and keep our religious observances, as his Persian Majesty has promised that we might. And we will not be at his Majesty's charge, but will defray our own expenses, as that too is our inflexible rule."

Habibullah Agha remained polite but adamant.

"It is the custom of this realm, as in others, that ambassadors, who are his Majesty's guests, be housed at his Majesty's expense, and greatly would his Majesty be offended if I were to agree, or you to insist, otherwise."

Father Paul fumed but gave in, asserting that this was a matter which he would take up with the Shah at the audience. The friars were now escorted to apartments consisting of several large rooms profusely curtained in silk, lighted by candelabra and thickly carpeted, but devoid of furniture except for several divans and taborets. The minister hoped that the friars would find everything to their comfort, and after assuring them that their slightest wish would be heeded, begged leave to depart.

In this vast palace, filled with servants coming and going, the friars managed to find a little seclusion by drawing the curtains, and immediately settled themselves by reciting the evening office. As they were concluding Complin they heard a clatter of horse in the courtyard and a moment later steps on the staircase.

A servant knocked and announced, "His Excellency, Sherley Khan, desires audience with your Reverences."

The friars had heard of the Englishman who was the Shah's master of artillery and a personage of importance though of uncertain favor with the Shah. He was the younger brother of Sir Anthony Sherley, whose embassy to Europe on behalf of the Shah's statecraft had resulted in this papal mission to the Persian court.

The man who was ushered in was handsome, not past his twenties, with a ruddy, chiseled face and flaxen hair that fell to his shoulders. He was elegantly appareled in Persian garb of tight-fitting satin trousers, a tunic of silk, and over the tunic, falling to his knees, a satin brocade redingote with buttons from the throat to the hem, but with the upper buttons unfastened. About his waist was a cummerbund of figured silk through which a scimitar was thrust, and on his head was a large turban of crimson silk with the peculiar pleat that, along with the crimson color, distinguished those in the imperial service. The profusion of silk in his apparel was less extraordinary than it would have appeared in Europe, since Persia was a great producer of silk and a principal supplier of this commodity to Europe. The same could not be said of the gold chain with its sunburst of diamonds that hung about the Englishman's neck, the ruby and diamond brooch in his turban, and the numerous rings upon his fingers, all of which set him off as a person of rank and consequence.

"I have come, Fathers," began the Englishman, "to welcome you to this realm as a fellow Catholic and, since it is some time since I have made confession, to inquire when it might be convenient for one of your Reverences to hear me."

"I am delighted to hear you say you are a Catholic," said Father Paul, "for, as I recall, your brother was not of the faith."

"We were reared as Protestants, our father, Sir Thomas, being an ardent supporter of Elizabeth. It was in Venice, before embarking on our Persian adventure, that I returned to Holy Church. His Eminence Cardinal Bentivoglio it was who received me and administered the rite of confirmation."

Father Paul bowed his head a moment, and then indicated that Fray Juan would hear the confession. He and Fray Vincent retired from the room.

It was immediately evident that the Englishman was unused to the confessional, and did not know where to begin.

"How long has it been since your last confession?" asked Fray Juan gently.

"I have never confessed—that is, not since my confirmation Mass. That was eight years ago."

"Indeed?" exclaimed Fray Juan in surprise. "We were informed that there was a convent of Augustinians here, and we have been looking forward to establishing fellowship with them. One of them might have heard you."

Sir Robert shook his head.

"Not a convent, but only a single friar, attached to the Portuguese legate as chaplain. You will meet the man, no doubt, but God spare you; and for the sake of your mission avoid him, for the Shah's relations with the Portuguese are strained over the matter of Hormuz Island, and moreover he especially dislikes this friar. Antonio de Gouvea is his name, a clever, pompous little fellow who imagines himself to be archbishop of the East. I would as lief confess to my stableboy as to him."

Fray Juan was disturbed by these words, and made a mental note to report this to the prior; he also considered whether he should instruct his penitent on the theory and practice of the confessional, but concluded that this was not the occasion.

"Do you have particular sins upon your conscience?" he asked, thinking that it would be somewhat difficult for his penitent to confess all the sins of omission and commission of eight years.

Sir Robert drew himself up.

"My conscience is clear," he announced briskly. "Being an uninstructed Catholic, you might say, there may be sins of which I know not, but by the rule of duty to God and man, as given me by a devout if Protestant father, I am innocent of any wrongdoing. 'Do your duty, Bob,' I can remember him saying to me, this Sheriff of Surrey and Sussex and the Queen's Treasurer of War in the Low Countries, my father, from the time I was able to perch upon his knee. That, I have consistently tried to do."

Fray Juan nodded approvingly. "Indeed, that may be said to be the summation of the Law and the prophets," he commented, "or, as said by Jesus, 'Thou shalt *love* the Lord thy God,' for duty without love may often be a vine without roots."

He was inclined to add something about the pitfalls of pride, by which the angels fell, but forbore, giving his penitent the benefit of a holy intention and making allowances for his English and Protestant upbringing. He pronounced absolution and pardon, but could not refrain a question: Why had his penitent abandoned the faith of his father and of his liege sovereign for that of Rome?

"Is it not obvious?" Sir Robert asked in surprise, as though the question were unworthy the friar. "The Protestant heresy adheres to the rule of conscience and individual judgment, which leads to anarchy, whereas the Catholic Church asserts universal sovereignty with the seat of that sovereignty in Rome by divine descent from the Apostle Peter. One can hardly travel as I have across Europe with its numberless frontiers and petty principalities interminably quarreling without grasping the significance of the Catholic view and recognizing the authority of the Church as the only answer to a confused and discordant Christendom. But now that I am again restored to communion with Holy Church," he concluded with the finality of a man who has balanced his accounts and can face the new day with peace of mind, "may I inquire if there is any service I can render your Reverences? You have not had an easy journey, I understand."

"We did not expect it to be easy," replied Fray Juan.

"You have been keeping to the byways, have you not, to avoid the attentions of the Shah's officers? It is a game of his Majesty—but you seem to have won the greater number of points."

Fray Juan spoke of the difficulty over the present lodgings.

"Habibullah Agha is not easily outdone," commented Sir Robert, "but perhaps I can have a word with him that may be effective. He is under his Majesty's orders, of course, but perhaps he can see his way clear to accommodate you as you prefer. Have you any news of my brother?" he asked suddenly.

Fray Juan shook his head. "It is three years since we left Rome. We heard that Sir Anthony had entered the service of the Spanish king."

"Which means that I shall never be free of this bondage," Sir Robert said grimly.

He was a man of great devotion, it seemed. When Anthony went off to sell his sword to the Shah, Robert accompanied him less from a sense of adventure than from brotherly loyalty. Anthony had persuaded the Shah to send him again to Europe as his ambassador plenipotentiary, but Abbas had shrewdly insisted upon a pledge, and Robert had generously offered himself as hostage for Anthony's return. But Anthony had not returned; rather, he had appropriated the proceeds of five hundred bales of silk which the Shah had given him to sell in the European markets, and had suddenly resigned his commission.

"I do not hate my brother," Robert asserted. "It is only that this imprisonment goes on from year to year, and each year, as my hope sinks a little lower, I grow more apathetic and tend to take to the accursed ways of these heathens."

There had been compensations, of course. Abbas was a monarch ever on the lookout for men of ideas and ability, and when Sir Robert admitted to some experience in cannon founding the Shah had promptly made him master of the royal artillery, and had given him an appropriation with which to set up a foundry.

"Until I began casting cannon the Persians were without ordnance, save for a few pieces they had succeeded in capturing from their enemies," Sir Robert explained. "But now we have them in ample supply, though Abbas still prefers to win his battles by feint and withdrawal, by thrust and parry, rather than by the overwhelming, the decisive stroke. Abbas is the grand master in the Orient of the art of maneuver and of the management of cavalry. There is not his equal in all Asia, and it is by his skill in the warfare of movement that he has won his resounding victories over the Uzbegs, and has withstood the Ottoman for so long, despite the formidable Turkish artillery.

"You must be wary of his Majesty, as one must be wary of Greeks bearing gifts," he went on to say. "Someday I shall tell you of the other boon which his Majesty conferred upon me, and which at times has been like an albatross about my neck."

Fray Juan remained discreetly silent, and as the Englishman did not seem inclined to discuss this boon the friar asked, "Do you have any counsel for us as to how we should proceed with our mission to the Shah?"

"I will say this," said Sir Robert: "Keep yourself from the grasp of the Shah, or he will squeeze you dry. You are—pardon my saying so, Father—as lambs sent into a den of wolves. Why his Holiness should send three friars on such a mission I cannot imagine. Surely he must know the character of the Persians, and above all the character of this monarch. I do not believe there is a shrewder ruler on any throne in the world, or a more unscrupulous, a more cruel, or a more dissimulating ruler. A Medici or a Sforza or a Borgia is not his equal."

"I can understand your pessimism," said Fray Juan, "but we must trust to the right arm of God, which is powerful beyond the calculations of men."

"Perhaps I am pessimistic," admitted Sir Robert. "Just what do you expect to accomplish here?"

"We have certain matters to present to the Shah, which are confided to our prior," said Fray Juan discreetly. "But as for myself, I think this is an opportunity to proclaim our faith, and to seek converts."

"It is a mistake, it is a mistake," said Sir Robert moodily. "These people were converted to Islam by the sword, and the sword is all they know. Persuasion is useless; you must have a weapon in your hand. You will see in time. They will listen to you politely and serve you coffee and invite you to ride with them, yet all the while they laugh in their sleeves. I have been here nigh on to ten years, that seem like twenty. I know. Do you bring presents? Do you offer them advantages? Then you are welcome. I happened to know artillery, and so I was well received; nothing was too good for me—palaces, parks, jewels, concubines, the revenue of villages, were mine for the asking. I am still useful to his Majesty, for like the clever magician who keeps always one trick more in his sleeve, I have not yielded all my art, for when I do, then will I be cast upon the dungheap.

"Finally," he said, "you must get used to comforts. The monastic life will not serve your purposes here. In the first place, while the climate is bracing, there are humors that attack the body as well as the spirit, and one must needs be fortified against them by good food, comfortable beds, and appropriate clothing. I have learned to be extremely careful. Aside from that, you will lose face, which is disastrous among these people. You are here on a significant embassy; you must comport yourselves as ambassadors. Here, you are judged by externals. It is to the man with a great retinue, whose outriders shout the loudest, that the crowds salaam. At night, you can judge the importance of a man by the size of the lanterns which his servants bear. Some of them are as large as hogsheads."

"I am afraid we shall be unable to make much of an impression, then," said the friar, "for neither by our rule nor by our means are we able to comport ourselves in this manner."

Sir Robert waved his hand, as though it were inconsequential after all, or as though the subject had suddenly bored him, and he now took his departure.

After he had gone Fray Juan thought for some time on what Sir Robert had said regarding the difficulty the friars faced in maintaining their monastic rule and way of life while carrying on the work entrusted to them by the Pope. It weighed upon him again that through his enthusiasm for missionary work, and by failing to curb his speech, he had been instrumental in involving his order in enterprises for which it was not adapted and for which its members were not prepared.

He arose and went in and made a complete report to the prior, ending with his own misgivings. Father Paul was unaccountably indulgent.

"Fret not your heart, Brother," he said. "We are in the hands of God, and with prayer we may rest our case in His hands, confident that He will see us through."

IV

The days lengthened into weeks and the weeks into months, and still the friars had not been summoned to audience. Sir Robert, as he had promised, had managed to inveigle Habibullah Agha into providing the Carmelites with a small house in a secluded district of the city, and there they erected an altar and were able for a time to maintain the observance of their rule. Then orders from higher up must have come, for the minister appeared before the friars with a long face and many apologies to tell them that this house was required for other uses and that he was providing them with another. This happened twice, and the game was brought to an end only when Father Paul said he would go to a public caravanserai if they were disturbed again.

It was now Ramazan, the holy month of fast, bringing with it irritability and license. Since no pious Moslem allows food or drink to pass his lips between sunrise and sunset during Ramazan, the fast brought stagnation to trade and virtual cessation of all public business. By day the streets were almost deserted, while at night the air was filled with the drone of sermons in the mosques and of merry-making in the gardens.

Early one morning toward the middle of the month, at the height of the fast, the friars were aroused from their devotions by a troop of scarlet-turbaned imperial guards in the street and a pounding at the gate. The officer of the troop, on being admitted, announced that he was to escort the friars to his Majesty, and that they must come at once. Father Paul, when he saw the troop in panoply and the three splendidly caparisoned horses that were waiting for them to mount, threw up his hands in dismay.

"Have you no mules?" he asked.

The officer's reply was a look of incomprehension that said, "Mules? What have we to do with mules? They are for peasants, not for ambassadors."

Fray Vincent, recalling his days as a lieutenant of horse in the service of the King of Spain, observed the horses with loving interest. They were magnificent animals. He now drew his superior aside.

"This would no doubt be accounted an act of God, would it not, like your illness, when we fed you meat stock?"

Father Paul surrendered and mounted. Long-forgotten skills of his youth revived his interest and reconciled him to this violation of the rule. He even found a mild satisfaction in uniting himself with the beast in the harmony of movement.

They rode out of the city by the broad four-laned boulevard known as the Chahar Bagh, or Four Gardens, across the imposing Allah Verdi Khan bridge and onto the Shiraz road. Soon they were crossing the shoulders of the Kuh-i-Sufeh. Behind and below them the sprawling city of Isfahan, with its glittering domes and minarets, was in the pangs of new birth. Everywhere, under the dynamic influence of the Shah, were the scaffoldings of new structures, and along the Zeyandeh Rud irrigation channels leading from that river were causing the desert to blossom with gardens and orchards. The officer pointed pridefully to these wonders.

"Abbas," he remarked, referring to his sovereign familiarly, "has too much vigor"—at this he lifted his arms, clenched his fists and flexed his muscles—"and he must have something upon which to exercise. This year it will be the Afghans."

He gossiped frankly, with a good-humored cynicism, and told how the Shah had risen to power through intrigue, bloodshed, and extraordinary ability. As a child, and the nephew of the reigning shah, Abbas had been sent off for his own safety to live among the nomadic tribes. The shah was assassinated, as were the various claimants to the throne—assassinated or poisoned or slain in battle—until only the young Abbas remained of the Safi lineage. A rivalry now arose among the chiefs of the tribes for his wardship. Using these divisions to his advantage, Abbas had maneuvered his election as shah, and then by a series of bold campaigns had subdued the tribes one by one to his suzerainty. Next he turned to the foreign enemies—the Uzbegs on the east, the Turks on the west, the Portuguese on the south, the Muscovites on the north. The Uzbeg power was smashed. A three-year-long war with the Sultan failed to settle the western frontiers, but it taught the Ottoman a great respect for the Persian cavalry. Meanwhile, internal quarreling in Russia following the death of Ivan the Terrible had abated danger from that quarter. There remained the Portuguese annoyance on the south. It was to be gathered that Abbas hoped for something from the Pope by way of influence upon the Portuguese to lessen their exactions on Persian shipping in the Gulf. Abbas, now at the age of thirty-eight, had been reigning for twenty years, and he was without question one of the leading rulers of the East.

"The Shah, I gather, is popular with his people," commented Father Paul. "To what do you attribute that?"

The officer pondered a moment before replying.

"It is because he is one of us," he observed with a light shrug of his shoulders. "In him each of us sees himself. He rides better than any of us, he loves more ardently, he gives more generously—and he lies more grandly."

"Lies!" exclaimed the priest.

The officer smiled broadly.

"Have you not discovered? We Persians outdo the world in lying. But yonder is the Shah's camp," he added, indicating with a sweeping gesture a city of tents that was now visible at the upper end of the valley.

Presently they were in the midst of the encampment. It was obvious that no fast was being observed here. In various fields men were drilling with arquebuses after the European fashion, marching in rows, by squads and by companies, painfully learning close-order drill. Upon an overlooking knoll, mounted on a gray Arab, sat the tutor of this art, Sir Robert Sherley.

As the Carmelites passed below him, the Englishman lifted his hand in salutation.

Beyond the infantry—higher up the valley, and symbolic of the greater esteem in which it was held—was the encampment of the cavalry. Despite Sir Robert's artillery, the horse still remained supreme in the mind of the Shah. Squadrons of horse were now engaged in exercises that brought an involuntary exclamation from Fray Vincent.

"Holy Saint Michael!" he cried, as a squadron charged down the field upon rows of pomegranates. Troop by troop they pounded by with lances lowered. The thunder of hoofbeats filled the ears, their impact shook the earth, and the dust they threw up made a pall that obscured the distant mountains and veiled the riders from view. When the dust subsided there were no pomegranates on the ground, and when the troops circled and returned each lance was tipped with a ruddy ball.

The officer glanced at the friars proudly, as if to say, "Have you seen better in Europe?"

Beyond the cavalry, still higher in the valley, was the encampment of the Shah and his principal lieutenants. Fray Vincent, for all his military experience, had never seen such tents: majestic in size, and of material and workmanship more familiar to palaces than to the open sky—roofs of woven wool and walls of corded silk, canopies of brocade, and ground coverings of fine-textured carpets.

The largest of these tents, guarded by eunuchs and Qizilbashies, was undoubtedly that of the monarch. The officer did not pause there, however, but rode on up the valley. Eventually they came to an extensive area, the boundaries of which were marked by sentries posted at intervals of twenty paces, with bows in hand and arrows in the notch, ready to challenge any comer. The appearance of this enclosure was that of a horse fair, with strings of tethered horses in charge of hostlers in various tribal dress. Near the center, on a little hillock, stood a small tent around which a group of richly garbed men stood, while below them horses were exercised and paraded.

At the edge of the field the officer and his troop dismounted, and the friars followed their example. The officer identified himself to the sentry, and then led the way toward the mound. Among the figures in front of the tent no one could mistake the Shah. He sat apart from his courtiers on a carpet at the edge of the mound, from which he could look down upon the horses being exercised. It was not the outward tokens of royalty about him that were so impressive; it was the sovereignty in the man himself that made him like a magnet that both attracts and repels—that and the naked simplicity of his appearance and his manner in contrast to the elegance about him. The carpet on which he sat was a mere rag, dust-covered; the Shah himself was dressed in nothing more than trousers of red cotton and a jacket of black—this bit of black a concession, no doubt, to the solemnity of the Moslem Lent. His only insigne of royalty was a large crimson turban with twelve pleats fastened with an emerald brooch—the pleats marking his descent from the Twelve Holy Imams. His face was freshly shaven, except for the long narrow mustache that fell below the line of his chin and was now powdered with a fine gray dust kicked up by the horses that trotted and galloped before him; his eyes were rimmed with red, the lids inflamed by the dust. But more striking than these externals was his complete absorption in what he was doing, an absorption that strained out all the various aspects of his personality of which the officer had spoken, that resolved its baffling paradoxes and focused his whole being in the rôle of the moment: a judge of horseflesh.

Abbas was judging horses which the tribal chiefs, in response to royal levy, had brought to him for his inspection. The officer whispered this to the friars by way of explaining his monarch's ignoring their arrival. Indeed, Abbas seemed completely oblivious of them, as he appeared oblivious of everything but the business in hand. One by one he examined the horses, and his manner was that of a dealer whose livelihood depends upon his abilities to judge horseflesh and to drive a bargain.

"A good horse is a man's life in battle, and Abbas sees that his troops are well mounted," said the officer proudly.

The horses being tested at the moment were part of a herd brought by Haidar Khan, chief of the Kermanshah Lurs. The chief, a tall man with a white beard, stood some paces below the Shah, awaiting the monarch's judgment. His anxiety was obvious. The horses he had to offer appeared to be far from mean; nevertheless the Shah did not seem pleased with them.

"You have offered me half starved nags," Abbas said shortly.

The chief apparently expected this, but he stood up to the attack with a kind of stubborn bravery.

"Your Majesty knows that the drought has been severe in Luristan this year, and the pasturage scant," he protested.

"Well, let us see their behavior."

Abbas spoke to one of his officers, who ran and seized the halter from the hostler's hand and leaped upon the bare back of the nearest animal. The horse reared, but the rider held; with the halter strap and the aid of knees and heels, he deftly guided his mount into the course. In a moment the horse was speeding before the Shah at a gallop, throwing up a veil of dust which the Shah did not seem to mind, and presently he returned at a walk. Abbas arose and went over to the animal, felt its knees, its withers and its fetlocks, and with a skillful hand forced open the mouth and examined the teeth.

"The horse lacks endurance for battle," said Abbas turning to Haidar Khan, "yet he is sound of limb. I will take him. Will the rest of your offerings stand up as well?"

"Upon my head," the aging chief avowed, regarding the Shah with dignity. "You have taken the meanest of my herd to test. Try them all, and you will find that, but for a little spareness—the effect of the drought—they will all compare with your best. We raise good horses in Luristan."

"Very well," said Abbas. "Then I will expect you to send me another five thousand, none worse than these."

At this the reserve of the chief was shattered. He threw himself prostrate before his monarch.

"Majesty," he begged, "the glorious Abbas Safi knows how our people have followed him in battle, how two of my own sons are now in his royal service, how there is not a sheep nor a goat nor a tent peg that is not his Majesty's to command. But five thousand horses, O Lord of the Worlds, are not to be had that are fit for battle; yes, not to be had of any kind, unless your Majesty wishes that our people no longer range for pasture, that our sons should grow up as muleteers, and that our tribes turn from herding to tillage."

Abbas regarded the man at his feet with an appraising eye.

"Well, then, four thousand."

"Not four thousand, Majesty, nor three thousand. Perhaps another five hundred."

Abbas's patience was wearing thin.

"I can withdraw the frontiers to Kermanshah, where they formerly ran, and then you could offer your five hundred to the pig's offal, the Sultan. Would that please you?"

At the words "pig's offal" there was a movement among the courtiers who stood about. One of them, glowering fiercely, half withdrew his scimitar from its sheath and then, with a smothered oath, violently thrust it back. The gesture did not escape the Shah's quick eyes, one of which closed in a sardonic wink as he waited for the chief's response.

"That," whispered the officer to Father Paul, with malicious amusement, "is the Ottoman ambassador."

Haidar Khan came to terms with the Shah, promising two thousand horses more, and the chief was dismissed, after he had kissed the Shah's foot and had received a gold medal—one of the new *abbasis* which the Shah was currently minting.

The inspection of the horses continued. The sun reached the zenith and began to decline. The Shah's energy seemed tireless, his concentration indefatigable. Not all that he examined pleased him, and there were times when his wrath mounted, and it seemed that the bowstring or the bastinado was to be the reward of some offending chief or noble. But on the whole Abbas was in a good humor, for he enjoyed this work, and on this day his subjects escaped with no more than a rebuke, and some received a purse of gold.

From time to time, Abbas would call for water, for the dust was choking, and occasionally he would draw from his pocket a handful of raisins and walnut meats. Finally, toward mid-afternoon, he waved his hand for a halt and called for coffee.

It was then that he first appeared to notice the friars, who had been standing for four hours awaiting his pleasure. He beckoned for them to approach.

V

If Abbas felt any resentment at the Pope's having sent him "dar-vishes" for envoys instead of men of the hierarchy, he did not show it.

He ordered his court to stand aside so that the Carmelites might approach, and when the friars were about to offer the Shah the same obeisance they offered their Pope—that of prostrating themselves and kissing his foot—Abbas extended his hand instead. He then spoke rapidly to his interpreter, who translated, with appropriate embellishments:

"My lord, his Majesty, God's Presence and the Sword of the Faithful, commands me to say that you are welcome. He inquires as to your health and that of your exalted sovereign, his Holiness, the Christian caliph, and desires to know whether you have been well received and whether you have been provided with all things necessary for your comfort."

"You may tell his Majesty," said Father Paul dryly, "that we have been so laden with hospitality that if we are held in attendance on his Majesty much longer we will be surfeited and unable to discharge our duties. We trust that his Majesty will not blame his officials whose kindnesses to us we have been compelled to decline because of the rule by which we are governed. In all things else, we are commanded by his Holiness to be his Majesty's loyal servants."

These words seemed to please the Shah.

"You are holy men, I see. Tell me about your rule."

The priest began to tell something of the rule under which they lived.

"You are not really bishops, then?" asked Abbas. "Have you no authority over the Christians of my realm?"

"We are the lowest of the clergy, giving but not receiving obedience."

"I wrote especially that his Holiness should send me a bishop to assume authority over the Armenians of my realm. Have you no instructions to do so?"

This was the delicate question which the Carmelites had been cautioned to avoid. It was the sort of question that had rocked Christendom for many years.

"We have no instructions on that point," said Father Paul simply and directly.

The friars felt the Shah's scrutiny. He was giving them the same appraisal which, a quarter of an hour earlier, he had been bestowing on the horses. His eyes traveled over the brown gaberdines, newly washed and ironed but threadbare in places and patched in others. He seemed satisfied; but something about Fray Vincent seemed to catch his eye, and he nodded to himself.

He asked Father Paul to continue. The friar now began his prepared speech, reciting the instructions with which the Pope had charged his envoys. Abbas listened to the translation with a preoccupied air.

"You have spoken well," he responded through his interpreter at the end. "Yours is an honest speech. I thank you for your kind words. You are a scholar, I see, and you will give me much pleasure, for I am unlearned in many things. You will be a valuable counselor at my elbow."

He turned to Fray Vincent.

"You have, I see, been a soldier."

A look of surprise passed over the friar's face, which caused the Shah to laugh.

"You are too erect and proud of bearing to have been long a man of God," he said, "for such a calling makes a man bowed and of downcast look. You see," he added proudly, "I am a judge of men or I would not be Shah of all Iran. You think I have been judging horses all morning. You are mistaken. I have been judging men. Besides, you have a quick eye. Some day I shall ask you what caused you to change your course in life; but for the moment tell me what you think of my army."

"Your Majesty," replied Fray Vincent, drawing himself erect—for a brief moment he seemed again the trooper—"had I known, before I came, your skill at reading the character of men, and had I known that you would question me on your army, I should have prepared my answer. True, I once called myself a man of war and of battle, but I was a youth when I did so. I know of war neither as a tactician nor as a quartermaster, nor would I, now that I am consecrated in my service to the Holy Church, speak on matters military except on express command."

"Then I command," said Abbas.

"Since you give me leave," said Fray Vincent, "it is this: Men versed in warfare may well differ as to whether battles are won with cannon or with horse. I will say that both are secondary to qualities of command. The Turks are past masters in the use of artillery. You are using it for the first time, but so skillfully have you handled it that you captured three hundred of the enemy's pieces. That news reached us even in Russia."

An expression of pleasure lighted the Shah's face.

"But beyond command is still a greater element of success," continued the friar, "and that is the cause for which one fights. Of course there are many, and some exact one measure of loyalty and some another. Yet, having soldiered under the greatest king of Europe, it came to me that there is only one cause for which to live, and hence only one cause for which to die, and that is the cause of God, and obedience to His will."

As the friar spoke Father Paul showed uneasiness at such boldness, fearful lest it annoy the monarch and mar the harmony of the audience. But Abbas seized upon the words.

"You have spoken truly, after my own heart," he burst out. "Does not our faith of Islam mean submission to God, even as your Christian faith? And I would have you know that I greatly revere men of God such as yourselves, and reverence your holy caliph, for that his service is in obedience to God."

He now turned to Fray Juan, who had not spoken as yet. He looked at the friar with the same appraising look he had given the others, and was about to address him, but seemingly finding nothing of interest in the man's face he turned away and spoke instead to Father Paul.

"You have, you say, messages from your sovereign?"

The prior drew from his gaberdine the wallet which he had so carefully guarded for three years, containing the letters from Pope Clement VIII and the supplementary letters from Clement's successor, Pope Paul V. Abbas brought them to his lips in a sign of reverence for their senders, and handed them to a court secretary.

Father Paul then produced the presents which the Carmelites had brought: first the crucifix in Bohemian crystal ornamented with gold and emeralds. Abbas seized it avidly and held it for a long time in his hands, admiring it.

"Beautiful," he murmured. "Beautiful." And he continued to gaze at it after he had laid it carefully on the carpet by his side. At last he turned and looked at the friars, his eyes surveying their tattered habits, as though mentally considering the contrast between the richness of the ornament and the poverty of those who brought it.

"This man—the Christ—means much to you," he said thoughtfully. "He means much to me also. Pray thank your sovereign, his Holiness, for sending me so appropriate a reminder of a common tie."

Father Paul, for all his dignity, was obviously embarrassed.

"This," he explained, "is not from his Holiness but from the Emperor of the Holy Roman Empire, Rudolph, as a token of his esteem for you. On our journey we passed through his dominions and he, desiring to be remembered to you, dispatched by us this gift."

An immediate change came over Abbas. His face grew dark with disappointment. "Is not this the emperor who, breaking his word, made his peace with the Sultan at the very moment when my armies were deployed against the eastern frontiers of the Ottoman realm? And now he sends a token of his esteem!"

"As to that, I cannot answer," said Father Paul with reserve. "We are neither his subjects nor his emissaries, and we are not informed as to his policies and affairs. I can only say that which is generally known, that as the Turks proved extremely powerful and overran his dominions, he was compelled to make peace."

"Well, let it pass," said Abbas, and turning again he eyed the prior's wallet with the eagerness of a child. "What else have you brought me?"

Father Paul took out the illustrated copy of the Old Testament which had been sent as a gift from the Cardinal of Cracow.[1] Abbas seized the book and opened it and began to admire the illustrations. Turning the pages, he came to a picture of the war in Heaven—the figure of St. Michael brandishing a sword over the fallen Satan. Abbas studied it.

"Who is this on whom the angel has planted his foot?"

The prior explained.

Abbas was suddenly amused and glanced wryly at the Turkish ambassador, who was still nursing his resentment at the earlier insult to his sovereign.

[1] A volume now in the Morgan Library in New York City.

"No," exclaimed Abbas, and broke into a hearty laugh, "it is the Sultan."

He signaled to one of his courtiers, a mullah in an enormous white turban. The ecclesiastic came and prostrated himself.

"I charge you," said the Shah, "to write in Persian on the margin of each of these pictures their meaning and interpretation."

The mullah accepted the volume gingerly, like a thing unclean.

"I charge you," said Abbas, continuing his joke, "that you consult diligently with these holy men concerning the meaning of the pictures. Perhaps"—a note of irony crept into his voice—"you may learn from them the secret of virtue of which you seem so ignorant."

"Pray thank your sovereign," he said, addressing the prior, "for his thoughtfulness in sending this book and assure him that I shall indeed have it read to me and shall treasure its words of wisdom."

Again the prior was compelled to explain that the book was not the gift of the Pope. Abbas's look showed puzzlement and a trace of petulance.

"Then have you brought me nothing from your sovereign?"

"May I explain to your Majesty," said Father Paul humbly, "that for a purpose we have brought no gifts from his Holiness, for the giving and receiving of gifts belongs to ambassadors, and we have come to your realm not as ambassadors but as simple religious, bearing letters from our sovereign; nor do we ask to be received and treated as ambassadors, but only to be at your service for such good as we can render in the name of our common Sovereign and Lord."

Abbas again gave the friars his characteristically penetrating glance.

"You are honest men," he said shortly. "Such are not common in these times. Do you have anything further to say?"

"Besides these letters," said Father Paul, "we have been charged by our sovereign with certain matters to discuss with you privately and we beg a time when you will have more leisure."

"That you shall have," said Abbas. "That you shall have."

The friars waited, hoping that the Shah would set a definite hour for such a private hearing, or that he might now dismiss his courtiers in order that they might speak to him without being overheard. But seeing that this was not the Shah's intention, Father Paul requested permission to withdraw.

Abbas, however, seemed to have taken a fancy to the Carmelites.

"Which of you," he asked, "was it that conversed with my niece and ward, the Princess Shamala?"

"It was I," said Fray Juan.

The Shah regarded him for a moment with narrowed eyes, but said nothing. And then, with a broad gesture, he motioned to the friars to be seated on the carpet beside him.

"Stay by me for a little," he said. "I have urgent affairs here, as you see, for these princes have come from great distances to offer me their aid in war, and I should not disappoint them. But sit here and we will talk while I dispatch this business."

Then Abbas, calling for the adjutant to approach, ordered the review of horses to be continued, and for another two hours the Carmelites sat with the Shah or walked about at his heels while he examined the horses, selecting this and rejecting that, now showing pleasure, now growing angry, now full of zest, now indifferent—spreading before them his humors and moods and treating them with the intimacy of boon companions.

VI

Shortly after the return of the friars from Serishabad, Sir Robert appeared and asked to speak to Fray Juan.

At that time the Carmelites were living in Julfa, across the Zeyandeh Rud from Isfahan. Julfa was the suburb across the river in which the Shah had settled the Armenian architects and artisans whom he had transported from the Caucasus to work on his various constructions. It was a thriving city in itself, connected with the greater city by the magnificent bridge of many spans named after the Shah's chief sirdar, the Georgian Allah Verdi Khan.

The house which the friars occupied had belonged to a baker who had forfeited his life and property to the state for having speculated in grain during the winter. It had fallen into disrepair, and workmen sent by the minister of court were still replastering, replacing broken bricks, and restoring doors that had fallen from their hinges.

Fray Juan received the Englishman in the courtyard, where there was a bench on which they might sit. As the friar was considerably taller than the Englishman and did not like to look down upon him, he sat and motioned the Englishman to his side.

"You made a good impression on his Majesty," Sir Robert began cordially. "You have played your game well."

The friar protested that they were playing no game, but that if they had gained any points it was simply through their directness.

"That is what I mean," said the Englishman quickly. "It took Abbas by surprise. He is not used to directness. That is your strength. Use it."

"That should be easy."

"I understand that his Majesty regards the conclusion of an alliance with the Pope as imminent and intends to observe the event by taking a Christian wife."

Fray Juan straightened up in shock.

"No, no, that would be impossible," he exclaimed. "A Christian could not marry a polygamist."

"Well, a sort of Christian, then."

"What would you consider a 'sort of Christian'?"

"Oh, a Georgian or a Circassian, many of whom are renegades. You will meet a notable one in the Sirdar Allah Verdi Khan. A Georgian, he was taken as a hostage while still a child and was reared in the royal service. He soon forgot his Christian faith. Or did he? A curious fellow," commented Sir Robert. "Dour and unfathomable he is; extremely able as a general and of undoubted devotion to the House of Safi; noted for his cruelty but also for his capacity for mercy; a most generous man, donor of funds for many public constructions including the great bridge across the Zeyandeh Rud." He paused. "The Shah's new bride might be the Princess Shamala, niece to his Majesty, another of the child hostages whom these Eastern monarchs are fond of taking and rearing," he remarked. "If so, I give thanks to God."

"You give thanks to God?" exclaimed Fray Juan.

"I would indeed, for that would relieve me of an involvement and an embarrassment."

Seeing the friar's astonishment the Englishman continued: "You recall that I mentioned at our first meeting how his Majesty had conferred upon me a boon that was like an albatross about my neck? He betrothed me to the princess."

The friar's perplexity increased.

"That was eight years ago," went on Sir Robert. "I had presented my first cannon to the Shah. A modest falcon it was, but I had cast it of iron instead of brass, as I had been taught by Henry Pit, gunmaker to our Queen, and it was light enough to be used in mobile warfare. We had a field test of it. Abbas was so delighted with the noise it made that he bade me come with him to the palace. He swore then and there to bind me to him with bonds stronger than the iron of my ordnance. Before his court he summoned the Mihtar Beg, as the chief eunuch of the royal Haram, or household, is called, and whispered into his ear. The official disappeared, and presently the curtains parted and he reentered, leading by the hand a childish figure veiled in snowy cashmere.

"Silence fell upon the court while the eunuch waited for those present to avert their eyes or bury their heads in their cloaks. Then Abbas turned to me and said, 'Behold your bride, to whom I betroth you this day by my imperial will and grace.' I had not time to protest before the eunuch lifted the veil and revealed a child no more than ten years old. She was appareled in a short skirt of white woolen, boots of white felt that came to her knees, and a blouse of fine linen gathered at the neck and embroidered at the throat and sleeves in yellow and red threads. Upon her head she wore a little coronet, a flat-topped cap of felt, covered with a veil that reached to her shoulders behind and down upon her forehead in front. Her eyes were large and solemn as she turned her face toward the Shah. Her manner was that of a child drawn from her play by her mother's call. But in fact she had been deprived of a mother since the age of five, and her expression made me feel that she regarded the Shah as father, mother, and God. Beneath the docility one sensed a wild, cat-like wariness that was no doubt the product of her Haram upbringing, combined with the Amazon blood that flowed in her veins, and in the veins of her people since the day when Queen Hippolyta yielded her girdle to Hercules.

"I was dumfounded, as you can imagine. Apart from the consideration that she was a mere child was the fact that I am a Englishman, and we Englishmen are as reluctant as the Jews to couple with an alien race. At least so I was brought up, and so I had resolved, long before I set foot on Persian soil. As you know, Father, the sin of venery is not upon my conscience. However, I told his Majesty only that it was not our custom to marry so early. Whereupon he retorted, 'She will grow up,' and added significantly, "If you knew how much I prize her, you would not be hesitant, but would leap to take her to your arms.'"

Sir Robert began to pace up and down the courtyard. The recital of the events had recalled to him his condition of exile, and the disappointment of his hopes of escape.

"But now that the princess is grown, could you not regard marriage to her in a different light?" asked Fray Juan.

"Possibly, though I fail to see a match. She is much too lively and headstrong for my taste and temperament. Besides, she still adores the Shah, only she will not unite with him, they say, except in marriage, and his Majesty still dallies with her, finding her charming, but wanting her without commitment."

"And how would that leave your betrothal, were the Shah to conclude to accept her on her terms?"

"What Abbas gives, Abbas, like Deity, can take away. Only his indecision deters him from saying to me, 'Friend Sherley, release me from this vow of betrothal.'"

Fray Juan was thinking of the princess as a soul to be saved, of one who belonged to the Christian fold but who had become lost from it, and who was now greatly in need of redemption. But redemption was not to be achieved by man, except by the aid of God, and by divine grace.

Still, the friar thought, the effort should be made. The Englishman had by the betrothal been given a claim upon her person. Would it be possible for him thereby to redeem her soul?

He discreetly brought these views to the attention of Sir Robert.

"Aye, and of course I would marry her if to do so were to save her from the arms of Abbas. She is a handsome, spirited lass, and could no doubt be quelled and subdued as was one Kate by her Lord Petruchio in a pleasant and witty comedy that I saw just before leaving London. Nevertheless, such is not my way and humor, nor would it be easy for me to forget an incident that always comes to mind at mention of her name."

Fray Juan did not inquire what the incident was, but the Englishman evidently felt a need to explain himself.

"A few days after the scene at court when his Majesty betrothed the princess to me, I came across her in the public square. She was upon her horse, accompanied by a quartet of Qizilbashies and her guardian eunuch. Seeing me, she reined up and spoke to me.

" 'So I do not please you?' she demanded with some asperity.

"I explained that she was indeed charming, but still a child.

" 'And how does this land please you?' she demanded next.

" 'As much as it may, seeing that it is not mine own country,' I answered.

" 'You speak as I have heard it said the English speak,' retorted the child. 'Full of boast and prowess. Is it true, as they say, that you draw a bow as tall as you stand?'

" 'That is approximately correct,' I replied, amazed at her precocity. 'I should not be honest,' I added, 'if I did not remark that the English have won many a battle with their long bow.'

"This produced a prompt response from the princess.

" 'Fie!' she exclaimed. 'Can you draw a bow?'

" 'If it is not too taut,' I replied.

" 'Can you do so well as this?' And suddenly a bow was in her hands. It was not a long bow—"

"I know the kind," interposed the friar, so quickly that Sir Robert glanced at him in surprise. But the friar's eyes were bent on the ground.

"It was rather smaller than the Persian archer's bow, but it served. Fitting an arrow, the child raised the weapon to eye level and drew aim at an object on a lance fastened to the barracks walls nearby.

"The arrow sang, struck its mark, and lodged, its shaft quivering from the impact. You can imagine my horror, Father, when I saw that the object at which this little girl had shot was a severed head, so blackened as to be hardly recognizable, with matted hair falling from the crown about the face, and hollowed eye sockets from which the carrion crows had already plucked the eyes."

"Nevertheless," persisted Fray Juan after a moment of pained silence, "as forgiveness is our Christian duty, if it were to serve to redeem her soul from hell, could you not conquer your aversion?"

Sir Robert was silent in his turn while he considered the question. Then, like a judge pronouncing an opinion, he gave his decision.

"If it were presented to me as my duty," he said solemnly, "then as my father the Sheriff of Surrey and Sussex taught me, I would do my duty whatever the cost."

Fray Juan nodded, though Sir Robert's statement somehow failed to give him any real feeling of satisfaction.

VII

It was the last day of Ramazan. Toward sundown all the rooftops were crowded with watchers eagerly scanning the evening sky for the thin sickle of new moon that marked the end of the fast. That evening the Shah returned from his Serishabad camp to preside over the feasting and games that on the morrow would celebrate the event.

Next morning, the minister of court appeared before the house of the Carmelites with an escort of troops to conduct the friars to the Shah for the private interview he had promised. When they were across the bridge and in Isfahan proper, the advantages of being mounted became apparent. Here the avenues were crowded with holiday makers bound for the great plaza—the Maidan-i-Shah—where the games were in progress. The nearer to the plaza, the thicker the crowds and the more difficult the passage, and it was only by a wedge of troops that it was possible to make a way.

They finally gained the maidan. This was the plaza that was the awe of travelers, unrivaled in extent by that of St. Peter's or the Kremlin. It was five hundred yards in length and two hundred broad, surrounded by palaces and mosques and other imposing structures. At one end reared the great portal of the Masjid-i-Shah, the royal mosque that was still in construction; upon one side rose the graceful dome of the Sheikh Lutfallah mosque with its faience work of bewildering complexity and glowing color; on the opposite side of the square stood the high, porticoed Ali Gapou, the Shah's official place of audience. It was toward this that the crowds pressed, toward the roped-off area where the games were being held.

Under the portico of the Ali Gapou, on a high dais, in view of the populace, sat Abbas, surrounded by court officials.

"Is this a Roman Caesar presiding over the combats, or a French king holding court, or the Shah receiving us in private audience?" Father Paul asked, bewilderment and vexation in his voice.

But the Shah had caught sight of the friars making their way through the crowd, and going to the balustrade he waved to them in an easy, familiar way. Father Paul again managed to contain his annoyance, and Habibullah Agha escorted them to the monarch's presence. This they reached by means of a steep, narrow, circular staircase that led from the ground floor to the elevation of several stories on which the portico rested. The Shah was expecting them when they appeared, and personally escorted them to the dais.

"I have been eager to see you," he said with such charm and obvious pleasure that Father Paul's countenance relaxed. "It is gracious of you to come. I could not send for you earlier, and today, as you see, is one of celebration over which I must preside. However, as your business is urgent, I beg that we may converse while we observe the games. But first, there are some here who I desire should make your acquaintance, and others whom you may find it convenient to know."

He gestured first to a stripling among his courtiers. The lad came forward and Abbas took him affectionately by the hand.

"This is my son, Safi Mirza."

The prince appeared to be in his teens—Abbas confirmed that he was seventeen years of age—and there was an inexperience and guilelessness in his expression that seemed to belie his spangled court dress.

"You are welcome, and I am happy to know you," the prince said simply and gravely, but there was a shining in his eyes that said far more.

"Safi is my eldest son, and has recently rejoined us after his education among the tribes," said Abbas. He went on to explain that since the age of ten the prince had been living among the Shamlus, with whom he himself had spent his childhood. It was the custom of the dynasty, the Shah said, and added that he thought well of it, for it took the princes away from the enervating influence of the Haram and of the luxury of city life.

"But now we must seek him a proper wife," Abbas concluded.

Fray Juan had been contemplating the prince, and he was startled to hear Abbas addressing him.

"His mother is a Christian," the Shah was saying, "and I hope that he may persist in his mother's faith."

These were the first words that the monarch had addressed to Fray Juan, and they were so astonishing that the friar was in confusion.

"I shall pray God that he may, your Majesty," he said plainly, and wondered whether he was being too forward.

Standing nearby was a tall, dignified man, elegantly but simply dressed, with a face as handsome as Lucifer's and an expression as cold and remote and lonely as that of the archangel. Abbas now introduced him.

"I would have you know also my right arm in war, the captain general of my armies, Mishevelli, whom we call Allah Verdi Khan," said the Shah. He addressed these remarks to the prior, but he leaned toward Fray Juan again and in a lowered voice added: "He too has been a Christian. He is of the race of Georgians, but alas, he reverences no God. He is a fit object for your prayers and preaching."

So this was the renegade of whom Sir Robert had spoken. The friar studied him with compassionate interest, and thought how lost indeed are those who live without faith. He was thinking also of the Shah, for the monarch had spoken of his sirdar with a mixture of seriousness and levity.

The sirdar's lips curled into a withering smile.

"I am a worshiper of the fire," he said quietly, "and I bow my knee only to the sun of this Empire—his Majesty."

The Shah and the sirdar exchanged glances, but they were so quick that the friar could not read what was in them, and then the Shah laughed and remarked: "My sirdar, as you see, is as adept at speech as he is at battle; he handles a phrase or a scimitar with equal ease. Beware that you become not involved with either the one or the other."

The Shah went on to other members of his court: the chief vizier, an inconsequential man for all his rank, rumored to be impotent; the royal treasurer; and a dashing young officer, who was apparently a favorite, by the name of Mohammed Ali Beg. He smiled and bowed and was about to say something, but at that moment a tremendous outcry arose from the plaza. The Shah rushed to the balustrade and further introductions were abandoned.

Two blindfolded bulls were being led into the plaza. They were small and gaunt, with long sharp horns. Pieces of red bunting had been tied to their horns, and hempen lines led from their halters and from their hind feet. There were three lines to each bull and each line was held by a man. The bulls were brought to the center of the roped-off arena and ranged face to face at an interval of twenty paces.

The shouting subsided while the crowd waited for the Shah to give the signal.

Abbas lifted his hand; the attendants uncovered the bulls' eyes and unsnapped the halter lines. The bulls faced each other stolidly; then as their eyes grew accustomed to the light and they saw their antagonists, they began to paw the earth and to bellow defiance.

The shouting of the crowd arose again, and mounted in excitement. Something of these human passions must have been communicated to the dumb brutes; or perhaps they became aware of what was expected of them. In any case they were charging at each other, their eyes glazed with madness, their nostrils distended and flecked with froth as they struggled against the ropes that held their feet. The attendants would allow the bulls to become locked in combat, goring each other, and then they would separate them until they had regained their strength. By means of the lines one bull or the other would be given the advantage, in order to prolong the sport.

Fray Vincent, more familiar with such spectacles than his companions, followed the contest with undisguised interest. But Father Paul refused to look at it, and kept his head sunk on his chest while his fingers told the beads on his rosary.

Abruptly, in the very midst of the charging and bellowing of the bulls and the roars of the crowd, the Shah left the balustrade and returned to the dais, where he seated himself and beckoned for his interpreter and for the Carmelites.

"Let us talk in peace," said Abbas. "What is it you wish to communicate to me?"

If this was the Shah's notion of a private audience, the Carmelites determined to make the most of it. Father Paul now spoke of the Pope's concern for the Christian subjects of the Shah, particularly the Armenians, and reminded the Shah of his promises to give them religious freedom. He suggested that a firman, or imperial decree, be issued to that effect.

The Shah listened attentively, and his manner appeared serious.

"Nothing is nearer to my heart," he assured the prior, "and you may tell your sovereign of my intention to do so at the earliest. But his Holiness must understand the fanaticism of the mullahs, and the exposed condition of the Armenians. You know, of course," he continued, "that nothing would assure their religious freedom so much as the interest and protection of his Holiness. The Armenians are now without a patriarch, since the death of Artavanes, and I have deferred the elections for a new head of their Church until I could hear your views on the subject. Now if his Holiness would send a bishop to govern them—for they are at present without a shepherd —it would serve to strengthen their faith and would simplify my relations with them."

Father Paul did not think it necessary to explain that the Pope was no longer a powerful potentate, for Abbas must surely be aware of that fact; nor did he consider the moment expedient to explain the present policy of the Roman See toward schismatics: the day of compelling dissidents to accept the authority of Rome was past; the Pope would under no circumstances assume authority over a Christian body such as the Armenians without their free election and accept- ance of such authority. It was not necessary to explain these things, for it had by now become obvious that the Shah was only engaged in baiting the friars in an effort to discover the actual interest of the Pope and the character of papal policy toward the Christians of Persia.

"I will communicate your wishes to my sovereign," said Father Paul, attempting to content himself.

"That will take time," said Abbas, "and the Armenians are greatly incommoded without a prelate." He leaned toward Father Paul in a confidential way. "You are holy men and, as I have noted, men of parts and discretion. Cannot one of you assume the bishopric in the interval?"

Father Paul avoided the trap.

"We are friars, your Majesty," he said firmly. "We have no au- thority to assume hieratical office."

There was renewed shouting from the plaza. The Shah again leaped up and ran to the balustrade, this time to watch the death of one of the bulls. Presently, he gave the signal for a second combat.

"You see what barbarians my people are," he remarked when he rejoined the friars. "We need such men as you who come from lands of gentler ways. We are happy to have you in our realm."

Fray Juan was prompted to speak up.

"We would not deceive your Majesty," he said. "There is equal or greater barbarity in Europe. In Spain, from which I come, bull- fights are common and, if possible, more horrible to witness."

The friar's speech produced a sudden uneasiness in the Shah. His hand crept inside his tunic where he seemed to have something—a talisman, probably—which he caressed.

"You are an honest man," the Shah said to Fray Juan. "You are all honest men and pleasing in my sight. Your sovereign the Pope I hold in the highest esteem for having sent me such worthy men."

"And will it be pleasing to your Majesty," Father Paul persisted, "to grant the assurances which his Holiness has requested?"

"Indeed, indeed," replied the Shah. "A firman shall be drawn up at once, as you desire." He waved his hand as though the thing were already done. "But your Reverences must stand in want. I shall appoint you a stipend. Is there anything particular which you require?"

"Your Majesty," replied the prior, all too conscious of how short of funds they were, "we are deeply grateful for your interest, but our order will provide for our needs."

Abbas, well informed on the friars' poverty, regarded them thoughtfully. "You are strange men," he commented.

"However, there is indeed one thing for which we must solicit your assistance," resumed the friar. "We desire to celebrate Mass and to maintain the regular observances of our order. We wish to invite attendance at our observances, to give instruction to those who seek it. For this we need a house which we can arrange to our purposes. But these things we are forbidden to do by the law of this realm. We beg therefore that you issue a firman granting us these privileges."

"Why, what need have you of a firman?" asked the Shah with an air of astonishment. "As my guests you enjoy every privilege of the realm, far more than those who rely upon the narrow terms of a decree. Surely you may use the house I have assigned to you in such ways as you please. Is the house not commodious enough? Then I will assign you another."

The prior reminded the Shah of the numerous dispossessions to which they had been subjected.

"That shall be remedied," assured the Shah. "That shall be remedied. Still, if it is your desire, I shall issue a firman."

At that moment there was another tremendous shout from the plaza, and Abbas arose.

"I shall not keep you longer," he said with finality. "This is not appropriate entertainment for men of God. Tomorrow I shall send you a letter which I shall entrust to one of you to bear to your sovereign."

As they bowed to take their departure, Fray Juan noticed the sirdar Mishevelli gazing upon him with an amused, cynical expression that seemed to say, "You see how little you mean to this monarch— or to me."

PART THREE

———•••———

The Princess Shamala

I

The letter to the Pope which the Shah had spoken of was two months in coming. Eventually the minister of court appeared at the friars' house with a silver tube, richly engraved, of the thickness and length of a forearm. This, the minister announced, contained the letter from his Majesty to the Christian caliph, and he laid it reverently in the hands of Father Paul. The priest bowed and said that he would personally see to it that it was placed in his sovereign's hands.

While waiting for the letter Father Paul's health had deteriorated so greatly that his companions had concluded that he should return to Italy. But it was plain that the prior was in no condition to make the journey alone, and Fray Vincent respectfully insisted that one of the friars should accompany him. Father Paul finally consented that Fray Vincent might see him across the mountains as far as Hormuz Island in the Persian Gulf, where he would be able to take ship with the Portuguese convoy and so reach Rome by sea.

So it was that the Carmelite friar, Juan Thaddeus of St. Elisaeus, became the sole papal representative at the court of Abbas, Shah of Persia. Of the five who had set out from Rome, two had now left to make this journey, and two had long since died in the Russian snows.

Hardly had his fellow Carmelites departed when Fray Juan was visited by a Qizilbashie with a summons dispossessing him from his quarters and assigning him to others. Fray Juan now found himself occupying a miserable hovel with broken walls, crumbling plaster, and dried-up gardens in a lower part of Isfahan near the tanneries, from which a nauseous stench continually arose.

The friar set to work to repair the house and make it habitable, and to install an oratory. In certain directions he was perhaps unimaginative: it did not occur to him that as a lone friar he could hardly maintain the observances as in a convent, or that before Fray Vincent could return he might be dispossessed from this house with all his work gone for naught. But in other directions his matter-of-factness was an advantage. He did not suffer greatly from loneliness or discouragement. There was work to do; he was occupied from morning to night. He maintained the conventual rule as best a solitary friar could: he celebrated Mass, observed the canonical hours, meditated daily on the goodness of God—and in the intervals was busy with trowel and mortar and plumb line.

During this time he was ignored by the Shah; he lived in Isfahan as one who had been transported there in the middle of the night, set down by some jinni, without knowing why or for what purpose. Still, Fray Juan soon managed to make himself at home in his shabby surroundings and to make progress with what he ever held to be his prime purpose in life, that of a witness to his faith.

To assist him in his house repairs Fray Juan had acquired the services of a young man named Javan—a word which meant simply "youth." The way this had come about may have been typical of the way things happened in Persia, but Fray Juan took it as a direct evidence of God's guidance and providence. The friar had gone into the bazaar to buy lime for plaster and was about to hoist the sack to his shoulder when the boy slipped in and with a nod to the kiln master indicated that it be put on his back instead. Fray Juan turned to him in wonderment. It was not unusual for porters to claim a load and to hoist it to their backs against the protests of the purchaser; but this boy was not a porter. He had sturdy legs, it is true, but he could hardly be past fourteen, and besides, he had no porter's bustle upon his back. Fray Juan said as much to him.

"I will be a porter when you have let me carry this for you," answered the boy. His brown eyes were bright with entreaty. "There must be a first time for everyone."

"I will give you the fee, and you may buy yourself a bustle and call yourself a porter, but as for this sack of *gach*, it belongs to my shoulders today," said the friar firmly.

He put a piece of money in the boy's hands, and took the sack from him.

The boy threw the money to the ground and began to cry.

"You starve me, you take the bread from my mouth, you rob me of my living, you steal my manhood," he wailed over and over until the friar, alarmed and embarrassed at the commotion he was causing, finally consented to let the boy carry the sack.

Once it was on his back again the boy started off at a lively pace, laughing and shouting.

"I know where the house is. You are the Firenghi darvish that lives in the tanners' quarter. Make way, there, make way for the Christian darvish; make way for the foreign ambassador."

At the house Javan fetched water for the plaster and brushed off the walls and wet them down, while the friar looked on in perplexity. Just as his Holiness had neglected to provide any presents for the Shah, so he had failed also to provide his envoys with means of subsistence, at the same time requiring them to be at no man's charge. For their expenses the friars had set forth with only some five hundred scudi. This sum had been largely spent in the three years of journeying and during their imprisonment in Russia. Of what was left, the largest part had been taken for Father Paul's and Fray Vincent's return journey. Fray Juan was not greatly concerned, for what he had in his wallet was enough to keep him in food and candles for the present—but he had no money to spare for journeyman hire. Furthermore, it was not the custom of the Carmelites in convent to hire services which they could perform themselves.

Fray Juan explained this to the boy and expressed his regrets. Javan looked at him with quizzical amusement.

"I like you," he said. "I work for nothing."

"I cannot accept your labor on such terms," said the friar.

The look of incipient tears appeared again.

"You turn me into the street?"

This was something that the friar could not combat.

"What am I to do?" he asked helplessly, more to himself than to the boy.

"Let me stay with you," said Javan promptly, and again laughter was in his eyes. "I serve you, I work for you, I be your man. Everybody needs somebody. Your friends have gone. I take their place. You need not pay. I can earn money. I bring you money."

And so Javan attached himself to the friar and became his man of all work. He proved far more sophisticated than his years suggested, and for loyalty a blood brother could not have been more devoted.

But his loyalty was all to the friar. Fray Juan would have liked it better had Javan been drawn by the faith which was the center of the friar's existence and shown some interest in knowing more about it, but as to this Javan was simply negative. It moved him no more than did the yelping of street dogs disturbed in slumber by a passing muleteer. This caused the friar a great deal of secret anguish, and he began to pray daily for Javan's salvation, but with no visible effect.

The friar considered his first task, that of preparing an oratory for public observances of the offices and the reception of inquirers for instruction in the Catholic faith. He went about this in the confident assumption that there would be attendance at the observances and a steady flow of people seeking instruction. While his official business in Isfahan was that of securing a firman from the Shah permitting the Carmelites to acquire land and build churches, his personal and private duty was that of winning converts. Land for a church would be desirable, but a congregation was more important. Fray Juan was confident that if he but let down his net figuratively, as had the Apostle Peter, the Lord would fill it. And so he made haste to finish his chapel, where he might receive this congregation.

It was while the friar was in the midst of this work that the eunuch who attended the Princess Shamala appeared at his door with a peremptory demand that he accompany him to the house of his mistress. Fray Juan argued with his conscience before acquiescing. It was against the Carmelite rule for friars to visit in houses, and to call upon an unmarried lady not in need of extreme unction would be a grave breach of the proprieties. Nevertheless, the friar concluded that this situation was unusual in any case, and that the rule should be regarded in a new perspective.

The Princess Shamala lived within the high-walled and extensive palace area known as the Haram. This was a large park filled with numerous palaces and lesser structures separated by gardens and hedge-bordered avenues and dividing walls. Each of the four begums had her own private palace; a number of the more favored concubines had houses of their own; some, from the nomadic tribes, unaccustomed to the confinement of houses, were provided tents according to their rank. The rest dwelt in a big dormitory-like structure. The princess, whose status was indeed especial, occupied a small house in a private garden walled from the Haram proper and accessible from the street without entering the Haram itself. It was to this that the friar was now escorted. While the eunuch went to fetch his mistress, the friar was left standing in a small but richly furnished chamber.

The friar began to tell his beads, and before he was aware of it the princess was in the room, or rather, standing in the curtained doorway, waiting for the priest to bid her enter. Gone was the Amazonian look, the barbaric imperiousness of their first meeting. Now, Fray Juan was struck by her resemblance to the Italian conception of the Virgin. He was amazed at the change. Was it an Oriental dissimulation for effect? Everything was there: the oval perfection of the face, the pinkish transparency of the skin, the large, oval eyes —green, however, beneath arching eyebrows—even the aura of tender, innocent virginity. Only there was more strength and maturity in the features, and a boldness to the nose, and the mouth was wider than the Italian Virgin's. The princess, he observed, had height; she would come above his shoulders—a fact he had not noted when she was mounted.

The princess was dressed with modesty and dignity. Her outer garment was a full-skirted redingote of white quilted satin with golden buttons; it extended from the throat to the crimson satin slippers of which only the tips showed. Upon her head she wore the remembered Caucasian coronet of red felt edged with ermine and covered with a wimple.

The princess's mood today was sedate, with a suggestion of deference in her manner. She glided into the room and waited for the friar to address her.

"You sent for me?" he asked.

The princess looked startled.

"Sent? Oh, yes. Please sit down." She was speaking Italian in her charmingly awkward way. The friar looked about. There were no chairs, but there was a thick ottoman. For her part the princess had settled herself on the floor, with the graceful movement of a bird settling on its nest, in a way that caused her skirt to fall in a circle about her. The friar took the ottoman. The princess clapped her hands and cried to the eunuch, *"Kavah."* While the coffee was coming she began to talk.

"When we met on the Ardebil plain," she said, "you said something to the effect that were I Christian I would be sole wife to sole husband, did you not?"

"I did."

"I can see some virtue in the Christian faith," mused the princess, "at least for a woman. It is better than being one of four wives, with innumerable concubines besides to contend with."

Her decision seemed made.

"Will you baptize me into the faith?" she demanded eagerly.

"Patience, patience," protested the friar, but inwardly his heart was beating with joy. "One does not become a Christian simply to take a husband. Moreover, how would this benefit your case with the Shah, whom, you gave me understand, you wish to marry?"

"Ah, you do not credit me with sincerity," reproached the princess with the suggestion of a pout. "Besides, are you not here to convert the unbeliever? And if I, by becoming truly a Christian, lead his Majesty also to the light—even through the path of desire—would that not also be an end greatly to your holy interest?"

The friar felt himself coming under the sway of the princess's mood. Yes, what a glorious conquest that would be for the Church! For if through the princess Abbas were saved, then were it not possible that he lead his people to Holy Church, which once in history they had almost entered? Still, something within him repelled the idea.

"You must be truly converted and baptized in heart before I could offer the promise of the sacrament of baptism," he said stubbornly.

"Very well," replied the princess equably. "What is it to be truly baptized in heart?"

The friar considered what, in view of the princess's obvious tendencies and interests, would be most to the point.

"There is much to learn in being a Christian," he said earnestly, "but it all begins with love, love of God in the Lord Jesus."

"Love?" asked the princess, wrinkling her brow in puzzlement. "Do I not know what love is—perhaps better than yourself—for all that we both are chaste? What is this love of which you speak?"

The friar was momentarily baffled as to how to explain what had always seemed to him obvious and axiomatic. The ordinary analogies of parental love, fraternal devotion, marital bliss, had no meaning here.

"Let me ask you a question," he said after a moment. "In your dreams, when you see yourself with the man you seek for husband, are there certain elements present which you do not find in the waking reality?"

"Yes," said the princess promptly.

Fray Juan wondered if he had allowed himself to be led into an alley with a different sort of turning from what he had intended. He was so very, very ignorant and maladroit in such matters, he told himself, as he closed his eyes for a moment to ask forgiveness of Heaven for his stupidity. Nevertheless, he decided to wade on, hoping for intuitive wisdom.

"What do you seek in marriage?" he asked.

"Something different from what one finds in the Haram," said the princess. "A relationship to which I could give my life with abandon."

The friar bit his lip and prayed again that his cast be true.

"Tell me what it is like," he said.

The princess regarded the friar in sudden helplessness. "How can I describe it in language with which I am so little familiar as Italian? It is like two threads of a carpet that cross and intertwine, upon which the Master Weaver casts his workmanship and the Tree of Life unfolds. It is like the string and the bow, both drawing and both responding, that together send their arrows as children into the path of the future. It is like the wick and the oil, like the flute and the wind that enters, for each is useless without the other. Yes, it is like the pot and the nothingness within, for what is the pot without the nothingness? Indeed, I would be the very nothingness within the pot that enclosed me as its own."

At this speech the friar was deeply moved. He experienced a strange but curiously familiar sensation, as though a distant memory had been summoned from forgetfulness—a memory of something left unsaid, an unclosed book, an unfinished song, a name that is known but eludes the mind. Above all this, however, was a welling admiration for the princess that caused him to exclaim: "Bravely spoken! It is not better said outside the Song of Solomon. I pray that God may send you such a husband.

"But meantime," he added, "since it is your desire to perfect yourself in the practice of the Christian faith and to experience its comforts, I will send you a copy of the catechism in Italian for you to study. You should begin the observance of the usages and rites of the Church. In all this I shall be pleased to instruct you."

"God send me a husband with such qualities and manners as you yourself possess," exclaimed the princess impulsively, and seemed quite unaware of the embarrassment it caused the friar.

They had drunk the coffee and had eaten little sugar cookies, and the princess, more at ease, began to tell the friar about her homeland in the Kafkas—about its towering, forest-clad mountains, so different from the gaunt and sterile ranges of Persia; about the wild free life of the Circassians, her people; about the hard-riding, harddrinking Prince Sampsov, her father. The prince, with forces and territory too small to maintain his independence, and forced to choose between Sultan and Shah, had allied himself with the Shah. In token of his fealty he had married his sister Tamara to the Shah and had sent his daughter as a child to live in the court as a royal hostage.

"Then the Prince Safi Mirza, whom I met at court, is your cousin?" the friar asked.

"Yes, and another, Khudabandeh Mirza, a few years his junior. You understand that it is not easy to be—the rival of one's aunt," said the princess, blushing. "Not to mention some several hundred others, whom his Majesty takes as his fancy directs, coddles, lavishing upon them his attentions, together with jewels and peacocks and slaves, and then forgets, leaving them to pine in bereavement worse than death."

Her tone as she said this was full of pain, and the friar, for all his innocence of worldly matters, sensed the deep ache in her heart, the nature of which perhaps the princess herself did not understand.

"Yet," she concluded languidly, with the weariness of one who has borne a burden too long but is still unwilling to surrender it, "there are thousands in the realm who would willingly spend a life of such bereavement for one day in these courts as the favorite of his Majesty . . . and perhaps with good reason."

The friar took leave of the princess feeling that for all her good intentions and for all the strength of purpose that had kept her from surrender these many years, she labored against a heavy cross current of desire. She was now, at eighteen, of the age in which her nature demanded some great object in life upon which to expend itself. It was no longer content to battle with negatives, with restraints and avoidance of evil; it must set itself toward some positive goal.

The princess's status was much in the friar's thoughts as he recited the evening offices and began his personal petitions to the throne of grace.

II

The vernal equinox was nigh, and the whole of Isfahan eagerly awaited the arrival of Noo Rooz, the Persian New Year. Streets were swept and door frames painted blue and yellow, and already thousands of beautiful hand-woven carpets hung from balconies as though in competition with the flowers blossoming on the steps below. All along the immense length of the Chahar Bagh were beds of hyacinths, jonquils, and early iris.

The Princess Shamala had gone to the bazaars to purchase new garments and presents for her servants, according to the custom of the Noo Rooz. In the past, visiting the various shops and stalls had always been an exciting adventure. Today the crowds were dense, and everyone seemed happy and enthralled by the wondrous displays. In the shops along the vaulted bazaar streets the shopper found a fantastic display of wares from all over the world. Usually, after she had remembered her household, Shamala would indulge her personal fancies in the purchase of some of these objects—a robe of brocaded velvet, or possibly an azure gown of mistlike silk, or a length of the down-soft woolens that were now being imported from England. Afterward, in the bazaar of the rose merchants, she would purchase some new attar—of jasmine or oleander or sandalwood—or perhaps some kohl to darken the eyelids, or Egyptian henna to use after the bath. Her tour usually ended in the street of the silversmiths, where she might choose a new comb of mother of pearl or tortoise shell, or perhaps a bandeau of pearls from Bahrein, or a bit of white jade, or possibly a ruby bracelet.

But today Shamala's heart was not in her shopping. The merchant Ali Seyyid noted the princess's preoccupation and protested.

"Hanim," he pleaded, "has your slave offended you? Why have you withdrawn the sunshine of your favor, so that this wretched earth still groans under the frosts of winter? You have bought only three hundred dinars of my wares, whereas in the past you bought ten."

"Have I forgotten some of my household?"

"Nay, nay. But you have cast hardly a glance at what I have displayed for the hanim who is renowned as the fairest moon that ever rose in the royal Haram—such merchandise as in Hind is only for maharanis"—here he lowered his voice confidentially—"merchandise which I have withheld from the eyes of one of the begums until your glance had rested upon it."

"It is not the fault of your wares," said Shamala, "but that I am tired of shopping, and the crowds."

She returned to her palanquin.

But Shamala did not wish to return home. It was springtime, and nature called her out of doors. She felt confined in the city and longed to be on a horse, galloping over the barrens in the midst of the great wastes and the empty deserts. She felt within her something that expanded and required release, so vital, so imperious, that even the wastes of the western desert did not seem vast enough to accommodate it.

"Take me out to the Hezar Jareeb," directed Shamala. The Hezar Jareeb was the park across the river, an extensive paradise, or *firdoos*, as it was called, that was being developed by royal command.

Fardoush, her attendant, nodded to the bearers to take up the palanquin.

The narrow, winding streets of the bazaars were choked, and they had to pick their way through crowds of shoppers, past queues of donkeys and grunting porters and around trains of camels. They finally emerged from the covered ways into the sunlight of the Maidan-i-Shah. A game of polo was in progress, and at the farther end of the plaza workmen were removing the last of the scaffolding that clung like a cobweb about the almost completed dome of the Masjid-i-Shah. The dust thrown up by forty pounding hoofs cloaked the base of the mosque in a haze, so that the dome, now revealed in all its splendor of blue and yellow faience, seemed suspended in mid-air, unreal, enchanting, sublime.

The sight of the horsemen exhausting themselves in sport, and the mosque, exhausting the resources of human art in the expression of worship, both served to lighten Shamala's mood, and her eyes brightened as she viewed the combined spectacle.

"Abbas is like the jinni of the *Thousand Nights and a Night*, is he not?" asked Fardoush, intuiting the princess's mood, as he had learned to do over a dozen years. "He but utters a word, and castles and palaces and mosques arise in his breath."

Shamala did not reply. A little later, as they entered the Hezar Jareeb, he remarked, "Travelers say that the parks of the Moghuls at Agra and Fatehpur Sikri do not exceed this in magnificence, nay, nor those of the French king."

"Why do you continually harp on his Majesty?" asked Shamala a trifle impatiently.

A look of innocence filled the eunuch's eyes.

"I only spoke of these gardens, which are truly Paradise now that it is graced by the presence of Nur Mahal, an houri without peer in this world or the next."

Shamala was reminded that the Shah frequently addressed her as "my *nur mahal*," which meant "light of the palace."

"You are in a flattering mood today," commented Shamala blandly. "First his Majesty, then the park, and last of all, your mistress. Well, I know where your interest lies."

"When every object of worth or grandeur we behold recalls his Majesty's greatness, his splendor, his benevolence, should I be blamed if his name leaps to my lips?" asked the eunuch, and then added insinuatingly, "or to your thoughts?"

"There is no gainsaying you, is there? You read my mind like a repeated prayer from the Koran."

Some moments later she left her palanquin and strolled down one of the many flower-bordered avenues, followed by the shadowing Fardoush. The branches overhead were filled with fluttering wings; the air was loud with bird song that mingled with the music of running water and sweet with the scent of fresh, damp earth and the faint perfume from masses of flowering daffodils.

"I saw his Majesty the other day," Fardoush remarked, making shrewd use of the solitude and the evocative setting of gardens and springtime to pursue his purpose.

"And you spoke of me, no doubt?"

Shamala's voice was taking on an edge that caused the eunuch to guard his speech.

"I am the princess's discreet and obedient slave," Fardoush replied quickly, "but I do not command his Majesty's tongue. He spoke concerning you."

There was no remonstrating with this person, whose sexless condition seemed to put the motions of his mind in an orbit distinct from that of ordinary creatures—a path that wandered through unknown voids of lonely darkness. He was a strange and pathetic person, whose inner workings were past divining, yet who had a quality of attaching himself to another, or to an idea, with the tenacity with which moss clings to rock. Shamala did not ask what the Shah had said, but Fardoush was not to be deterred.

"Why do you not accept the Haram?" he now asked directly. "Abbas attends your coming as a hushed nightingale awaits the rising moon. You are indeed the Light of the Palace, which has lain in darkness since your return from the Kafkas."

"Why do you say such things?" asked Shamala plaintively. "You know my resolve in this matter, and that I have become a Christian, and as such cannot accept to yield myself in this fashion."

"Accept the Haram, where warmth envelops you and delights caress," urged Fardoush.

As Shamala did not respond, the eunuch altered his strategy. "Perhaps it is the darvish to whose house I escort you regularly who draws a veil over the effulgence of his Majesty?"

"Quiet that evil tongue!" cried Shamala hotly, "and take me home."

The eunuch, finally subdued, subsided and waddled petulantly ahead to summon the bearers.

III

In her house again Shamala paced restlessly from room to room. She paused in the kitchen where Ahmet and his helpers were heating milk to be fermented into *mast* and preparing a special curry for the rice, and from there wandered into the garden to see how the new tulip beds were thriving. A magpie was scolding the gardener and the gardener was scolding his apprentice. But nothing held her attention. She returned to her chamber and called for Parvin, her maid.

Parvin was the widow of a Shirazi who had been killed in battle. Shamala had often pitied her bereavement, but now she thought that Parvin must be happier than she, for her maid had at least known the actual meaning and joy of love. As for herself, she had thought she knew its meaning, but now she was doubtful.

"Dear Parvin, tell me a story," Shamala coaxed, for Parvin was not easily drawn out, but like a darvish storyteller of the bazaar had to be put in the mood.

Parvin regarded her mistress searchingly, and said: "My mistress is not happy today. I will tell her the story of Prince Hassan and the peri Banou."

Shamala knew the tale by heart—of the prince who, hunting in the wastes for his lost arrow, came upon a magic cavern, and of the peri who offered him wealth and kingdoms and jewels, and would have offered him her heart had she not been a peri, to whom love was forbidden, and who, unwilling that the prince fall in love with a mortal, made herself so beautiful that no earthly creature thereafter pleased the prince.

Parvin told the story in a singsong fashion to the soft accompaniment of her three-stringed lute. She was midway in the tale when Shamala interrupted:

"My head is in too much of a whirl today. Sing me a song only, and leave off the story."

"One of the songs of Nizami, then," said Parvin gently. "They are sweet and soothing to the weary heart." And she began to recite the love poem of Laila and Majnun, the tale of Laila, whose beauty was the delight of the tribes, with "ringlets of a thousand curls, and ruby lips, and teeth of pearls," upon whom Majnun looked, and as he looked, "distraction filled his burning brain—no rest he found by day or night: she was forever in his sight." But the wandering tribe to whom the girl belonged folded their tents and slipped away into the solitude of the mountains. The love-stricken youth wandered through the mountains in search of his beloved, "swelling the mountain streams with his tears, starting avalanches with his sighs."

"No more, no more," exclaimed Shamala, holding her head.

Parvin broke off her recitation, but continued to touch the lute with her fingers, drawing forth beguiling chords.

"Tell me," Shamala said with an affected casualness, "what it is to be loved."

But having revealed herself she became embarrassed. It was ridiculous that one who spent her life in the royal Haram, in the very citadel and marketplace of love, should know so little of its meaning. Yet it was true that her knowledge was as theoretical as that of an observer of the stars, who has spent his years gazing at them, contemplating their movements, but has never grasped one.

Parvin grew pensive, and then her expression became languorous, her eyes soft and voluptuous.

"Oh, my mistress, how can I say? It is like being in the bath, except that all is reversed. Instead of the warm water, followed by the cold, and then the anointing and the perfumes, it is first the anointing and the perfumes, then the shock of the cold water, like ice, and then the warm water, foamy with the soap sponge, falling all over one, until one wishes to drowse and dream forever."

"Oh, Parvin, Parvin," exclaimed Shamala impatiently, "how can you say such things! Then any bath attendant would serve!"

"I have heard of those who go from bath to bath," said Parvin contentedly, a little wistfully, "and compare those of Samarkand with those of Stamboul, and of Tiflis, where the water flows hot and sulphurous from the rocks, and I have heard also of those who search the wastes for the oasis where spring the fountains of eternal youth, desiring to lave only in those mystic waters. But as for me, I will quaff from any stream that refreshes, and let others thirst for the fountains of Paradise. There is no Paradise, mistress, for our sex, and such little joy as our kismet allows we should seize, remembering that the rose blooms but for a day, and the nightingale sings but briefly in the springtime."

Shamala felt a kind of suffocation. This was the sort of talk she had heard since childhood. She yearned for a clearer atmosphere, and her thoughts turned upon the friar, and the instruction he had been giving her.

Actually, she had been taught little concerning the mysteries of his doctrine. There was a Christian catechism which she had been learning by rote, but the friar did not place much stress upon memory work. He talked to her about the simple duties of life, which she was beginning to look upon from the Christian viewpoint, and through these he had gradually enlarged her devotion to the deeper mysteries of the faith. There was the matter of industry, for instance, which in the Christian light became the touchstone to a happier natural order and explained also a fundamental nature of the Godhead. The friar placed a great emphasis upon industry as a manifestation of Christian living. Work, he explained, was not just something for servants, not something one did from necessity or because the Shah commanded it, but something that brought one into closer communion with God. Fray Juan frequently quoted the words of Jesus, "My Father works, and I work," and made the point that the believing Christian should always be engaged in some useful activity. Under this prodding Shamala had taken a new interest in embroidery and needlecraft.

There were other things of which the friar spoke, to her soul's welfare—but there were also things of which he did not speak. There was so much to learn! Just now, Shamala would like very much to hear the friar explain to her his views on marriage and love. . . .

"I must speak to the darvish of what you have said," Shamala said to Parvin, but really to herself.

Parvin threw up her hands.

"A darvish, mistress! I did not mean so much. Go to any but a darvish, for such men are ashes and water that leach the flesh for a bit of gold."

"I mean the Christian darvish from Rome."

Parvin regarded her mistress shrewdly.

"What is it like to be a Christian and attend upon the darvish?" she asked.

"That I cannot rightly say," Shamala responded lightly, "except that I must go to him regularly to confess all that I have done of a sinful nature."

"What a strange man he is! The Sufi darvishes speak only of the pleasures which are reserved for us, but I have never known them to show one. What is sin?"

Shamala shook her head.

"That I have yet to learn. I am receiving instruction."

Parvin laughed. "In sin, mistress?"

"You naughty woman!"

"I have seen the Christian darvish," Parvin went on composedly. "He is a handsome man. Would that I could be so instructed!"

Shamala dismissed her with a sharp rebuke, but she was obliged to admit to herself that she was not so shocked as she had pretended.

IV

Abbas disliked formalities. He prided himself that he needed no retinue or panoply to mark his dignity, and enjoyed a freedom of movement such as other kings did not. His entertainments were accordingly casual and generally impromptu.

Now, after a protracted absence, during which he had been in the provinces making levies of troops for his forthcoming campaigns, he had returned for a brief sojourn in Isfahan before rejoining his army. On his last evening in the capital he announced a durbar, and then suddenly took the notion to have a small supper party before the reception. To this party he summoned the Princess Shamala.

The party was to be held in the Chehel Sitoon, the newly completed summer palace which was already renowned for the grace of its architecture, the beauty of its garden setting, and for its murals.

"His Majesty will have Firenghi guests," said Fardoush, who brought the summons to the princess, "and the entertainment will be after the Firenghi custom. You will apparel and behave yourself accordingly."

The evening was mild, and supper was served on the great portico of the palace whose twenty slender columns reflected in the pool gave the palace its name of "Forty Columns." In deference to Firenghi custom the platters were not set on the floor but on tables—rather taborets—and the guests sat on thick ottomans for chairs. Besides Shamala, the guests were the Carmelite friar, Sir Robert Sherley, and two Armenians and their wives. The Armenians were Mattios Hagopian, the venerable *khwajeh nazar*, or dean, of the Armenian community, and Petros Ashkhanian, a wealthy merchant who handled much of the monarch's personal business. None of the Shah's household was present, and Shamala surmised that the Armenian ladies were included in order to provide her with appropriate chaperonage. Eager as she had been, she found herself now somewhat disquieted by the intimate company. Her glance met that of the friar, and for the moment that they exchanged looks she seemed to see an answering disquiet in his eyes, though with it was a mild good humor that reassured her.

Fortunately, Shamala was not forced into the midst of the company, but sat apart with the Armenian ladies. These two, clad in black that set in dazzling contrast the white and crimson of the princess's dress, accepted with quiet submissiveness their role of framing the princess with appropriate dignity.

Abbas was at his most ingratiating best, and his conversation touched on a multitude of topics: he was like a merchant displaying his wares to a hesitant customer, drawing out one object and then another until he finds something that brightens the eye. It was mainly upon the friar and the Englishman that he plied his craft, but from time to time his gaze would embrace the others, and when it fell upon Shamala it would linger for a moment with a questioning, assessing expression, until Shamala began to suspect that this whole affair was for her benefit, that she might see how well Abbas compared with the best that Europe had to offer.

Shamala's attention was drawn to the Englishman, to whom she was nominally betrothed, but with whom she had hardly exchanged a word since their encounter in the plaza nearly ten years before. She studied him with a new interest in the light of the ideas being imparted to her by the friar. He was handsome enough, she thought. His yellow hair that came down upon his shoulders after the Firenghi fashion, his cloud-gray eyes, his fair skin that years of campaigning in the Persian sun had given a golden sheen—all spoke in his favor. Shamala knew that he was accounted moody and aloof, and that he led an austere, remote life, and that while he commonly wore Persian dress, this was his only accommodation to Persian custom. He held himself to be a Firenghi, and above all an Englishman, and it was well known that he pined to return to his native land.

"Your Reverence is acquainted with the man who has reformed my armies and revolutionized the art of warfare in the East," said the Shah, addressing the friar, and then to Sir Robert, "but I have wanted you, Sherley Khan, to explain to this excellent ambassador sent by the Christian caliph the military situation of the realm, and why an alliance with the powers of Christendom is to our mutual interest."

The Englishman now spoke.

"Persia," he began, "is an extensive realm of forest and desert, oasis and pasture, yielding many delectable fruits and an abundance of cereals, lambskins, and silk, besides many excellently wrought wares of brass and copper and the like. It is, however, confronted by enemies on all sides, but particularly on the west and in the south. His Majesty's major preoccupations today are three: the frontier with the Ottoman, the situation in the Persian Gulf, and an outlet for the silk produced in the realm. The silk is of great importance, and supplies probably half the demand of Europe, but it moves thither under great vexations by the Sultan and the Portuguese, as well as by the Muscovites for such as is transported through their realm.

"Against his enemies," he continued, "his Majesty has won several notable victories. His greatest—against the Uzbegs on the east— ended for all time, I believe, the threat from Central Asia, and was achieved against cannon and musketry by use of the traditional bow and pike and scimitar, and by skill in maneuver of horse.

"Nevertheless, the issue with the Ottoman remains in doubt, and the present status is one of uneasy truce. It is for this reason that his Majesty is deeply concerned for the alliance with the powers of Christendom which his Holiness has offered to promote."

Shamala had listened to this explication with increasing interest. She thought that Sir Robert had spoken with dignity and intelligence, and it struck her suddenly that Sir Robert had more the qualities of an ambassador than those of a man-at-arms, and that the Shah should have sent him to Europe rather than his brother. The friar was speaking, however—and with unusual boldness for one addressing his Majesty.

"His Majesty persists in calling me an ambassador," he said, "despite the fact that I am not received at court, live with the simplicity of my religious calling, and have not obtained those testimonies of confidence which his Majesty promised his Holiness. I must therefore repudiate the title of ambassador. While I find myself here as the representative of my sovereign, his Holiness, it is only in the capacity of a courier and humble attendant upon your Majesty."

The friar's outspokenness seemed to amuse the Shah.

"How modest you are," he murmured. "How you enchant me with your modesty. But tell me now, will you not assume ecclesiastical jurisdiction over my Armenians? I have explained to you that they are without a prelate. Is this not so, Mattios Hagopian?"

The khwajeh nazar meekly bowed in assent.

The friar sighed to himself, wondering how to find new words with which to counter the familiar theme.

"Your Majesty is well aware that as an alien I would only antagonize your Armenian subjects were I to attempt to exercise authority over them, and would involve them in divided loyalties. In any case," he added firmly, "I have no instructions to such effect, and I can assure you that his Holiness has no intentions in this regard."

Shamala thought the friar had made a good impression upon the Shah, and she wondered why the Shah had neglected him for so long. In his friar's habit he looked cadaverous and insignificant, and he ate with the frugality of a man to whom food was a matter of indifference; but Shamala noted that his voice was strong and that he moved with effortless coordination.

The musicians had begun to play, and their music stirred the princess. Below the terrace lay the palace garden, and above the dark outlines of the foliage the new moon was now visible, a thin golden sickle suspended like a scimitar above the trees. From the foot of the terrace, extending into the depths of the garden, was the pool which mirrored the tender foliage of willow trees, the twenty columns of the portico, the lanterns hung among the trees, and the diffused radiance of many stars. From the garden was wafted the scent of lilacs in bloom, and mingling with the strains of the music were the splash of water in a distant fountain and the night song of the bulbul caroling from the recesses of the plane trees.

Shamala thought this garden must be very like the gardens of love in the verses of Nizami, and she was enchanted. At the same time she was vaguely disturbed by the interrogations of the Shah, for it was plain to her that he must be probing for the friar's weaknesses, to the friar's ultimate disadvantage.

"Yes, we need such men as you in this realm," Abbas was saying. "Something has happened to our people for which I understand you have the cure. Once we were a mighty people, and the ruins of the

ancient grandeur are to be found on every hand, but something of
the ancient manhood has disappeared.

"I can tell you what has happened," he continued. "The people
drink a strange poison that sucks their vigor worse than the juice of
the poppy. Do you know what it is? It is Islam. In former times the
people worshiped Ahura Mazda—the Lord of Great Knowledge, the
Lord of Light and Life, as revealed to them by Zoroaster. Then came
the Arabs bearing the sword of zeal and the banner of Islam and the
cry of the faith: 'There is no God but God, and Mohammed is His
Prophet.' And such was the edge of their sword and the burning
fire of their zeal that our people were compelled to accept the faith
or perish."

Shamala glanced at the friar. He was listening attentively. Her eyes
crossed those of the Englishman, and for a moment the two gazed
at each other, while the Shah continued to speak, and then Sir Robert
looked away.

Abbas was speaking.

"How has this faith of Islam corrupted us? That, I do not rightly
understand, for how can one be corrupted by acknowledging the one-
ness of God? Yet such is the case, for honor and truth have disappeared from among us, and an upright man is not to be found; and
without uprightness there can be no greatness, and without greatness
there can be no kingdom, and without a kingdom this pleasant soil
will revert again to desert."

Abbas was speaking now with such earnestness, such deep feeling,
that it was impossible to doubt his sincerity.

"Ah, my friend," exclaimed Abbas, addressing the friar, "even as
Sherley Khan here has aided me in restoring the political integrity
and greatness of this realm, so must you assist me to restore its moral.
That is your duty here. That is your kismet which has brought you
here. I am glad you have come. You are welcome. Is there anything
you desire?"

The friar again went on the offensive.

"It would be most gracious of your Majesty," he said, "if you were
to grant the firman which has been the subject of correspondence
between you and his Holiness, confirming the religious freedom of
the Christians in your realm, and granting us the right to acquire
land for churches and religious institutions."

"Ah, of course, the firman, of course." The Shah smiled as though the matter had simply slipped his mind. "Well, that shall be attended to shortly. Meanwhile, let us enjoy this evening which Heaven has so graciously provided us."

Abbas paused abruptly. It was as though the weight of his thoughts —the vastness of his dreams and the magnitude of his responsibilities —was too heavy for him, and he was too greatly burdened. Above the garden, against the curtain of the evening, the stars moved in their orbits, as they had moved in the time of Darius, and from the garden a bulbul suddenly began a new song—a song of spring and of the mating season.

The company was silent, and Abbas turned his head slightly to listen to the song of the bird. Then he turned further, and his gaze moved over the garden, drinking in its beauty, absorbing its message of the present, which had nothing to do with history and the grandeur of nations and the monuments of kings, but was a reminder rather of the fleetness of days, the silent dropping of the moon, the quenching of fire, the urgency of the seasons. Tomorrow, he would be with his troops, riding among the windblown and silent wastes, far from these gardens, far from this lovely Chehel Sitoon, far from Shamala.

"Would you not like to visit your aunt?" he asked, turning to Shamala with the abruptness to which his courtiers had long since grown accustomed. "She is in her quarters in the palace, and she would, I am sure, be grateful for a visit from you."

Shamala was surprised, for she had understood that her aunt was not in Isfahan, having gone to spend the season on the Caspian. She suspected a ruse, but the idea intrigued her.

"Why not?" she replied lightly. "It will be refreshing for both of us."

V

Abbas had no sooner escorted Shamala through the door at the rear of the portico than he seemed to be diverted by another idea.

"I must show you the palace," he said, "before the court gathers. You will be the first to see it completed."

The Chehel Sitoon was more a summer pavilion than a palace

proper, its chief feature being the portico on which they had sat for supper. Behind this was a solid structure enclosing an imposing banquet hall and several smaller adjoining chambers. The hall had a vaulted ceiling intricately decorated with arabesques of blue and gold and was enclosed at the ends by high, semicircular windows formed of panes of colored glass combined in a pattern of jeweled splendor. The opposing walls were filled, with the Shah's bland disregard for Moslem religious prohibition against portraiture, with four immense murals. One depicted the Shah's battle with the Uzbegs; another, his battle with the Turks; the other two were court scenes, the first depicting the reception of Humayun, the Moghul emperor, by the Shah's forbear Tahmasp, and the second showing Abbas banqueting with his principal courtiers.

Abbas conducted Shamala with the delight of a man who has newly come into a fortune and is showing off his treasures.

"Such paintings are the mode in Europe," he explained, "and I engaged a French artist to supervise their execution."

Shamala sensed the game that Abbas was playing and perversely reserved her admiration.

"I have others I must show you," continued Abbas, unperturbed by her equivocal enthusiasm. He led her through an adjoining chamber, the walls of which were also covered with life-size depictions, to a small side portico.

"Behold!" he exclaimed.

There, on one wall, appeared a heroic portrait of Shamala herself, appareled in Circassian garb. Shamala gave a gasp of astonishment and pleasure, but promptly recovered.

"So, you must display me, one way or another, before your court," she scolded. Nevertheless she was greatly flattered.

"Forgive me," begged the Shah, "but should not ambassadors and envoys from abroad obtain some inkling of what loveliness, what charm of womanhood, our country produces? And is there in my realm a more glorious exemplar of these qualities than Shamala, Nur Mahal? But let us sit for a moment and talk," he added, "here with the garden at our feet."

He clapped his hands and a servant, as though awaiting his summons, appeared with a ewer of steaming coffee on a tray.

Shamala knew that when the Shah was indulgent she must be doubly wary.

"Will you not serve me?" Abbas asked, as he seated himself on a convenient ottoman.

Shamala busied herself with the coffee and avoided the Shah's eyes.

"This is better than a banquet with princes," said Abbas as he took the cup. His manner grew pensive, tender. "To be out of your presence is to be crossing the wastes of the western *lut* without water."

"If that is your metaphor," responded Shamala distantly, "then Abbas is an island in a lake."

"An island in the sea, rather," retorted Abbas, without offense, "for compared to the purity of your disposition, all other women are like salt water, bitter and unfit to drink."

He waited expectantly, a hurt look in his brown eyes, as though he could not believe it possible for anyone to deny his wish.

"Nur Mahal—Light of my Days—" he began again.

Shamala lifted her head but her eyes refused to meet his.

"How beautiful you are," Abbas whispered. Shamala thought he was going to use one of those expressions so common—"like a moon on the fourteenth night," "the rose to which the nightingale sings," or the like, but he did not; he simply repeated, "How beautiful."

The simplicity of the words and their obvious sincerity caused Shamala to lift her eyes to him. Instantly Abbas had them as in a net. It was impossible to avoid his look, royal in its dignity but like that of a nomad gazing upon a prize mare, imperial in its challenge yet with the wonder of a tribesman standing before the portals of the Great Mosque. A kindred response was awakened in Shamala; the tumultuousness of the Caucasian mountains responded to the desolation of the Persian desert; her eyes met his in an instant of understanding; for a moment she was prepared to ride out with him into the wastes.

Then the lightning faded as it had flashed, and Abbas was quick to discern the change. His long mustaches trembled, but not from anger or impatience; he seemed instead crestfallen and his expression was one of regret and humility.

"Shamala," he said diffidently, "is it that I cling to the faith of my fathers? Would you have me adopt this Christian faith? Would you have me send away all others of the Household and abide with you only? That would I do gladly, for you are the pearl, as says the Christian story, to gain which the merchant sold all his possessions."

This was the surrender for which Shamala had long hoped and for which she had schemed. But now she was not ready for it—even though the offer were genuine, which was, her better judgment told her, to be doubted. She hid behind an evasion.

"Your Majesty knows that, were you a Christian, you would be forbidden to ask such a question, for you are already married to my aunt."

The reminder irritated the Shah. He arose and began to pace up and down to keep his composure. It was plain that he was doing everything possible to make himself agreeable, aware that to lose his temper now would spoil all that he had achieved. At last, no longer able to restrain himself, he faced Shamala.

"Words, words, words—mere words," he fumed. "As long as I am a Moslem I am married by Moslem law, and I can divorce by Moslem law. I can divorce, and then become a Christian."

Shamala's ideas and deepest desires gradually cleared before her vision. It was like a mist clearing, revealing the outline of the distant mountains sharp and clear against the sky. She understood now that she did not love Abbas, as she now understood love. And it was equally clear that her nature could not allow her to yield herself on any other terms. Her back straightened and her eyes took on a rebellious, defiant look.

"And then, after I had married you, you would renounce your Christian faith and become again a Moslem?"

Abbas accepted reverses, but never defeat. He recognized now that his strategy had failed. He must retire gracefully and await another day, a more favorable opportunity. He understood the value of patience. He smiled now, a little ruefully, and bowed in acknowledgment that Shamala had won the contest. He held out his cup and Shamala refilled it.

"You see a great deal of the Christian darvish," he remarked casually. "How is that?" The stroke was adroit. Shamala's face crimsoned.

"I go to him for instruction in the Catholic faith, to which I have been admitted," she replied defensively. "That is all."

"I mean," said Abbas, as though he had been misunderstood, "what is he like?"

"Your Majesty needs no one to instruct you in reading human character. You are acquainted with him."

Abbas laughed.

"Still, a woman's insight is to be valued. What is this game of his? The Christian caliph who calls himself Holy Father, but who plays with kingdoms as though at chess, has not for nothing sent ambassadors to me in the guise of sandaled darvishes. What is the meaning of this? He will find that Abbas is not a fool, though he was reared among the tents and never learned to read and write. Tell me, what does this man seek?"

"I have never spoken to him of his affairs," said Shamala firmly. "But he is an honest man, I assure you, and what he says, I would believe."

"So you find him an honest man also, do you?" asked Abbas penetratingly.

"I do."

Abbas's expression became grim.

"Then let him keep himself so, and all who consort with him," he muttered.

He turned toward the door.

"Shall I take you now to your aunt?"

Shamala's eyebrows rose.

"Are you sure," she said, "that my aunt is not on the Caspian?"

The question was to Abbas like the lifting of a curtain.

"Ah, Shamala," he exclaimed delightedly. "How I have been deceived! You thought your aunt was on the Caspian, yet you permitted me to draw you away on the pretext of seeing her. You have not entirely forgotten me, have you?" He laughed. "But your aunt, I am happy to say, has just now returned, and so Abbas is not the liar you would believe him to be. She is not far away, in the Little Haram across the garden, and she is waiting now to embrace you."

With a mocking smile Abbas left to rejoin his guests, while an attendant escorted Shamala across the garden.

VI

Shamala returned from her visit to her aunt in a depression, strongly affected by the older woman's lonely, unhappy state. Tamara, it struck her, was an example of what it meant to have had Abbas's favor. Tamara had long been the Shah's favorite—the adored, petted, spoiled darling of the Haram, lavished with every delight her whim demanded. As the mother of the royal heirs she was pre-eminent in the Household, the sovereign's viceroy in this kingdom of women. Yet how insecure had proved this life, how dangerous, and now to what sad and bereft state it had come at the very maturity and splendor of womanhood! In all the household of women Tamara had not a single friend, not a single person of her sex in whom she could confide, or whom she could trust. Everywhere she was the object of such jealousy, envy, or awe as forbade approach. And there was one who hated Tamara with such fury that her life was never secure. This was the embittered, half mad, loathsome hag Faridje, the Shah's first wife, who lived a solitary, almost caged existence under constant observation lest she do harm.

Abbas no longer visited Tamara. Tamara's two elder sons had been taken from her when they reached the age of ten, and they were seldom allowed to visit her now. At the age of thirty-five she had become a lonely old woman, whose only comforts were her third son, a boy of five who like his brothers would soon be taken from her, and the shreds of her Christian faith. This faith had ceased to have any concrete meaning for her; not since her marriage had she attended any of its observances, for she had nominally apostasized; its liturgy and teachings had become only vague memories; yet because of it she retained a mild, sweet resignation that filled Shamala with sadness and misgiving.

Tamara had greeted her niece eagerly, with all the affection of her hungry soul; she had bade Shamala sit beside her, and while she stroked her niece's hair she had asked her about her life. When Shamala gave evasive or noncommittal answers Tamara was not surprised, but nodded understandingly, as though disappointment and dissatisfaction were the expected lot of women. She asked about her sons. Had Shamala seen them? Were they well?

Shamala could tell her only what she had heard—that Safi Mirza appeared to stand high in his father's esteem, that Abbas held his hand at state receptions, and that recently he had put the prince in charge of an army corps.

At this news, Tamara's large, dark eyes, still beautiful for all that they had become sunken with loneliness and grief, filled with anxiety.

"That is bad," she said. "Safi is bright, and he is brave, and he will win glory, and his father will grow jealous."

And she began to recite, plaintively, a verse from one of the poets:

> *"Quake not at the lion's roar,*
> *Laugh at the fox's cunning,*
> *Prod boldly with your lance the wild boar*
> *And flee not from the coiling serpent—*
> *Fear only the smile of a king."*

Tamara now wanted to know what news there was of her second son, Khudabandeh Mirza. Her ignorance of her sons' welfare or where-abouts was pathetic, and drew from Shamala all the sympathy of which her spirit was capable. Shamala closed her eyes, seeking to re-member some verses of Christian Scripture which the friar had been teaching her, for the comfort they might afford. None came. Khuda-bandeh Mirza was less docile and more temperamental than his brother; he was a youth of hot passions, fond of the hunt, and Abbas, who did things by contraries, had not sent him to the tribes but was employing him in one of the ministries, and had betrothed him to a daughter of the khan of the Kashgais. The young man chafed under what he considered an insult to his manhood.

Shamala was reserved in what she told her aunt, but scraps were enough, and Tamara was satisfied.

"Would you like to see my Yusuf?" she asked.

"Yusuf?"

"Mohammed Mirza, but I call him Yusuf, for he is the crescent moon before whom the stars bow in obseisance." She summoned her eunuch attendant, and the boy was presently brought to her. He was an attractive child with large, solemn eyes, and a way of clinging to his mother's skirts that filled Shamala with a sudden aching of un-fulfillment, and she thought, Can agony be so richly rewarded?

After caressing her son and asking him some questions to which the child replied in the distant monosyllables of one whose thoughts are upon play, Tamara let him run off. She fell to toying with the network of heavy pearls that laced her bodice. Beyond her children she had no interest in life. She asked neither about Abbas nor about his empire, nor about her homeland. After some increasingly desultory conversation Shamala begged her leave. Tamara gave it absently, and as absently kissed her niece farewell.

When Shamala returned to the Chehel Sitoon she found a great change in the courtyard. A silken curtain had been drawn to enclose a portion of the portico and behind it were the Armenian ladies together with the wives of a number of the Shah's courtiers. In the garden, now illuminated by a great number of lanterns, musicians had been assembled, and the park was thronged. Shamala recalled now that the summons had referred to a durbar and that Abbas had remarked casually that he was expecting other guests later; actually, a big state reception had been ordered.

There was nothing ritualistic in the affair. Everything was as informal as a circus, and Abbas was like a juggler, entertaining those about him while he balanced repartee with introductions, and disposed of state business as he jested. Just now he was on the lowest steps of the portico, conversing with the Carmelite, while turbaned khans and solemn *mujtahids* and lean-faced tribal chiefs came and made their salutations. No prostrations were permitted—at most a low bow —and to many of his favorites the Shah offered his hand. He prided himself that his imperial dignity did not require abasement.

Abbas was not averse to a bitter jest. The two Turkish pashas, ambassadors of the Sultan, approached. Abbas immediately turned his attention to the Carmelite, and began to praise the Pope, while the pashas were kept waiting and compelled to listen. A servant passed, bearing a tray with a wine bottle and goblets. Abbas seized the bottle and now affected to recognize the pashas.

"You are welcome," he explained, "and you have come at a propitious moment. We are about to drink a toast to the Christian caliph, who has promised alliance with our power. Will you join us?" And so saying he thrust goblets into their hands.

The Turks, more observant than the Persians of the Islamic prohibition of wine, accepted the goblets sullenly, and only at Abbas's insistence did they drink. Having properly humiliated these envoys of his most hated enemy, and still holding them at attention, Abbas turned his attention again to the friar.

"What think you of this holy man?" he asked of one of the courtiers standing nearby. "Does he not have the manner and dignity for patriarch of the Armenians?"

At this the friar spoke up.

"Here, as elsewhere, your Majesty, I must make clear that I am not of the order from which governors are chosen."

Abbas clicked his tongue.

"When we want a vizier whom we can trust, we go to ordinary men. Was not Nasrollah, the vizier of Ismail Shah, a porter when my great ancestor made him chief counselor? We are not like the kings of Europe. What is it to be king, if not to be free? You see, I go where I please, I dress as I please, I consort with whom I will, and if it pleases me to pluck the beard of an ambassador"—here he leaned forward playfully as though to take the beard of one of the pashas—"that I do. Which of your European kings has such freedom? And so, when I choose a vizier, I choose a man of merit though I find him among the water carriers along the riverbank, or take him from the dyeing vats—"

At that moment the palace chamberlain signaled to the Shah, and Abbas, draining his goblet, handed it to an attendant and hurried down the steps.

In the garden, illuminated with its thousand lamps and candelabra, and the dazzling reflections from cloth of gold and jeweled turbans and brooches, and filled with the music of drums and cymbals and the fluttering notes of the flutes, Abbas could be seen passing from group to group, nodding, conversing, laughing. The music, or perhaps the wine, combined with something that was said, put the Shah in an even more jovial mood. His imperial dignity completely disappeared, giving place to a wayward abandon born of his youth among the nomads. He began to sway to the rhythm of the drums, and with arms akimbo started to leap and turn in the movements of a tribal dance, that of the Shamlus among whom he had been reared.

The chamberlain, to prevent the Shah from making a spectacle of himself, signaled to one of the officers, who in turn signaled to some of the Qizilbashies. The troopers were eager, and they leaped to form a circle. The music became louder and more barbaric. The Qizilbashies were leaping and gesticulating in an Oriental fandango the temper of which affected the whole company until the garden was filled with shouting and clapping and the bobbing of turbans.

It was near midnight. In the midst of the dancing, with the same impulsiveness he had shown in beginning it, Abbas signaled for the music to cease, and called for his horse.

Just before he rode off, his eyes traveled again to the portico, behind the silken curtains of which Shamala had been observing all that happened. The monarch's look rested for a moment upon her half hidden figure; his head inclined ever so slightly, and then, without a glance to the company in the garden, he galloped off to join his escort waiting at the gate.

PART FOUR

———•·•———

Affairs of Empire

I

Abbas did not remain long with his troops. A restlessness had gripped him, and to shake it off he went on a hunting excursion. Abandoning that, he made an inspection of the mulberry district of the Caspian, heart of the silk industry of the Empire, but before long he was back in the capital.

The fact, which Abbas disliked admitting, was that he could not dismiss Shamala from his thoughts.

This was extraordinary—and annoying. Abbas's spirit was magnanimous, and moved upon an inner landscape as vast as those which the mountains and plains of his Empire presented to the eye. His interests ranged from the condition of the silk trade to the pilgrim accommodations at the Shrine of the Imam Reza, from the art of warfare to the mechanics of clockwork. He had large dreams for the course of his Empire—the consolidation and settlement of the tribes, the construction of roads and caravanserais and bridges, the development of the carpet industry, the draining of swamps and the digging of wells and irrigation ditches. But everywhere, in these preoccupations, the thought of this woman intruded. Why it was that a man with six hundred women to amuse him should be unable to rid himself of the thought of one he could not say.

Shamala's image was not, however, his only distraction at the moment. Another was a concern extraordinary in that it should bother him at all, and even more so in that it should continue to bother him, like a thorn under the nail. This came about through an incident on his hunting trip.

While hunting wild boar along the Caspian Abbas had observed a stirring in a rice field, and with the swift reaction that had been his safety on so many fields of battle he had drawn an arrow and sent it at the object. On approaching he discovered that what he had taken for game was only a poor peasant who had curled up for a nap and who had evidently stirred in his sleep. Abbas's aim had been sure. The man was dead. Abbas made a jest of the matter and dismissed it with the words, "I found him sleeping, and I left him—sleeping." Afterward he felt irritated with himself, and irritated with his courtiers for having laughed at his joke. Just why he was irritated he could not say; but the irritation had a habit of returning to him at moments when Shamala was in his thoughts, and that annoyed him all the more, and added another kind of anxiety, of a sort that he had seldom experienced, but that was becoming more frequent. . . .

Abbas decided to inspect the markets, and summoned the Darugha of Isfahan. It was an ancient practice made famous by Haroun-al-Raschid when he ruled his Persian Empire from Baghdad. The practice had fallen into decay, but Abbas had restored its usefulness; it was never known when he would go abroad; and when he did it was in his own person and not in disguise. This was simple, for Abbas seldom dressed otherwise than as an ordinary man, except for his enormous turban, and he went about with the fewest of retainers, often with no more than a single Qizilbashie.

The Darugha was not allowed to leave the Shah's presence once Abbas had announced his purpose, but then and there was required to lay aside court dress for a goat's-hair jubbah like the one Abbas was wearing.

The two set forth. The Darugha would have liked time to send word to one or two merchants of his acquaintance, whom he had been favoring by remitting certain taxes, but it did not greatly matter. To sell privilege was a perquisite of office, and he was sure that the merchants would be discreet.

Abbas avoided the bazaars, however, where the trade in silk and commodities and exchange was conducted, and went around by a narrow *kucheh*, known as the Zard, from its ancient yellow walls, down to the lower part of the city, below the bridges across the Zeyandeh Rud, where the abattoirs were and where the tanners and potters worked. It was muddy in the street, and the water that ran down the gutter was discolored with tanbark and the blood of animals. Bits of skin and hair from the dressing of the leather floated on the surface.

The Darugha, wondering what game Abbas was pursuing in this forlorn quarter, and inwardly cursing his kismet for such a day as this, stepped gingerly from cobblestone to cobblestone to keep his shoes dry, while with one hand he held the corners of his cloak to keep it from trailing and with the other held his nostrils to avoid the stench.

Abbas paused before a tannery where a number of men, nearly naked except for leather aprons, were at work at a bench scraping the hides of sheep that had been treated with lime. The skin of their hands was cracked from the caustic, and their faces were as wrinkled as the leather they worked. Abbas watched them silently, and again the Darugha wondered what thoughts occupied him, for in his face was a look new to the official—a look of anxiety mingled with pre-occupation. Abbas turned to leave, but a half naked boy, playing in the gutter, recognized him, and exclaimed, "*Allah Hazrat!*" In an instant the workmen had prostrated themselves, and the foreman was crying, "God's Presence, have mercy on us, that we were unaware of you among us."

Abbas, speaking kindly, bade the men arise and return to their work, and after making a few inquiries of the foreman directed the Darugha to give each of the men an abbassi, and two to the boy who had recognized him.

Before going on, Abbas asked if it was not nearby that the Christian darvish dwelt, and the boy ran ahead to show him the way.

The quarter in which the Carmelite's house lay was even more squalid than the tannery district, but as they came to the house itself Abbas saw that the walls had been newly plastered and that workmen were repairing the wall that enclosed the garden. There were two workmen, one a tall, lean man with close-cropped hair and no turban, the other a youth. The lean workman was singing a song. Abbas could not make out the words, but the melody was like that sometimes heard in the courts of the Haram, sung by one or another of the younger concubines from the Kafkas.

"Is the Christian darvish within?" Abbas asked, and then he recognized the friar.

It was a moment before Fray Juan recognized the Shah, however, and then:

"Majesty!" he exclaimed in surprise, and added without thinking, "How I have prayed for you!"

Fray Juan had seen the Shah but once since the departure of his companions—on the occasion of the supper party at the Chehel Sitoon—but something about that meeting had left him with the feeling that the Shah was not satisfied with himself, and that there was a wedge, a crevice, that led into his heart. By sympathy and by prayer that crack might be widened sufficiently for the Holy Spirit to enter. Fray Juan had been praying for that eventuality, and this unexpected appearance of the Shah seemed to him now a partial answer to his prayers.

"So you have prayed for me," said the Shah, visibly touched, and he put his hands upon the friar's arms affectionately. "I am grateful to you. I have never had anyone do that for me. But—do you believe in prayer?" he asked with a kind of incredulity.

"Of course."

"I mean, do you believe that God really answers prayer? We Moslems must pray five times a day, but that is like so much incense burning under the sky. We know not where the smoke and the odor are borne. Our fate is written on our foreheads at birth and is as unchangeable as it is unknowable."

The friar touched briefly upon the doctrine of Christian prayer—that God heard and answered, though not always in the manner prayed for. The notion of a Supreme Being so different from the aloof, unapproachable and unknowable God of Islam—of a tender, loving God with whom communication could be achieved—was captivating to the Shah. He had heard these ideas before, of course, but always they were beclouded with mystery and theology. The friar's simple explanations held him spellbound. He wanted to know what was the Holy Spirit of the Christian Trinity. The friar considered how best to explain this Being, so often misunderstood by Christians.

"The Holy Spirit," he said, after a moment, "may be likened to the Breath of God blowing into the windows of the heart—that is, if the windows are left open."

The Shah's expression was one of delight and wonder.

"I shall remember that," he said, and then, as though for the moment surfeited, he said, "But where are your companions?"

"Our prior returned to Rome with your letter, as you know, and Fray Vincent accompanied him as far as Hormuz. From there I have letters saying that he met such welcome and such need that with the prior's consent he is remaining to establish a house."

The Shah frowned at the news, for Hormuz was held by the Portuguese.

"Then as you are sole representative here of your sovereign, I must see you more often and make sure that you are properly entertained. I shall expect to see you at court regularly. You know," he added, "Abbas is one who likes to see his courtiers on every occasion. You must not deny me the frequent sight of your face."

Fray Juan was puzzled at the Shah's new interest after such long disregard, but he thanked him for his consideration, and promised to attend court functions.

"Meantime," added the Shah archly, "can you not invite the Shah of Persia into your abode?"

Fray Juan used the opening to renew the matter of the firman which the Shah had promised.

"If the house were mine to command," he said, "you would have been invited before now; but as you know, it is ours only by sufferance, and it is your Majesty that commands one's presence or demands one's departure."

Abbas's eyes narrowed, but he chose to ignore the reminder.

"Then I command my presence," he answered lightly. "Shall we enter?"

"Tell me," Abbas asked, as they passed into the courtyard, and he saw the work that the friar and Javan had been carrying forward, "why must you be grubbing as a laborer? Did not my Darugha here give you the hundred tomans I appointed you?" And he glanced sternly at the magistrate as he said this.

"His Excellency did indeed give me the money," said Fray Juan, "but as he has no doubt advised you, I returned all but ten tomans, which were sufficient to supply the materials for our needs. As for the work, I enjoy it, as refreshing to both body and soul, and as a duty to God."

"To God?"

The friar explained, as he had explained to Shamala, the Christian concept of labor. Abbas was impressed.

"That is good statecraft," he commented. "Our peasants and workers toil from morning to night, but only from compulsion, and no one has ever told them that it is an honor to their manhood. Rather, among us, it is considered a degradation, and so everyone regards idleness as the mark of position and freedom. That is why, between seasons, you will find so many idle peasants. I must think about that."

The friar now showed Abbas through the house, and Abbas paused for some moments in contemplation before the altar. With a curt nod to the magistrate, that sent the official hastily out of doors, Abbas turned to the friar diffidently, and asked him about the song that he had been singing earlier. Fray Juan explained that it was an ancient Greek hymn of the Church, which he had been teaching to Javan—for, he said, "it is comforting to the heart, and full of promise."

"Then teach it to me," said Abbas, "for the cares of kingship are heavy, and I need comfort."

Fray Juan sang the hymn:

> "Jesus, Name all names above;
> Jesus, best and dearest;
> Jesus, fount of perfect love,
> Holiest, tenderest, nearest;
> Thou the source of grace completest,
> Thou the purest, thou the sweetest,
> Thou the well of power divine,
> Make me, keep me, seal me thine."

"That is a love song," interrupted Abbas in surprise.

"Yes," acknowledged the friar. "Shall we not love the Lord who has so loved us and shown us such mercy and compassion?"

"I have not found God compassionate and merciful, though the Koran hails Him as such, but rather a taskmaster. Do you hear our mullahs singing glad songs? No, for music is forbidden in our mosques.

How is it," Abbas asked in perplexity, "that you can be so joyful, who by your rule are so confined in your enjoyments of the pleasures of life? You know nothing of women, nor of the chase, nor of battle, nor of the wine cup, and you have neither servants nor kingdoms to command and you go about in mean raiment and eat only the simplest food."

"There is no joy like that of a pure conscience," said Fray Juan, and then to avoid any inference of complacency, he added, "I am the greatest of sinners."

"Really! How can that be?" asked the Shah, amazed.

"In being unfaithful in the small things entrusted to me. It is like this: one may forgive a courier, sent on a distant errand, for becoming lost in the mountains, but how hard it is to forgive a servant who stumbles in crossing a room. A man may fail in swimming a river, but how could one fail in crossing a ditch? Unlike yourself, I have only ditches to cross, and so I must continually seek God's mercy. Our joy and solace is not that we sin not, but the sweetness of God's grace, that washes away all sin, and the remembrance of sin."

The friar's words seemed to relieve a weight of disquiet in the Shah, and he regarded the friar with respectful interest.

"Tell me more," he said.

Fray Juan attempted to explain, in simple language and with homely illustrations, the doctrine of the Incarnation, so difficult to the Moslem mind, reared in the teaching of the aloofness and unapproachability of God. Abbas listened with attention, but seemed to listen in the manner of a student who has become lost somewhere in the lecture. Fray Juan sensed his failure and began to go over the doctrine, but Abbas interrupted him.

"Do not try to explain," he said kindly. "I know that there are mysteries past explaining. But that your faith has the truth I can see by the example of yourself and the good works that you do. I would that such reforms might be effected among my subjects. Meantime, the palace doors are always open. Come as you can, and freely. If there is anything I can do for you, please speak out."

Fray Juan took the occasion to press again for the firman.

"We would do that for which we are sent, your Majesty, which is to preach freely the Gospel by which we live, and we crave your permission to do so."

"That you have, that you have," said Abbas, but added, "Only do not do so out of doors, for the mullahs are fanatical, and your life would be in danger. Yet you may freely receive into your house all who come, and instruct them in the doctrines of your faith."

"And baptize them?"

Abbas was thoughtful, and a frown appeared on his brow.

"That would be a dangerous thing to do—unless they are of Christian parents, and born into the faith—for should the mullahs hear of it they would vex you beyond measure, and I have a responsibility to your sovereign for your safety. And beyond that, any Moslem who was renegade to his faith would suffer instant death at the hands of the mullahs—and that I know you would not wish. Let baptism wait until your position here is stronger."

As the Shah was leaving he turned, as if struck by an afterthought, and asked, "The Circassian princess—does she still come to you for instruction?"

"No longer so frequently, your Majesty, for she has learned her catechism, and has been confirmed in the faith, and she comes now only for confessions and the observances."

Abbas hesitated, and then said, with a diffidence unusual for him, "If opportunity occurs, will you tell the princess that the Shah does not look unkindly upon the Christian faith, that though he is precluded from adopting it himself, nevertheless he holds its beliefs and rites in the utmost respect."

"If the opportunity presents itself," said the friar. It struck him that Abbas had spoken from policy rather than from conviction.

Abbas seemed to sense the friar's dubiousness. His face became earnest. "Ah, you think I am speaking with guile. Let me show you this." And tearing open his jubbah, and unbuttoning his tunic, he showed the friar a cross hanging by a chain about his neck. It was very old, and encrusted with a few ordinary gems. It was not something a Shah would wear for adornment, but was such a cross as some village priest might have borne.

"I have worn this about my neck since my youth," said Abbas. "Once, while pursued by the Ustajlus, I took refuge in an abandoned church, tenanted by an ancient and purblind priest of the Nestorian faith. He sent me off with it as a token of God's compassion. I have worn it ever since. It has been a good talisman."

The reference to the cross as a "talisman" spoiled for the friar most of whatever effect the story might otherwise have had. Nevertheless, he was impressed. Here, it seemed to him, was tangible evidence that Abbas might be good ground for the seed of the Christian Gospel. There revived in him the hope that he had vaguely entertained on leaving Rome, of converting the Shah of Persia, and of thereby turning the tide of Islam in the East. For with the monarch converted, what powerful example that would be for his subjects! It would mean, at the least, official tolerance for the propagation of the Gospel.

After the Shah had gone, Fray Juan retired to his chapel and sang a quavering, excited, exultant *Gloria in excelsis Deo*. Here, he thought, was the beginning of the fruition of his work, and of the eventual answer to the countless prayers that had been laid on the altar since the days of the Crusades.

II

Abbas's resentment against the Pope for his failure to negotiate an alliance against the Ottoman power, or to form any concerted policy against the Ottoman among the Christian princes, seemed to have died. Likewise, his suspicion of the friar, and of the Pope's policy toward the Armenian Christians of the realm, had also seemingly dissolved. The Shah was showing evidences of benign regard for his Christian minorities.

Thus, he had finally sanctioned an election to fill the vacant patriarchate of the Armenian Church, and he made contributions toward the completion of the cathedral church which the Armenians were building in their Julfa suburb. The new church was an ornate structure of quasi-Moslem architecture, with garish murals on the walls. One large mural depicted in macabre detail the persecutions suffered by St. Gregory, the founder of the Armenian Church.

Toward the Carmelite, Abbas's favor was conspicuous. In obedience to the Shah's behest Fray Juan regularly attended the durbars and state functions, and he was becoming a familiar figure at court. At first somewhat timid, and seldom speaking, with the monastic rule of silence strong upon him, gradually he began to unfold. He learned to speak freely when opportunity presented, and being accustomed to only a few ideas, his speech had a directness and simplicity that gave it favor. The Persians, he discovered, were used to flowery, devious ways of talking—manners of expression he could never acquire—but he found that his manner of speech was just as effective, and seemingly appreciated. In any case, he seldom wanted for listeners when he began to talk.

Occasionally the Shah would summon him to private audience—at first usually in connection with the growing correspondence between the Shah and the European princes, but now often on matters of administration. He was avid for information, and persistently curious as to how this or that business was handled in the courts of Europe. Fray Juan of course had had no experience in such affairs and he told the Shah so; but Abbas liked to quiz him, and the friar gave the best answers his common sense and his limited experience could summon. His answers seemed to satisfy the Shah; at any rate, Abbas seemed to find him more and more indispensable.

The Shah's intimacy with the friar did not fail to attract attention, and the friar was finding himself surrounded by flatterers and favor seekers. It puzzled him how to deal with them, particularly as he did not wish to cultivate suspicions of others' motives. Moreover, he seemed to sense—perhaps it was the blindness of hope—a genuine interest among some of them for the secrets of trustworthiness and a desire to learn more about the religion to which he witnessed.

As he dwelt in thought upon the various ways of presenting his message, the conclusion emerged again and again that the most effective presentation of the truth which he held as Truth was by means of the Scriptures themselves, which through so many centuries had been the means of faith to countless generations of disciples. To this end, he determined upon a labor of translation, beginning with the Gospels and the Psalms.

There existed, Fray Juan learned, a translation of the New Testament into Persian, but its language was so obsolete that a new version was necessary. Mattios Hagopian, the khwajeh nazar of Julfa, who was something of an antiquarian, showed the friar a copy of this earlier work, an ancient text on Chinese laid paper, with a notation that it had been transcribed in the reign of the Ilkhan of Arghun, in the year 1282, at the behest of the Franciscan Juan de Monte Corvino. The Ilkhan, it appeared, had shown favor to the Christian religion and had solicited relations with the powers of Christendom, and the Franciscan had traveled throughout his realm and had established numerous churches.

The thought occurred to Fray Juan, as he saw himself treading in the footsteps of this missionary of three centuries earlier, that all that remained of this earlier enterprise was a decaying copy of the New Testament, and that his own labors might be equally fruitless. For a moment, he was troubled by misgivings—but not for long. Fortunately, he was not educated in the pursuit of philosophical speculations or historical parallels—and besides, he was too busy. Having early in life hired himself out, as it were, as a penny-a-day worker in the Lord's vineyard, he must work while it was day; just now, the harvest seemed at hand, and there was much to be done.

To assist him in the task of translation—for despite his growing ease in the Persian tongue he recognized his incompetence for such an exacting labor—Fray Juan found, after much inquiry, a mullah who was a thorough scholar and willing to undertake the work. Khodja Ibrahim had been reared in Baghdad; he was familiar with Arabic, Hindustani, and Latin; he was precise and assiduous. His chief disqualifications were his Moslem faith, to which he was fanatically attached, and his persistency in arguing the veracity of the Gospels, and in disputing the various doctrines of the Christian faith. He was, however, courteous, like all his race, and he would always apologize profusely for taking issue with the friar.

"The Christian *khodja*," he would begin, always referring to the friar as "khodja," either to show that they were both ecclesiastics of the same rank, or to deny the validity of any other religious term, "will forgive the forwardness of this unworthy person, but it seems to me that the ancient texts must have been altered, through ignorance or fanatical devotion, for the account differs from what we are told in the blessed Koran, which as you know is infallible, having been revealed to the Prophet by God himself in divers visions."

And then he would expound what the Koran had to say about the matter. Fray Juan often grew impatient, almost to the point of dismissing the man. But his good humor came to his rescue—fortunately, for he had been acquiring the most valuable knowledge of all—that of the enemy's defense, so to speak, that of the strength and weakness of Moslem theology.

"I will tell you why I hold to the textual integrity of the Christian Scriptures," he said one day, thinking that at least there was great argumentative strength in the fact that the Prophet of Islam had acknowledged their divine inspiration—so much that the Christians were properly called the "People of the Book"—and that the matter of their textual integrity could not be so difficult to resolve. "Our Scriptures declare that Satan is a liar and the father of a lie. That being the case, no scribe, no compiler or translator of the Scriptures, would distort them by falsification, for that would make him a servant of Satan and not of God. If he be not a servant of God, and a follower of the Lord Jesus Christ, why should he be devoting his energies through his work as scribe and translator to the spread of the Christian Gospel?"

The khodja considered this for some time, but could find no effective answer.

Fray Juan took delight and found comfort in recasting the Gospel narrative into Persian. In putting the ancient account into a new tongue he found new beauties and new meanings in the familiar narrative. Perhaps it was because the manners and customs of life in Persia had changed so little in comparison to those of Europe that the idiom of the Gospel narrative was so much more understandable and meaningful.

Fray Juan had begun his task with the Gospel of St. John, partly because the language lent itself to translation better than the other Gospels and partly because it expressed the mysteries of the Christian faith in terms more familiar to the Persian mind. The friar had soon discovered that mystical and metaphorical language was characteristic of the Persian tongue, and that the Persian mind grasped the abstract concepts of mysticism more readily than the European. A whole school of poetry, the Sufi, existed in which poetical and symbolical expression had been given to a philosophy of life that had been affected, at some time or other, by Christian mysticism.

It was while Fray Juan was in the midst of this work that the hopeful trend of affairs was broken by the extraordinary events of *Khatchaturan*, or Blessing of the Crosses.

III

The Khatchaturan, commemorating both the Lord's baptism and His manifestation to the Jews, was the principal event of the Epiphany season in the Armenian Church calendar and one of the most colorful ceremonies in the Gregorian liturgy.

Since the establishment of the Armenian colony at Julfa the Khatchaturan had been held on the banks of the Zeyandeh Rud, where it drew crowds of onlookers from Isfahan. Abbas, signifying his newly awakened concern for his Christian subjects, now announced that he would attend the forthcoming observance. Public interest multiplied, and the Armenians made elaborate plans for a celebration worthy of the royal patronage.

Fray Juan had been notified that the Shah wished his attendance, and early on the morning of Epiphany the friar was at the Ali Gapou. Abbas, with unusual attention to attire, was wearing satin trousers and a scarlet jacket and his famous twelve-pleated turban with aigrette and emerald brooch. He moved out of the palace on a white charger to the accompaniment of trumpets and a troop of scarlet-clad soldiery. The blare of trumpets, the roll of kettledrums, and the shouts of the populace filled the Sunday air while pennons waved in the morning breeze and the scarlet plumes of the horses rose and fell to their prancing. Down the length of the Chahar Bagh the cavalcade moved to the acclaim of thousands, and crossed the Allah Verdi Khan bridge over its thirty-three graceful arches.

Above the bridge a cleared space by the riverbank had been roped off for the Shah and his company. All along the river, on both sides, great crowds watched the proceedings. To amuse them until the Shah's appearance there had been games and dancing and hymn singing, and now, as the Shah descended the bridge ramp the singing was drowned by the shouting that filled the air.

Awaiting the monarch were the principal personages of the Armenian community. Chief of these was of course the patriarch, resplendent in chasuble, pearl-embroidered cope, and miter thickly encrusted with rubies and emeralds. About him were grouped the clergy of the ten Gregorian churches in Julfa and the two in Isfahan proper, accompanied by their acolytes bearing lighted candles. Massed before the patriarch were the cross bearers in surplices, a hundred of them, each bearing aloft a cross of silver and rock crystal.

As the Shah advanced, the patriarch was on the point of prostrating himself, but Abbas waved his hand.

"It is I, holy Father," he exclaimed heartily, as he dismounted, and gave his horse to an adjutant, "who should kneel before you and before these blessed crosses." And he humbly bowed his head.

The patriarch stammered his greetings:

"Your Majesty is most—most gracious to honor these ceremonies of our faith. We are—grateful, and welcome you most gladly."

"Then let me observe these holy rites as one of the humblest penitents and devotees of the blessed Jesus," said Abbas piously. He signaled to his attendants to fetch his throne, which was nothing more than a low dais spread with a carpet, and on this he seated himself, his feet tucked beneath his cloak in the attitude of a pious Moslem in a mosque. The patriarch, ill at ease in the presence of the Shah, advanced toward the river's edge, and began to chant the litany.

Hardly had he begun, however, when Abbas was on his feet and down by the water at the patriarch's side.

"May I suggest to your Reverence," he said with the diffidence of a courtier addressing a superior, "that the crowds are not yet in the proper attitude of reverence for such holy matters? I beg you to wait a moment until the disturbance is quieted."

And he called to the Qizilbashies to press the crowd back and to require everyone to kneel. Then he nodded to the patriarch to proceed. Hardly had Melchisadek begun the liturgy again when Abbas interrupted a second time, to suggest that the clergy stand farther back in order that none of the proceedings be obscured from the spectators. He now had questions about the way the crosses should be held, and he instructed the acolytes as to how they should carry them to the waterside. The patriarch waited helplessly to proceed.

The sky had grown overcast; the air had a January chill. Finally, Abbas appeared satisfied; he returned to his dais, and tardily the rites began. The ceremony itself—the litany, the chanted prayers, the pouring of the chrism upon the water—were all preliminary to the great event of casting the crosses into the water, and their recovery by the people.

The crowd was intent upon the climax, and to the rumbling of distant thunder the liturgy itself advanced with increasing pace, with mounting tension, toward the great prayer of consecration, the blessing of the crosses, and the blessing of the waters, followed by the petition that they be contained to their proper uses, as ordained by God of old, in his covenant with Noah, that they make fruitful the fields, and refresh the weary. The prayer concluded, the patriarch stepped to the edge of the river, lifted the cross which he held, and cast it into the river. At the same moment all the cross bearers did the like; the air was filled with a glitter; the water received the emblems with a rippling splash, and they disappeared into its depths.

At once a company of young men, who had been waiting along the banks of the stream, flung off their cloaks, poised for an instant in their loincloths, and plunged into the icy waters. One by one they returned to the bank, like retrievers, bearing the crosses. As each cross was restored to the waiting clergy, a shout arose from the crowd; an attendant threw a cloak over the dripping swimmer, and he was led before the patriarch to receive the patriarchal blessing.

When the last cross had been recovered the ceremonies were ended —and it was opportune, for the sky was now leaden and the atmosphere was heavy with the threat of rain. The crowds began to disperse, though many would have waited to see the display of the Shah's going; Abbas, however, seemed reluctant to leave, and remained questioning the patriarch about the various symbolisms of the ceremony.

"We have no such celebrations in Islam," he remarked to Fray Juan. "Everything with the mullahs must be sad and full of weeping and tortures. Do you have such ceremonies in your Catholic Church?"

Fray Juan explained that the observance was known but seldom used in the Roman rite.

"We have two Christian sects in my Empire," remarked Abbas, referring to the Georgians of the Orthodox rite, and the Armenians of the Gregorian, "not counting the Assyrians, called the Nestorians, who are fewer in number and dwell in the mountains of Kurdistan. Of these, whom do you consider to be the truest Christians?"

Fray Juan hesitated lest he be drawn into argument.

"That is for God to say, but since what a man believes governs his conduct, his beliefs are important. As a Catholic, I believe the Catholic Church to contain the purest truth, while the Armenian has the closest affinity to it."

"A sound and sage answer," commented Abbas, with evident satisfaction.

Drops of rain had begun to fall, and the patriarch, who had been standing all the time, was showing great weariness. Abbas saw the old man swaying, on the point of falling, and he rushed to support him.

"Let us go under shelter," he commanded, "but as we are on the threshold of important truths let us not abandon our discussion." He addressed the khwajeh nazar. "Shall we go to your house?"

Mattios Hagopian was overwhelmed. Never in his long memory had such a thing occurred hat the sovereign should come under an Armenian roof. He qu   ed his welcome, and hastened a servant off to prepare for the Shah's reception. The house was small, and though the Shah had dismissed all his courtiers save only his chamberlain and Fray Juan, the company filled the narrow room. While Abbas continued his discussion of theology with the patriarch and the Carmelite, the servants managed to put together a supper, which was presently served. When the wine was brought, the Shah took the goblet and, holding it to the light, said:

"Ah, blessed dispensation, that denies not to mankind the cheering consolation of the cup. With the Moslems, wine is forbidden, but they debauch themselves nevertheless by means of hasheesh and the juice of the poppy, which take men's senses and drive them to stupor or to crime."

He drank freely of the wine, and his mien grew jovial; he frequently leaned over to pat the patriarch on the back as he urged him to further exposition of the mysteries of the Christian faith. He wanted to know about miracles, and the relics of the saints, and the miracles wrought by the relics.

"You have here, I am told, certain relics of St. Ripsima," he said, referring to the famed virgin and martyr of Armenia. The patriarch glanced at the khwajeh nazar in anguished consternation and despair and was silent.

"Yes, it is true," exclaimed the Shah in delight. "And surely you will not deny your monarch, in his great need, the joy and spiritual satisfaction of gazing upon such precious mementoes of your faith?"

The question was a command. The patriarch looked like a man condemned. In hopeless resignation he nodded to one of the clerics;

the man went out, and after some interval, while the Shah continued to talk about his sins and the great refreshment this holy discourse was bringing him, the curtain parted, and four priests entered garbed in sacramental vestments, accompanied by acolytes bearing candles, and set before the Shah a casket of walnut wood, with bindings of gold, which the priests carried by poles set through hoops, like the ancient Ark of the Covenant. The patriarch felt within his cope and drew out a key; mumbling a prayer he opened the casket.

The box contained the slim radius and ulna of a female, together with the bones of the wrist and hand. The latter had become separated from the forearm, but the radius and ulna were still joined by a paper-thin fragment of cartilage. The bones were white as ivory, almost transparent, as though they had been polished.

Abbas gazed at the objects with the utmost reverence. Then, bending over them, he carefully lifted the radius and ulna and kissed them and placed them on his head in sign of veneration.

"Ah," he breathed, enraptured, "how cleansed and uplifted is the soul from gazing upon these objects!" He turned to Fray Juan. "You are far from home, far from the fountains of spiritual refreshment. You should not be denied the solace which these holy objects confer. With the permission of the patriach I shall confide one of them into your keeping."

Abbas glanced at the patriarch, but the old man was too far gone in exhaustion and horror to protest. Fray Juan did not understand what the Shah meant until he saw him take up the forearm and with his hands suddenly wrench the ulna from the radius. He handed the ulna to the friar.

A feeling of sickness swept over Fray Juan, and he was on the point of vehement protestation when he glanced at the patriarch, who had been trying to catch his eye. In Melchisadek's look, filled with despair and resignation, was also a mute warning. Fray Juan understood, and kept silent.

The Shah now seemed satisfied, and bidding the assembly good night, took the friar by the arm and went out.

As the Shah was returning to Isfahan, descending from the bridge and entering the Avenue of the Four Gardens, an arrow sang from the darkness of the plane trees. There was a grunt from the Shah, and his horse reared.

"Your Majesty!" exclaimed the chamberlain, reining to the monarch's side.

"Assassins, assassins!" cried the Shah. "Have at them, and I will burn Julfa to the ground."

The Qizilbashies spread in all directions, and within a matter of minutes the criminal was brought before the monarch, screaming. It was not one of the Armenians, as the Shah had suspected, resentful at the parody he had made of their holy celebration, but a woman of Zinjan—Ladika, formerly concubine to the Shah, whom he had used and then had given in marriage to Sadik, keeper of the sumpter mules. Her hair was disheveled, and the look of madness was in her eyes as she strained in the grasp of the guards, and glared at the Shah, the while she shouted in frenzy, "Long live Shah Safi Safavid! Long live Shah Safi Safavid!"

"Did not the Armenians put you to this?" demanded Abbas, his hand gripping his shoulder to stifle the pain.

But the insane woman only cried the louder, "Long live Shah Safi!"

"Put her to the rack," commanded Abbas, "and when you have had the truth from her, quarter her and throw her to the dogs."

IV

For God so loved the world, that he gave his only begotten Son, that whosoever believeth in him should not perish, but have everlasting life.

Fray Juan was reading these words from a beautifully handwritten and illuminated text which had just come from the copyist.

As always, when he came upon this passage, he involuntarily paused, and his breath ceased at the wonder of it, at the immensity of its meaning, in which was compressed the whole message of Christianity, in which was revealed, as in a flash of lightning, the gulf that separated the Christian faith from all other religions, that summed up the whole relationship, from the Christian viewpoint, of mankind with the Creator, and of man with man—the message that would, if its promises were accepted, reconcile all the conflicts of life, remove its discords, restore harmony, and heal all wounds.

As he dwelt upon this passage the friar thought that he should not wait for the completion of the other Gospels, but should present this Gospel at once to the Shah, whose relations with his own son Safi Mirza had been strained ever since the abortive attack upon his life by the woman Ladika.

Safi Mirza had hurried from his post in Nestoria to throw himself at his father's feet and to protest his innocence of the business. Abbas affected to believe his son, and he let it be known also that he absolved the Armenians from any implication in the attack. The Armenians had fallen into a paralysis of fear. "He has a long memory," confided Mattios Hagopian to Fray Juan, "and it is as hard to allay his suspicions as it is to restore the bloom of a spent rose."

After his wound had healed, Abbas joined his troops, and it was spring of the following year before he returned to Isfahan. At the durbar held to celebrate his return the Shah honored his son by embracing him and placing a gold chain about his neck. Nevertheless, the rumors persisted that Abbas secretly feared Safi Mirza and sought opportunity to disgrace him. Fortunately for the prince, he was popular with the masses.

It was shortly after the durbar that Fray Juan set off for the palace carrying the copy of his newly translated Gospel.

Fray Juan's spirit had been especially lifted within the fortnight by the arrival from Rome of two young friars with letters from the Pope. It was now nine years since Fray Juan had left Rome, six since he had arrived in Persia, and four since he had been left alone to represent the Pope at the court of the Shah. Few and sporadic had been the communications that had come from Rome. Indeed, for long intervals Fray Juan had been seemingly forgotten. The arrival of the friars, bringing with them letters, reassured him that the work in Persia still held the papal interest. The letter commended Fray Juan for his diligence and bade him continue to be at the service of the Shah while persisting in his negotiations for the firman.

The names of the friars were Silvester and Anselm. Seeing them, Fray Juan was acutely aware of the years that had passed since he left Rome, and that he was no longer a youth himself. He was also made aware of how well defined had become his new pattern of life—one not divorced from the monastic rule, but one in which meditation and asceticism had been subordinated to activity and movement in behalf of the Gospel message. These new friars were young men, eager, pious, obedient, and scrupulous in their prayers and meditation. They found it difficult to understand all the things which Fray Juan was called upon to do. They were convent-minded, attached to the cloistered life and to the rule of silence and contemplation. To go about the city, to attend court, to engage in conversation and to witness openly to their faith, were strange matters to them, if not actually repugnant to their notions of their vows. Nevertheless, Fray Juan found great comfort in their companionship, and thought their influence was good for him. They also gave him what he needed, an opportunity to taste again the pleasures of community life, and to draw renewed strength from conventual worship.

Besides the two young friars and Javan, who remained devoted to Fray Juan but remote from his faith, there was now in the house a young native Christian of the Nestorian race, by name Grigor, who had attached himself to the friar and whom the friar had accepted for lay orders. These persons, Fray Juan thought, comprised the hopeful beginnings of the working of the leaven of the Gospel in Persia!

What a victory it would be if only the Shah were brought into the Christian fold! In a monarchy of such absoluteness everything hung upon the Shah's will. At his nod, everywhere doors would be opened to the propagation of the Christian Gospel. More and more Fray Juan began to see himself as the possible instrument of God to this glorious end—the conversion of Abbas, and the reorientation of this extensive Empire in the direction of Christianity, the restoration of that glorious period of the fifth and sixth centuries when the Church of the East was spread throughout this land, as far as China and the Pacific, with over thirty-two metropolitan sees, within each see from seven to fifteen bishoprics.

Abbas was in conference with his viziers when Fray Juan was announced, but on hearing that the friar attended him he adjourned the meeting and directed that the friar be admitted.

"You have been long in coming," Abbas reproached him gently. "I have been back a week, and you have hidden your face from me."

"Your Majesty must know that concern for your many responsibilities led me to avoid disturbing you."

"Ah, it is true. I am pressed on every side. But no affair of government should draw one from his duty to God, and you remind me of that duty. I have thought of you much since our last meeting. Have you been well; has your work prospered?"

Fray Juan now spoke of the work on which he had been engaged, and drew out the volume he had brought.

Abbas was delighted. He removed the wrapping, and his eyes brightened with pleasure as he beheld the green leather binding, hand-stamped in gold, its cross embellished with arabesques.

"Ah, it is beautiful," he whispered, with the same manner of awed reverence with which he handled all articles of the Christian faith, from the cross of Bohemian crystal that Father Paul had presented to him at the first interview to the relics of St. Ripsima which he had profaned in the house of the khwajeh nazar. Fray Juan recognized that these objects were to Abbas in the nature of talismans, but he was reassured somewhat by the Shah's next words.

"It is not this wondrously worked leather," Abbas said, "nor this fine paper, nor the calligraphy, but the precious words themselves which are important—the words that tell of the life and teachings of the Prophet Jesus. Do you read some of them to me."

And he sat down on the floor, disdaining the ottoman nearby, sitting with his feet tucked underneath, his hands folded respectfully in his lap.

Fray Juan took up the book and began reading from the opening:

In the beginning was the Word, and the Word was with God, and the Word was God. . . .

And the Word was made flesh, and dwelt among us, (and we beheld his glory, the glory as of the only begotten of the Father,) full of grace and truth.

"Ah, that was the Lord Jesus," interrupted Abbas, his eyes shining. "He who is acknowledged by all to be the Spirit of God. Read on. These words have more comfort than wine or the caresses of women."

Fray Juan continued to read and came to the passage over which he had paused earlier in the morning, the passage declaring God's great love for mankind, a concept of such vastness and profundity that it could be taken only on faith. As he came to these words Abbas looked up questioningly, and Fray Juan hesitated.

"You Christians make much of that passage, do you not?" asked Abbas.

"Yes, Majesty. It is, in a sense, the heart of the Christian Gospel."

"Which is?"

"That God Himself suffers for the sins of men."

"And we are told elsewhere, are we not, in that or another Gospel," said Abbas thoughtfully, "that we should seek to be like God?"

"Be ye therefore perfect, even as your Father which is in heaven is perfect," quoted the friar.

"Sometimes, then, we must sacrifice what is dearest to us, for the sake of the people?"

"Yes," said the friar, not comprehending the direction in which Abbas was leading him.

"There is a story in the other book which your prior gave me, about Abraham and how he was required to sacrifice his own son for the good of the world. The story is also told in the Koran—"

The terrifying point of the Shah's twisted logic was suddenly revealed to the friar.

"But Abraham was not required to make the sacrifice, your Majesty," he hastily interrupted, "for as the Koran itself bears witness: *We cried unto him, Oh Abraham! Now hast thou satisfied the vision. . . . And we ransomed his son with a costly victim. . . . Thus do we reward the well doers, for he was of our believing servants.*

"God made the sacrifice once, for all mankind, when His Son suffered on the cross, crucified by wicked men, and we are all saved by His vicarious offering. And being saved by grace, we are commanded to live in love, forgiving others their trespasses, even as God forgives us our trespasses."

Abbas was silent, and it was evident that he had heard enough of the Gospel for one day. Fray Juan waited for his will. Presently Abbas looked up and said:

"It is plain that you know by what you live, for you have not confined yourself to reading that which was given you from youth, but have also acquainted yourself with the writings of the faith which you find around you. That is good. You will prosper in your work, and you have my good wishes."

"The greatest prosperity with which my mission could be blessed," said Fray Juan, at last daring to speak, "would be that your Majesty himself acknowledge the claims of Christ, and that you surrender your life into His keeping."

"Ah, that is a boon which I sometimes think of granting you," said Abbas heavily, "not only for the sake of the love which I bear you, but for my own happiness." He stood up. "But a monarch cannot surrender his crown to another, for to do so is to take his hand from the task to which he has been appointed by God."

"You are not called upon to surrender your crown," said the friar quickly. "Some, like myself, are called upon to lay aside all material possessions for the sake of the Gospel, and to make ourselves hirelings for the Kingdom, but there is a diversity of callings as there is a diversity of gifts. Some are appointed ministers, and others servants. You would remain on your throne, which would then become all the more glorious, haloed as it would be by the light from the throne of God whom you serve, and from your crown would flow out to the ends of your Empire a blessing, like a life-giving stream gushing from the rocks upon the arid plain."

Fray Juan paused, caught up by his enthusiasm, fearing lest he had pressed his point too far.

Abbas regarded him with the kindly, benign look which he so often visited upon the friar.

"Ah, you speak well," he said, with an access of sadness. "But still you are not a man of the world. You must know that over every sovereign of your faith stands the Pope to whom the king is beholden, and if he obey not the behest of the Pope he stands in danger of damnation and excommunication. That, indeed, is the blessing of Islam. The True Believer crooks his knee to no man for his eternal salvation, neither to priest nor to king, but only to God, who has neither ministers nor clergy nor mediators.

"But do not feel discouraged," said Abbas, seeing the look of disappointment in the friar's face. "You have deeply touched me with your discourse, and I shall ponder your words." He sighed. "The cares of a king are heavy," he said. "Do you know what troubles me at this moment?"

Before the friar had an opportunity to consider his answer, the Shah went on:

"It is the state of the silk trade. The prosperity of our country rests upon silk, and all my wars with the Ottoman, and all my diplomacy with Europe, have been to find an avenue by which this merchandise may journey unmolested to the markets of Europe. For some time it has been moving by way of Muscovy, but difficulties have arisen there, and if they are not resolved it will mean loss of a year's revenues from the silk harvest and untold suffering to the peasants who have grown it, to the artisans and workers who have reeled and carded and baled it."

Fray Juan became discomfited at the turn the conversation had taken, knowing the Shah's habit of going just so far along a road and then abruptly turning off.

"Your Majesty," he said dryly, "has skilled ministers to advise him on every aspect of his administration. That is one of the marks of his greatness as a ruler. When the silk trade really perplexes him he will turn to one of them and not to a simple religious whose competence, whatever it may be, lies not in such an area."

"You do not know your own worth," said Abbas. "Had you been reared in court instead of in a convent, you would have made a fine vizier. Tell me," he said, breaking off, "are you well settled in the house I have provided you?"

Fray Juan thought now to raise yet again the question of the firman.

"We can never be settled so long as we do not have a house of our own," he said. "For while we have had evidence of your Majesty's benevolence, yet without a firman we are still the strangers in the house who must be prepared to yield their beds to the need of the householder. May you live a hundred years, your Majesty, yet the Church has existed for sixteen hundred and it must look beyond the lifetime of any individual sovereign. Did we have a firman, then we could establish in confidence the work which you have so graciously permitted us to begin—that of founding a house of our order in this land."

"Well, as to that, do I look sickly?" Abbas asked, drawing himself up, and looking at the friar quizzically.

"Indeed, your Majesty appears to be in the best of health."

"And I shall continue to remain so," asserted the Shah, "and I shall continue to sit upon the throne of the Safavids despite the conniving and intrigue of those who would see me in my grave."

His tone was soft but ominous, and Fray Juan was impelled to say, "God forbid that your enemies should prevail!"

"Thank you for your support," said Abbas. "But let us come to your desire in the matter. Perhaps it can be arranged. I have spoken of the necessities of the silk trade. I need someone to go to Moscow and treat with the Muscovites regarding transit rights for the traffic. You are a man of sense and judgment. There is no one in my realm in whom I place more trust than yourself. If you will execute this commission for me I promise you that you shall have this firman on your return."

The friar paled. All he could think of was the legend he had heard as a child, of the Greek demigod Hercules bound to King Eurystheus for the performance of twelve difficult and dangerous labors. He recalled the repeated vexations that had been put upon the Carmelites from the moment of their arrival in Persia—the unwelcome entertainment pressed upon them, the continual change of their quarters, the long neglect at court, and now this extraordinary embassy.

"Your Majesty," he protested faintly, "you jest, surely. Who am I to journey abroad as your Majesty's ambassador?"

"Did not your Pope entrust to such as you an embassy to *my* court?" demanded Abbas. "And surely whom his Holiness trusts I can trust. I recall, moreover, that in his Holiness's letters he confided you to my service in such ways as I might consider appropriate."

This was true. The Carmelites' instructions were to be at the Shah's service. Both by these instructions and by the Shah's wish Fray Juan was bound to accede. Perhaps, Fray Juan thought, this would be the last of it. Perhaps by this proof of his fidelity he would gain the firman to preach and to proselytize and to found a convent. He bowed his head in assent.

"Ah," exclaimed Abbas with satisfaction, "would that I had a dozen like you in my Empire. Then would it be an Empire indeed! But fear not for the gratitude of Abbas. Whether you succeed or fail you will have the reward I have promised, for should you fail you would do no worse than countless others who have tried to deal with the Muscovite. The only language they understand seems to be that of the lash and the arquebus."

Fray Juan returned home in a state of dejection. The Carmelites on their outward journey had spent two years among the unfriendly Muscovites, much of that time in prison or as unwilling guests. Fray Juan could still shiver at the recollection of their last horrible winter in Russia, when they had journeyed south from Moscow by sledge. For days they had traveled over a desert of blinding white. They had holed up for more days in thatch huts while the wind howled across the plains and the storm blew out its fury. More than once they had been overtaken by sudden blizzards. To sit in the sledge was to freeze slowly and painlessly to death in a dream of the sunlit coasts of Spain, and so they had run alongside, clinging to the boards lest they be lost in the swirling snow, while the driver in desperation whipped the horses to exhaustion to gain the inn before the way was wholly covered by drift or the night overtook them on the wastes. If a horse stumbled, there could be no mercy; it was cut from the traces and left to freeze, and there it would lie, a frozen carcass, until the spring should thaw it for the vultures.

Still, it was not the thought of the Russian climate or of Russian inhospitality that disturbed the friar. It was the thought of how, in the years since leaving Italy, he had been insensibly drawn further and further from the profession of a contemplative monastic to which he had vowed himself, and into the orbit of worldly affairs. Again the misgivings of the aged General, Father Peter, returned to him, and the unanswerable questions which his decision posed: What could the Carmelites hope to accomplish by foreign journeys which they could not accomplish equally well in the confines of the monastery? What could preaching and proclaiming achieve that appeal to God in prayer could not? Was it man by his actions, or was it the Holy Spirit, that redeemed the world?

In its practical applications the question was whether a strong man's force lay in his comings and goings or in the moral influence of his inner integrity, whether a nation's security lay in its armies or in the rectitude of its policies.

Nevertheless, within the week, during which he was instructed by the Shah's viziers as to the details of his embassy, Fray Juan took leave of his brothers and set forth for Muscovy. Convinced of the purity of his intentions, and trusting to God for guidance, he kept before his eyes a saying of Jesus:

No man, having put his hand to the plough, and looking back, is fit for the kingdom of God.

PART FIVE

A Royal Pilgrimage

I

With the departure of the Carmelite, Abbas began to suffer again from severe inner gnawings of dissatisfaction with self; he was preoccupied, irritable, and restive.

Ordinarily, when the Shah became depressed and morose, the palace chamberlains would discreetly send to him, through the chief eunuch, some young and tender fruit of the Household, demure and soft-spoken, gentle in deportment as a spring zephyr, hitherto concealed from the Shah's eyes against just such emergencies.

But the delights of the flesh did not appease the Shah's restlessness, nor did an extensive hunt for the *mouflon*, the wild sheep to be found in the Bakhtiari hills, nor did certain baser excitements in which the monarch sometimes indulged. The Circassian princess still haunted his thoughts, her image strangely mingling with that of the friar, her voice melodious in his ears, but in the alien accents of Gregorian plainsong. The maturity of her twenty-three years had only increased her charm, enriched her beauty. She had become for him a kind of ethereal creature, like the cloud of pink that hovers above the almond trees in spring, elusive and unpossessable but clinging and lingering like a fragrance in the air. He was still unreconciled to the fact that she had somehow slipped his grasp, that she no longer gave him the worshiping adoration of her younger years; but he could not drive her from his thoughts. He had fantasies about her that disturbed and excited him—fantasies that could not be realized with any other woman of the Household.

In the midst of these vexations, the Shah's ministers brought him word that the repairs and reconstructions to the shrine of his ancestor the Imam Reza, which he had ordered some years before, were now completed. They suggested that he might like to inspect the work.

The Imam, from whose offspring the Safavid dynasty traced its lineage, was one of the twelve descendants of the Prophet Mohammed, whom the Moslems of Persia held to be the lawful successors to the Prophet, as opposed to the line of caliphs generally accepted by the Moslems of the neighboring countries. This difference had been the cause of a notable schism in Islam, and the tomb of the Imam Reza had therefore both a religious and a political significance. Under the encouragement of the Shah's predecessors, it had become increasingly an object of pilgrimage for the Persian Moslems, and as such served to divert the lucrative pilgrim traffic from Kerbela and Mecca, which lay under the dominion of the Sunni Ottomans.

The shrine was in Meshed, capital of Khorasan and the principal city in the northeast. Abbas decided to inspect the shrine, and to make his visit in the nature of a pilgrimage. He had no sooner come to this conclusion than his fertile mind began to see the various possibilities it presented. He would set his subjects such an example of piety as the times had not recorded. He would make this event memorable in his reign. He would, in short, make the whole pilgrimage on foot, like the humblest penitent. From Isfahan to Meshed was a distance of eight hundred miles.

Abbas's entourage for the pilgrimage was itself impressive. The Shah set out accompanied by one hundred members of the court, two thousand horsemen, and as many servants and tent strikers, together with three hundred camp women who rode astride and dressed themselves in men's apparel, and twoscore concubines from the Household, especially chosen by the chief eunuch of the Haram to companion the Shah and relieve the tedium of the journey.

The entourage made a grand display as it collected before the Ali Gapou in the great plaza, and then passed down the broad avenue to the city gate, pennons flying in the breeze. The entire city of Isfahan collected in the streets to watch the procession pass, and continued to huzza until it had disappeared in a vapor of dust upon the desert. News of the pilgrimage was carried to every part of the realm, and at Qum, at Veramin, and at other cities along the route great crowds came out on the road to greet the monarch, and to escort him on his way.

Abbas, with his usual attention to administrative detail, had organized the itinerary with admirable skill. The court, transported by a great company of horses, litter camels, baggage camels, and pack mules, made two encampments some *farsakhs* apart. The Shah would walk from one encampment to the other in the course of the morning, setting out at three hours before daybreak and arriving at the second camp before the midday heat. Accompanying him would be a hostler leading his horse, fifty horsemen riding in his rear, and after daybreak, such secretaries and court officials as were required to transact business en route.

Abbas was in no haste, since he carried his court with him and continued to conduct state business while traveling. Several secretaries would ride beside him on mules, taking his letters as he dictated them, and courtiers were always at hand to hurry off with his dispatches and orders. Often he would call together his viziers and conduct a council while he walked.

Walking did not tire the Shah. Nevertheless, as he was more used to the saddle and ordinarily would mount to ride across a courtyard, his stages were never longer than fifteen miles. When he had arrived at the end of his stage, he would retire to the royal tent where his personal servants would have warmed and perfumed water ready to bathe him. After a nap the chief eunuch would send him some unexpected darling to amuse and comfort him until evening, after which he would go forth to supper with the principal nobles and chiefs.

The journey consumed two months. The route skirted the Dasht-i-Kavir—the great salt plains—and led eastward following the general course of the Elborz range. Here was country abounding in game—gazelle, bustard, wild pig, and leopard. Hunting was a passion with Abbas and he was sorely tempted to spend a few days in the chase; but, after several times trying his famous, rhinoceros-bone bow, stringing and unstringing it, he put it aside, determined to keep his eyes resolutely fixed upon the holy object beyond the horizon. He was resolved to keep his thoughts innocent of earthly desire, that he might enter the Shrine with appropriate piety.

It crossed his mind that he should avoid dalliance with his women. However, he came to no immediate conclusion on this question. The pleasures of women were among the chief joys of Paradise as set forth in the Holy Koran—which, for some reason, failed to mention hunting as a sport for the faithful who had crossed the bridge of Al Sirat. Moreover, coition was especially recommended as a means of purging the thoughts of lustful desire, and in the environs of the Shrine there lived a large number of women who offered themselves in temporary marriage to pilgrims in order to refresh them and to purify their thoughts before they entered the holy precincts.

Actually, as Abbas discovered, the invigorating exercise of walking in the early morning was itself a marvelous purgative. He had never been a city man, and the vast solitudes of the early morning when he began his day's stint elevated his thoughts, lifted his imagination, and sent his aspirations soaring on high. About him were evidences of a supernatural world which he could not control and which seemed to beckon to him for communion and understanding. There was the wonder of the stars overhead, never so multitudinous, never so brilliant, never so close as upon the desert. There was, in these early morning hours, the refreshing breeze upon the cheek, cold and stimulating, wafted down from the heights of the ranges. There was the solemn stillness of the wastes, broken only by his own footsteps upon the desert gravel and the distant hoofbeats of his troopers in the darkness behind him.

All these evidences of an immeasurably vast yet intimate and friendly natural world, this cold air sucked into the lungs, drew Abbas in the train of great thoughts. He could see his position in a clearer light. He became aware of himself, of his own identity, in a new and different way. Always he had been dominated by his own wants, which were chiefly for the physical pleasures of life—food, the chase, the mattress; by his fears, which were innumerable and nameless, both of the seen and of the unseen world, of people whom he knew and people whom he did not know; and by his ambitions, which were inordinate, like his appetites. In these early-morning moments, however, his hunger and his fear would disappear, and his ambitions subside. Then he seemed to stand up on an eminence, exalted and relaxed, and a mood of magnanimity possessed his heart. He would see himself as the father of his people—as the Safavid, who had been brought to this eminence by kismet and the will of God to restore the ancient luster to the crown, to resurrect the greatness of Iran of the days of Cyrus, Darius, and Shapur.

God had given him extraordinary gifts: Abbas was quite aware of them. Though not a large man physically, he enjoyed health, vitality, and a power of endurance beyond that of ordinary men. He was now in his forty-fourth year, and his teeth were sound, his eyes clear. He could draw a bow with the best. Among his achievements since he had mounted the throne was the mastery of half a dozen crafts, smithery and surgery and the making of locks among others. His mind was as clear as his eye and as sharp as his scimitar. He could see into the purposes of others and read their minds, and that gave him a great advantage in dealing with them. There was no man in the Empire who could match his wit or challenge his judgment.

It sometimes happened, however, that the release which Abbas experienced in these early-morning communions with nature and self would be followed by a familiar but never predictable depression of his spirits. At the very moment that his soul was being lifted up by the thought of his superiority to other men, he would become, oddly enough, aware of profound deficiencies that renewed in him the mood of dismay and self-dissatisfaction of which he was never free for long. Then he became fearful for his very life, and mistrusted everyone who approached him, suspecting a concealed dagger or a hidden bowstring or a napkin with which to strangle him. At these times he would be vaguely aware that he was an evil man. He was far from being troubled by conscience, for nothing he had ever heard from the mullahs or shamans had warned him that what he did was wrong; indeed, as a shah, as a ruler of any sort, he was a privileged person, exempt from ordinary duties and obligations in proportion to the measure of the power he exercised. Did not the Prophet Mohammed himself give such a rule of privilege to the powerful? Had not the Prophet exempted himself from the law he had just given his followers that limited a man to four wives, and in other ways had he not asserted special personal dispensations? The ulema had frequently assured Abbas that he, too, as a *seyyid*—a descendant of the Holy Prophet—as a shah, as a descendant of the Imam, was specifically above the common law.

No, it was no sense of wrongdoing, no weight upon the conscience, that would suddenly plunge Abbas into the blackest of depressions at the most unexpected times, with a sense of evil within and evil without; rather it was a vague and wholly impalpable sense of loneliness and separation. Separation from what? He could not say. It was only such a sense of separation as would leave him feeling miserably isolated, abandoned and friendless, surrounded by all the menacing powers of darkness, by threatening jinn and *devs* and afreets. And in these moments, as a lightning flash will illuminate the dark surface of water in a well, Abbas could see momentarily into the depths of his own soul, and what he saw there was black and glistening and hard and evil—as though the eye of Satan himself were peering up at him, gloating.

But on this pilgrimage, it must be said, these moments of despair were infrequent. As the arduous and continued exercise burned out the bodily wastes and the excess fat from his limbs and brought a revived vigor to his step, Abbas experienced more and more a contentment of spirit, a sense of satisfaction in doing what was wise, what was statesmanlike, what was edifying to his people. He grew more devout, anxious to hear about the God of whom both Moslem mullahs and Christian priests preached such wonderful things. He resolved to purify himself of all attachments of the flesh, and to devote himself, on this pilgrimage, to godly meditation.

At Shahrud, therefore, on the border of Khorasan, he astounded his court by ordering all the women in the company to be packed back to Isfahan. He also dismissed his secretaries and ceased to transact state business, refused to hear petitions or causes, and gave leave to his court to return to the capital. A number of his staff, whose offices demanded attention, did take advantage of this release and returned to Isfahan, but the greater part of the court remained with the Shah.

Abbas now called for a mullah to read to him. This the mullah did, joining the monarch each morning as soon as the light was strong enough to see by, sitting on a mule that padded along by Abbas's side. The two made a picture which many of the court remembered for years and recounted to their grandchildren: the Shah of Iran, in cotton trousers and jacket, trudging along in the dust, and by his side a jogging donkey bearing a mullah in an enormous white turban, holding a large book in his hands, and reading from it to the majesty plodding afoot.

Abbas, of course, did not understand a word of what the mullah read, for it was all in Arabic, but it sounded glorious, being chanted with a marvelous resonance, and the reading affected Abbas with a sense of truly mystical exaltation. This, he thought, was a supreme moment in his life. What could be more wonderful than to be on a pious pilgrimage to his ancestor the Imam, going humbly on foot, companioned at night by the stars and by day by the voice of God, speaking from His Holy Koran, the sonorous roll and cadence of the verses sounding in the ear like a divine sea flooding in upon the wastes?

In the second month of the pilgrimage, however, as they approached Nishapur, where had begun the train of circumstances that had brought Abbas to the throne, Abbas's sense of mystical exaltation gradually evaporated like the springtime lakes of the lut that, receding, leave exposed the desolation of the salt flats. Not the increasing chill of the air, the rising elevation of the plateau, the proximity of the holy object of his journey, nor the sublime and mystical words of the Koran chanted in Arabic, could now recover the Shah's lost afflatus. Abbas lengthened his stint and walked until late afternoon, far beyond the point where the court had encamped, until he was exhausted; then he called for a litter to bear him back to his tent, where he remained secluded for the rest of the day.

One morning his court waited for him to appear, as usual, in the early hours of the false dawn, but though he was awake he did not come out, remaining in his tent, moving about restlessly like a man racked by indecision. Finally, as day began to break, he called for his horse.

Taking a half dozen Qizilbashies with him for escort, the Shah rode off into the hills.

His customary geniality when riding with his troops was absent. His eyes were unwaveringly fixed upon the line of hills ahead, as though he were searching out some enemy or some landmark; he kept his Arab in check, but at intervals would allow it rein and would dash ahead at a gallop. At one of the lateral breaks in the range he drew up, then turned toward a defile through which a thread of water flowed.

Some miles up the narrow valley the party came to the ruins of an abandoned village, now no more than a formless heap of mud, with here and there the rounded outline of what had once been the cupola of a peasant hut, and a handful of scraggly trees. Above the village, among the scrawny herbage, stood a stone wall, one of four that must once have been the base of some structure, for there remained also the stump of a tower.

On the hillside a few sheep grazed, herded by a beardless youth wearing a tattered cloak and carrying a crooked stick. Abbas called to the boy, who at first was on the point of fleeing at the sight of the armed horsemen, but then came running, to stand with head bowed, in awkward peasant fashion, before the Shah.

"What is the name of this village?" Abbas asked.

The boy was dumb, but presently replied, *"Namidanam"* (I do not know).

"How long since it was inhabited?"

Again the same negative. After all, how should a boy know the name of this deserted village? It was nearly thirty years since Abbas, a fugitive from his enemies, had taken refuge in its broken, half ruined church, and had been sheltered by its ancient, half blind priest. The village even then had been abandoned, its inhabitants driven off by the predatory nomads. Abbas had promised the old priest to restore the church and to rebuild the village. He had never done so. What was one village, one church, one priest, among so many? What was one promise considering the myriad cares of administration?

Strange it was that this incident should remain so present in his memory, that this one broken promise should so frequently rise to darken his thoughts.

Strange it was, indeed.

II

Abbas entered the city of Meshed one day in late October. The pilgrimage had been made in fine weather, beneath clear skies. But this day had turned wintry and a fine dust from the desert had begun to blow, veiling in a yellow mist the immense gold-sheathed dome of the shrine toward which the Shah was journeying. Dust filled the mouth and gathered upon the saddle mountings of the horses and the trappings of the camels, as though Nature was mimicking the Shah in his symbolic pilgrimage.

The provincial dignitaries had gone out on the road to meet the Shah and escort him into the city. The roads were lined with people and the housetops were crowded with gaping humanity.

The Shah walked slowly through the suburban streets followed by his court. He gave no heed to the cheers and salutations of his subjects, but kept his eyes downcast, as befitted a pious pilgrim. Despite the cold which had caused others to draw their cloaks about them, the Shah wore nothing more than his habitual cotton trousers and the jacket of quilted cotton fastened with a belt of goat's leather.

The procession came to the city walls, surrounded by their dry moat, and here Abbas could not resist raising his eyes and making a quick survey of their condition. They passed through the gates and entered the broad Khiaban-i-Shah, the plane-tree bordered avenue which Abbas himself had laid out. It was an impressive avenue, that ran like an arrow to the great portal of the shrine, now visible in the distance between the trees.

At that moment a woman, garbed in a black chuddar which covered her from head to foot, appeared from behind one of the trees and ran up to the Shah. A Qizilbashie rushed to drag her away, but Abbas raised his hand. The Qizilbashie waited, scimitar unsheathed, ready to defend his monarch.

The woman in her dingy black covering appeared to be one of those pious crones that affect to prophesy.

"Blessed art thou, Majesty," she cried in a loud voice that was not without a musical quality. "Blessed art thou who hast gained sainthood by thy piety. Blessed is our nation to be led by such a Shah."

Abbas regarded the woman gravely.

"Thank thee, daughter, for thy blessing. Would that all my subjects were like thee. Then would my labors be blessed indeed and I could go to my grave in peace, knowing that I had so lived as to have won the esteem of my people. It is no easy task to sit upon the throne and to judge a people, or to lead an army into battle in defense of our security," he added thoughtfully.

"Thou art a saint! God leads thee by the hand!" exclaimed the woman with passionate fervor.

"No saint, my daughter, but a simple wayfarer on the Path, seeking by this pilgrimage to win merit and Paradise and to set an example to my people by pious exercise."

"A saint, a saint," the woman insisted. "A descendant of the Imam! Behold our Mahdi who comes to redeem the world!"

The cry was taken up by the multitude: "A saint—the Mahdi—*ya Abbas.*"

The Shah regarded the woman benignly.

"I thank thee again for thy blessing, daughter. With what boon can I recompense thee?"

The woman drew near to the Shah.

"To live and die in thy presence, O Lord of the Worlds," she breathed passionately.

Abbas's eyes narrowed.

"And were that enough?" he asked, a trace of steel finding its way into his voice.

"Aye," answered the woman, and dropped her voice to a whisper, "and to feel thy hand upon my neck and under my thigh and to bear thee children."

"Show me thy face, daughter," said Abbas.

The crowd stood at a distance. The woman stepped close to the Shah and drew aside her veil, shielding her face so that none but Abbas might look on it. It was a face that was neither youthful nor virginal, but handsome, and the lips were full and moist. The bodice of her dress was rich with threads of gold, and a massive chain of rubies hung about her throat.

The Shah regarded the woman for a moment and then remarked, "Hast a husband, woman?"

"Aye, the merchant Tadmor—but him—and all that I possess—would I sacrifice for thee."

"Does he not feed thee and keep thee well?"

"He is miserly, and strews food upon his beard. It is to suffer the pains of Hell to abide with him."

"Hast charms?" asked Abbas coolly.

The woman's lips formed a provocative smile.

"Aye," she whispered, "and I will show thee such caresses—"

A look of calculation passed over the Shah's face.

"What is thy name?"

"Dilka," said the woman eagerly, "and my husband, as I said, is Tadmor the merchant, and to send for me note that we live in the Street of Shirvan that lies just beyond the mosque of Sheikh Kahmel, behind a gate remarkable for its narrowness as well as for its solid brass studding."

"Well, Dilka," said the Shah, "return thou to thy husband and show him thy devotion. Thy lord is upon a pilgrimage to gain his soul and merit in Paradise and to set an example of piety to his people. Go and set thyself as an example to thy kind, and purify thyself with holy thoughts lest thy flesh be made the meat of dogs and thy bones fare for the jackals to gnaw."

His voice had risen sternly as he said these words and his face had hardened with cynicism, but seeing the woman's look of horrified dismay he relented and with an enigmatic smile said, "But I will remember thee—in my prayers."

The Shah motioned to the soldier to lead the woman away. And as he walked along he muttered to himself, half aloud, "Lies, lies."

III

Early the following morning the dignitaries of the court and the city gathered to accompany the Shah on his entry into the shrine of the Imam. Among them was Allah Verdi Khan, whose largess had provided the gilding of the dome and whose presence now was at Abbas's command. Atai Beg, the palace chamberlain, and Habibullah Agha, the Shah's minister of court, were also in attendance, as were the Maboob Agha, the aged governor of Khorasan, the Darugha of the city, together with the Naib Tollieh and the chief mujtahid of the shrine.

The Shah had abandoned his simple dress, and in honor of the Imam had appareled himself in robes of state—crimson trousers and tunic of satin, and a redingote of crimson damask embroidered in gold. About his waist was a scarf of silk, many yards long, twisted into a girdle, through which was thrust a scimitar in a gold-embroidered and gem-encrusted scabbard.

The sun was just rising on the horizon as Abbas emerged from the gate into the street. Its beams were like a benediction, and in the morning light the golden dome of the shrine shone with a heavenly splendor. Abbas walked slowly, in silence, with downcast eyes, his whole manner seemingly imbued with the solemnity of the occasion, but he did not fail to take note of the remarkable transformations in the city in the fifteen years since its reconquest from the Uzbegs. Prosperity, he observed with satisfaction, was everywhere evident.

The procession moved down the broad esplanade, the Khiaban-i-Shah, by which Abbas had entered the city. At the end, five hundred yards from the city gate, rose the portals to the outer precincts of the shrine. Beyond was an imposing space framed by the outer portals and by three immense gateways—*ivans* as they were called, works of extraordinary construction—half-domes sixty feet in height, set in square frames. Except for the one leading to the shrine, the façade of the *ivans* consisted of glittering faience of intricate design. That which led to the shrine, known as the Golden Ivan, was plated with gold in geometrical patterns.

As Abbas entered the outer court he was shaken by the sudden realization that he had neglected to remove his Christian talisman before setting out. He could not reason away his qualms at entering the holy Moslem shrine with the Christian cross on his breast. For all that the Christians were accepted as "People of the Book" by the Moslems, an irreconcilable antagonism separated the two faiths, and Abbas recognized that he must accept the one and reject the other lest his soul be split in twain.

But there was nothing he could do about it now. He rallied his shattered nerves and passed on.

In the center of the court was the ablutional fountain, octagonal in shape and covered with gold inlay. Pausing there, Abbas washed his arms to the elbows and his feet to the ankles. The act seemed to relieve some of his uneasiness over the cross inside his tunic. His attention was drawn by the ivans, and for a moment his spirit was captured by the splendor that rose about him.

What was the mystery of the art which by means of line and form had such power to elevate the soul? Before the marvelous patterns of line and color that were displayed upon the immense surfaces with an intricacy of detail past imagining, Abbas felt himself to swim in mystic exaltation. For a moment he was removed from mundane existence and dwelt in the very presence of the Godhead.

It was an experience, however, that was tinctured with loneliness; it was glorious to be so uplifted into the very airs of heaven, but it was also devastating for one whose umbilical ties to the hungers of the earth had never been severed. Abbas's spirit reached out for a companioning handclasp, and as it could not quite touch the Godhead it groped for something more immediate. As so often happened, it was upon a vision of the Princess Shamala that his soul was transfixed. Shamala—green-eyed and mysterious, aloof and distant, like the Godhead in that neither Abbas's manhood nor his majesty nor all the wealth of his Empire could entice it to his grasp . . .

The spell passed, and the vision dissolved. Abbas felt a distaste at this pilgrimage, a cynicism at this pious fraud he was perpetrating. The presence of the crowd that had pushed into the court, gaping in wonder and curiosity, sharpened his irritation.

He controlled himself, however, and allowed his guides to conduct him into the sacred precincts. From the doorway of the Golden Ivan, he entered the Dar-ul-Saada, the Gate of Majesty, which was not a gate but a vast chamber nearly one hundred feet in length, with central and supporting domes of equal vastness and grandeur, the whole paneled with gold and blue tiles and ceilinged with glass facets which dazzled the eyes with their scintillation. Beyond this was a gate, a high grillwork of solid silver, that admitted to the Dar-ul-Hefaz, the Place of Receivers, the immediate forecourt to the shrine. Here the Shah, like any common pilgrim, prostrated himself, touching the ground with his cheek—as only in honor of God may the forehead touch the ground—while a mullah intoned prayers for his well-being.

And now, through a golden gate, he was admitted to the Haram, the holy ground of the shrine, where stood the tomb of the Imam, a shrouded catafalque enclosed by a golden grille. Abbas approached the grille, kissed the lock, recited a prayer, and then made a thrice-repeated circuit of the tomb, crying aloud at each circuit a curse on Mamun, the caliph who had in jealousy poisoned the Imam with a dish of fruit.

The veritable dish in which the fruit had been served to the Imam was still in existence. It was a basin of gold, with a small hole in the center, set in one wall of the Dar-ul-Saada. It was commonly believed to have wonder-working properties, and pious pilgrims would insert a finger in the hole and rub upon their eyes the dust that adhered. This sacred dust conferred a blessing. For some, their spiritual eyes were opened, and they saw truth like a supernal splendor. Others experienced a benignity of peace, and for still others the sacred dust brought healing of physical infirmities.

Something like this last now happened. As Abbas completed his last circuit of the tomb and uttered his final curse upon the wicked Mamun, a murmur arose within the vast edifice of the Dar-ul-Saada; the murmur mounted, and became a shouting of wonder and rejoicing. The shouting was not for Abbas, that he had completed his long and arduous pilgrimage. Those in the royal entourage looked at one another in puzzlement. The shouting became more distinct. There were cries: "A miracle, a miracle! Holy dust, miracle-working dust!"

Abbas turned to the Naib Tollieh in mute inquiry.

The ecclesiastic appeared embarrassed.

"It seems that there has been a miracle, your Majesty," he said diffidently.

"A miracle!" exclaimed Abbas, his eyes brightening. "Then not in vain have I made this pilgrimage. Let us know more about it."

The Naib Tollieh was relieved. He nodded toward his attendants. The shouting redoubled.

"Holy dust, miracle-working dust!"

One of the attendants hurried back with the news that a blind man had just been healed of his blindness.

"What is this wonder-working dust?" Abbas inquired.

The Naib Tollieh explained about the basin. "There have been instances of cures," he said cautiously.

"Of blindness?"

"Aye, your Majesty."

"I suppose then, that if it can restore sight to the blind it can improve the sight of the living," said Abbas penetratingly. He did not believe in miracles; he was skeptical of such things; yet he would like to see a miracle. There might be some truth in the claims of miraculous power from on high. He was willing—yes, secretly, he was eager —to be convinced that there were men who had drawn nigh to God, held converse with Him and received strength and courage and peace and hope from Him in some tangible way.

The ecclesiastic was slow in answering the Shah's question.

"That would follow," he said at last.

"Is there anyone who does not need to see more clearly?"

"None."

Abbas peered sharply at the Naib Tollieh.

"Even your Shah?"

The Naib Tollieh was confused.

"Can one bring light to the sun?" he asked, neatly evading the dilemma.

Abbas turned on his heel.

"Fetch me this man who has received his sight," he directed his officers.

The man was brought before the Shah. He wore a dirty jubbah around which was wrapped a green sash that signified him to be a seyyid or descendant of the Prophet. That he was not a mendicant, however, was indicated by the small black turban of the petty trader which he wore.

"You are he who has received the blessed gift of sight from the Holy Imam?" Abbas asked gently.

"Aye, your Majesty."

"This was accomplished by rubbing a little dust from the golden plate onto your eyes?"

"Aye, your Majesty, but seventy times I had made the course about the tomb, at each course beseeching the Imam's favor."

"What is your business?"

"A merchant, your Majesty. I bring silks and shawls soft as maidens' cheeks from Agra. I know the country of Hind. If your Majesty requires services in those parts you will find me one to trust. The Holy Imam has given me his blessing, as you can see."

"How long is it, my good man, that you have been blind?" asked Abbas, as softly as before.

"I was born blind, your Majesty."

"And how did you find your way to Hind?"

"For finding the way in the mountains, it is better to be blind than to be possessed of sight," responded the man glibly. "Besides, I have a brother."

"And you can see well now?"

"Aye, Majesty. My eyes but now are dazzled by the brightness of your incomparable glory. I see the light of our people standing before us in majestic effulgence."

"Nay, I am but a man," said Abbas slowly. "See," and he quickly drew back the sleeve of his *gaba* and showed his arm. "Is this not flesh?" he asked.

The man was abashed.

"Aye, your Majesty, but such flesh—like alabaster."

"And the color of this tunic?"

"Red," said the man. "The royal purple that belongs to shahs and *kaisars*."

Abbas smiled grimly.

"You say you were born blind, and yet you can distinguish colors and know what each is called."

"Nay, your Majesty," protested the man, suddenly horrified at the trap into which he had fallen. "It is well known that the Shah wears crimson and that, true Persian that he is, his flesh is white."

"Then thou liest to flatter," said Abbas, "for my skin is burnt black from my youth in the tents and from years in the wars, and my face is blacker still that my Empire should be possessed of so many liars."

Turning to the Darugha he said in a voice like distant thunder:

"See that this man's eyes are removed from their sockets. He claims to be born blind. We will see that he dies blind. It must not be said that a liar entered these sacred precincts."

And with these words Abbas strode from the sanctuary.

PART SIX

Return and Departure

I

Fray Juan's Russian embassy proved an abject failure. Just before he set forth, the Shah, with his usual expansiveness, had enlarged the friar's embassy to include most of the courts of Europe, and he had given the friar letters of credence to the various princes. Hardly had the Carmelite crossed the Russian frontier, however, when he was arrested. The fact that he was a Catholic had been sufficient to arouse antagonism. Russian-Orthodox fanaticism against Catholics had been inflamed ever since Polish arms and influence had been used to set the pretender Dmitri on the Russian throne. Fray Juan had been searched; the letters to the Catholic princes were found; they seemed to confirm official suspicions, and the hapless friar was accused of fomenting military alliances against Muscovy. He was thrown into prison.

When the Shah learned how his envoy had been treated he was furious and sent a dispatch threatening war unless the Carmelite were released. This seemed to have no effect upon the Russians, however, and presently Abbas, in his absorption in other affairs, forgot about the matter.

It was the Grand Duchess Marina Georgina—the Polish Helen for whom Dmitri sacrificed the support of the boyars and eventually his life—who finally effected the friar's release. While the Carmelite languished in the dungeon of the Astrakhan kremlin, political confusion mounted in Russia. It was the "Time of Trouble" in Russian history, the period of political anarchy between the death of Ivan the Terrible and the establishment of the Romanoff dynasty. Dmitri had gained the throne with Polish aid and on the claim that he was the actual son of Ivan the Great. But the boyars resented the Polish influence with which he surrounded himself, and when he insisted on going through with his marriage to the Polish princess Marina Georgina, the boyars conspired and assassinated him during the wedding festivities. His bride escaped, however—by witchcraft, some said. She was a remarkable woman, of extraordinary beauty and with an extraordinary power to sway others to her desires. She was an out-and-out Catholic, and her well known piety, coupled with her magnetic presence, seemed to fence her with awe. In any case, it was not long before she appeared with another Dmitri, who she claimed was the true Dmitri, and with the support of the Polish king obtained his election to the throne of Ivan. But shortly afterward he too was assassinated. There followed a third Dmitri, her son by the first Dmitri, who was crowned but subsequently seized and strangled, and a fourth Dmitri, another son.

Marina Georgina, while on a journey to Astrakhan, had learned of the imprisonment of a Catholic friar. She visited him, made her confessions to him, and sought his absolution, and subsequently managed certain favors for him, among them the privilege of receiving visitors and of celebrating Mass according to the Roman rite. It was another year, however, before the grand duchess succeeded in obtaining Fray Juan's release.

Fray Juan was put ashore in a small boat with money enough for only a night's lodging. Still dizzy from the closeness of the hold, retching from the lingering seasickness, and weak from his long confinement, the friar stumbled across the beach and through the reedy marsh toward the caravanserai set against the hills. From the innkeeper he learned that he was at Kevsar, a fishing hamlet on the Caspian, and in the Shah's dominions. The innkeeper showed him a dry stall. He found strength enough to recite the office, and then, exhausted, with his beads still clutched in his fingers, he fell asleep in the straw.

When he awoke it was morning again and an aqueous light filled the courtyard. He got unsteadily to his feet, bracing himself against what seemed to be the familiar swaying and rolling of the vessel, and then, discovering that he was on dry land, fell to his knees and murmured a *Laus Deo*.

During the morning the sound of mule bells, accompanied by a sickening odor of decay, crept into the courtyard. A corpse caravan had arrived bound for the sacred burial ground about the tomb of the Imam Reza at Meshed. The *charvadar* needed a man to help him with the mules in crossing the passes. Fray Juan, penniless, offered his services for hire.

They left the warm Caspian lowlands the same day, mounting the Elborz slopes through fields of tulips and purple iris in bloom and forests of pine and walnut, but the stench from the corpses was so great that Fray Juan was continually nauseated. Then, at the second pass, they met the gales that still raged on the Iranian plateau. They struggled through the mountain snows for three days, and Fray Juan, still prison-pallid and soft of muscle, lived again in three days the long winter of his first terrible journey through Russia. Finally they were out of the mountains and came down, by way of the ancient Caspian Gates through which Alexander had pursued the last Darius, upon the Veramin plain. Here the snow had turned into intermittent rain which flooded the flats and made the road a miry waste. At the village of Aivan-i-Kaif, famous for its melons, where the great caravan route from Asia—the ancient Silk Road—joined the road from the north, Fray Juan was met by Javan, who had heard of his master's release and had set out to meet him. Javan had a warm room ready at the caravanserai, and while he rubbed the friar's frost-bitten feet and fed him hot coffee he volubly cursed the Russians.

"They are not so bad," protested the weary friar. "It is only that they are a very suspicious people. Some day, perhaps, when they know us better—and we know them better—we will get along."

"You are still a child," commented Javan. "The only way the Muscovites will learn courtesy is to stuff it down them."

He went on to berate the Russians with the vehemence of a *ferash* beating a carpet. Fray Juan was too tired to protest further. He was no longer thinking of the Russians—that incident was ended—but he looked ahead to the Shah, to the Carmelite house and the young friars he had left behind. Perhaps the three years of his imprisonment had not been wasted. Perhaps his sacrifices in the Shah's interest had softened the monarch's heart toward the Carmelites, and Silvester and Anselm had garnered many sheaves in his absence.

He heard Javan mention the Shah's name and looked up.

"Abbas?" he inquired.

But Javan was suddenly silent.

Fray Juan waited.

"How you have changed!" he commented after a moment. "Three years ago you were still a lad; now you are a grown man. It was good of you to come and meet me. Have things gone well in the house, and how are the fathers?"

Javan busied himself rubbing the friar's feet with renewed vigor before answering.

"Three years is a long time, Father," he said, and his voice was harsh, as though he were bitter about something which Fray Juan could not perceive. He was still the ferash beating a carpet. "In three years you have—may God pardon my boldness—grown gray and aged in the Shah's service, and as thin as a tent peg. And how does this Shah recompense you?"

"Why, how?" asked Fray Juan uneasily. The young man's mood was not reassuring. To hide his feelings Javan left off rubbing the friar's feet and busied himself with the brazier and the coffee. He poured a cup and offered it to the friar. Fray Juan accepted it, but set it down untouched.

"You know I did this thing not for the Shah's remembrance, but for God's," Fray Juan said placatingly. "Abbas, you know, has promised a firman for a house on my return."

Javan stood erect and faced the friar, his eyes blazing.

"Abbas has forgotten you, and likewise his promises," he exclaimed violently, and Fray Juan was suddenly struck by the depth of the young man's devotion to him. He thought that was more important than any bad news of which he might be the bearer. If only Javan's devotion were to the Cross and the Church . . . His bullet head, with its tightly curled black hair, the heavy nose, the fire of loyalty and impertinence that shone in his black eyes—all these made Fray Juan think of the Apostle Paul. And there were other things about Javan —his ready speech, his tirelessness, his sharp logic and passionate zeal

—that could make him a new St. Thomas, or another St. Gregory in this land. Even while his thoughts were anxiously turning upon the meaning of Javan's intimations, Fray Juan prayed that Javan might be touched by the Holy Spirit and led at last to the Christian faith.

"You have not told me how the house stands," he reminded Javan.

"The house is not," said Javan shortly. "That is to say, we have been dispossessed, and the reverend fathers Silvester and Anselm have departed, and only the lay brother Grigor remains. With him I lodge in the public room of the caravanserai near the Qum gate."

Fray Juan felt himself growing giddy. He closed his eyes and bowed his head, and prayed for strength. It was some little while before he could summon himself to speak. Outside, the rain dripped steadily in the courtyard; men shouted; a mule brayed loudly. The Tartar charvadar was continuing on his way to Meshed with his caravan of forty corpses. Fray Juan thought of those forty former habitations of the soul, now decaying flesh, oozing putrescence through the joints of the coffins, filling the air with their fetor. In his anguish the words of the Prophet Jeremiah came to his lips:

Oh that my head were waters, and mine eyes a fountain of tears, that I might weep day and night. . . .

For death is come up into our windows, and is entered into our palaces, to cut off the children from without, and the young men from the streets.

It was a proper thing in the friar's view that one should wish to be buried in hallowed ground, and he thought of himself falling asleep in this Moab's land with his body left to moulder on these sterile plains. At that moment there were steps on the earthen staircase, and a knock at the chamber door. The charvadar stood in the opening.

He was a big rotund man, with a plump face and eyes that were little more than slits. His name was Kazim Sarkis.

"I have come to say goodbye, my friend," he said. He had a big voice that could at times soften to the gentle pitch of a cooing dove. "You have entertained me well with your stories of your Christian prophet, and they have made the days pass quicker and the cold seem less bitter."

"But did I not care well for your mules?" Fray Juan asked.

"As to that, your knowledge of the nature of mules wants something of that of my stable-boy Ali," the charvadar replied. "But the way you broke a way through the snow with only a mattock is some-thing I shall long remember. Men here, even for gold, do not strive so hard. But you are bound for Isfahan, you say. Where do you lodge there? For I shall seek you out. You are an odd Firenghi, and you intrigue me like a Chinese puzzle."

"Really?" asked Fray Juan, his face suddenly suffused with a glow of pleasure. "What is the name of the caravanserai, Javan?"

"The Caravanserai of Shah Ismail."

"At the Caravanserai of Shah Ismail seek for me, and if not there, the *arbaab* will direct you. I shall indeed be happy to see you again."

The charvadar's visit had lifted Fray Juan's spirits, and after Kazim Sarkis had gone the friar turned again to Javan.

"Do you hear from Fray Vincent at Hormuz? Has he sent you funds?"

"Such is the enmity that now exists between Abbas and the Portu-guese that little commerce passes between the two sovereignties. We have not heard from Fray Vincent since the arrival of the English."

"The English?"

"Agents of the English Company of the Indies are now in Isfahan, and they offer to take all the silk of the realm, and moreover they offer their aid against the Portuguese. To please the English, the Shah no longer shows his face to the Catholics, for the Pope, he says, has not met his promise of an alliance against the Turks."

Fray Juan's reviving spirits were sobered.

"Is there anything else I should know, Javan?" he asked intently.

"Abbas, it seems, grows daily more suspicious of his son Safi Mirza, though he has again put him in command of troops. He suspects more-over that certain members of the court would like to see him de-throned. For that reason he does not go about freely as he formerly did, but sleeps, they say, in a different room every night; and it is also said that he has become an eater of the dried juice of the poppy."

Fray Juan in his anxiety rose and walked about the room in his bare feet.

"Please, Father, you will take your death of cold," protested Javan. "Sit again, I beg, until I have rubbed the frost from your feet."

But Fray Juan was too agitated to sit.

"You treat me too well," he said, and sat down, but not to allow Javan to rub his feet. Instead he drew on the Russian felt boots that had been drying near the brazier. They were badly frayed and were open in places at the seams, enough to allow the cold snow water to seep in and chill his feet. "It is not well for us religious to be so pampered," he added, "especially when there is work that calls. We must find means of travel."

"We have means, Father. Horses are in the stable, and we can ride in the morning."

"Horses!"

"Yes, horses."

"Provided by whom?"

"By the Princess Shamala."

The friar was silent. To ride horses was forbidden, and Father Paul had made the prohibition an issue with the Shah. Fray Juan, however, had long since come to terms with the restriction. By specific instructions of the Pope, this and all other rules of dress and diet and comportment had been mitigated according to the necessities of the case, leaving only the basic vows of poverty, obedience, and chastity in full effect. Accordingly, whenever there was need for speed, Fray Juan had ridden horseback; at other times he used a mule, or walked.

What was his necessity now? What were a few days more to his three years' absence? What could his excuse be for accepting the horses if mules were available?

"How is the princess?" he asked, unconsciously seeking for time in which to make a decision.

"More beautiful than ever, Father, and more kindly, if that is possible."

Fray Juan felt a faint sense of confusion.

"Why do you call me 'Father'?" he asked, but the question was flat, almost mechanical. It had occurred to him that Javan had never before called him by his ecclesiastical title. Could it mean that he was taking a new interest in the Christian Gospel?

But the young man evaded the question.

"Why not?" he asked innocently, and changing the subject said, "Grigor will be eager to see you."

"We will ride mules," said Fray Juan finally.

But Javan, who had known how to attach himself to the friar, knew now how to have his way about their mode of travel.

"Very well," he said meekly, "but in that case I must lead the horses, for they belong in Isfahan."

The two sat in silence. Presently, however, the friar began to show restlessness. To compose himself he took up his breviary and read. After a while he glanced out of the window.

"The rain has abated, and there are still three hours of daylight," he commented. "We could make Sharifabad by nightfall."

Javan's face puckered in anxiety as he scrutinized the friar.

"It is as you wish, Father, but it seems to me you would do better to rest awhile in bed. You don't look well."

"Nonsense!" exclaimed Fray Juan, suddenly impatient, rising and throwing back his shoulders. "Now that I am on these uplands my strength revives. Let us be going."

Javan understood that they would ride the horses after all, and went to saddle them. Fray Juan gathered together his belongings. He folded and replaced in his haversack his stole and alb that had been drying by the fire, and carefully rewrapped his chalice and vial of wine. Besides these articles there were a frayed missal and his breviary, a small crucifix on a stand, a change of undergarments, and a copy of the poems of the Persian mystic Jalal-ul-Din Rumi bound in green leather—a volume which the Princess Shamala had given him on his departure. Fray Juan was never sure in his own mind as to why he had kept this little book with him—unless it was as a memento of his first spiritual child in this land, and a work by a Moslem Sufi poet who had come to comprehend something of the depth of Christian revelation and had expressed his understanding in admirable Oriental imagery. There might be some question as to the propriety of a religious such as he having a work of this character in his possession, since it did not bear the imprimatur. On the other hand it was not on the Prohibitory Index, and indeed many of the odes were so close in spirit and in mood to those of the Carmelite poet and mystic Fray Juan de la Cruz as to be almost indistinguishable.

Fray Juan held the book in his hands, and turned the pages absently, thinking perhaps he should now rid himself of it, yet unwilling to do so; and then his eyes fell upon a particular verse and his throat suddenly constricted. It was from the *Masnavi*, and was entitled *The Music of Love*, addressed, of course, to the nature of Divine Love:

Hail to thee, then, O Love, sweet madness!
Thou who healest all our infirmities!
Who art the Physician of our pride and self-conceit!
Who art our Plato and our Galen!
Love exalts our earthly bodies to heaven,
And makes the very hills to dance with joy!

. . . .

Did my Beloved only touch me with His lips,
I too, like a flute, would burst out into melody.

Fray Juan closed the book, wrapped it in a piece of colored silk, and placed it in the haversack with the other articles.

When Javan re-entered he found the friar sitting on a stool, his head bowed.

"Are you ready, Father?" he asked anxiously. "Do you still wish to leave?"

The friar's eyes were bright when he looked up, and Javan thought he was feverish.

"I am ready," said Fray Juan composedly. "Let us be on our way."

II

The friar, Javan thought, seemed well enough as they set out, but before the two reached Sharifabad Fray Juan was swaying in the saddle, and on arriving at the caravanserai Javan put him to bed with a raging fever. Nevertheless, on the morrow Fray Juan insisted on continuing the journey. Fortunately, the weather turned mild, and as they journeyed south the air grew balmy. They reached Isfahan safely within a fortnight, but by then the friar's reserves of strength were exhausted; his fever returned, and he lay in a coma.

The Princess Shamala had engaged a house for the friar when she heard that he had been released by the Russians and was returning to Persia, and it was to this that Javan took his master. It was a pleasant place with a garden and windows overlooking the river and the royal park. After putting the friar to bed Javan hastened to advise the princess of his arrival.

The day Fray Juan opened his eyes was one of those precursors of spring which the region of Isfahan knows, more glorious than spring itself. Through the window the storks could be seen repairing their nests on the wind towers. Sunlight glittered upon the gilded cross of the cathedral church in Julfa, pigeons circled in the air, and the dome of the Masjid-i-Shah shimmered in the distance; but what the friar saw when he looked up were the green eyes of Shamala gazing down at him.

Seeing the friar awake, the princess, with the familiarity of an old friend and with the impulsiveness of her Circassian blood, settled herself on the floor beside his pallet, swirling her redingote to form a circle about her—the graceful gesture the friar remembered from his first meeting with her in her house.

"Ah," she exclaimed, "how happy it makes me that you are safely returned!"

She said this joyously, but for all her attempted gaiety her eyes grew moist, and even as the friar watched, her tears flowed uncontrollably down her cheeks. This was something new to the friar, to see her so affected. Alarmed, he put out his hand and touched her sleeve.

"God in His infinite mercy has taken care of me," he said. "Let us rejoice in that."

The princess brought her tears under control and dabbed the corners of her eyes with her handkerchief. She smiled.

"You do not know how many prayers I have sent winging to heaven for your safekeeping, how many tears have stained my pillow during your absence," she protested. "Should I not be allowed to weep a little at your return?"

Fray Juan was so deeply touched that he could not find a proper response. He felt vaguely that Shamala deserved rebuke, but for what he could not say; he himself was conscious of a sensation alien to his experience and perhaps repugnant to his calling, yet so tender, so beautiful that he had no heart to dismiss it. Fortunately, the princess relieved him of the necessity for reply.

"Was it not Nizami who said, 'After the black cloud the white rain'?" she exclaimed. "So now we walk in this glorious splendor-shot shower of blessings, and I shall not speak to you again of your Russian experiences—though I dearly love a tale as much as any bazaar urchin, and I am certain that you could entertain me, if you would, with such that could hold herdsmen from the campfire and dogs silent under the moon. But I shall not ask you; nay, I shall keep silence on that subject."

She did keep silent on that and on all subjects for a moment, her green eyes gazing down into those of the friar with such solemn intensity that he felt in the grip of forces which he could not recognize.

"Have you kept the observances faithfully?" he found himself asking in a dry voice. How arid he felt, in the phrase of Mother Teresa of Ávila, how much spiritual zest had he lost, how starved he was for the nourishing food of the conventual worship, the strength imparted by the rigorous discipline of the monastery! How had he survived those three years in his Astrakhan cell without the comfort of holy companionship? There came the faintest perfume from Shamala that was like sweet-scented apothecary's balm upon a wound. As out of a mist, as out of a cloud of almond blossom, he heard her say:

"May I be forgiven, Father Juan, but it has been so long since I have made confessions—not since the departure of the reverend fathers Silvester and Anselm—and I fear I have forgotten all the wicked things I have done. When you are feeling better, I must come to you for penance."

"A priest never considers himself too ill to offer the sacraments of salvation," protested Fray Juan, and forced himself up on his elbows to show that he was well enough to perform his duty. But he fell back almost immediately upon the pillows. The princess was on her knees at once, arranging the bolster and calling for a basin of water with which to bathe his forehead. Presently the friar opened his eyes again.

"It is not necessary," he said firmly, almost roughly, and removed the wet cloth from his forehead. "Let Javan attend to me."

It was plain that the friar was in no condition to have visitors, and Shamala quietly withdrew.

It was Lent, but the friar refused the indulgence granted to the sick to eat meat, and his health was slow to mend. Shamala visited him daily, either to bring him some fruit, or fresh mast, or flowers from her sun garden, always attended by Fardoush and bringing sometimes one or another of the Armenian ladies of her acquaintance. On one of these days, when she was accompanied only by Fardoush, she renewed her request to make her confession.

This she did, kneeling by the friar's pallet and speaking in Italian while the watchful eunuch remained in a corner of the room.

The Princess Shamala had over the years changed greatly from the hoyden who had accosted the friar on the Ardebil plain; she had changed marvelously and charmingly in the three years of the friar's Russian adventure; she had acquired maturity and new dignity and added grace and graciousness. Nevertheless, she had not lost entirely her Amazon instincts; there were grievous sins of which she had been guilty since her last confession. Her violent temper had not been conquered; she was covetous too often and squandered her allowance on luxuries she did not need; she had neglected her prayers.

And there was something besides, which the confessional did not explicitly reveal and which neither the friar's experience as a priest nor his native intuition was able to uncover. Fray Juan had long been convinced of the essential purity of Shamala's nature. It was evident in the simple directness and candor of her confessions, in her willing acceptance of spiritual counsel, in the sincerity of her contrition under rebuke, and in the immediate release of her spirit upon absolution. But now there were matters which did not come to the surface as they should. It became acutely evident only that Shamala was subject to certain stresses and distresses, manifesting themselves in fierce emotional outbursts and strange longings and perverse dislikes, the cause of which defied explanation or analysis.

It was only after he had given the absolution that an intuitive light seemed to illuminate the problem.

"Does his Majesty still seek your consent?" the friar asked.

Shamala's response was a pensive shake of the head.

"Not since his return from his pilgrimage has he visited me or commanded my attendance," she said.

Something like the suggestion of nostalgia was a goad to the friar, leading him to ask:

"And you? You have dismissed him from your thoughts?"

Immediately he regretted such prying. It was a question hardly warranted by the priestly prerogative of the confessional, and Shamala was not now confessing.

She turned to the friar with appeal in her eyes.

"You, Father, are the only fixity in my life. You are the only one to whom I turn with confidence."

There was in her tone such urgency, such joy mingled with such desolation that the friar was speechless. And then he felt a sickening sense of guilt for having been so obtuse. At the same time his soul was raked by a mortal fear.

III

The following day the friar, driven by a sense of great urgency, sent Javan to inquire if Sir Robert Sherley were in the city, and if so to urge him to attend him. At the Englishman's house Javan was told that Sir Robert was with the troops in Mazanderan, and that his return was uncertain.

Two days later, however, Sir Robert appeared at the friar's house, and begged the friar's forgiveness for not having come sooner, explaining that he had but now arrived from the provinces. The Englishman was as handsome, as distinguished, as ever, but his habitual melancholy seemed more pronounced; his face showed the strain of responsibility unrelieved by contentment. It occurred to the friar that all this was propitious for what he had in mind. He spoke cordially, inquired as to the other's health and the course of his affairs, and then indirectly reminded him of the obligations of a good Catholic.

"The blessed celebration of Easter approaches," he commented. "I trust that you are preparing to enter into these glorious Mysteries."

Sir Robert recalled that he had had little opportunity to make confession, and asked the friar to hear him.

Afterward, the friar spoke more directly.

"His Majesty still holds you to his service?"

The sacrament had lightened the Englishman's spirits somewhat.

"His Majesty needs my services," he said. "Even though he were to release me I would feel myself attached to him by a kind of pity. We are both lonely souls, each suffering from his own private despair. I have, however, this news to bring you: his Majesty has decided to send me to Europe on an embassy. I have on this account returned to the capital in advance of the Shah, in order to arrange my affairs for my departure."

"And when will you leave?"

"Directly his Majesty returns to Isfahan—within a fortnight, I expect."

"You will remain in Europe, then, and this marks the end of your Persian sojourn?"

"Nay, for I remain bound to his Majesty, as I see it, since my brother has never returned nor discharged his debt, and my conscience requires me to return at the completion of my mission."

Fray Juan found in this only another instance of Sir Robert's deep attachment to duty, as he saw his duty, and his respect for the Englishman was renewed.

"Now that you will be among your own people," he said carefully, "you will no doubt find yourself a wife to return with you and comfort you in the discharge of your duty."

The Englishman's expression relaxed. A faint smile formed on his lips.

"Ah, you are always thinking of my welfare, Father," he said. "But do not allow me to be morose. It is a sin which I acknowledge. This land, even as Europe, has its charms, and I confess that, having grown accustomed to these sterile plains, these brass-bound mountains, these pleasant gardens set in the midst of desolation, I will long for them when I am away. No, I shall return and with as much eagerness no doubt as that with which I leave.

"And I shall return celibate as I leave. For it is one thing to grow accustomed to bondage; it is something else to ask another to share it with you. It would be too much to ask an English lady, reared on our green and pleasant island, to accept my hand in marriage and expect her to undertake the arduous journeying and existence here which would be her lot as my wife."

The friar protested that Sir Robert was making imaginary difficulties and was too modest regarding his own worth, but his protest was faint. The match he had in mind seemed all the more logical in the circumstances.

"You reminded me once," he remarked, "that it was not your English custom to marry outside your race, and that you were very sure of yourself in this respect. You surely do not intend to forswear, as we religious do, all hope of conjugal bliss and all hope of paternity, and go down into the grave without issue?"

Sir Robert's smile broadened.

"So you think it imperative that I take a wife?" he asked. "Whom would you suggest that I could make happy?"

Fray Juan was disconcerted, guessing that Sir Robert knew what was in his thoughts. He plucked up his courage to speak.

"You have been betrothed for many years now to the Princess Shamala," he said boldly. "She has matured marvelously in the Christian graces. Could you not think of her as wife and helpmeet?"

The Englishman gave a gesture of decision.

"Father," he said, "I grant what you say, and more. She has been under your tutelage, and can hardly have failed to learn much of Christian virtue and obedience. Still, I find it impossible to look at her without recalling the barbarous child."

"You must think of her in a different light now," Fray Juan protested, "and this you could do had you kept up your acquaintance with her. The fact is, I feel concern and pity for her. She is of marriageable age—has been for some years; she is in that rich and spiritual condition that requires a husband for the perfect fulfillment of her aptitudes and spirit. If she fails to find a husband of her own faith and rank and quality she may, I fear, from natural necessity turn to his Majesty, who has so often proffered her a status in the Household. That, I am sure you agree, would be a catastrophe which no devout Christian, zealous of his faith and with any spark of charity toward a less fortunate being, could contemplate with good conscience. In view of your own reluctance to espouse her, therefore, do you know of some other upon whom the princess might look with favor?"

"Another? Before God, no!" exclaimed the Engishman with sudden alacrity and surprising force. "I am her lawful betrothed, and I would go down into Hell before I would see her married to that lecher Abbas."

"Every man has the right and the duty to save his own soul," reminded the friar. "You could hardly save the princess's at the cost of your own. You could hardly contemplate matrimony except under the conditions of Christian marriage, the foundation of which, I need not remind you, is mutual love."

"Nevertheless," exclaimed the Englishman, "since it is my duty, as God has given me my duty, so He will also give me the love with which to discharge it. Can there be a worthier love than that which comes with doing one's duty? And if to marry the princess is my duty, then to marry her is my love."

Sir Robert had arisen, and was pacing the floor with a kind of feverish excitement. His eyes were glowing and he rubbed his hands together like a man in from the cold with a congenial fire before which to warm them.

"Yes, yes," he continued, "I must thank you, reverend Father, for having shown me so clearly, yet so delicately, where both my duty and my happiness lie. Will you speak to the lady on my behalf? Will you convey to her my sentiments, and beg her, if she be willing, to name a day for the nuptial rite? Will you tell her of my European journey, and of the distinction which a person of such charm and lineage as herself could add to his Majesty's embassy?"

The friar was overwhelmed by the success of his proposal, so much so that he began now to doubt its wisdom. A nervousness overcame him and it was a moment before he could ask:

"Are you not overhasty in this? If what I have suggested be wisdom, is there a reason why you waited so long to embrace it?"

"Father," said the Englishman fervently, "no man is capable of seeing his own good, for in that case there would be no mistakes in this world—no sin and no unhappiness. Why have you, who are responsible for my soul's welfare, never shown me my duty before? But now that you have, the veil has been torn aside, and I see my destiny clearly. Was there not the hand of God in this betrothal in the first instance? Yea, I am inclined to believe it. Therefore, let us talk no further of it, but go you, I beg you, to the lady, and tell her that I solicit the honor of her hand in marriage."

The following morning, after Tierce, the friar went out and called on the princess at her house. It was the first time he had stirred abroad since his illness, and the princess, noting his exhaustion after his long walk through the city, made him rest upon an ottoman while she ordered hot coffee and milk for him. As before, she settled herself on the floor beside him. She waited for the friar to speak, and he sensed that she had an inkling of his business. But he had difficulty in bringing himself to the matter, and only after having sipped the coffee for some minutes did he speak.

"You have heard that his Majesty is sending Sherley Khan on an embassy to Europe?" he asked.

The princess nodded her head and said nothing, but her eyes, as they looked into those of the friar, were filled with apprehension. Fray Juan found himself stopped for speech. Did he know what it was that stirred within his heart? He did not ask to know; he resolutely refused to discover. Instead, he thanked God for the grace that had been vouchsafed him when the Holy Spirit sent this delicate and vibrant creature to him in the midst of the wastes. His aches and weariness dissolved in the sunshine of her presence.

He compelled himself to speak again.

"My child," he began, and then, "Shamala," he began again, and finally blurted out, "Sherley Khan, who has long been betrothed to you, desires now the fulfillment of the engagement in honorable and Christian matrimony. Can you accept him?"

Shamala grew pale, and for a space she did not answer.

"Is this of his own prodding?" she asked at last, her voice fallen to a whisper.

Fray Juan was silent.

"You need not reply," Shamala said. "What Sherley Khan accepts he performs, and between his duty and his desire there is not room to pass a hair. Do you think, Father Juan, that I can make him an acceptable wife, comforting him and giving him joy?"

"If so be your will, God will mightily strengthen your power."

"Then tell Sherley Khan that I yield myself to him, and that if he will have me, I will endeavor to render him every earthly and spiritual due that is his in the rite of marriage, cherishing him and obeying him until death. He is an honorable man, noble in all his attributes, and the greatest lady of Europe would not feel herself unfortunate to be his spouse."

Fray Juan thought nothing could have been said more admirably or more sincerely. He was choked for words, and to prevent Shamala from seeing his reaction he quickly stood and, signing her with the cross, blessed her and departed.

Next day the friar read the nuptial Mass over the princess and Sir Robert, and a week later the two set out for Europe on the embassy for the Shah.

On the eve of their departure, the princess came to the friar to say goodbye. It had been a warm day of spring, and the friar had moved into the garden. On a bench among the almond trees, which made a cloud of tender pink against the blue of the sky, the two sat and silently absorbed the charm of the scene. Presently the princess spoke:

"Pray for me, Father, that I may be pleasing to my husband in all ways, and a channel of grace and love to strengthen him in his work."

"That I will do, that I will do daily," said the friar fervently.

They continued to sit in silence, while from over the garden wall came the muffled sounds of the street—a muleteer cursing and grunting to his beasts, a string of camels, their bells jangling in heavy rhythm, a seller of eggs crying his wares, and finally the muezzin of a nearby mosque calling the Faithful to prayer. Almost at the same moment, from the house, came the tinkle of a bell in the hands of lay brother Grigor.

"It is time for Vespers," said Fray Juan. "Will you come?"

They arose and went into the house, to the chamber which the friar used for a chapel. Fray Juan donned his vestments, approached the altar, and began to recite the office.

Grigor and Shamala gave the responses, and Fray Juan found himself hesitating during the liturgy, waiting for that mysterious, poignant voice which for so long he had heard only in memory and which soon again he would hear only in memory.

After the service the princess stood before him to say goodbye. The image of her in a close-fitting jubbah of azure wool, that enclosed her from her throat to her feet, and her arms to her wrists, yet delicately revealed the outline of her slimly rounded and graceful figure, was one Fray Juan knew he would carry with him until they met again —if God willed they should meet.

"I must say goodbye now," Shamala said diffidently.

"Goodbye," echoed the friar, not comprehending the finality of her words.

"We leave tomorrow at three hours of sunrise, for we go south, to India, and we will journey before the day grows hot in the desert," she continued. Fray Juan felt an abyss opening before him. He had prepared himself for this separation, but he had not imagined it so soon.

"Yes, you must journey before the day grows hot," he repeated mechanically.

Shamala knelt before him, her palms together.

"Will you give me your last blessing?" she said, almost in a whisper.

Fray Juan made the sign of the cross over her.

"*In nomine Patris et Filii et Spiritus sancti . . .*"

His voice stopped. Gathering himself, he spoke in Italian:

"Go in peace, and may the Lord of Peace be with you. Go with God's blessing, and the blessing of Holy Church. Go with my prayers for your peace, your joy, a safe and secure journey, and a safe return. Go with the remembrance—"

His voice choked again. He made the sign of the cross once more to regain his composure and concluded:

"—of our paternal interest and solicitude."

Shamala was gone. Lay brother Grigor and Javan, sensing the friar's need, had quietly gone out, and Fray Juan stood alone on the steps of the house, gazing into the velvet dusk. There he stood, fixed as a statue, for a long time, while the stars one by one were hung upon the curtain of night, and the sounds of the city stilled, and the earth lay in a starlit radiance.

PART SEVEN

Of Faith and Morals

I

Though Abbas had returned to his capital, he did not send for
the friar, and indeed seemed to have forgotten his very existence.
Easter came, and Ascension, and in the celebration of these glorious
events Fray Juan recovered his spirits and his health. Finally, on the
eve of Pentecost, a Qizilbashie came and summoned the Carmelite
to attend the Shah at the Chehel Sitoon. The friar went prepared to
give an account of his Russian mission, but as he saw the palanquins
and outriders in the avenue it was plain that Abbas was interested
in something else, and from the street chatter the friar learned that
a reception to the newly arrived representatives of the English East
India Company was in progress.

There was a crush at the gate, but in the spaces of the great garden
there was more room. As the friar passed around the reflecting pool
he came upon the Shah's sirdar, Allah Verdi Khan, standing quite
alone under a willow tree. The dour-faced Georgian appeared oblivious to what was going on; he was staring at the reflections in the water.
He looked up, however, as the friar approached, and saluted him with
exaggerated deference.

"You have escaped the clutches of the Muscovite, I see," he remarked dryly.

"Yes, praise God, Sirdar," answered the Carmelite, "as I thank

God that I find you safe also after your Turkoman campaigns."

"And why should you thank God on my behalf?" asked the sirdar, with what seemed like veiled cynicism. "Have I ever done anything to befriend you, that you should remember me in your prayers?"

"Is it not something to thank God for," the friar responded evenly, "that forces which could be hostile have been negative? You are of his Majesty's court and are held in high esteem. Should I not—as indeed I have done—remember you in my petitions to our heavenly Father?"

The Georgian seemed a little surprised. Fray Juan noticed that he had taken on weight since their last meeting, and that his long silky mustaches were graying. His eyes, still sardonic and defiant, had lost something of their fierceness, and Fray Juan detected in them uncertainty and questioning. He wondered if possibly the sirdar was out of favor with the Shah. Allah Verdi Khan was one of the few who had been with Abbas during his rise to power and who throughout the years had survived the vagaries and vicissitudes of the Shah's caprice. There was a famous story of how during the early days of his reign Abbas had become infuriated with the Georgian, even then his chief sirdar, and had sworn to have his head. Mishevelli had promptly handed the Shah his scimitar and as much as dared the other to make good his word. From that time the Georgian's favor, like his loyalty, had gone unquestioned.

"And so you are able to remember me, among all the many lost souls for whom you pray," commented Mishevelli musingly.

"And why not? I have all day for prayer, and a thought is as quick as a flash."

"Then you consider my life in danger, my position insecure?" asked the sirdar, who must have divined the thoughts running through Fray Juan's head.

"What happens to the body is nothing," replied the friar. "It is for your soul that I pray."

"Oh, yes, my soul. I had forgotten. But not my body? I have much more of it to be prayed for, as you see. Do you think I have too much —for my good?"

This was the nearest to humor that Fray Juan had ever seen the sirdar.

"I might bargain with you," continued the sirdar, "that what I abstain from eating, you agree to consume. For, by the beard of Noah, you are wasted away. Come to my table some time, and I will see you well stuffed."

"When I am in need of stuffing, I will come," said Fray Juan, and then daring at last to take his stand with the Georgian he added, "and in return, when you feel hungry for the Body and Blood of God —of which, I understand, you once partook—I attend your Excellency."

At this the sirdar's eyes suddenly glowed, like a brazier to which the bellows has been applied, and it seemed that resentment and hatred were like heat from a furnace.

"And re-enter the community of Christian followers who seized you in Muscovy, for that you worship images and they pictures, and held you in prison for three years?" Allah Verdi Khan demanded. "The benign faith from which I was sold as a child to serve this Majesty of Persia?" The voice was crackling now with the lightning of a spring storm. "The sublime mystery whose hierophant in crimson and purple and sitting on a marble throne has sent you barefooted friars on this weary, hopeless journey, and then has forgotten you, left you here to starve and wither in the mercies of this Majesty?"

The voice suddenly subsided into a whisper.

"No, my brave and foolish man. I thank you for your interest, but your prayers are like salt poured out on the desert."

He bowed to the friar, and turned away to resume his contemplation of the reflections in the water.

Fray Juan thought that the sirdar was seeing life as it looked in the pool—a confusion of glittering, broken reflections rather than as it appeared on looking toward heaven, whole and harmonious. Nevertheless, his own spirit, still suffering from the shock of his Russian experience, was profoundly disturbed, and he thought how after a dozen years he was farther from his goal than when he had started.

A sense of disenchantment for having been summoned on such an occasion dominated the friar as he made his way toward the palace. Here he found the monarch deep in conversation with a tall Firenghi —a spare man in a tight-fitting black cassock with a starched ruff. Abbas beckoned the friar.

"Welcome, holy man," Abbas exclaimed affably enough, but with less than his usual warmth. "I have been wanting to see you, but as you must know I am much plagued these days by affairs of state. I have heard of the barbarous treatment you received from the Muscovites. It appears that they could not understand the Shah of Persia sending a darvish as his ambassador. Well, they should have heard how the Pope sends darvishes to my court, and how Abbas is quick to learn the ways of the West." He laughed. "But," he continued, "you must become acquainted with this gentleman who, like yourself, is a priest of your faith—Mr. Cotmore, chaplain of the English company now in Isfahan. I have just been talking with this reverend gentleman regarding the tenets of his persuasion. He is of those who do not recognize the sovereignty of the Pope."

The Reverend Mr. Cotmore, it seemed, was deaf in one ear, for he turned his head to one side when he listened, and he asked to have the friar's name repeated. He was a hard-faced, hollow-cheeked man of swarthy complexion. Fray Juan thought he showed distant courtesy, if not something of defiance; but this might have been the effect of the friar's own depression and disinterest.

Abbas, moving like a country landlord among his guests, introduced the friar to others: the head of the English party, a ruddy-cheeked, portly man with pale blue eyes, exuding confidence and good cheer; a young man in velvet doublet who appeared to be the Englishman's son; a thin, reserved gentleman with a scholarly bearing, who spoke faultless Persian; several Hindustanis, handsome men with enormous dignity, lords of the earth in jeweled turbans and close-fitting silken jackets and trousers; and several new courtiers who had risen in the Shah's favor during the friar's absence, one of them a vizier in charge of the royal treasury, who was precise and very courteous in speaking to the friar, although it was plain that he regarded with suspicion Fray Juan's acquaintance with the Shah.

A youth stood apart in an attitude of sullenness, and the Shah called him over.

"This," Abbas said, "is my second son, Khudabandeh Mirza, whom I don't believe you have ever met. If Safi Mirza is simple but shrewd, this youth is wise and mad. Beware you leave him not alone with a dog, for by morning the dog will froth."

This was said in a gay manner, and with a show of affection, for the Shah put his arm about the young man's shoulder, but Fray Juan felt the barb in the words. And if his sympathy had once gone out for Safi Mirza it went out tenfold for Khudabandeh Mirza. The young man had rings of sleeplessness under his eyes, and the eyes themselves, small and black, darted back and forth like those of a caged animal. He bowed in acknowledgment of the introduction, and then, as though his tongue were suddenly loosed, he began to babble.

"You are the Christian darvish; I have heard speak of you. Is it true that the bones of your saints work miracles? I have heard that in Constantinople the Sultan has made the chief church there—the Aya Sofia—into a mosque, and has painted over the pictures of the saints, but that at unforeseen times, in the midst of the services, the saints cry out imprecations from the walls upon the mullahs for having desecrated the Christian house of worship. And I have read also that in India they worship a god called Jagernath, whose image, of enormous size, is drawn in a great cart by thousands pulling on the ropes, and that many, in the excess of zeal, throw themselves beneath the wheels and perish. Can you tell me the truth of this? And I am told also that among a sect of the Hindus, called the Jains, the people wear a mask before the mouth lest their breath kill the innocent living motes of the air. Is this true?"

The prince paused, but before Fray Juan could find words to answer this extraordinary battery of questions, the Shah had drawn him away.

"He is—mad," said the Shah, touching his forehead. "But he breeds fine offspring," he added. "His child Fatima for sweetness and charm surpasses anything I have ever seen."

The Shah, having extricated the friar from Prince Khudabandeh, now excused himself to speak to other guests. Meanwhile, dusk had fallen and servants were passing through the audience chamber lighting the candelabra; the long, vaulted room with its four great murals glittered with myriad reflections from polished brass, from satin tunics, from jeweled scabbards, from diamond and ruby pendants. The servants brought linen cloths and spread them upon the floor. Abbas seated himself before one of these squares and motioned to several of his guests to join him: Mr. Fenwick, the head of the English company; Mr. Fenwick's son; the new royal treasurer, Kazemi Khan; the Reverend Mr. Cotmore, and a Moslem ecclesiastic, Abdallah Meshedi Seyyid. Then, looking about and seeing Fray Juan, Abbas called to him and, moving over, bade him sit by his side.

All this was no sooner arranged than Abbas was taken by a thought.

He summoned a servant and almost at once there was brought to him a child whom he set beside him in the most affectionate manner, holding her hands and stroking her hair.

"This is my granddaughter Fatima of whom I spoke," he said to those about him, and Fray Juan gathered that she was the daughter of Prince Khudabandeh. She appeared to be about six years of age, and was docile and well behaved, with large round solemn eyes that looked up at her grandfather as though to the sun and source of her being. The servants were bringing in the dinner. There was a caravan of silver dishes—trays supporting mounds of rice like new-fallen snow, tureens containing sauces, enormous platters on which rested whole roasted lambs. The Shah filled a plate for the princess, and fed her with a spoon, a service she meekly accepted, while he conversed entertainingly with those about him on a dozen subjects. He himself ate sparingly, but from time to time he would sip some of the *sherbet*. This was a drink made of the juice of oranges and lemons, sweetened, flavored with spices, and served to all the guests in little China porcelain bowls. Presently, when his little granddaughter showed signs of sleepiness, he wiped her mouth and fingers and, taking her in his arms, carried her off to her bed.

When Abbas returned he resumed his conversation, but now turned it to the subject that seemed always to tantalize him—that of religion.

Fray Juan listened in silence and weary detachment. It was not good, he thought, to allow religion to become a preoccupation of logic or knowledge. Religion was something to be felt, to be lived, not to be argued over.

During the meal the friar had been even more abstemious than the Shah, drinking only a little of the sherbet. To the Shah's urging that he eat, he had explained that he was fasting.

"I observe that you English do not fast," said Abbas turning to Mr. Fenwick. "Is that according to your faith?"

"God has given us food to eat, and appetites to enjoy it," said the Englishman heartily. "I know of no rule of Scripture that requires us to abstain beyond the limits of moderation. Am I not right, sir?" He addressed this question in a loud voice to the chaplain.

Mr. Cotmore nodded.

"And what is your view?" asked Abbas turning to Fray Juan.

The friar agreed that fasting was not prescribed by Scripture, but added that it was a useful spiritual exercise, practiced also in Islam and among the Jews, and that example was offered in the frequent mention of fasting to be found in the Gospels, and in the life of the Lord Himself, who had fasted forty days in the wilderness.

Abbas nodded like one conceding a contest and turned the conversation, but it was not long before he was back again to his favorite topic. He had evidently been quizzing the Anglican on the differences between Protestant and Catholic dogma, for he wanted to know now about images and the authority for their use in worship. Fray Juan had been confronted with this question before. Among Moslems, whose religion, like the Jewish, strictly forbade the use of images as tending to idolatry, the Christians were regarded as idolatrous for the images in the churches and for the veneration offered before them; Fray Juan had discovered that even sincere inquirers who had been touched by the Christian message were repelled on entering a church containing images.

"As to that, your Majesty, in your Moslem faith, in which you are strictly enjoined against idolatry, do you not make use of *mohr* when you say your prayers?"

He was referring to the little pellets of earth which the devout put before them in praying, and to which they touched their foreheads in making their genuflections toward Mecca.

"I never bow toward Mecca," said Abbas, "and so I cannot answer you, but Abdallah Meshedi Seyyid here, who like myself is a descendant of the Prophet and one who also has studied such questions, can no doubt answer you."

"Their use is well understood," said the seyyid, given permission to speak. "We recognize that we are clay—that from earth we came and to earth we return. This earth, which enshrouds so many of our ancestors, is worthy of veneration. It is out of piety and in reverence for that soil that we place a bit of it before us when we pray. But we do not worship these mohr."

"It is the same with us Catholics," said Fray Juan. "The images are clay reminders of the saints they represent; we bow our heads to them to remind us to imitate their virtues. We believe also that as the soul is immortal these saints are not dead but alive, and close to

God, and that they intercede for us, and thus we address them in prayer, which is a form of communication with the invisible world of the spirit."

Abbas now wished to know how many nails there were in the cross.

Fray Juan was growing restive at this discussion of the minutiae of faith. He was sure that he was being baited; he thought that Abbas had been put up to this question by the cadaverous English clergyman.

"Your Majesty," he said, endeavoring to control his voice, "that is a matter as to which no evidence exists. According to some Church fathers there were four, but tradition has generally accepted that there were but three."

"That is right," exclaimed Abbas gleefully. "That is the way I have always seen it in the pictures and in the images." And he crossed one foot over the other to show how the feet of Christ were both impaled by a single nail.

The English factor, Mr. Fenwick, who had been trying all evening to divert the Shah's interest to the silk trade, now spoke up.

"May I ask this learned Catholic how many wounds Christ had in his body?"

Fray Juan lifted his hands in a little gesture of resignation. There were five, he said—in the two hands, in the two feet, and in the side.

"Wrong," announced the Englishman. "By your own admission there were but three nails. One nail pierced the feet—one nail, one piercing, one wound—hence but four wounds."

Fray Juan was stung by this attack.

"May I ask," he retorted, "whether the wounds made by the nail were continuous or contiguous?"

"Continuous, and for that reason but one wound."

Fray Juan turned to the Shah.

"This goes contrary to philosophy," he said, "for that which is continuous is that which is joined by a common end; but the wounds in Christ's feet were not joined by a common end, and in consequence there were two wounds, and not one."

Abbas spoke to the Anglican clergyman.

"Do you agree with this view?" he asked.

The clergyman cupped his hands and asked to have the question repeated.

"I am not versed in such matters," he answered, "and to me they have little to do with the verities of faith, of sin and redemption."

What the clergyman said, Fray Juan knew that he should have said long before. The friar felt humiliation at the way he had allowed himself to be entrapped into quibbling.

Abbas had enjoyed the argument hugely.

"Well, my friend," he exclaimed to Fray Juan, "it seems that you have won all the arguments. What can I do for you?"

Fray Juan turned weakly upon the Shah.

"Should I ask anything further of you, who have shown yourself so remiss to the promises you have already made me?"

Abbas's look was innocent.

"In what way have I been remiss?"

"I have been gone three years in your service, and where are the firmans you have promised me on my return? Instead, I find myself dispossessed and occupying a house only by the kindness of friends."

"Why, how your feathers ruffle," exclaimed Abbas, but not annoyed. "I had not thought it in you. I am glad to see that you are a man and not one of your plaster images. It endears me all the more to you. But tell me, when is the Pope going to declare war on the Turks?"

"His Holiness does not dispose of any army, as your Majesty is well aware. But the Christian princes have maintained such a threat to the Turks that thereby you have been able to hold undisturbed your northwest provinces."

"I have asked what the Pope is doing, not what the princes are doing," said Abbas acidly. And then, with a swift, ingratiating smile, he leaned toward the friar and whispered, "I am greatly indebted to you for what you have done in my absence to remove all cause of friction and misunderstanding between us."

Fray Juan felt a concealed barb in this, and his neck grew cold.

"To what do you refer?" he asked.

"Why, this," shot back Abbas, glitter in his eyes. "Have you not married off my ward, the Princess Shamala, to the Englishman, and prevailed upon him to take her with him to Europe? By doing so you have taken away any possibility of her becoming a bone of contention between us."

"Your Majesty," Fray Juan answered with as much reserve as he could summon, "if there has ever been any difference between us over the princess, it has been due to my desire to see her strong in the faith which is hers by heritage, and observant of its dictates."

"Among which, of course, is to marry neither a heathen—*nor* one vowed to the service of the priesthood," responded Abbas pointedly. "But let us not make an issue of the matter," he added mollifyingly. "Let us rather rejoice at our reunion and reconciliation."

Then, tiring of conversation, the Shah proposed that they have the dancing girls in. Fray Juan begged and received leave to depart. As he was passing through the gate he felt his sleeve plucked and, turning, beheld the lean English clergyman.

"I wish to beg your pardon for anything I may have uttered this evening to lead into disputation," the Anglican said, "and at the same time to offer my admiration for the way in which you stood your ground before his Majesty. Only by such forthright witness will the world be won to the kingdom of Our Lord."

Fray Juan looked at the Englishman and felt his soul suddenly washed with a flood of grace. His eyes were moist as he held out his hand.

II

Fray Juan did not have the means to maintain the house the princess had engaged for him, and as the Shah failed to provide him with one he went with Javan and Grigor to live in the Caravanserai of Shah Ismail. It was hardly an ideal shelter for a religious whose rule was written around a dedication to the contemplative life; but for an evangelist inspired with zeal to preach the place could not have been better. Among the medley of camels, donkeys, and heaped-up bales of merchandise, one met merchants and porters and tax gatherers, those who harvested and those who scattered; one saw beggars and harlots and surgeons whose business was that of converting young boys into eunuchs; there were letter writers and notaries and darvishes who told stories for the coins that were tossed into their gourd bowls, as well as mullahs and royal couriers and passing companies of soldiers.

Here, in a corner room overlooking the courtyard, Fray Juan resumed his work of translating the Gospels. Under difficult conditions he continued to observe the canonical hours and to celebrate Masses.

Occasionally there were those who came to inquire and to be instructed in the faith, and many nights the friar was awake late, writing reports to the headquarters of the order in Rome. His housekeeping problems were simple: Javan did such shopping as was necessary, Grigor prepared the meals over a charcoal brazier. Flat bread did for plates, a pot and a pair of skewers for cooking, and a single spoon for serving.

It was in this place and during these days that two simple souls, porters in the caravanserai, Baghir and Mahboob, were baptized into the Christian faith and now, every morning early, came to assist in the celebration of the daily Mass. It was here also that the shopkeeper Jafar Kerbeli sought out the friar, begging baptism. Jafar was a peculiar case in the friar's experience. He had been at death's door with asthma when one night he dreamed that the prophet of the Christians came and breathed on him. Miraculously, next day, he felt better, and shortly afterward he seemed completely cured. In recompense for his healing, he considered himself bound to be baptized. Fray Juan's position was that of his Church: he accepted such supernatural visitations in theory, and the evidence of miraculous healing, but he was suspicious of them in fact. Only after considerable deliberation, and probation on Jafar's part, did the friar receive the shopkeeper into the faith. Nevertheless, Jafar proved to be devoted, and took pride in publicly declaring his allegiance to the Christian darvish.

It was in the caravanserai also that Fray Juan met again the charvadar Kazim Sarkis, with whose forty corpses the friar had journeyed up from the Caspian to the Persian plateau. Kazim was as rotund, as jovial, as good-humored as ever, but it seemed to the friar that there still clung about him the nauseous, musty odor of decayed flesh. He brought the friar gifts. The relatives of one of the deceased whose remains he had transported to the holy ground at Meshed had been so grateful that they had given the charvadar one of the dead man's properties—a prosperous village in the region of Shamakha. Kazim had sold the village for two thousand tomans; in his turn he had been obliged in all conscience to give a pious gift of a twentieth. He insisted that Fray Juan, though not a Moslem, should receive the hundred tomans for the "good luck" he had brought the charvadar.

The gift was welcome. Despite the intermittent correspondence with Rome, few funds were received from that source. In the Congregation of the Discalced there were influential elements that still looked with suspicion on missionary enterprise, and the view apparently prevailed that if God's blessing were on the Persian venture God would find means to sustain it. This did not mean that the Congregation did not pray for the success of the mission, but as for financial aid the Congregation of the Discalced was new and without endowments and this was, after all, considered the Pope's mission. Kazim's gift permitted Fray Juan to pay the arrears of rent to the caravanserai —the arbaab had been a lenient creditor—and to meet other pressing needs.

The following summer Fray Vincent came up from Hormuz. It was nearly nine years since he had left Isfahan. The two men embraced affectionately, and then stood and regarded each other.

"Oh, how ageless you are!" exclaimed Fray Vincent heartily. " 'Tis true your hair has grayed, and your face is more gaunt, your eyes more hollow—but youth refuses to abdicate to age in your expression, in the resilience of your spirit, in the sprightliness of your gait—which I observed from the gallery as you entered the courtyard."

"Kind words, kind words," murmured Fray Juan warmly, "which show only the quality of your affection. Have you had a quiet journey?"

Fray Vincent had changed but little—at least outwardly. He was firm, erect, and his hair had only a trace of gray at the temples, but Fray Juan had a feeling that something had gone out of him. What it was he could not say, but beneath the heartiness there seemed to be a tension and a restiveness not there before. That could be, Fray Juan thought, the effect of a long and tiring journey.

"A splendid journey," responded Fray Vincent, as if to belie Fray Juan's doubts. "What a relief it is to come to this upland air after the heat of Hormuz and of India!

"But we have a good work there," he went on, and began to tell about the convent. There were a half-dozen religious in residence, and a church with a congregation of over a score. Besides this establishment, there was another on the Indian mainland, at Tatta, where several friars were carrying on the observance.

Fray Juan could not repress a feeling of humiliation at Fray Vincent's enthusiastic account of the successes farther south. At the same time, he asked himself why the order, which had evidently been able to find recruits for that work, had been unable to send reinforcements to Persia, where the need was so great. Had he failed in his letters to make the need clear, and if so, how? After a little while Fray Vincent remarked that they were really trespassing the rule in talking so long, and indicated he would like to retire for private meditations after his journey. Fray Juan nodded toward the corner of the room.

"You mean that you have only the one room—that you do not have cells for yourself and Brother Grigor?" asked Fray Vincent in consternation.

"Our means are so limited that we have been unable to engage more than the one room," Fray Juan explained, a little surprised that Fray Vincent regarded the matter as of such importance or that he had not appreciated the difficulties under which the work in Isfahan was carried on. He went on to tell, what Fray Vincent must already have known from the letters they had exchanged, about their being dispossessed of the house, and the failure to receive funds from Rome. Without a house, they could not even grow their own food, as had been their practice previously.

Fray Vincent retired to his meditations, while Grigor cooked supper, and Fray Juan thought of the change that had come over his fellow friar. Fray Vincent had never been a stickler for the rule, he recalled, and he thought that perhaps something in the Hormuz climate, or perhaps the associations there, had led him to give more attention to the discipline of the observance.

As they sat at meat together—the two friars, Grigor, and Javan— Fray Vincent showed a surprise that had in it a pinch of annoyance. "The rule that the friars should not eat in the presence of the laity, or admit the laity to the refectory or the cells, merits observance," he remarked. He was gentle in his manner, but the rebuke was even more positive than before. Fray Juan avoided taking issue. Even though they had but the one room he could, of course, take his meals separately from the others, but that seemed to him hardly gracious and more a perversion than an observance of the rule.

That evening, as he lighted a lamp upon the little altar against the wall, Fray Vincent remarked: "I see you are using ordinary *naft*. You surely recall that in the sacred lamps olive oil must burn."

"Father," said Fray Juan directly, "have you forgotten that olive oil is not expressed in Persia, and is not obtainable from abroad, as in Hormuz?"

Fray Vincent seemed at last to be aware of his captiousness.

"I have been forward," he said, "but, my dear brother, this situation of yours cannot continue. It is an anomaly. You cannot carry on without a house."

"But the situation *has* existed—for nearly a decade now," responded Fray Juan. "Though we have for periods had enjoyment of what passes for a house—that is, four walls and a roof—yet at no time have we had the sense of shelter which indefeasible right confers. But then, what is indefeasible right? Is it, after all, not an illusion? All things are in God's disposition. We have survived, and until I have received instructions from his Holiness I must remain where I am."

Fray Vincent gave Fray Juan a penetrating look, as if to measure how much mettle was behind the words. He seemed satisfied. He grew more cheerful, and something of his former ebullience returned. Disregarding the rule, they postponed Complin for an hour, which they spent in an animated discussion of John of the Cross and his doctrine of illumination by darkness.

Fray Vincent remained in Isfahan a week, and in the time Fray Juan thought that he had come around to a more liberal view of the situation. When he left he gave Fray Juan a hundred tomans for the support of the work and promised to send him remittances regularly until a decision had been wrung from the Shah.

Nevertheless, some time afterward, when Fray Vincent's letters could have reached Rome, Fray Juan received a letter from the prepositor of the order sharply though paternally critical of the laxity of Fray Juan's observance, and complaining also of the small number of converts that he had made.

Fray Juan's patience, long tried by the Shah, now broke. He brooded upon the lack of faith and vision among those who had sent him here until he remembered that he himself had been the instigator of missionary work, and that in truth he should not blame the Congregation.

In his reply to the prepositor, Fray Juan explained without rancor that it was not possible to maintain the observance except there be two or more brethren, and as his superiors were well aware, Fray Juan had been alone now for several years.

As to the small number of converts, he wrote, *may I remind your Reverences that I was not sent to make converts, but to preach the Gospel, for, as your Reverences are well aware, the making of converts is the special work of the Holy Ghost.*

This letter Fray Juan sent by an Armenian merchant who was traveling to Rome, and after it had gone he spent the night in prayer for forgiveness for the exhibition of impatience it contained.

III

Fray Juan's thoughts were filled with the memory of failures and dissatisfactions, of which his letter to the prepositor was only the most recent. He thought of the Shah's neglect, of Fray Vincent's want of sympathy and understanding, of the narrowness of his own scope, the feebleness of his accomplishments. He thought of his physical misery. It was summer in Isfahan, and the heat was intense. The corner room in the caravanserai, cut off from the breeze, was stifling. In his dejection even the voice of prayer was stifled; he could not hear the voice of his Lord speaking to him with reassurance, reminding him of all that He had suffered. Finally, when prayer and meditation and hours of silent contemplation proved fruitless of relief, Fray Juan turned to an ancient and sensible and well tested remedy: vigorous physical exercise.

Not far from Isfahan was a peak of no great size that was a resort for young men and picnickers—the Kuh-i-Sufeh—a remnant of an ancient range that once perhaps had dominated the Isfahan plain but was now only a rocky ridge that rose gaunt and bare like the vertebra of an ancient dragon protruding above the sand. A trail led up the sloping shoulder of the peak to the foot of a cliff. Here were a spring, a little grove, and a coffee house. Holiday makers usually made this their objective. Beyond the coffee house a narrower trail led along the face of the cliff to its crown; from here those who insisted on achieving the summit pursued their way over a steep slope of shifting and treacherous detritus.

The friar took Javan with him, and the two set out at two hours of sunrise in order to make the ascent before the heat of the day. Fray Juan had discarded his habit, as much to avoid attention as for comfort; he wore instead the customary cotton trousers of the country and a loose jacket bound at the waist by a broad leather belt. He carried a small sack of mixed walnut and raisin meats for their breakfast, and Javan bore a bottle of water.

In the early morning the air was bracing, and the two walked along at a good rate, passing on the way parties of peasants driving their donkeys to market and singing quavering love ditties to the setting moon. They passed a suburban village, and in the darkness could smell the fragrance of melons in the gardens. They crossed a strip of desert and reached the base of the cliff. There in the grove they paused to breakfast. A violet pallor still lay over the landscape; in the early morning stillness they could hear, faintly from the plain below, the peasants singing as they drove their donkeys along the trail, some women talking, and the wail of a child; a shepherd on the slopes piping to his flock, and the rush of gravel started by the hooves of many goats.

Along the face of the cliff the trail lay well marked, but was narrow and at places tapered off into a mere foothold on the rocks. In one of the crevices they paused to watch the unfolding of the dawn. The plain below was now like the face of an opal, a shimmering expanse of nacre in tints of pink and mauve and blue; the sun began to color the eastern horizon and like the opening of a furnace door to spill upon the plain a liquid gold that spread to the foot of the cliff; at the same time the summits of the ridge seemed to be showered from above with golden rain, which began to run down the sides, meeting the flow from across the plain.

Fray Juan had forgotten his problems in the exhilaration of the climb. His muscles, of late, had received too little exercise. It was tonic to him now to stretch for a hold and to cling by the strength in his hands and arms to an outjutting rock, to brace his feet and spring for foothold. Fray Juan was no longer a young man, but this recalled his youthful days in Calahorra, and something of his youthful zest returned to him. They were now at the brow of the cliff and were following a goat trail that led toward a grove of stunted oaks watered by a spring. Above them a party of young men were resting on the ledge while two of their number were in contest drawing bows against the eagles that circled overhead in the morning sun.

An arrow flashed in the sunlight, making a silver arc in the blue. It was as though the eagle soared to meet it; the arrow lodged in its breast; the great bird fluttered for a moment in mid-air, then, turning over and over, fell into the chasm.

The youth, turning to follow its fall, observed the friar, and called a welcome, addressing him by name.

"Ah, Khudabandeh Mirza!" exclaimed Fray Juan. "Forgive me that I did not recognize you in these surroundings. You have, I see, your father's fondness for plain dress."

The reference to the Shah caused the young man to frown, but immediately he was gay with the reckless, enigmatic, capricious abandon that was characteristic of him.

"You are forgiven," the prince exclaimed, "but as I understand your doctrine, you must do penance for your fault. I impose upon you and your companion—"

"My good friend of many years, Javan," interposed the friar.

"—your companion Javan the duty of breaking bread with us."

"You call that penance?" asked the friar smiling.

"'Tis only bread and cheese, and a little wine, which I believe is not forbidden you by your rule," explained Khudabandeh Mirza; "but you will find it a sore trial to converse with us, as I shall require you. You may recall that I am a very inquisitive person."

"I can sustain such a penance," responded the friar, cheered by the prince's familiarity with the Carmelite rule, at the same time recalling that Abbas regarded him as a little daft. The "bread and cheese" proved to be a collation of cold roast meats, rice balls, fresh fruit, sugar cakes, and bottles of wine, that had been fetched on the backs of servants. The prince introduced one or two of his companions, but the others, a half-dozen or thereabouts, remained in the background. The friar recognized with dismay that the reticent ones were not young men but young women in men's dress. Their reticence did not last. After a little, when the wine began to take effect, they were talking and giggling and making free with their companions, much to Fray Juan's embarrassment.

The Carmelite made excuse to withdraw, but the prince detained him, clinging to the friar's company.

"Do not go," he begged, and drew the friar aside to a little rock shelf overhanging the cliff. "One must have a little amusement in this world, must he not? And to be here on the mountain heights with my friends, who ask nothing of me but a little money for their needs, and my indulgence in their whims, is far better than spending my days in curtained rooms, with a cabal, plotting against my father."

At the friar's look of astonishment, the prince went on:

"Ah, but do not stare so, for if you have not heard, at least all Isfahan has heard and whispers that my hand is against the Shah's. But it is not so, I assure you. I avoid my father, that I may not think ill of him. Yet he loves me not, whether I am with him or absent from him. My face annoys him when I am with him, and when I am absent he fears that I am talking about him, And so I come here" —the prince gestured to the abyss that yawned at their feet—"where I may gaze down into the serenity of the depths and think what peace it would be to float upon yonder mist and drop gently as a feather into this nothingness. They tell me that is bad, that thinking leads to doing, and that I am far too heavy to float upon a cloud, and so my friends accompany me here, though as you can see they are not made for mountain climbing and it wearies them—yet they do it for love of me."

Fray Juan was trembling at the thought of the need that opened before him, like a maw that could swallow all that the world had to offer and reach out for more. Here was such loneliness as his own could not compare with, and he felt ashamed of himself for the doubts and dissatisfactions he had allowed himself. He asked himself what help, beyond intercession, he could offer the prince. As if in answer an impulse led him to stoop down, as though in contemplation, and scratch upon the soil with a piece of rock.

"I know what that is," said Khudabandeh Mirza, with the eagerness of a child who has recognized the letters a teacher is putting on the board. "It is the Christian cross. My father has always worn one around his neck. My mother was a Christian. I know some of the stories about the Christ."

"Can you tell me one?" asked Fray Juan hopefully.

But Khudabandeh Mirza evaded answering.

"When I come to tell them they grow confused in my mind," he said. "But tell me what I have long wanted to know: What is it to be a Christian?"

Fray Juan meditated before replying. To one filled with the message of Christianity, as to one who has spent a life in any study, a simple answer to the prince's question was not easy. Fray Juan had learned that the greatest evangels were those whose instructions in the faith had been very plain—but often to make instruction plain was a highly complex matter. Thus, while the axiom that one and one make two appears simple, the question "What is one?" leads directly into the baffling mystery of the universe and the ultimate affirmation that can be made only on faith—that to which the ancient Jews laid hold by revelation, "God is One, and not many."

"To reduce it to a sentence," the friar said to the prince, "to be a Christian is to find the completest joy and satisfaction of this life, and the hope for the world to come, in the adoration of the Lord Jesus Christ as God."

Khudabendeh Mirza found this answer fascinating.

"How clear, how beautifully explicit!" he exclaimed. "With the mullahs all is inscrutable, all is mystery in the mind of God, for He is the Unknowable, the Past Finding Out. And if one cannot know God, then all else is likewise mystery, and no friend, however close, can be accounted as familiar. Thus, suspicion breeds and multiplies. But with you, as you know the life of Christ, you know the mind of God, which is full of love and compassion. But what does this do for me? How does this knowledge give me satisfaction?"

Again Fray Juan chose his words carefully, seeking to express from his experience the purest truth he could offer, truth that would be meaningful to one who stood outside the faith.

"To those who have accepted Jesus Christ as their master and guide in all affairs of this mortal life, promises are given of peace in this world, and of bliss in the world to come. That the promises are true has been certified by the experience of generations of men, and the final assurance is the experience itself, that begins to work within one the moment one has declared his faith."

The prince was looking at the friar raptly, but even as he looked a glaze came into his eyes, and Fray Juan was aware that his attention had wandered and was lost. At that moment another eagle circled overhead, and the prince called excitedly for his bow.

"Excuse me, your Reverence," he exclaimed, "while I show you the way I shall deal with my enemies."

As Fray Juan watched the prince take aim, he had a sudden vision of the powers of darkness, and a premonition of eventual tragedy.

PART EIGHT

Ascent of Carmel

I

Fray Juan was awakened one night by the arbaab of the caravanserai, Ali Askar, who ruled his establishment with the temper of a Tamerlane. With a garlicky breath he whispered into the ear of the Carmelite:

"One of the Shah's begums to see your Reverence. I have put her and her eunuch in the room above the gate, and I beg you to summon me after you have spoken with her, for this business must be handled skilfully. Neither of us wishes the bowstring about his neck as recompense for entertaining one of the Haram."

The woman was standing with her eunuch when the friar entered. She was heavily veiled, but something about her—the erectness of her figure, the grace of her movement as she turned—identified her as a Circassian. She announced herself as the begum Tamara, and when she lifted her veil the friar recognized at once the resemblance to her niece Shamala. The queen's face, beautiful as it was, showed lines of grief and anxiety. It was about her son that she had come to see the friar.

"Shamala has told me of the warmth of your tenderness, the nourishment that is in your sympathy, the wisdom in your counsel," the begum began.

"Pray go on," said Fray Juan, and he bowed the begum to the bench against the wall.

"I have come to speak about my son, and to ask you to appeal to the Shah in his behalf," Tamara began in great agitation. "Abbas seeks his life."

Fray Juan felt an immediate solicitude. Unfortunate was the man upon whom Abbas's displeasure fell. Nevertheless, he was not convinced that Tamara's fears were justified. He waited a moment for the begum to collect herself.

"I have met and talked with Khudabandeh Mirza, and I have heard Abbas speak of him," he said reassuringly. "I cannot believe that the prince is such an one as to cause his Majesty jealousy or anxiety, nor do I believe that Abbas has such feelings toward the prince."

This increased rather than quieted the begum's agitation.

"No, no, not Khudabandeh Mirza. It is not of him that I speak," she exclaimed distraughtly. "It is of Safi Mirza—though I have no doubt Abbas hates Khudabandeh also."

"But Safi Mirza—no, that cannot be," protested the friar. "Abbas heaps honors upon him—and justly. He has shown ability both in war and in administration. A true heir to carry on a great work of rulership. He has worth, he has promise."

"Yes, he has worth and he has promise," said Tamara bitterly. "It is for these that Abbas hates him with a passion no medicine can cure. But he will listen to you, I am sure." She was looking up at the friar with hands clasped in appeal. "You can tell Abbas the truth which he will believe from no one else, for he has had so many lies from his courtiers that he distrusts them all."

In the flickering light of the candle Fray Juan could see the begum's eyes fixed upon him, dark and challenging.

"Let us begin at the beginning," he urged earnestly. "Let us examine the sources of your anxiety. Why do you charge the Shah with designs upon the prince?" Fray Juan waved his hand. "I know," he said, "about the Ladika affair, and how the woman seemed to implicate Safi in her attempt upon the Shah's life. But all that was disproved long ago, and has been forgotten—"

"Abbas never forgets," broke in Tamara. "When his mind is once bent, it remains forever crooked. He appears to honor Safi, only to conceal his hatred from the public. Of late, reports come to me of increasing jealousy of Safi because of his popularity among the troops.

Abbas's soul is possessed by Shaitan, I tell you, and Shaitan is driving him to do away with Safi."

Fray Juan recognized the logic of all that Tamara was saying, but he could not accept her conclusions as reasonable.

"There is no one Abbas hates more than the Turks," he said thoughtfully, "and he is now in campaign against them. No commander in his army knows the northwest country so well as Safi. It is hardly likely that Abbas would at this crucial moment be plotting the death of one so important to victory. Besides," he added feelingly, "must we conclude that Abbas's soul is already the possession of Satan? Does not the Lord's angel also contend for the prize? I cannot but believe that in Abbas's heart fatherly affection governs his attitude— that Safi, as Abbas's eldest, may even be his dearest son."

"His eldest and dearest son!" exclaimed Tamara harshly, and struck her bosom with her fist. "Abbas has forty sons by so many concubines, and I know not how many daughters and other children unacknowledged. He cares not for sons. He cares only for the female sex, for females cannot threaten his throne. Do you know who is his favorite? A mere child—my granddaughter, the daughter of Khudabandeh Mirza. Toward her he leans with incest in his heart—his own granddaughter! Upon her he dotes as once he doted upon my niece Shamala as a child. But does Abbas cherish Safi Mirza? He fears him rather."

Fray Juan shook his head.

"Even if what you say is true," he asked, "what can I do?"

Tamara's eyes lighted with hope.

"Go to Abbas and plead with him," she said eagerly. "He respects you. He will listen to you."

"Go to Abbas," said Fray Juan, "and say, 'Your Majesty, I hear rumors that you hate your son and intend his life'? I need not tell you how that would be received. What do I or you know of what is in Abbas's heart? Only God knows, and only God can touch his heart. I will pray, which is my proper service."

Tamara's eyes flashed.

"This is a crisis that calls for something more than prayer; it calls for action!"

"In a case like this, what prayer cannot accomplish nothing can," responded the friar positively.

The begum stood up.

"You give me the same advice I hear from the mullahs," she protested bitterly, and she began to pace back and forth in the narrow chamber, her golden ornaments giving off a clanking sound, like that of prisoners' chains in the distance, it seemed to the friar. "The mullahs say that God is all-powerful, that if He wills it, my son will live and reign; if not, that it will not be so. They say that God has from old written his fate on his forehead. What is ordained to happen will happen, and nothing we can do or say will make the least difference— But I had thought to hear better advice from you," she added.

The friar was silent. He wanted to declare his faith in a God who answers prayer, but at the moment he had neither the confidence nor the vigor to do so. His own failures weighed too heavily upon him. Tamara, seeing his hesitation, spoke again, confidentially:

"I am a Christian, or I should say I *was*. While my sons were yet with me in the Haram I gave them such instruction in the Christian faith as I could. Safi once declared to me his desire and his determination to be baptized in the Christian faith. From word that comes to me—for I do not see him directly—he still holds to that purpose, and it is for this as much as for anything that Abbas hates him, seeing that he possesses something which Abbas does not, yet which Abbas would like to have. Surely," she added insinuatingly, "for a life bearing such seed of promise for the future of the Christian Church in Persia some effort should be made."

Having said this, Tamara drew her chuddar about her and sat, her head bowed, a picture of despair.

Fray Juan was stirred. He knew something of the prince's inclination toward the Christian faith, and he could see what it would mean for the spread of the Christian Gospel should a prince of his persuasion come to the throne of Persia. All the ground lost since the sixth century, when the Church of the East succumbed to the Sword of Islam, might be regained. Through Safi Mirza those hopes which had so far proved barren in the case of Abbas might yet be realized.

Despite this appeal, Fray Juan found himself rejecting the begum's plea.

"I can do no more," he said firmly.

Tamara, no doubt taking his words as another manifestation of God's inscrutable will, meekly bowed her head and left.

II

For some days after the begum's visit Fray Juan continued to censure himself for his unresponsiveness to need, for his failure to rise to his responsibilities, to his opportunities. He raked his imagination to invent some excuse by which he might yet go to the Shah and speak to him—though to what effect he still could not say. It was a profound truth that the door to a man's heart hinges outward, and only he within can open it. To broach the subject to Abbas, Fray Juan feared, would only stir resentments and gain no end.

As it happened, however, a fortnight later the court minister, accompanied by a Qizilbashie, came to the caravanserai seeking Fray Juan, and bringing him a summons to the Shah. Abbas was then at his army headquarters at Kermanshah, and the Qizilbashie was waiting to escort the friar.

Fray Juan begged a few moments in which to recite the office with Grigor and Javan, to give Grigor a few words of counsel concerning the management of the "house" in his absence, and to say something privately to Javan of encouragement and cheer. Javan was a mystery to Fray Juan. He had become like a brother to the friar—a brother who kept the friar against all bodily need but who obdurately concealed his own needs, both bodily and spiritual. As with the Shah, so with Javan—the friar dared not broach the subject, for if his yearning for the young man's conversion were not obvious to him, words would not make it clearer, and they might curdle their relationship as vinegar does warm milk. Javan's disinterestedness seemed to sum up for the friar his own total failure and incapacity, for how could he hope to bring others to discipleship by his example when one who had lived intimately with him for a decade and knew his secret thoughts and desires was so unmoved?

It was a dispiriting journey. They traveled in a mode repugnant to the friar—as estafettes, commandeering changes of horse as they went along and food and quarters at night in whatsoever house pleased the Red Head. They reached Kermanshah, but learned that Abbas had moved on in the direction of Maragha, where his army could be more rapidly deployed against the Turks. It was possible that they would see the bloody marks of warfare before their journey was done. In the rugged country through which they now journeyed the army quartermasters had already raked the villages for provisions, and to pass through them was like traversing a conquered territory. This did not seem to perturb the Qizilbashie, who continued to demand horses, food, and lodging as though he were among the substantial suburbs of Isfahan, and if they were not immediately provided he did not hesitate to use his whip, laying it about him indiscriminately.

Fray Juan felt an increasing pessimism and depression. This ambassadorial role he was playing, this diplomatic mission to the Shah to which he had been dedicated, with its persistent dilemma and futility, revolted him; he was appalled at the falseness of his life, at its baseless pretensions, at his inadequacy for the work with which he had been charged. His real service, he was reminded, was to God; it was to Him that his life belonged, and to His glory that his efforts had been dedicated when he took the vow of a Carmelite. Yet how could he, riding on a horse in this miserable village, attended by a trooper and accoutered as an ambassador, tell these people about his Lord who had been born in a stable, who had died on a cross, and had risen again—who had taught humility and had given the kingdom of heaven to those who were poor in spirit? In what language and with what sincerity could he, a friar sworn to poverty and abstinence, address these cowed and poverty-stricken villagers who were being left not even their seed grain, that the Shah's forces might be fed?

He would not eat their bread. It was yesterday since he had eaten, but he would keep his fast. He must preach the Gospel.

The Red Head had gone off with the village *katkhoda* to inspect the barley jars, to see for himself that they were empty. Fray Juan dismounted. Tethering his horse to a stone he set out walking through the streets. In one of the deserted alleys, where a trickle of water flowed in a gutter between narrow walls of sun-dried mud, and the air was a dusty haze, he drew his breviary from his pocket and began to chant in Latin the Penitential Psalm:

Have mercy upon me, O God, after thy great goodness; according to the multitude of thy mercies do away mine offenses. . . .

A group of half naked children, playing in the water of the gutter, looked up at this strange figure speaking in an unknown tongue, and fled. Presently they reappeared from the doorway of a courtyard and, seeing the man still reading, crept out and huddled against the wall. At the turning of the alley other faces began to show tentatively from behind the wall. One by one they appeared, and as the friar continued reading they drew near. Then, as their confidence grew, they gathered about him—men with gaunt faces, with turbans of frayed and greasy cotton and trousers of coarse woolen much patched; women in gaudy but tattered muslins, holding their shawls in their teeth and their babies upon their backs; more naked children with dirty faces and ulcerated eyes.

Fray Juan ceased his reading; he closed his eyes, prayed wordlessly for his Lord's presence, and then addressed the villagers in Persian.

"I speak to you of Jesus," he began, "who is known among you as a prophet, the Spirit of God, whom your holy book the Koran declares to be Messiah Son of Mary, *illustrious in this world, and in the next, and one of those who have near access to God.*"

Some of the men, hearing him speak in a familiar tongue, nodded in understanding and pleasure. The women, less reserved than the men, nudged and whispered to each other in delight, and the children, to whom the friar's speech, even in their own tongue, was hard to follow, gave attention.

"Jesus," Fray Juan went on, "was born in a village such as this. The *malek* of the country had laid heavy burdens upon the people and had issued a firman that every man should go into his own village with his household to be taxed. In obedience to this firman the man Joseph and his wife Mary, who was heavy with child, went up to their village, which was named Bethlehem. There was no chamber in the caravanserai, and they lodged that night in the stalls with the camels and the asses. During the night the woman was delivered of her firstborn, whom she named Jesus, and whom she laid in swaddling clothes in the manger."

Fray Juan thought he had caught the interest of his listeners. He was sure of it. He could tell by the look in their faces. This was an experience that they understood—a familiar story in a familiar setting. Others had joined the group about him, and now the narrow alley was thronged with those who came to see the Christian darvish and to hear his story. Fray Juan was happy. This was the work he had come so far to do. This was the fulfillment of the vision he had had in the cell of the monastery in Naples, the vision which had been imparted to him by the old Baron di Cacurri, now gone to his rest in God's peace.

Fray Juan continued his account of the Gospel narrative. He told of Jesus' youth and of His ministry, of how He went forth preaching and healing and calling men to repentance, of the enmity He aroused among jealous men, of His last journey to Jerusalem, His arrest and trial. As the friar came to the story of the Crucifixion he could hear the responsive murmurs among his listeners, their exclamations, their sighs, even their wailing, for they were simple people who understood suffering.

This, Fray Juan told himself, was pure preaching—to tell the Gospel story as the Gospel writers had told it, and to let the story itself, working with the Holy Spirit in the hearts of men, unfold its own mystery and understanding and desire for salvation and discipleship. There was no need for theological explanations, for ritual, or for liturgical embroidery. The words themselves carried their own framework. Here was the justification of his efforts to translate the Gospels into the vernacular.

He continued. He told the story of the Resurrection, of the women coming to the tomb on Easter morning, of the disciples gathered together and of the Lord appearing mysteriously in their midst—of the breaking of bread, of the injunction to the disciples to go into all the world preaching the Good News—and finally of the Ascension into heaven on the hill outside Jerusalem.

It was a glorious story, and often as he had read it, often as he had recounted it to himself, Fray Juan was moved by a new exaltation. He was sure now that some hearts had been touched, that the seed had been planted in fruitful soil. Of that he was certain by the exclamations, the "*Ai's*" that arose on all sides.

The friar turned and looked about him. And then his heart sank. For there, behind him, stood the Red Head with his insigne of the Sword and Lion of the Shah's household troops on his red turban. He stood there impassively, but with a look of authority in his steady, cold eyes, and Fray Juan wondered if the villagers had not been listening out of obedience to the command they read in the eyes of the Shah's officer, habituated as they were to yield to all in authority, and regarding the friar not as one who spoke from conviction of the heart but as one who repeated what he had learned and had been directed to recite.

In his confusion, he thought that it was as it might have been with Thaddeus, after whom he had been surnamed by the Pope, had the Apostle appeared in a Syrian village, preaching his message of the glorious Word while holding aloft a Roman standard.

Fray Juan was unable to continue. His chagrin was too great. There weighed upon him the burden of the dual capacity in which he served—missionary and envoy, mendicant friar and the Shah's counselor. He muttered a hurried benediction over the congregation and returned to his horse.

III

They had reached Senna in the Kurdish country to find the town almost deserted, everyone having fled to the hills with his belongings for fear of one or the other of the armies. The Qizilbashie with difficulty found a man who told him which way the Shah's troops had moved. Somewhere among the Zagros ranges the Ottoman and the Persian forces were maneuvering for battle. The Qizilbashie asked the friar whether he feared to go on, and indicated doubt whether in the circumstances the Shah would now have any interest in seeing the friar. Fray Juan replied that as the Shah had summoned him, he would not rest until he had presented himself.

It was toward Galajan that they met the first signs of the battle—a long caravan of camels with bloodstained panniers coming down over the gray hills, bearing the wounded. Near Farmaz they encountered straggling bands of haggard men in tatters, and cavalrymen with empty arrow cases, torn mail, broken lances, and battered shields. These were not the signs of victory, and lines of anxiety appeared on the stolid countenance of the Red Head. Seeing an officer of his own rank, he saluted and asked him for the news.

"We have beaten them," the officer answered wearily, reining up and allowing his horse to nibble the sparse grass. "The Turks—may dung be their bread—are in flight. But at what a price!" He covered his face with his hands in a gesture of despair. "*W'Allah, W'Allah,*" he wailed in sudden release of grief. "Our great leader—may God receive him into Paradise!"

"Abbas killed!" cried the Qizilbashie. "*W'Allah, W'Allah!*"

"Not Abbas, not Abbas," cried the officer bitterly. "A jinni watches over Abbas. The prince Safi."

He stared at the Qizilbashie and remembered his loyalties.

"But what is that to you?" he demanded. "If you ask me, I am of Safi's party, but ask me neither my name nor tribe, for I have no yearning for the bowstring." He wheeled his horse and was off.

Fray Juan recalled the visit of the begum Tamara to his cell, and knew that there was something here to be explained; but by the time he had recovered his presence of mind the officer was far down the trail. The friar wheeled his mount and spurred it after the officer.

"Stay!" he called.

The officer's mount was as jaded as the man, and in a moment the friar had overtaken them.

"What were the circumstances of the prince's death?" he asked.

The officer reined up and let his bloodshot eyes rest upon the friar in dull curiosity.

"What is your interest in this affair?" he asked. "Are you not the Christian darvish whom I have seen in Isfahan living in the Caravanserai of Shah Ismail?"

"I knew Safi Mirza," said Fray Juan quietly, "and held great expectations for him."

"There were many who held such expectations," said the officer bitterly, "but it was not his kismet to realize them."

He gave his horse its head and rested his hands on the saddle pommel.

"I will tell you how it befell," he said. "We were fifty thousand in number, holding a fortified ground at the opening of the Rowanduz Gorge, through which the Turks would have to pass to bring their forces upon the plains of Nestoria. We could have held the gorge with half that number, so narrow was the way, so high and abrupt the enclosing precipices. But word came from Abbas to withdraw to the heights and to allow the Turks to enter. For a time Safi Mirza debated with the chief captains whether to obey the order. Being an adjutant to our brigadier I was present at the deliberations. Certain it was that in circumstances other than these to yield this ground without a fight would be treachery warranting the bowstring.

"But there was Abbas's order, and Abbas is not one to give the enemy a slit through which to send an arrow. What was his strategy? Was it to admit the enemy, as flies into a bottle, and then to stopper the bottle? The order was received, and the order issued. From the cliff heights we looked down through the trees and beheld the enemy advancing, and our hearts sank, for great was their number, and their cannon in number beyond counting, and we cursed the Shah for his foolishness in forbidding us to fall upon them as they passed.

"And then we cursed and rejoiced when, a few days later, Abbas sent a messenger for half our forces to depart and to come to him by roundabout route, for he was sore-pressed and in need of reinforcements. And the day following comes another messenger directing the prince to disengage another half of his command and send it to the aid of Abbas. And on the third comes still another, so that we have left a bare five hundred men to guard the gorge."

"And you were among that number?" asked the friar, who knew nothing of military tactics, but sensed the significance of what he was hearing.

"I will not tell you the name of my brigadier," replied the officer, "who was a bosom friend of the prince, but it was he who directed that I remain at the prince's side when the prince ordered him to go with his command. I obeyed, for I am liege both to my brigadier and to my prince.

"And so the days passed, and no word came to us of battle. This was not unexpected, for the Shah, as is well known, plays a game of cat and mouse with his adversary. At last the Turks, weary of meeting the Shah in battle, weary of dragging their cannon over the hills and through the sands and up the gorges, and their horses growing gaunt from want of forage, begin to retire.

"At this moment comes another order from the Shah to refuse them passage through the gorge. An easy thing to order—and an easy thing to execute had we five thousand men—but we are five hundred.

The prince made his prayers to God the Compassionate, the Merciful —and to your Christ, it will please you to know—and prepared for battle.

"The enemy approached, and then we began to see the strategy of Abbas. From all the surrounding heights his men were upon the Turks, like a swarm of gadflies upon a stallion, and furious was the rearing and the snorting; and then they were like a hacked serpent threshing in death pangs but with his head struggling to reach its hole, which is the gorge we defend. And this serpent lashes out its tongue, and Safi Mirza falls, as did all of us who remained by his side.

"After the battle was over, and when the earth had begun to stink with the smell of rotting flesh, I awoke, and throwing off the coverlet of death by which I had been protected, I discovered that I was still a man, lacking only some draughts of blood which I had poured out upon the soaked earth. And I crawled to the stream that flowed in the gorge and drank and found strength to bind my wounds, and then, cajoling a wandering horse to my side, I mounted and rode away, and presently came upon this caravan of the wounded. That is my story. What else would you know?"

"That is parcel enough of news," said the friar. "I shall pray for the soul of the prince, and the souls of all that were lost, as well as for your recovery of strength and health. Where may the Shah be found?"

"At Souj Boulak, they say, where he rests himself from his victory —though I do not know for certain, nor do I care so much as that"— he flicked a grain of dust from his sleeve—"whether he rests there or in Hell."

The friar and the Qizilbashie pressed on, the friar wondering at the change in the popular attitude toward the Shah, if the wounded officer were an example. On the way they encountered other trains of wounded, and then overtook caravans of camels laden with barley and provender, and they knew that the camp was nigh.

The following day they came in sight of the army, encamped on the plain before the city of Souj Boulak, and on a knoll saw the great tent of the Shah flying the pennants of victory. A sentry blocked their way while word was sent to the Shah of their arrival, and then they were escorted to his presence.

Abbas was in the quartermaster's camp, where the camels were tethered and where sacks of barley had been piled. He was in company of a group of officers, and he was superintending the allotment of grain among the troops. He wore the soiled uniform of a common soldier, the only mark of his rank being the crimson turban with the aigrette and the emerald brooch.

He looked up in surprise when he saw the friar, and said shortly: "You are welcome. But what brings you here?"

"I came on your Majesty's orders, and as soon as I received them. I am at your Majesty's command."

"Well, I have no need of you now," said Abbas. "We have won the victory. But you can write to your sovereign what you behold with your eyes. Look about you and you will see that we have put the enemy to rout and have captured four hundred of his guns. Now is the time for the princes of Europe, if they would seal this victory, to declare war upon the Sultan. Thanks to Abbas, he will now be helpless before their arms."

"I shall inform him," said the friar, "and I shall pray God that your great success be not lost."

"Lost?" exclaimed Abbas. "There is no loss to concern us now. But what matters whether you write or not?" he added irritably. "What care I now what the Christian powers do? They have lied and lied, promising alliances and joint war against the Ottoman, but while I have gone out and won the battle they have dozed in their palaces and feasted themselves."

He turned as if to dismiss the friar, and began to go over the list which the quartermaster handed him.

Fray Juan felt that the decisive moment in his mission had come.

"Then," he said, "since this is the case, and since you have so long neglected the firmans which you have so often promised, there remains no further duty for me here. I would, therefore, return to my country, where other work awaits me. Do you grant me permission to depart?"

Abbas looked up from his list.

"No," he said, "not yet. I would speak with you."

He handed the list to the quartermaster, and gave him some directions. Then he set off walking, nodding for the friar to follow.

IV

Abbas led the friar to the royal tent and entered. A young village woman, dressed in gauzy silk, her arms covered with bangles, lolled on an ottoman, and stared insolently at the friar. Abbas shot her an imperious look; the girl sullenly glided from her seat and disappeared behind the curtains.

"You have come at a good hour," said Abbas, in a more friendly vein, though his irritation was still obvious. "I have need of you. Will you thank the Lord of life whom you worship—whom we both worship—for this great victory, and pray that it may persuade the Ottoman of the virtue of peace with his neighbors."

"Of that I have already assured your Majesty," said Fray Juan.

Abbas clapped his hands for his orderly, and asked for coffee. Seating himself upon a carpet next to a pile of leather war harness, he motioned the friar to the crimson-covered ottoman upon which the village girl had been lying. Fray Juan would ordinarily have acceded to the Shah's caprice in reversing the precedence of seating, but now he remained standing in an attitude of respect.

"What may I do for you?" he asked.

"Oh, talk to me. That is enough—and sit here beside me, as formerly."

"Talk of what?" asked Fray Juan wearily, seating himself on the floor beside the Shah.

"Talk to me as you would—to a penitent. What do you say to one who comes to confess?"

"That would depend upon the matter confessed. As you are not a Christian, you are not under the obligation of confession and absolution."

"But I am close to being a Christian," protested Abbas, beginning to wheedle. "You know I wear the cross."

"Yes, but not openly."

Fray Juan wondered at the object of this conversation.

"You understand why this is," urged the Shah. "I rule over a nation of Moslems. If I were to declare myself openly to be a Christian, the Empire would be in uproar, especially that large element of it dominated by the mullahs, and the nation would fall into anarchy, and then we would be as straw for the Turkish flail, as ripe grapes for their winepress."

"Whence such doctrine?" asked the friar, unmoved. "Is it not from your ulema, and is it not known as *taqia*, or dissimulation of the faith—the propriety of concealing one's religious conviction for a purpose? You may not be a Christian on such terms," the friar said firmly, and continued: "To be a Christian you must be afraid neither for yourself nor for the world, but you must be bold in testimony. For St. Paul declares that if you confess with your mouth the Lord Jesus, and believe in His Resurrection, you shall be saved."

The orderly brought the coffee, setting the tray on the carpet before the Shah. Abbas poured and gave a cup to the friar, then taking his own lifted it with slow deliberation to his lips. Fray Juan sensed that Abbas was avoiding a direct approach to the matter uppermost in his mind, and was trying to attain his ends by the same means he employed in battle—retreat and feint until he had exhausted his adversary. The friar kept silent and gave his attention to his coffee.

It was late afternoon of the summer day. Through the tent door the slanting rays of the sun in the areaway made a golden haze filled with dancing dust motes, golden in color; the light, penetrating the tent, glinted upon the brass of the platters and the lanterns, and upon the steel of the Shah's battle harness. It also lighted the Shah's face, which had a curious appearance of bronze, as though it were a mask, carved rather than cast, glowing as from internal heat and covered with little drops of perspiration. The light that fell upon the face came seemingly from below, as though the Shah were standing over an alchemist's brazier, in which mysterious substances had been ignited that emitted light of strange and oppressive colors—green and sulphurous yellow and the purple of the strangled—and suddenly it occurred to Fray Juan that Abbas was in pain and was in the grip of a terrible fear.

Abbas set his cup down and spoke.

"If I were to proclaim openly my devotion to the Christian faith," he said slowly, "then all my sins would be forgiven—is that the meaning of the words you have quoted?"

"God has the power to make you pure as the new snow," the friar said simply.

At that, Abbas's expression showed profound relief. The manner of crafty negotiation that characterized so much of his conversation disappeared. Suddenly, he seemed to have reached a decision. He regarded the friar tenderly, as with a new sense of brotherhood.

"Then I shall do it," he said firmly, and leaped up and began to walk about with the eagerness of one who has made the kind of decision he cannot wait to execute. "Oh, what joy this gives me!" he exclaimed, and then clapped his hand to his forehead. "The firman," he cried. "I had well-nigh forgotten. I will give you the firman at once—and I shall do more. I shall proclaim to all my subjects that their sovereign is devoted to the Prophet Jesus and desires that all his subjects give heed to the words of the Prophet and receive him into their hearts."

He clapped his hands for his orderly, and sent him running for his scrivener. While he waited for the scribe he paced about feverishly, rubbing his hands together like a bazaar merchant who has just driven a good bargain. Fray Juan was disquieted. Doubt showed in his face.

"You shall see, you shall see," exclaimed Abbas, noting the friar's expression. "You shall see how Abbas ransoms his soul. You will have no cause for dissatisfaction."

At last the scribe appeared. Fray Juan recognized him as the mullah Ibrahim Reza Kerbeli, who besides being an ecclesiastic was a famous penman whose court title was "Prince of Calligraphers and Glory of the King's Household." He had, in his time, entirely alone, executed an illuminated copy of the *Shah Nameh* in which every one of its thirty thousand couplets was embellished with arabesques in gold, vermilion, azure, and several other colors—a tremendous undertaking that had taken the better part of twenty years of the mullah's life and was almost as great a work in its field as that of the original composition of the poet Firdausi. The mullah was now an old man in his sixtieth year, with a long white beard, but his hand was still firm and his eyes were undimmed.

Mullah Ibrahim bowed to the floor before the Shah, and then squatting on his heels and removing his turban—his head was not uncovered thereby, for beneath the turban he wore an embroidered skullcap—he drew out his writing materials: a number of quill pens, a small blade for sharpening them, and a bottle of ink, all of which he kept in an old and minutely embellished and lacquered pen case, together with a roll of fine Chinese paper. He took the paper in his left hand, dipped his quill in the ink, and waited.

Abbas began to dictate. Fray Juan held his breath. What the Shah dictated was the firman that had been the object of the friar's diplomacy and prayers for the past dozen years—a royal decree granting the order of Discalced Carmelites the privilege of acquiring land and erecting churches in whatsoever part of the realm they desired, of celebrating Mass and receiving inquirers, of preaching in the open and holding meetings in all cities, lands, and territories owing fealty to the Shahinshah, of receiving converts, of baptizing them into the Catholic faith; further, it commended the order to all governors and other officials, and enjoined all subjects of the Shah to receive them kindly, to minister to their needs, and to give heed to their words. Further, these privileges were extended to all other orders and agencies of the Roman Church.

When Abbas had finished, he turned to the friar.

"Is that satisfactory? Does it please you?" he asked triumphantly.

"It is more than I could have desired or prayed for," said Fray Juan fervently. "God Himself is the One who will seal His approval, by the peace of your conscience."

Abbas now spoke to the scrivener.

"Bring it to me when you have written it carefully," he said, and added significantly: "This is the most important firman of my reign, one on which I have deliberated for many years. See to it that it is done in your best calligraphy, such as will equal your *Shah Nameh*."

"Upon my eye," replied the mullah knowingly, "I will make it a labor of devotion to your Majesty—a firman the very beauty of which will certify to its royal importance, one that men will in after years behold with wonder."

At this Fray Juan felt like one being awakened from a pleasant dream. It would be days—months even—before the document was ready for the sovereign's seal. Such was the Shah's capriciousness that by then the document might never be signed. Could Abbas, knowing himself, have had that in mind in the instructions he gave the scribe? To control his disappointment, Fray Juan began to whisper, "*In my distress I cried unto the Lord, and he heard me. Deliver my soul, O Lord, from lying lips, and from a deceitful tongue.*"

The monarch's look was one of piety and serenity.

"Oh, what joy to have a clear conscience!" he murmured. "Already a heavy load is lifted from my heart. A king has much to bear," he added fervently. "You know, I have suffered a great loss."

The friar was regarding the monarch broodingly, but now he felt impelled to speak.

"I have heard the news," he said.

This statement appeared to take the Shah by surprise. He turned swiftly and faced the friar with a suddenly blank expression.

"You have?" He frowned. "News travels fast. What have you heard?" Then, not waiting for the friar's reply, he added harshly, "I know what you have heard." He began to pace back and forth, in his agitation kicking up the corner of a carpet, and a moment later stumbling over it. The tent seemed to grow perceptibly smaller, and to become like a cage in which a restless desert animal was continually circling.

"What do they say?" he demanded, pausing in his nervous pacing and standing before the friar, and for the first time in the years since he had been in court Fray Juan was aware that he was taller than the monarch. "What do they say?" repeated Abbas.

Fray Juan hesitated, recalling what treasonable language the officer had used in telling him the story. He thought also that Abbas had forfeited any right to his confidence, and that it were perhaps better, all things considered, that Abbas realize that the friar was reasserting his independence of will and action.

"That, I will not tell you," he said deliberately, after a moment. "I have treasured the words of the Psalmist, *Lord, who shall dwell in thy holy hill? . . . He that backbiteth not with his tongue . . . nor taketh up a reproach against his neighbor.* I am no bearer of gossip."

The Shah stared at the friar with vacant eyes, as though struck with amazement at the friar's speech.

"They are bound to talk," he muttered. "They are bound to have their lies. Lies, lies. They hedge me in; they are like the jungles of Gilan. How can I escape them or penetrate them?"

His eyes focused, and fixed upon the friar's.

"Yes, they will tell you that I killed him, that I sent him to his death—that I did it because I was afraid of him. The prince was popular with the people—but should he not be? He was my son.

Should not the son of the Shah, the heir to the throne, be loved by the people?

"They say that it is our Safavid blood, that we have a madness to slay our young, like the wild boar, and that I am only doing what my grandfather and my uncle did. But that is a lie. How have we Safavids, who trace our ancestry back to the Eighth Imam, the holy Reza, persisted so long if that lie were true? Members of our family have held the throne for a hundred years. Why have we labored to build up the Empire? To what end have we fought in battle and waged war? Surely, is it not for the glory of Iran? Should we allow these splendid victories, these fruits of conquest, to be lost by a spendthrift, given away by a wastrel, squandered by a fool? If former shahs have been pushed to the hard decision, between paternal love and love of country, should not mercy temper judgment if the choice lay toward love of country?

"Consider what I have done to strengthen the Empire—the rich provinces I have regained, the roads and caravanserais I have built, the mosques and public buildings I have erected, the splendid cities that I have raised. Of what account is all this, if after I am gone the throne fall to a weakling? The scepter would pass, the golden throne would crumble, civil war would rage, anarchy pursue the just, and the Empire would cease to be.

"And so, why should I wish the see the prince Safi dead, who has won such notable victories, who has shown such skill in administration, such marks of true majesty—in his clemency, in the affection he has won among the people? Why should I wish his death? They cannot answer you. But they must lie. Yes, they must have their lies."

Abbas was standing before the friar, like one in supplication, his hands clasped, an intense agony in his eyes, yet in them bright sparks of shrewdness which no burning contrition could quite consume.

"They say I gave him a battle station, and then withdrew support. They say I risked his life needlessly, well knowing the fatal outcome. But who can judge? Who can say to a commander in battle that he should do this, or avoid doing that? None but the commander himself, and at times he cannot say, but acts as the voice of God directs. Is a general to sacrifice his chance of victory because his son happens to be in peril? What about Ibrahim the water carrier and Baba the quiver bearer who are in constant peril? Shall they be ignored? When the battle rages, is one to be accounted better than another? Are not all men equal when they face death? Then, the only difference is in the strength of the arm, the quickness of the eye, the skill in wielding the ax, the lance, or the bow.

"Should Safi Mirza—though he be my own son—be shielded from danger more than any other soldier? Should he not be tried as his father was tried? Was I not thrust, at an age younger than Safi Mirza's, before the oncoming horse of the Ustajlus, helpless before their lowered lances but for my own wit and will and stout legs? Yet there are those that say that princes should lie on mattresses of cotton down and drink honey from flagons. They forget that this Shah was not so reared, that he did not gain the throne of the King of Kings by sitting on a mountain and watching the thunderclouds roll in the valley."

The Shah's voice had grown strident as his passion rose.

"Ingrates!" he cried out. "They hate me. They hate their Shah. The more he does for them, the more they hate him."

The Shah was standing facing toward the tent door. The setting sun illuminated his face—ruddy and contorted and terrifying in the rage it mirrored.

"This will I remember," he uttered hoarsely, "and as God is my witness, I will make their backs to ache and their feet to burn for it."

Had the Shah threatened death and destruction, slitting of tongues and throats, the bowstring and evisceration, there would have been something to match the awful majesty of his mood; as it was, the mildness of his threatenings filled Fray Juan with a sense of anticlimax and pity.

Abbas perhaps expected some rejoinder from the friar, but as there was none, and Fray Juan stood unmoved, facing him, the Shah's manner underwent a further transformation: the anger and the majesty were now melted away as a waxen image before a fire, and in their place were only surrender and abjectness. Suddenly the Shah was on his knees before the friar.

"Tell me, reverend Father," he cried brokenly, "that I am guiltless of sin."

Here, it appeared to Fray Juan, was being offered him again that for which he had prayed so long, the opportunity to win an empire for Christ at a single stroke. It flashed through his thought that here was a moment as pregnant with significance for the history of the

East as that, for the history of the West, when the Emperor Henry stood in the snow before Pope Gregory.

Fray Juan was unable to move, stricken with amazement and uncertainty. The sight of the Shah of Persia on his knees before him, the thought that Abbas was close to, if not in the very act of, surrendering his soul to the Christian God, the realization of what vast consequences hung in the balance of a hair, filled the friar's head with a swirling as of many waters. His knees trembled, and his breath was choked. But some inward sense of proportion steadied him and cleared his mind. He closed his eyes. "Father in heaven," he prayed, "lead me not into temptation; deliver me from evil."

He opened his eyes. Abbas was still kneeling before him, his head bowed in an attitude of patience and penitence. Fray Juan recalled that Abbas had just now, and for the first time, addressed him by his ecclesiastical title of "Father." "Deliver me from temptation," he prayed again. Aloud, he said, "God alone, your Majesty, can remove the guilt of sin."

"But you have the power—which the mullahs have not—of forgiving sin," murmured Abbas. "Tell me that my sin—if I have committed sin—is forgiven."

And now certainty came to the friar. He knew now that if God willed Abbas's conversion to the Christian faith, this was not the moment. He recognized also that the success of his mission and the future of Christian missions in Persia depended upon the skill and discretion with which he conducted himself at this moment. He must get the monarch to his feet without his being aware that he had been on his knees. But how? And then, without conscious thought, Fray Juan knelt beside the Shah.

"Let us pray," he said quietly.

Fray Juan addressed his prayer to God the Compassionate, the Merciful, to Him who was not only God of the Christians but God of the Moslems as well. In the acceptance of one God the two were on common ground.

"God, our heavenly Father," he prayed, "deliver us from false judgments, from blindness, from sin. Help us to know Thy truth, and to obey Thy voice. Forgive us our sins as we forgive the wrongs done to us by others, and lead us not into temptation, but deliver us from evil. Amen."

The friar remained with his head bowed, in silent prayer, in a Hail Mary, and in a prayer of intercession. When he looked up, dusk had fallen, the tent lay in a gloom, and Abbas was nowhere about.

As Fray Juan left the royal tent he saw, lolling against the tent ropes, the village odalisque who had been in the tent when he entered. She gazed at him now as he passed, and in her yellow eyes, glowing in the dusk, was a look of contempt and, it seemed, of secret knowledge.

PART NINE

———•———

The Rejection

I

Rome received comprehensive reports regularly from its Persian mission. Although Fray Juan's work had multiplied many-fold and communications had frequently been closed he had always managed to keep the General of the order informed. These reports were usually prepared in triplicate. One copy was sent by some merchant or traveler going to Europe. A few inquiries at the caravanserai generally produced such a courier. A second copy was dispatched to Fray Vincent at Hormuz, who relayed it on to Rome by some Portuguese convoy. The third copy was kept in a brass-bound box, labeled "Archives of the Carmelite (Discalced) Convent in Isfahan." After the Shah's forces laid siege to Hormuz in 1621, it was no longer possible to communicate with Fray Vincent, and thereafter only two copies of letters were made.

In one of the reports written during this period the friar said:

For all his pretenses, the Shah is a Moslem at heart who contemns the Christian faith, and all the favors he has shown our mission, all the benevolence he has manifested toward the Armenians, are but sham, which he carried so long as there was hope of gaining an alliance with Christendom against the Turks. But now that he has been victorious over the Sultan, an alliance no longer interests him, and his blandishments are now directed toward the English, whose aid he hopes to gain against the Portuguese.

We have lost all prospect of gaining the firman to establish a convent here, and hopes for a firman establishing religious liberty for the Christians are equally baseless. Rather, the Shah's antagonism toward them grows, and he uses every means, including persecution, to compel them to apostatize and to become Moslems.

Another report spoke of the English gains in Persia and of the growing coldness of the Shah toward the Carmelites.

The Shah no longer receives us as formerly, it continued. *This is partly due to the arrival of the English Company and their ascendancy in court because of the moneys they bring him in the silk trade. Now they are inflaming him against the Portuguese . . . but the coolness of the monarch toward us is due to other causes: as I have written to your Reverence, two angels war within his soul. Once I had hope, a pride-begotten illusion, of assisting the angel of the Lord against the spirit of Satan, but some defect of mine has driven me from the field. The Shah's life has become shadowed with suspicion and pride and the lust of the flesh. The motions of his soul are dark and shrouded with mystery.*

Fray Juan tried to be perfectly truthful in his reports to his superiors, but inevitably in drafting his letters he forgot to some extent the depth of his loneliness in the mere labor of writing. In fixing his thoughts upon the Congregation at Rome, in composing what should be read by his superiors, he absorbed some of the comfort to be had from being in the physical presence of a company of like-minded brethren. By the powers of memory, fortified by distance and yearning and by constant exercise, he could attend a celebration of the Mass in the convent church at Valladolid, where he had made his novitiate, a quarter of a century earlier; he could hear in his ears the droning of the celebrant and the antiphonal chanting of the brothers facing each other across the choir stalls; he could smell the incense in his nostrils, and he could all but taste and consume the holy Wafer that was offered him.

Some powerful nostalgia must have overcome the friar while drafting this letter, a nostalgia born of the reverses to which he had been subjected, born perhaps of the intuitive knowledge that the Congregation of the Discalced did not as yet see with one eye the missionary task of the Church, for the writing broke off suddenly, and ended on a note of appeal:

*Pray, Fathers, I beseech you, for the security of this little flock I
shepherd here, that the all-loving Father may spare us until these
lambs in Christ have been strengthened against the day of trial. For
snug as we are, blessed as we are beyond our expectation, yet am I
never free of the feeling of the blast upon our necks, of a cold wind
brewing in the hills, ready to descend upon these poor defenseless
creatures. Pray, Fathers, that they may be spared from the wrath of
evil and hatred.*

II

The Shah seemed to have forgotten the friar entirely, but he could
remember his existence when he had some business to transact that
required fidelity and discretion.

Such a business now arose that caused Fray Juan to be summoned
peremptorily to Kasvin, where the Shah was in residence. This business
was the arrival of the Spanish ambassador Don García de Silva y
Figueroa, charged with diverting the Shah from attacking Hormuz
and of making a general settlement of the Persian Gulf question.
Fray Juan was called to act as interpreter for the audience.

King Philip—who was king of both Spain and Portugal—was not
making again the mistake of niggardliness he had made in his former
embassy, but had exhausted his treasury to equip his ambassador
properly. Don García traveled with a train of nearly two hundred
attendants, and his baggage required a caravan of five hundred camels.
The caravan took a whole day to enter the city, and the population,
accustomed as it was to pomp and circumstance, had never been quite
so impressed. All business ceased for the day.

The ambassador himself entered the city at two o'clock in the afternoon, mounted, appareled in a velvet suit of old rose, with a massive
gold chain about his throat, and on his head a hat with a diamond
band and three long ostrich plumes that, when the breeze caught
them, fluttered and hid the ambassador's face from the crowd. Each
of his attendants was garbed in mauve-colored velvet embroidered in
gold and silver.

The Shah received the ambassador early the following morning
in the palace garden. Fray Juan, uncertain as to Abbas's mood, dreaded

meeting the monarch, but Abbas was excited over the presents and hardly noticed the friar, though he was directed to sit between the monarch and the ambassador.

Fortunately, the ambassador's hat and sense of decorum relieved the strain of the audience. Don García, whenever he mentioned the name of his king, would ceremoniously remove his plumed hat and place it on his knee. If he mentioned the name of the Shah in the same passage, he would shift the hat from one to the other knee. Abbas, to whom the removing of headgear was a sign of disrespect, found this highly amusing. He would wink to the friar, and then, mentioning the King of Spain, remove his turban.

Don García was a man of magnificent composure, but he gradually began to show impatience at the way the Shah evaded, with one or another ruse, every attempt to take up the business of the embassy. Abbas began to talk about his battles, causing the ambassador to squirm, and Abbas guessed that Don García had a tender stomach.

"I am accounted an excellent surgeon," Abbas remarked. "You must know that I circumcise all my sons myself, and with my own hand emasculate all the young men brought in for palace service."

Noting that the ambassador blanched, he jumped to his feet.

"Come," he cried. "It happens that some boys were sent me this very day by Kashgai Khan as hostages for his tribe. You shall see how skilful I am. I tell you that in all my years I have lost not more than a dozen in the operation. They were, unfortunately, past the age when it can be done delicately.

"Translate that, translate that!" cried Abbas to Fray Juan sharply, seeing the friar hesitate.

Fray Juan looked away.

"Would you have it reported throughout Europe that his Persian Majesty is but a barber, and worse?" the friar asked.

The Shah was quieted, and the ambassador now thought the moment appropriate to make his presentation of the gifts. He signaled to his adjutant, and presently from over the palace walls a great shouting could be heard as the laden porters came through the street and entered the palace gates with their burdens.

There were four hundred porters, all garbed in velvet and silk, and they came down the garden walk one by one to where the Shah sat with the ambassador and Fray Juan on a dais, and knelt before the monarch to exhibit their offering for his inspection.

The first gift was the sword which King Philip had worn at his wedding. Don García explained through the friar the symbolic significance of the sword, but Abbas had taken too many wives and concubines in his time for any such symbolism to affect him; he was curious only as to the workmanship and the value of the jewels in the hilt and scabbard. He wanted to know where the blade, which had a wonderful temper, had been forged, and Don García explained something of the excellent metalwork done in the Spanish king's dominions, in the city of Toledo.

Afterward, there were twenty-two porters, each bearing a necklace of emeralds worked in gold. The emeralds, Don García explained, came from the king's mines in Peru, in the New World. These were followed by a number of golden salvers, and then a silver brazier so large and heavy that eight men were required to carry it.

The Shah was overwhelmed, but such extravagance could not go on endlessly, and to relieve the wonder the next gift was a table service for the road, including candlesticks. The service consisted of some three hundred pieces, and a hundred and fifty porters were used to display the gift, a porter being assigned to each two pieces. The table service was followed by a kitchen service of knives, hammers, shovels, tongs, pots and pans, all made of steel or copper.

The table service fascinated the Shah, and he wanted to know about the use of knives and forks at table, as practiced in Europe. His questions had not been exhausted when porters brought in what Don García considered to be the most striking of his presents, one which he thought would testify indubitably to King Philip's eagerness for settlement of his differences with the Shah.

This was a great glass secretary, with the shelves supported by golden pillars, an object that had cost as much in money and labor to bring hither as to execute in the first instance. But there was a story behind this piece of furniture. It seemed that Abbas, in a mood of extravagance some years before, had ordered it in Italy through one of the envoys he was continually sending abroad. The envoy, whose name is not known, had bought the secretary with royal funds, but afterward had pledged it for a personal loan of five thousand ducats. The matter somehow had come to the attention of Philip's minister, who saw some political advantage in redeeming it and sending it to the Shah with Philip's compliments.

Actually, Abbas did not appear too happy to receive the secretary, reminder as it was of another misplaced confidence, and when Don García related the story of how it had been obtained, Abbas muttered an aside to Fray Juan: "Does he make me out a fool?" Nevertheless, he asked the friar to express his gratitude to the king through the ambassador; and to show his satisfaction he got up and examined the secretary in some detail.

But there was more to follow. There were porters bearing bolts of velvet and damask from the best Spanish and Italian looms, and helmets of Toledo steel, almost as intricately engraved as the Persian, a sheaf of lances, a collection of fine arquebuses and muskets, and finally thirty camels laden with pepper and spices from the Portuguese Indies. The procession ended with a young page in yellow velvet leading a massive Pyrenees dog, with silky coat of white and black, that stood to the page's shoulder.

The dog was a fitting climax to the procession, for Abbas was immensely fond of dogs, of all breeds, and the Pyrenees immediately captured his fancy. He fondled it, stroking its coat and calling it endearing names, and then, with a sigh, peered down the avenue of poplar trees to see if there were more porters coming. As there were no more, he sighed again, and lay back against the cushion, like a child filled to bursting at a feast.

It was now toward noon. After a while, Abbas stirred himself and, clapping his hands, ordered dinner to be served. All this time, of course, Don García had been unable to get in a word about the high objects of the embassy—the regularization of relations in the Persian Gulf. Don García thought to try again, while the Shah was in a glow over the gifts he had received, but when Fray Juan attempted to translate what Don García was saying, Abbas cut him short, and began to talk rather of hunting and other amusements he had in store for the ambassador, by way of hospitality.

Abbas had had prepared a dinner worthy of the occasion. This was served in the banquet hall of the palace, a large barrel-vaulted chamber not unlike that of the Chehel Sitoon in Isfahan except that the walls were bare of ornament, immaculately white and cool, with niches all about with honeycomb arching, inlaid with tiny mirror work, and the ceiling was a mass of mirrors inlaid in arabesque design, the whole giving a sense of overpowering brilliance. To heighten the effect, in the niches were tubs of sparkling snow, brought down by runners from the heights of the Elborz, and in the tubs were wine carafes of cut glass. Finally, on an immense white cloth spread on the floor, as they sat to eat, servants placed enormous platters piled with rice so delicately cooked that the heaps trembled like jelly.

The dinner began with wine drinking. Abbas insisted that the ambassador finish off three large bowls of wine before he would allow him to eat, all the time carrying on, through the friar, a running flow of inconsequential conversation. Gaiety, jesting, lively comment, flattering references—all these filled Don García with satisfaction. He took it as good augury for his mission; but Fray Juan, as he translated, grew more and more despondent, recognizing Abbas's strategy of feint and diversion. Finally, when Abbas himself began to grow slightly stuporous from the wine—Don García held his liquor far better than the Shah—the ambassador again opened up the subject of his embassy.

"Your Majesty," he began—and the high hat with the ostrich plumes and the diamond band, which he had kept on his head while at meat, now came off and rested on his knee—"my sovereign the King of Spain"—at this the hat was shifted to the other knee—"being greatly desirous of amicable relations with your Majesty, has sent me to your presence to hold converse with you regarding the grievous conditions existing in the Gulf, particularly the occupation of our island of Bahrein by your Majesty's forces."

"His royal Majesty," replied Abbas, mimicking the ambassador by removing his turban and placing it in his lap as he spoke—his hennaed hair, which was no longer thick but was sparse and stringy, was reflected in thousands of facets in the ceiling—"does me great honor to dispatch to me one of such distinguished rank and attainments as yourself. I understand you have had formidable service in the wars. You have also, I believe, fought against the Turks. Tell me of your exploits."

"I did have some service against the Turks, your Majesty, but our great victory was at sea, near Lepanto."

Don García did not want to be diverted, but he had to yield; nevertheless, he thought some advantage might be gained by the opening offered. He began to tell the Shah of the great naval engagement of

Lepanto, in which nearly two hundred galleys engaged. Fifty years had passed since this battle, but it had marked the end of Turkish naval supremacy in the Mediterranean, and it still made a moving story. Don García spoke in stilted, even bombastic Spanish, but Fray Juan managed to render it into simple, direct Persian. The effect was better than might have been expected: the Shah sat like a child drawn from his play. Don García thought he had gained a point, and at the end he referred casually to the power of the existing Spanish navy, which, he indicated, was considerable despite the loss of the Armada, and intimated that it would be unwise to press this sea power into battle for the recapture of Bahrein. It would be better to give up the island and reach a settlement on the Persian Gulf.

All this Fray Juan softened as much as possible, sensing the effect it would have on the Shah. Abbas took it thoughtfully, but his next comment showed that he was not yet prepared to bargain. He began a new diversion.

"His Spanish Majesty," he said, "as I have long understood, is an ardent champion of your Christian faith, and I gather you also are much interested. Your compatriot, his Reverence here, has translated into our tongue certain portions of your holy book, and I wish to inquire whether he is now ready to present me with this work."

Fray Juan had indeed brought the work along. Some hope had led him to place the volumes, wrapped in oiled cloth, among his belongings when he set out with the ambassadorial train, and this morning he had been prompted to bring them with him. He now brought them forth. Abbas seized them with the avidity with which he always treated religious objects, and taking the parcel reverently, but with a kind of madness in his eyes, he kissed it fervently and placed it on his head before opening it. He examined the volumes for some minutes, and then asked the friar to read from them. The friar opened the Book of the Psalms and read. When he came to the passage, *Yea, though I walk through the valley of the shadow of death*, Abbas interrupted him, and began to speak of the uncertainty of death, and then, with the maudlin sentiments with which the friar had long since become familiar, he began to hold forth upon the immortality of the soul and the blessed state of those who died with the promises of the Christian faith.

Fray Juan could not restrain distasteful memories of other occasions when Abbas had shown such a mood—the day of the Khatcha-turan, the session at the army headquarters at Souj Boulak, and the first occasion when Abbas visited the friar in the house in the tannery district. When Abbas was in such vein there was nothing to be gained by forcing his attention elsewhere. Even now, he was becoming like one possessed. His eyes had grown glassy, his face was strained, the cords at his neck were taut, and he had began to gesticulate. Don García was dismayed, and after a while, seeing the dejection in the friar's face, he begged leave to retire.

"How thoughtful of you," exclaimed Abbas, at once recovering, "for you know that I leave tomorrow with forces for the Kafkas, where the Muscovites have been stirring up trouble among the Kevsurs and the Abkhasians. I will have an army of twenty-five thousand arque-busiers and eighty thousand horsemen armed with bows and lances —enough, I think, to meet the threat. I will see you again when I return. Meanwhile, I have given orders that you are to be comfortably entertained."

That evening, as Don García sat with the friar, he commented:

"The Shah is a madman or the greatest liar the world has ever known. I do not wonder that you have had such disappointments in him over so many years."

But Fray Juan now thought otherwise. Mad as Abbas might be, lying and deceitful as he could be, Fray Juan felt a great pity for him, for he could not believe Abbas's interest in the Christian faith to be al-together feigned. It seemed that he was like the possessed from whom Jesus had driven the legion of devils. But Fray Juan recognized sadly that the gift of casting out demons had not been given to him, and so their shrill cries continued to sound in his ears.

III

Two young Carmelite friars who had volunteered for missionary service in Persia arrived with the Spanish ambassador. Their names were Balthazar and Dimas. They came expecting to find a house in which to resume the monastic life they had left in Italy, and Fray Juan was mortified when he had to tell them that there was no Car-melite house, that he was still living in a caravanserai.

One indirect result of Don García's embassy, however, was the remedying of this condition. Shortly after Fray Juan returned to Isfahan, he received a visit from the minister of court with news that Abbas had instructed him to assign quarters to the friar. The minister did handsomely by the Carmelites. He gave them a house in the quiet Maidan-i-Amir district with a plot of ground adjoining it, well watered by the same stream that supplied water to the royal gardens of the Hezar Jareeb. Balthazar and Dimas had brought a contribution of funds from the Italian Congregation, and with it Fray Juan was enabled to pay off some of the debts that he had incurred and to put the new house in order.

With the indifference to disaster of a honeybee that promptly commences rebuilding and restocking its cells no matter how often its house is despoiled, Fray Juan now set the whole community to rebuilding, replastering, restoring, and to erecting a wall around the land. He divided rooms into cells so that a proper conventual life could be followed, painted and decorated a large room in which he installed an altar, and over the gate put up a cross and a sign, *House of God and Jesus Mary*. In the camel-keeper's bazaar he found an enormous bell, designed for some gargantuan bull camel, which he thought would serve admirably for a church bell. He bought it and installed it in a cupola just above the refectory. He also set out vines and trees and dug a network of irrigation channels to water them.

As for Don García, he did not see the Shah again, and all the hundreds of thousands of ducats' worth of presents which King Philip had amassed to woo the Shah was so much money wasted. Abbas spent the summer campaigning, and the winter at his palace at Ferrahabad on the Caspian. When he did return south it was to go to Ab-i-Kurang to supervise the work he had started there on a tunnel to divert the flow of the Karun into the Zeyandeh Rud. Finally, Don García, his dignity much offended, left the country.

Fray Juan was content to be rid of court duties and official responsibilities. The loneliness that had traveled with him like a dogging shadow since the departure of his first convert was not relieved. He tasted again the sweetness of life that distills from companionship with those of one's own faith and outlook. Balthazar and Dimas were both Spaniards, and their rich Spanish speech, their strong Spanish faces, the glow in their dark eyes, affected Fray Juan with a swelling of paternal pride, with an overpowering rush of patriotic fervor. Of a sudden, looking at them, he could see in his mind's eye the whole of Spain—or at least as much of it as he had known—the blue skies and the fleecy clouds above the rounded hills; the gorges, and the rushing torrents; the olive groves and the cork forests, the groves of orange and lemon trees, the peasants trudging along the road and bent over in the fields. And sounds too were recalled—the rhythmic clatter of a castanet under the trees and the shouting of peasants as one danced a fandango. And he could smell the dust of the road and the fragrance from the orange groves. All this he drank in with his senses, in a moment, in the hurried pause between the responses as they recited the afternoon office together, and the thought would occur to him: Was Shamala passing through those scenes? And he was tempted sometimes to inquire of the brothers whether by any chance the princess had worshiped in the church which they served, and whether they had encountered her. But such a question was useless, of course, for they would not have spoken with her in any case.

Of the two friars, Fray Balthazar was the elder. He was twenty-six years old; he came from Pampilona, in the Basque country, and had early dedicated himself to the Church. He had been drawn to the Jesuit order, for the ancestral castle of the Xaviers was nearby and he had heard a great deal of the missionary labors of the noted Jesuit Francis Xavier. It was at Valladolid, where he had been sent to school, that he became acquainted with the Barefooted Carmelites; attracted by the contemplative quality of their observances, by their seeming detachment from the world, he had chosen this order in preference to the Jesuit. When the need for recruits for the mission houses arose and he was asked if he would volunteer, he was at first shocked at the thought of interrupting his contemplative existence; but seeing in this the will of God made manifest, he had offered to go. Actually, Balthazar was by temperament hardly the sort one associates with contemplation. He was short and sturdy, and looked like a woodcutter. In his deep-set dark eyes was a perpetual twinkle, like the reflection of lanterns in a pool. He was a gay-humored man; his basic good cheer came out in the ejaculations which, despite the rule of silence, continually escaped his lips: "By the grace of God, what a glorious day!" "By the mercy of Providence, what a tasty salad!" "Praise be to God for this work before us!" Everything pleased him; he thought there were no days and nights like those of Isfahan; he found the fruits of the countryside unsurpassed; he considered the people the most charming imaginable, wanting only the Christian faith.

Nevertheless, for all his willingness to be serving abroad, for all his appreciation of the opportunity to win souls for the Christ, Fray Balthazar was not a missionary. He was content to remain within the walls of the compound: the garden was an ample universe in which to lift his eyes, a kingdom sufficient for his needs. It was not that he lacked zeal for the faith; it was, as Fray Juan resolved it in his mind, that his joy was a species of contentment: the world was good, and in time men would learn to praise their Maker for His goodness, for His wonderful works to the children of men; and, if men did not, the Lord of His abundant mercy would make Himself so known to them that they could not resist His appeal. Fray Juan did not think this theologically sound, yet as he could find no errors in the logic he was hesitant to urge another view—the view that time was passing, that the end of all things was nigh, and that men must work, for the night would fall. Fray Juan had a great pity of an errant humanity, and the thought that the least of the little ones to whom he ministered might be cut off by some neglect of his from glorious salvation drove him continually to be about, preaching and speaking, and lifting his voice in appeal.

Fray Dimas, two years younger than Balthazar, was even more the contemplative by calling than the other. He could have been a courtier —he had the qualities for ambassadorship the lack of which Fray Juan felt so keenly—but Dimas's thoughts were turned to God. The young religious was quick of wit and had a dry Spanish humor, but he preferred to curb these tendencies and to lose himself in meditation. At these times his lean, swarthy face began to glow, and his seemingly unseeing eyes were lit with exaltation, fixed on something invisible to the others. One day he came to Fray Juan, his dark eyes large and troubled.

"Father Juan," he said, "I have come to you for confession and forgiveness. I have sinned greatly against your Reverence."

"Not against me," protested Fray Juan, perplexed. "Against God, and against God only, have you sinned, whatever your fault may be."

He wondered what could have happened, for the young man had made his morning confession only an hour before.

"Father Juan, on leaving Rome I was entrusted with a letter to you by a former penitent of yours, the Donna Sherley, and grievous is my fault, most grievous is my fault, that I forgot its existence until a half-hour ago."

"A letter!" exclaimed Fray Juan. "A letter! Where is it? Where is it?"

"Here, Father Juan," said Dimas, producing a missive sealed in parchment and secured with a crimson cord. "I came upon it only a little while ago, between the pages of the *Apology of St. Justin*, where, had I given them more devotion, I would have discovered it long before."

Fray Juan took the letter, and to hide his feelings bowed his head.

"Your forgetfulness is nothing to be censured, but rather we should be thankful that the letter was not lost entirely," he said. He cleared his throat. "The lady was the first to be baptized here by one of our order. For that we hold her in tender remembrance. Tell me, did you speak with her?"

"But briefly, Father. She came to worship in the Church of Santa Maria della Scala, and Father Jerome, the celebrant, discovering who she was, told her of Balthazar and me, and of how we were soon to leave for Persia. She asked then if she could send a letter by us, and the following day brought it to me. I was with her for only a moment."

"Did she—look well?"

"She appeared in excellent health, Father. There was a lively light in her eyes. She seemed in good health."

"The letter was, of course, unsealed, that it might be read by the father prior?"

"It was, Father, and as there was nothing warranting censorship, it was sealed as it is now."

No purpose would be served by asking further questions. Fray Juan excused Dimas and hastened to his cell. What Shamala had written was simple and direct, like herself. She wrote to him as to her father confessor, as to the one who had admitted her to the mystery of the faith. She told briefly of the arrival in Rome of Sir Robert and herself, and of how, while Sir Robert was busy on state business, she had visited the various churches of the Eternal City, but how, most of all, her footsteps continued to return to that of Santa Maria della Scala.

There was a reference to a sermon that Shamala had heard there on her first visit.

The reverend father prior dwelt upon the parable of the talents, the letter read. *It was an excellent sermon, addressed to the congregation, among whom were several Carmelite novices and postulants. The prior expounded the idea—which is one that animates you —of the necessity of carrying the Word abroad, and of propagating the Gospel in the distant regions of the world, lest the riches of grace that have been entrusted to the brothers be like the talent wrapped in a napkin.*

The passage closed with a wistful statement:

I feel as though I were a talent wrapped in a napkin.

Fray Juan paused in his reading to dwell upon this cryptic intimation, and he felt an outgoing of pity and understanding. At the same time he was struck anew by the dreadful thought that he might have urged the princess into an unfortunate marriage. . . .

The letter continued:

At the palace of Del Fonte, where Sir Robert and I were invited the other evening, among the entertainment offered was a play called Hamlet, *by the English actor-producer William Shakespeare, which has had, they say, a great success in London. It was given in a wretched Italian translation, but so powerfully moving it was that it left me weeping, and a few days later Sir Robert brought me a copy of the English folio edition, which he had from an English merchant, a friend of Sir Robert's. There is a passage in it—among many noteworthy passages—that deeply impressed me, for it was counsel given by a father to his son departing for distant parts, and to those like myself, removed from familiar scenes and having no permanent abode but living in a state of continual movement, it is wisdom of the finest natural order. The counsel runs:*

> Give thy thoughts no tongue,
> Nor any unproportioned thought his act. . . .
> Those friends thou hast, and their adoption tried,
> Grapple them to thy soul with hoops of steel.

Following this counsel I shall therefore guard my present thoughts; but you may guess of whom, when I consider the friends I have, I think particularly and how grateful I am for his fatherly devotion.

*But I have written enough. I write to you, as one ever grateful for
the counsel and inspiration you have given me, and pray our heavenly
Father to keep you in good health, to prosper your work in the Lord,
and to save you until we are privileged to meet again.*

Ever your faithful
Shamala

The Vespers bell had rung, but Fray Juan was unable to bring himself from his knees, to which he had fallen, seeking to pray, yet unable
to compose his thoughts to do so, unable even to resolve the mingling
of images and feelings that troubled him, that seemed almost to
separate him from his God and from his brotherhood. Grigor came
to his cell and peered in. Seeing his superior bowed down, he crept
away, and the service was conducted without the prior.

Toward dusk, Fray Juan found his feet and walked slowly into the
garden. He felt stifled. Opening the gate, he went into the street. He
made his way to the Caravanserai of Shah Ismail, that his own inner
turmoil might be absorbed by the confusion of the great throng there.

Here the friar heard astounding news which drove away for a time
all personal reflections: Khudabandeh Mirza had fled Isfahan to the
protection of Mansur Khan, head of the powerful Kashgai tribal con-
federation, and was hurling public defiance against the Shah his father.

This was sheer madness, of course, for it was doubtful whether
Mansur Khan, restive as he was, would dare put the tribes behind
Khudabandeh Mirza, and, if he did, whether the prince was the man
he would trust to lead them in rebellion against such a military genius
as Abbas.

Abbas, however, was returning to his capital posthaste, and this
was a baleful omen.

IV

Excerpts from a letter from Fray Juan Thaddeus of St. Elisaeus,
of the Carmelite convent in Isfahan, to the General of the order in
Rome, written in the year 1622:

*Besides the lay brother Grigor, the number of our communicants
is now eight, all of whom are converts from Islam, so that we now have*

in fact a Catholic Church in Persia. The first of these are the porters Baghir and Mahboob, and the shopkeeper Jafar Kerbeli, whose conversion I have previously reported to you. There is also Jamileh, a widow of a soldier who died at the battle of the Rowanduz Gorge; Zamdar, a beggar, but now gardener in our vineyard (the yield of which commands good prices in the market and now provides most of our income); and Abdallah Massih and his wife and son. Abdallah is the former Abdallah Meshedi Seyyid with whom I sat at dinner given to the English Company some years back, as I have previously reported to you. In what surprising fashion does the Holy Spirit work! I had come away from that affair much discouraged and much conscience-stricken for my own ineptness and lack of humility. But about a year ago—long after I supposed what I might have said had been forgotten—Abdallah came to our house seeking instruction in the faith. When we baptized him he dropped his Moslem name of Meshedi Seyyid, which means "the descendant of the Prophet who has made the pilgrimage to Meshed," for that of Massih, which means simply "Christian."

I look for great fruit from Abdallah. He is a brilliant scholar, but after his conversion he was compelled to give up his court post as jurist of the Shariya—which is the Moslem domestic law—and is now earning a meager livelihood teaching Arabic and Hindustani and assisting me in translating the Scriptures. He also lives in continual fear of his life from the fanatic element and the mullahs, for he was too high an ecclesiastic for his repudiation of Islam to be ignored. Nevertheless, so bold is he in witness, so unafraid, that he has already made a great impression on many, and we have as result a steadily increasing attendance at our Masses and other services.

It would be most helpful, in propagating the Gospel, and in fortifying the faith of those who have declared their adherence to it, if the Mass could be said in the vernacular, and if authority for such could be granted by the Holy See, as I have urged in former reports.

It was Saturday, and Fray Juan had been hearing confessions in preparation for the Sunday Masses. All had been heard except Jafar. The grocer, who ordinarily came promptly, during the mid-morning lull in the market, was late. Jafar usually made his confessions in a leisurely, singsong manner, and after he had been shrived he liked to linger and give the friar the gossip of the day. In the greengrocers' bazaar people shopped early while the vegetables were fresh from the fields, and Jafar did good business because he knew how to gossip with his clientele. In consequence he usually had all the news before anyone else.

Today, however, Jafar could hardly run through his sins of the week fast enough.

"Bad news, Reverence," he burst out the moment Fray Juan had pronounced the absolution and assigned a penance.

The friar nodded absently. He was still in a mood of detachment and spiritual reverie after his morning's labor, thinking of the blessing which God had vouchsafed his work, full of compassion for the grocer, who seemed, for all his miraculous cure of asthma, not yet to have found the true grace of the Christian faith.

"The city is in an uproar!"

Excitement made Jafar's lips twitch like a rabbit's nostrils over a lettuce leaf. He was small and wizened of body, and his head was narrow like a rabbit's, and nearly bald, with the baldness concealed by a tight-fitting turban.

"In an uproar?" repeated Fray Juan musingly.

"You heard, of course, that Prince Khudabandeh had been arrested? He had only reached Kerimabad."

"You told me as much a week ago, I recall."

"Yes, the prince was brought home in state and lodged in his own house—the surest sign of the Shah's contempt. And then this morning the executioners came and blinded him."

"Blinded him!" the friar whispered, startled.

Jafar went on to give the details. Khudabandeh, after his arrest, had been allowed to resume his ordinary mode of life. Everyone acted as though nothing had happened, as though the Shah had not been offended, as though Khudabandeh did not stand in the same awful shadow as his brother Safi had.

"The prince was idling in his garden where several of his concubines were disporting in the pool," continued Jafar, with the assurance of an eyewitness. "There the chief eunuch finds him and informs him that his presence is desired. The prince leaves his women and enters his high-roofed chamber. There stand the black-turbaned, black-aproned executioners. They have with them a lighted brazier and thongs, and one of them bears in his hand the prince's own scimitar.

"The prince asks no questions, but quietly allows himself to be bound, thinking no doubt that it were better to lose his head swiftly and cleanly than otherwise. But the executioners have another use for the scimitar. They thrust the blade into the coals and fan the brazier to a heat. The prince now sees what is reserved for him, and he begins to weep and to cry aloud. But too late. One of the executioners has thrust his arm into a heavy sleeve of leather, and from behind he locks it about the prince's throat. No longer can the prince protest; his voice is muted and his eyes began to start from want of breath. At that moment the other executioner snatches up the sword, by now white-hot, and passes it before the prince's eyes."

It was all done very deftly, according to Jafar, who had it from a relative of the prince's eunuch. The hair of the eyebrows curled, but the face was not burned beyond a blistering of the forehead and the cheeks. The scimitar was turned edgewise, so that only the eyeballs were seared. After the third pass the work was done: the prince had lost his sight beyond recovery. The prince was then released, and he stumbled among the cushions and threw himself upon them, screaming. Presently the physician came and bandaged his eyes and anointed his face, but the prince continued to sob and moan.

"The people are aroused," concluded Jafar. "All through the bazaar the talk is of nothing else, and at the name of Abbas the ground is spit upon. The people ask themselves whether it is indeed Abbas or the terrible Ismail again on the throne."

Reports of the people's attitude apparently reached the Shah, and his usual indifference to public opinion must have been shaken, for he left his Serishabad residence that day and returned to Isfahan, and promptly ordered a court durbar. Immediately, in response to his command, carpets appeared on all the balconies and bunting in the windows, as though it were Noo Rooz.

The following morning, while Fray Juan was celebrating Mass, a Qizilbashie appeared at the gate to summon the friar to court.

It was not yet sunrise when the friar let himself out of the gate and set out for the Ali Gapou. The streets, ordinarily filled with traffic at this hour, were half deserted, and the shops of many of the merchants were closed, while such business as went on had a curiously muted quality that was very different from the semi-quiet of Fridays and religious holidays. There had been times like this before in Fray

Juan's recollection, as when the attempt had been made on the Shah's life after the Khatchaturan. The temper of the people was plain.

In Isfahan proper, the streets were thronged with people going to the durbar, but the crowds were undemonstrative, and it was as though they were gathered for a state funeral, or other somber occasion. When Fray Juan reached the Ali Gapou he found the entrance heavily guarded, but the lieutenant in command was Afsar Malek, the officer who had escorted him to the Shah at his Souj Boulak headquarters.

"May God be merciful," the lieutenant murmured as he nodded to the sentry to admit the friar, and Fray Juan could not tell whether it was by way of greeting or whether it was the password for the day, so impersonally were the words uttered.

Fray Juan reached the elevated portico to find Abbas so surrounded by officials that he could not go near him. Most of the officials were new favorites whom the friar did not recognize. Only Allah Verdi Khan's status had not changed. The sirdar's position, never explicit in name, was explicit in fact. The Georgian seemed neither to rise nor to fall; his place was never close nor distant, but always mysterious, just as his face was a mask. He glanced at Fray Juan now with his customary look of veiled amusement, as though there were something ridiculous about the friar's presence here—and the friar would have agreed with him.

The crowd about Abbas parted a little, and now the Shah was visible in his court apparel. It had become increasingly elaborate: his gaba was of emerald-colored satin embroidered with seed pearls; he wore trousers of crimson; about his neck were several chains of heavy gold with jeweled pendants—one of them the gift of the Spanish king —and upon his head was his crimson turban, loftier than ever, with the familiar aigrette and emerald brooch.

Abbas now noticed the friar. Fray Juan bowed and offered his greetings, and Abbas murmured something by way of reply. At that moment there was a fanfare, and the minister of court advanced to the balustrade. Through the crier, he addressed the crowd below:

"Abbas Safi Safavid, Shahinshah of Iran, the Protector of the Faithful, the Sun of the East, the Majesty of the Kingdoms, God's Presence, Lord of the Two Seas and the Lands Between, gives greetings to his loyal subjects and deigns now to hear their supplications and petitions."

A hush fell over the plaza, and the Shah's chief vizier—now Shams-ed-Din Agha, formerly a merchant dealing in lambskins—came forward and prostrated himself before Abbas, kissing the Shah's foot. He stood and said in a loud voice:

"Imperial Majesty! As your humble slave, to whom you have deigned to entrust the affairs of your capital during your absence, I beg to lay before you my life, and to bring you word that your subjects, from the meanest porter to the highest grandee, hold you in august reverence, and that among them their chief and highest desire, after that for your long life, is that you now remain in their midst, nor depart again. What is your will?"

All this was repeated by the crier for the benefit of the crowd below.

Abbas gave a nod. His eyes were lackluster, indifferent. His jowls, the friar remarked, had grown flabby, and there was a looseness of the skin at the throat. The monarch now indicated that he would hear the petitions. Several of these were of importance to the people of Isfahan: one was for the repair of the ancient and famous Jumma Masjid, which had been damaged by the recent earth tremors; another concerned the division of water from a newly built channel; and still another was for relief from the recently imposed house tax. The Shah was conciliatory, and his decisions were received with huzzas of satisfaction from the crowd.

Everything was going smoothly—too smoothly. The friar's attention, wandering over the scene, was caught by the lean figure of a palace eunuch issuing from the Pearl Palace, on the distant side of the plaza. This, the friar remembered, was the palace in which Khuda-bandeh had been confined since his blinding. The eunuch approached with a diffidence in contrast to the customary insolence of the palace servitors, and made his way to the Ali Gapou. The expression on his face, when he appeared at the door to the antechamber in the rear, was that of a bearer of ill tidings. Unable to catch the eye of the courtiers, who were too shrewd to be involved in the disaster, whatever it was, the eunuch turned appealingly to the friar. The Carmelite thought swiftly, and went over and plucked Allah Verdi Khan by the sleeve. The sirdar glanced around and nodded for the eunuch to approach.

There was an exchange of whispers. The sirdar's expression remained enigmatic, but his hand went to the hilt of his scimitar. He turned to the dais and fell on his knees before the Shah. In all his years in Persia, Fray Juan could not remember ever having seen Allah Verdi Khan on his knees. Until this moment he alone among all the court had never knelt to the Shah. But he was on his knees now, and he would not rise, so that Abbas must bend over to hear what he said.

A frightful change came over the monarch. His face turned livid and puffed as though he had been struck with a stone. And then he uttered the scream of one who has been mortally wounded, a single word issuing from his slavering lips:

"Fatima!"

The matter was no longer a secret. Sham-ed-Din Agha rushed to the railing, and cried in a loud voice, "The audience is over!"

Abbas had risen to his feet, but his strength had gone from him, and he swayed dazedly, his face yellow and his eyes rolling. His personal guard—an innovation in the form of a gigantic Negro—stepped to his side and assisted him to the staircase. As he passed by Fray Juan, and his glassy eyes came to rest on the friar, the Shah recovered himself momentarily. Shaking off the Negro, he stood swaying before the Carmelite.

"Ah," he gasped, "your God has taken his vengeance."

"Your Majesty—" exclaimed Fray Juan earnestly, but Abbas turned away and, leaning on the arm of the guard, staggered down the steps.

That night the news was all over Isfahan. Khudabandeh Mirza, in revenge upon his father, had sent for his little daughter Fatima, and as she rushed into his embrace the crazed, blind prince had plunged a dagger into her heart.

PART TEN

The Martyrdom

I

Jafar's keen ear for news was sometimes helpful. It was he who now brought the Carmelite word that Abbas, to divert public resentment against him for having mutilated his son, was throwing the blame upon the Christians. The story he had set afloat was that Khudabandeh Mirza had been indulging in an orgiastic Christian rite and that to purify his house the Shah had had him blinded.

Jafar urged the friars not to ring their bell until popular feelings had settled. For some time Fray Juan debated the matter with himself before discussing it with the others. In the end, they decided upon the course of discretion, and the bell, that had rung daily ever since it had been installed the year before, was silent.

There was another reason for heeding Jafar's counsel: the Ten Days of Moharram had begun. This was the most solemn festival in the Moslem Shia calender, commemorating the martyrdom of the Imam Hussein. This year, it was announced, the back beating and the head cutting that for many years had been forbidden by the Shah as barbaric and inflammatory would again be permitted.

For nine days the recitation of the offices and the celebration of Masses were drowned by the wailing from the streets as the processions of the back beaters passed. Mingled with the intoxicated shouting of the crowds could be heard the unnerving *swish, swish* of the steel whips as they circled in the air and came down in unison upon the bared backs of the flagellants. On the Tenth Day the processions of back beaters gave way to the head cutters. All morning long, until the sun reached its zenith, the air was filled with the sound of wailing as the procession of head cutters passed through the crowds that lined the streets. The monotonous threnody of a continually repeated "*Shah Hussein, Wah Hussein,*" degenerated into a pounding "*Shahsy Wahsy, Shahsy Wahsy,*" chanted in time to the thud of unsheathed swords upon naked heads.

Within the Carmelite house the friars recited the offices almost in shouts, but even their greatest concentration could not quite shut out the din. They seemed to be on the edge of an immense sacrificial fire into which people were throwing themselves in paroxysms of ecstasy and hate; one could almost smell the burning of flesh. The overcast of tension seemed at any moment about to break into a deluge of released passions; the cries that arose were like a universal imprecation, monotonously repeated, like the throbbing of a drum: "Kill the heretics; slay the unbelievers!"

The murderers of the Imam Hussein had not been Christians but fellow Moslems, hated Sunnis who denied the succession of the Caliphate through the Imams. As there were no Sunnis nearer than the Ottoman frontier, and as fanatical emotions demanded an object, it was not long before the cry was raised against the Armenians.

The night passed. The Carmelites were unable to sleep, but morning came at last and there had been no disturbance in the Maidan-i-Amir quarter. Fray Juan learned from Jafar that the Armenians had not been molested. Mysteriously, miraculously it seemed, just as the frenzy of the populace reached a climax and a movement toward the bridges to Julfa started, troops of grim-faced, mail-clad Qizilbashies appeared at all the approaches and sternly, sharply, turned the crowds away. Qizilbashies had also taken up positions at the head of the street leading to the *House of God and Jesus Mary.*

It was whispered, though without confirmation, that Allah Verdi Khan had posted these guardians of the peace without having consulted the Shah—perhaps even contrary to the Shah's wishes.

After a few days, when the volatile passions of the populace had evaporated and quiet had returned to the city, the troops were withdrawn and shortly afterward the Carmelites again resumed the ringing of their oversized camel bell.

One evening, after Complin, when the lights of the house were darkened, and only the candles in the ruby cups before the image of the Virgin were burning, there was knocking at the gate. Javan, who answered, came to Fray Juan's cell.

"The convert Abdallah Massih wishes to speak to you," he whispered.

The friar was instantly awake and went out to meet the convert.

Abdallah Massih appeared to be his usual gracious, courteous, contained self. He inquired as to the friar's health and apologized profusely for having aroused him from slumber.

"You are always welcome," the friar said, and added, "especially when you are in need."

Abdallah Massih was surprised that his troubled state of mind was so obvious, and came to the point.

"I think it would be desirable for me to remove my family from my native land," he said.

Fray Juan sensed the immense reserve in the simple statement, and his heart sank within him even as a dozen questions rose to his lips. Controlling himself, he waited for the convert's explanation. The former mullah bowed his head.

"I am prepared to bear the blows that I see coming," he said, "but should I not consider those who have followed me along the path that I have taken?"

"What are the perils that you foresee?" asked the friar.

"It is true that the city is quiet," said the convert, "but my position is different. As a former mullah my apostasy is not kindly taken by the Moslem hierarchy. As with the Apostle Paul—with whom I am audacious to make comparison—a band of young men have sworn not to put razor to the head until I and my household be dead. This oath was taken during Moharram, but they have been hindered in executing it by the military watch that Allah Verdi Khan posted at all the entrances to Julfa. As their beards grow steadily longer so their patience grows steadily shorter. Today the watch was restored to the civil police—and you know what those fellows are. It is my conclusion that I should leave the city."

Fray Juan marveled at his convert's self-possession in the circumstances. In Abdallah Massih's long, intellectual face there was no fear written; the look was rather that of a scholar seriously explaining to another the necessity for a hard decision he has made. Fray Juan felt a strength emanating from the convert, on which he himself was drawing, for the thought of this man leaving him, with whom he had spent so many profitable hours in translating the Scriptures into Persian, left him with a sense of personal disaster that for a moment overshadowed his proper anxiety for the convert's safety.

"Where would you go?" he asked.

"No place in Persia is safe for me," said Abdallah Massih slowly, weighing his words. He seemed deliberately to avoid any inference, any inflection, that would indicate the least anxiety on his part. "I would go to Hormuz, or perhaps to Hind, where I may be able to find work with the merchants who have trade with Persia."

Fray Juan nodded.

"I approve your decision," he said, and indeed it seemed to him the only wise one. "I shall give you a letter to Father Vincent, in our convent in Hormuz."

The friar went to the cabinet and took out paper and ink, but his heart sickened as he wrote. He thought of the break it would be in the ranks of the Christian brotherhood that had been collected around the house of the Carmelites in Isfahan. Abdallah Massih, his wife Arzima, and his son Sohrab—together they represented nearly half the number of converts, and more than half the friar's hopes. His affection for them poured out in the letter which he addressed to Fray Vincent. Finishing, he handed it to Abdallah Massih to read, then sealed it and returned it to the convert, who carefully folded it within his turban.

After they had prayed and sung a hymn together, Fray Juan escorted the convert to the gate and gave him a blessing. The two men embraced. Abdallah Massih cautiously opened the gate and peered out. Almost at once he closed it again.

"Is there another door?" he asked, with the same courteous and self-possessed manner as before. "It appears that someone is waiting for me in the alley."

"May I show such calm in danger!" exclaimed the friar to himself, and said aloud, "Fool that I am, I should have guessed. Come—this way."

He led the convert around the house and into the garden until they came to the water channel that supplied the vineyard.

"This ditch leads under the garden wall to the Hezar Jareeb," the friar explained. "Fortunately, the water was diverted a few days ago to permit its being cleaned, and you will be able to pass under the wall without difficulty. Once you are in the royal gardens you will be able to pass unobserved, I am sure."

Leading the way, the friar crawled under the wall and showed the convert the direction to follow. They silently embraced again, and then Abdallah Massih moved away. In the starlight his form was visible against the silvery trunks of the poplar trees and against the tawny soil of the garden. Presently he was lost from view. Fray Juan stood for a long time, gazing into the immensity of the night overhead, at the countless stars that wheeled in the clear Persian sky, and he thought of the inscrutable wisdom of God in having sent Fray Vincent to Hormuz so long ago, that he might establish there a refuge to which this brother in Christ could flee in his need.

II

It was Thursday morning after Ash Wednesday, and a mist, such as occasionally arose from the river in winter, was creeping through the streets as Fray Juan let himself out of the gate and made his way toward the Caravanserai of Shah Ismail.

The Caravanserai of Shah Ismail had a deep hold upon the friar's affections. During the years when he had lived there with Grigor and Javan, he had come to know many of the merchants and charvadars. The big arbaab Ali Askar was a particular and devoted friend. After moving to the house in the Maidan-i-Amir quarter, the friar came back to the caravanserai at least once a week to revisit his friends, to make new acquaintances, and to take every opportunity offered to give witness to his faith and to explain it to those who wished to learn more.

There was astute missionary strategy in this. The Caravanserai of Shah Ismail was not the largest of the eighteen hundred that Isfahan boasted, but it was one of the most important. Here it was that the caravans from abroad generally unloaded their wares, and here one could get first the latest news from distant parts. A better place to preach the Gospel could not be found. The Word, dropped here and there, was like the seed burrs that are picked up by the camels in their wool as they journey; one never knew in what distant land the holy Seed might be dropped, there to sprout as the beginning of a new congregation of the faithful. The thought of the possibilities that lay within one uttered word—of how its echo might mingle with the whisper of the sands in some Arab encampment, with the rush of wind on the high Pamirs, with the rustling of palm trees on the coasts of Coromandel—filled the friar with a renewed sense of his God-given mission.

The day began early in the caravanserai, and Fray Juan liked to get there before dawn, for it seemed to him that the Word he had to offer, like the cucumbers hawked by the peddlers, had an added freshness and appeal in the dewy hours of morning.

A pallid moon was dropping among the tree tops and the shapes of cupolas and turrets were indistinct in the gossamer mist that floated in the streets. The friar knew the way by heart, and though he could not see the high ogive archway to the caravanserai he knew that he was approaching it by the mingled odors of spice and dung that rose in the street and by the muffled outcries and the clangor of bells.

As he drew near the gate a huge figure in a cloak stepped from the shadows.

"Reverence—"

"Ali Askar!"

"Not so loud," said the big arbaab, and drew the friar into the deeper shadow of a niche. "I have been waiting for you. Your life is in danger."

The friar's literal mind took command of the situation, for Ali Askar was plainly unstrung.

"More than usual?" asked the friar. He could think of nothing that had happened of late to inflame fanaticism against the Carmelites.

"Yes," panted the arbaab, finding difficulty speaking. "News from Gambrun. Terrible news, that came but an hour ago by a friend who rode in with the courier. By mid-morning it will be all over the city." Ali Askar took the friar by the arms and held him so, peering into his face. Fray Juan could smell the sweetish, sickly odor of opium, and it occurred to him that the arbaab was under its influence. "You must leave while you can," Ali Askar almost hissed into his ear.

"What is this news from Gambrun?"

"You have a friend by the name of Abdallah Massih?"

"Yes, and more than a friend, a Christian brother."

"That is the one," breathed Ali Askar. "He was caught crossing the frontier and was killed."

"God forbid!" Fray Juan sank down, groping for the curbing. He thought of Abdallah Massih's family, so far away. What could he do? "And his family?" he asked, fearing Ali Askar's answer.

"They too. All captured, all executed. Abdallah and his son sewed up in the skins of asses and impaled. The woman beheaded."

Ali Askar was growing impatient; he stooped down to help the friar to his feet. "You have no time for tears," he muttered, as he felt the shaking of the friar's shoulders. "You must be going."

"What band of fanatics did this work?" asked Fray Juan.

"*Aziz darvish barader-i-man*—my dear darvish brother," exclaimed the arbaab, now really impatient, "do you not understand? By orders of the Shah, which means that Abbas has gone mad again, and that now it is your life that is in peril. You must flee at once."

Indecision gripped the friar like a chill, leaving him both hot and cold. Yet had he not faced down the Shah before, and could he not face him down again? Abbas could thwart the spread of the Word; but the friar's calling was here to preach the Gospel, and preach it he would.

Fray Juan turned toward the caravanserai gate, but Ali Askar caught him firmly by the arm.

"The letter, the letter," the arbaab was moaning. "Will you not understand?"

"What letter?"

"To the Portuguese governor of Hormuz that you sent by your convert. It was found, and the sirdar Teymour charges you with treason to the Shah. That is the news which the courier tells me is whispered all over Shiraz."

"There was no letter to the Portuguese," the friar protested, "and there is no treason. Why," he demanded, "should there be treason in any case?"

"Since Gambrun is under siege by the Shah's troops, and Hormuz by the English ships—"

Fray Juan interrupted. "Ali Askar," he said quietly, "do you imagine that I, as an envoy to his Majesty, if not as a Christian priest, would engage in treasonable correspondence against the Empire?"

"My friend, my dear friend, my darvish," pleaded the arbaab, and his voice became like the shrilling of a pipe, "I care not what you have written. I only know what the report is in Shiraz. Praise God it is not yet news here, for the moment it is your life will not be worth a wormy date. You know the Shah's sensitivity about such things. Will you be warned?"

Fray Juan was sobered.

"I trust I have good sense, and can follow good counsel. What do you suggest?"

"There are horses ready in the caravanserai. There is a caravan trail across the Zagros that takes you into the Bakhtiari country. No, it is not the one into which Khudabandeh Mirza was betrayed, but known to only a few. From there you can go down to Basra and take ship home, or cross the domain of the Ottoman to Aleppo. But you must leave at once. Half the escape is in the start."

It was all so incomprehensible that Fray Juan was in a daze. Why should his life be in danger, and even if so, should he flee? He had no experience in flight. Flight was not among his instinctive defenses against danger. His defense was the armor of salvation which was trust in God for his immortal soul.

The dawn was breaking, and activity in the caravanserai was commencing. A camel caravan lumbered through the high gate into the street, the bells filling the air with a great din. When the sound died down the friar gave his decision.

"No," he said with finality, "this is no time to run away. But I must go and speak to the brothers. I shall remember your solicitude, Ali Askar, in my thanks to God for His goodness to me through you."

Fray Juan turned away, and the arbaab recognized the firmness of his purpose. Perhaps it was his kismet. Nevertheless, he called after him, "Remember me if you do decide on flight, that I may have horses ready, and a man to show you the road."

III

Fray Juan was met by Javan when he returned to the house. He greeted the young man with forced ease.

"*Pedar*—Father," Javan said, as though he might be petitioning Heaven itself, "I have a request."

Mechanically Fray Juan took up his breviary.

"Yes, Javan?"

"*Pedar*," Javan repeated and then seemed lost for words, "I . . . I . . . wish to become a Christian. Will you baptize me?"

Fray Juan dropped his breviary with a clatter. His mind was suddenly far, far away. So long ago he had given up. Years ago he had searched his soul, many times he had examined himself to discover where and how he had failed to understand and interest the loyal Javan in the faith. So many failures. It was strange . . . for the youth at their very first meeting had all but thrown himself at the foot of the cross.

"Baptize?" he echoed.

"Yes," exclaimed Javan, finding speech. "For fifteen years I have been your servant, and now I would also be the servant of Christ."

Fray Juan felt his throat tighten. To gain time to collect his thoughts, he asked, "You would now, after all these years, accept the Christ and the cross?"

"I would," said Javan firmly.

Enlightenment suddenly dawned on the friar.

"You have just returned from the bazaar?" he asked.

"Yes."

The friar stiffened. "I see," he said. "Come to me after this trouble has passed, and if then you be so minded, I will examine you for baptism."

But Javan was suddenly on his knees before Fray Juan; his fingers clutched the friar's habit; in his look was terror and supplication.

"No, now before it is too late," he pleaded. "I would be one with you in Christ, and then I shall know that whatever happens, whether we be parted and separated, yet we cannot be separated, for we are together in Christ."

Fray Juan marveled at the young man's grasp of the absolute reality and meaning of the Christian faith. He hesitated no longer; he had no right to deny the boon of the faith to one who so sincerely sought it.

"Come then," he said, "for time is precious."

Taking an earthenware jug of water from its niche, the friar led Javan into the chapel, where the brethren were still gathered, assembled in silent adoration of the Mysteries, and interrupting their meditations he called upon them to witness the sacrament. After asking Javan if he had a Christian name by which he wished to be called, and being told it was Yusuf, Fray Juan dispensed with the liturgy. Pouring water into his hand, he placed it on Javan's head, making the sign of the cross as he did so, and intoning, "I baptize thee, Javan, whom I now name Yusuf, the faithful, in the name of the Father, and of the Son, and of the Holy Ghost."

Fray Juan had hardly finished speaking these words when they heard the sound of horsemen in the street, and the sharp blow of a mace on the gate, accompanied by the cry, "Open, in the name of the Shah!"

Fray Juan himself answered. Opening the gate he saw his old acquaintance the lieutenant Afsar Malek, sitting stonily on his horse, his expression as grim as a dungeon.

"*Salaam aleikum*—Peace be to you," said the friar, using the customary Moslem greeting. "It is always good to see you, whatever the occasion."

"You speak boldly, for you know not the occasion," said the lieutenant without warmth. "I have orders to place you under arrest, and to close and seal the doors of your house."

"I am prepared to accept arrest, though perhaps you can tell me with what I am charged. As for the house, since it is occupied by several of us and is dedicated to the service of God by royal permission, I must object to its being closed."

"You do not understand. All the Christians within are placed under arrest, and must remain within the house, which I shall close and seal for your safekeeping. Have you any Moslems within?"

"There are none."

"I mean, have you any Moslem apostates within?"

Fray Juan felt the blood draining from his face. He had not expected this. Fortunately, the gardener Zamdar, who had lodgings elsewhere, had not yet come to work. He prayed that Zamdar would be late. Then he thought of Javan, and the spirit went out of him, but he answered the lieutenant firmly.

"That," he said, "is something you must discover for yourself."

Afsar Malek dismounted and entered. Fray Juan assembled the household in the refectory, where the officer questioned each in turn. There was no doubt as to Balthazar and Dimas, who were Firenghi and obviously Christians by birth. As for Grigor, the lieutenant was not sure, but after many proddings satisfied himself that Grigor, as a Nestorian, had never been a Moslem. Javan was ignored. Malek whispered a few words to his men and they went about the house closing the cells and affixing the royal seal to the doors. The chapel was also sealed, but the refectory and the kitchen were left open.

"You will all remain in this room," he now announced, "and if you have occasion you may go into the garden, but all the rooms are to remain sealed, as well as the gate."

"Will you tell me now with what we are charged?" asked Fray Juan.

"My darvish, I do not know," said the lieutenant, "and if I knew, it would not be my business to inform you." He came a little closer to the friar, so that his men, who were standing in the courtyard, might not hear, and added in a low voice, "From all I have gathered, however, it is serious—treason to the Shah."

He turned almost at once to Javan.

"Why are you here?" he demanded, and made an impatient gesture of dismissal. "Begone!"

Fray Juan seconded the injunction with a furious nodding of his head.

"I am one of these," said Javan quietly. "I belong here."

"What mean you?"

"I am a Christian," said Javan, and a little lilt crept into his voice, like that in the voice of a bride who says aloud for the first time, "I have a husband." He seemed entranced by the words and repeated, "I am a Christian."

"You wear the turban," exclaimed the lieutenant impatiently. "What madness is this?"

Javan adopted an insouciant attitude.

"Is it madness, you think?" he demanded of the lieutenant, with a manner that recalled to the friar in a flash of remembrance that lighted the darkness of the moment, his first meeting with Javan in the bazaar of the gach sellers. "Perhaps it is," continued the young man, "but why not? Perhaps I am one who has stood on the edge of a pool too long, and at last have dared to plunge. In any case, it is not bad. I recommend you try it."

Afsar Malek looked at Javan with a gathering comprehension. "I have traveled with this darvish," he remarked, "and see the reason for your foolishness." He shrugged his shoulders. "Nevertheless, I feel sorry for you, my friend, for I am afraid you will soon be cut off, like a cucumber plucked from a vine." He signaled to one of his men to take Javan into custody.

Fray Juan wanted to cry out in protest against this outrage, but at that moment he was diverted by a familiar sound in the street. Such had been the rapidity of events that the rising sun was still entangled in the almond trees and Zamdar the gardener was just coming to work. He was singing a *Laudamus* in his quavering treble. Fray Juan shouted to him to flee, but it was too late: already he was entering the gate. One of the guards laid hands on him and challenged him; he promptly confessed that he was a Christian convert and was taken into custody.

At this the friar rushed up to the lieutenant in a frenzy.

"Afsar Malek—*Saldan!*" he cried out supplicatingly.

"Yes, my darvish?"

"These men are guiltless of wrongdoing. It is I who have trespassed the law in baptizing them. Release them, and carry me off to prison instead."

Afsar Malek regarded the friar admiringly.

"You speak true to your preaching," he said, "but it cannot be. Perhaps something worse is reserved for you."

"Fear not, Father," spoke up Javan, "'twill be nothing. A few days of fasting in a dungeon, perhaps—no more, I assure you. And if more, why, 'tis soon done. Eh, Zamdar, what say you? You have no quaking, have you? Speak up, man, tell the *kasha* how it is."

The gardener was a man of little speech.

"What shall I say, Father Juan? I have never had my head cut off, but it must be soon over, and not so bad. Have I been a good gardener, Father?"

"Oh, Zamdar," burst out the friar, "such as the Lord saw in Adam before the fall."

" 'Twill soon be time to transplant the geraniums," said Zamdar reflectively, with a kind of anxious perplexity, as of one starting on a journey and not certain of his return by a stated day.

"You can smell spring in this chill!" exclaimed Javan. "What a nose you have! For myself, I see a freeze coming. I can feel the cold on my neck."

"No, no freeze," protested Zamdar. "No killing freeze in any case —not here, at any rate. Now, in Hamadan, where I tended the kitchen garden of his Highness the Nizam-ul-Mulk, I never sowed radish seed until Noo Rooz, but in this climate you may do so before the middle of Esfand. Well, let us be going, for I know how these judges are, and they grow irate if one delays the officers. I remember once, before I was saved, having taken a quantity of opium, and having fallen upon a police officer that had annoyed me. That did not go down well. One must cater to these fellows." He turned to Fray Juan. "What thanks I owe to you, Kasha, for releasing me from that bondage!"

"Thanks be to God rather," said Fray Juan, his voice choking.

"Now, should there be a delay in my return," Zamdar went on, "you will not forget that the geraniums and the potted oleander will need water shortly? Not much, little more than a cupful to each pot save for the oleander, which can drink a bit more."

Fray Juan threw his arms around the gardener's shoulders.

"Zamdar," he cried, "do not be deceived. You may not return. Are you ready to die?"

A look of surprise filled the gnarled, ancient face.

"Why not?" the old man asked. "Have I not been preserved beyond my time? For I was well-nigh dead when I was in my opium dreams, and all the years since then have been a free gift of God. Besides, I have buried too many seeds and made too many cuttings not to know that that which is dead is not dead if within it is life, and now I know that within me is planted a life which shall never die. No, Kasha, this troubles me not. Be at peace."

But Fray Juan was not at peace. He could say nothing, and to hide his anguish, he embraced the two men, Javan last, and then, grasping at straws, begged the officer to unseal the chapel and allow him to administer the viaticum. But Afsar Malek was adamant, stating that he had been under orders to forbid any incantations, lest his men be bewitched, and for that reason had sealed the sacred chambers.

He led the two converts away, and his men then barred and sealed the gate. Fray Juan stood like a man in a trance, incapable of movement. He tried to utter a prayer, but his lips remained motionless and his thoughts whirled in a chaotic void.

Fray Dimas was whispering in his ear: "I have here the Host and the elements and the sacramental vessels which I was able to spirit from the chapel while the officers were sealing the cells."

Fray Juan turned and regarded the young friar. In the younger man's face was the expression of triumphant satisfaction of a Trojan warrior who in the midst of the holocaust and the sack of his city has rescued the image of Apollo from his burning temple. That the young man was right, that his sense of values was correct, and that he had done the appropriate thing was a proposition to which all Fray Juan's training and beliefs gave assent; yet at the moment the Wafer that was God under the appearance of bread was unimportant; Fray Juan wanted to rush headlong into the flames.

"Would it please the father prior to celebrate Mass, for it would be comforting to the souls of all of us?" Fray Dimas asked solicitously.

Fray Juan could not speak, but nodded mechanically.

They retired to the refectory, and Fray Dimas removed the crucifix from the refectory wall and set it on the table for an altar. There were no vestments, since the vestry had also been sealed, but they proceeded without them. Fray Juan dipped his fingers in a bowl of water and sprinkled the drops on his companions. After the *In nomine* and the *Judica me*, with Fray Dimas giving the antiphonal responses as minister, Fray Juan uttered the *Confiteor* and then gave the Absolution.

But whatever release the others experienced, Fray Juan felt no such remission; his soul remained heavy within him. This was the sacrament that for sixteen hundred years, in various forms and for uncounted millions—those facing the morning sunshine and the day's work, and those facing death in horrible forms—had been a solace and a source of strength. This was the eternal, recurring Mystery that would continue to be enacted for a thousand years to come on untold millions of altars, until the seventh trumpet should sound and

the kingdoms of this world become the kingdom of the Lord Christ.
But today the sacrament was powerless to soothe the friar's troubled
spirit, to relieve the bitter sense of sin and failure that was like an
acid eating into his very heart. It was powerless to still the voice of
reproach that kept leaping up like a flame. "O God!" the friar
moaned inaudibly, "Why did you give these children into my keeping,
to let them be snatched from before my eyes? Why must their blood
be upon my hands? Why have you made me as the servant that was
set to filling the basket with water?"

IV

"Recant, recant," pleaded Afsar Malek, who had had so much of
the pushing crowd and the screaming mullahs that he would have
been glad to turn his pike outward. At the same time he felt a cold
contempt for these Christians who offered no resistance, who did
not even return the obscenities of their accusers. The whole affair
had become repulsive to him; his sympathies were neither with the
crowd nor with the victims.

Besides Javan and Zamdar, the Shah's officers had arrested the two
porters, Baghir and Mahboob, and in addition they had seized a
little merchant from Hormuz, a Hindu who had been baptized by
the Jesuits of Agra. The widow Jamileh they did not bother with, and
Jafar they did not find, for he had hid himself well in a great heap
of stinking cabbage at the bottom of the greengrocers' bazaar. The
five made, however, sufficient hecatomb. Abbas sent criers throughout the city calling upon all the Faithful to assemble and stone the
apostates, and by mid-day the city was in an uproar more frenetic than
at the mourning for Hussein during the Ten Days of Moharram.
Abbas himself did not come into the city, remaining instead at his
Serishabad camp, but he allowed the most fanatic of the mullahs to
have their will.

The five victims were brought to the Maidan-i-Shah, followed by a
howling mob. From the parapet before the great mosque mullahs
had been haranguing the crowd already assembled. Here the victims
were released to face the unleashed frenzy of the pack. Cries went
up from all sides: "Recant! . . . Recite the Creed! . . . Death to

the Christians!" But the five men remained dumb, and stones began to fly. The poor Hindu fell at the first blow, bleeding from a long gash from his forehead to his chin.

For a moment the crowd was subdued by the sight of the fallen victim's blood, and then a wizened shoemaker, who spent his days cobbling under a plane tree near the Madresseh, croaked shrilly:

"Gut the renegades bewitched by the barefooted devil!"

Baghir and Mahboob were bent over the bleeding Hindu. Zamdar had his hands clasped and his eyes were lifted to heaven while his lips moved soundlessly in prayer, and on his face was an expression of contented unawareness of his surroundings.

Another stone was thrown. It struck Zamdar on the head and felled him.

Javan faced the crowd defiantly.

"Kill us!" he cried. "Kill us! But we die Christians!"

"Gut him! Gut the apostate!" screamed the little shoemaker, and the cry was taken up by the crowd.

The mob now took control, and Afsar Malek could not say who were the actual perpetrators of what followed. There was no leader, no directing mind, but only what seemed to the lieutenant to be an unseen genius, the Spirit of Evil hovering over the plaza with beating wings, moving with a susurration in the air, a grimacing jinni, whispering obscenities in the secret ear, a savage upward thrust—and the mob was upon its victims like wolves upon a flock of sheep.

The five Christians scattered and ran amid a hail of stones; one by one they fell, were beaten senseless, were stoned until they lay lifeless on the ground of the plaza, their blood soaking into the earth. All but Javan.

Javan had been swept up and carried to the nearby parapet. A lance, snatched from an unwary Qizilbashie, was affixed upright to one of the merlons, and to the hysterical screaming of the crowd Javan was hoisted into the air and forced upon the pike. He uttered a cry of agony and revolt as his body settled down upon the point and the point itself issued from his abdomen; and then, as the pain passed, and numbness took its place, and thought became incoherent, words issued from his slavering lips which only those immediately below could catch: "*Dominus . . . Deo gratias . . . Oremus . . . Kyrie Eleison . . .*"

Presently the straining ceased. The head lolled to one side. The eyes, open and glazed, stared down at the crowd below. To Lieutenant Afsar Malek the young man's dying was passing strange, for after that first outburst his face had mirrored a marvelous gentleness and contentment utterly unlike the agonized contortion so common on the faces of those who died on the field of battle. . . .

V

In Armenian Julfa shops were shuttered and doors barred. The streets lay silent and deserted, but, as during Moharram, strong detachments of Qizilbashies at all the bridges to Julfa kept the Moslems to the Isfahan side of the river.

Qizilbashies also barred the entrances to the street that led to the *House of God and Jesus Mary*, but the cries of the mobs surging through the avenues and alleys beyond floated over the walls like a miasmic dust. How soon the friars would be called forth to face the wrath of the mob no one could say.

When Fray Juan considered the question of his personal danger, his spirit revived. There had been a time in the friar's life when the thought of dying was governed by his emotions, and was surcharged with fear and anxiety—but that was long ago. For many years now he had been able to take a rational view of death, at least so far as his own death was concerned. He had come to view dying as the greatest event he would ever experience next to his birth, and he had no desire to run away from it. He prayed, of course, the petition of the liturgy to be "delivered from *sudden* death," but that was simply that he might have opportunity properly to prepare himself for the event, as a child for his first Communion, as a postulant for his initial vows. He wished to enter upon the great occasion with faculties alert, and with soul in readiness. And so, as he prepared himself for the events of the day by prayer and fasting and the sacraments of the Church, he prepared himself in like fashion for the great moment when he would pass through the portal of this life into Purgatory.

For Fray Dimas and Fray Balthazar, however, Fray Juan felt that the passage might not be so easy. They showed no panic, but he thought he detected signs of uneasiness. They were young men; the humors of youth still flowed strong within them: they slept soundly, they had good appetites, the smell of a well cooked porridge caused their nostrils to expand. . . . These young friars deserved to live. But if they were to die the death of martyrdom, they must know the meaning of it.

In the refectory were a number of devotional books, for it was a rule with the friars to eat in silence while one of their number read from the Scriptures or some other comforting work. Fray Juan now took one of these volumes from the shelf, and assembling his companions he began to read. The volume was from a collection of the writings of the Apostolic Fathers; it opened with the account of the first martyrdom after that of St. Stephen for which an eyewitness report had been preserved—that of Polycarp, Bishop of Smyrna during the first half of the second century:

From the Church that dwells as a tented pilgrim in Smyrna to the Church in pilgrimage at Philomelium, and to all the faithful everywhere—mercy and peace be unto you through the love of God the Father and of our Lord Jesus Christ:

We write to you, Brethren, of the death and martyrdom of the blessed Polycarp, who by glorious witness to the faith confounded the adversary and sealed the bottle of wrath, and put an end to the persecution of the Church. . . .

The story of the fortitude of this eighty-six-year-old man who resisted the pleas of the proconsul that he swear "by the genius of Caesar" and who allowed himself to be led to the stake and there burned alive, and whose serenity brought such humiliation upon his adversaries that further persecution of the Christians was abandoned, had a powerfully reassuring effect upon the friars; there was an immediate lightening of tension. They continued to read, by turns, throughout the day, interrupting the reading only for the observance of the canonical hours, and once to break their fast with a little wine and a palm's breadth of bread. They read the New Testament through, and began again on the lives of the martyrs: St. Polycarp, St. Laurence, St. Anthony. They lighted the lamps, and continued reading.

They were reading the life of St. Catherine when there was a scratching on the door. Fray Juan arose and went outside. There, within the shadow of the porch, loomed the huge form of Ali Askar. Fray Juan gripped him by the arm.

"How came you here?" he demanded in a whisper. "But that can wait. What of Javan and Zamdar and Jamileh and Jafar and Baghir and Mahboob? What has been happening in the city?"

"I do not know Jamileh and Jafar of whom you speak, but your young man Javan and the porters Baghir and Mahboob, and another of your house, an old man whom they called Zamdar, besides a fifth, a Hindu, have paid with their lives for their apostasy.

"And now you will be next, unless you flee at once. I have horses ready," he concluded urgently.

"How did they die?" asked Fray Juan. "Did they recant? Did they die bravely? Did they die in peace?"

"Answers to those questions I cannot give you, for I do not attend such affairs; but such news as passes through the caravanserai—and the talk is of nothing else—is that they died like men who were sure of Paradise, which is as no Moslem dies, willingly as he may surrender to the kismet written upon his forehead. But I, for one, never cared for such talk. Again I say, I have horses. Will you be wise and come, or do you also wish to show your entrails to the populace?"

"For myself, I could not leave any more than you could abandon your caravanserai before a band of marauding Afghans," replied the friar; "but I have three companions upon whom life still has some claim. Come with me and we will consult them."

In the refectory, Ali Askar made an impassioned speech to the friars and to the lay brother Grigor on the horrible fate that awaited them if they remained; he dwelt upon the ease of flight, the beauty and the delight of living, and upon the opportunities for other service that lay elsewhere. He proved to be quite an orator, and his appeal was most persuasive. Fray Juan was touched. Yes, life was sweet, he reflected; and his thoughts irresistibly traveled over the sweet and precious memories of the past. As he looked into the bearded, ferocious face of the arbaab he marveled at how the friendship between himself and Ali Askar had begun, and he whispered to himself a *Deo gratias* at the mysterious forces that sustained it.

In the end, however, the arbaab's appeal was futile. Not Dimas nor Balthazar nor Grigor was interested in escape. They too had somehow been captured by the eagerness to behold the angel of death garbed in white ready to lead them through the portal of life into Purgatory.

When Ali Askar had gone, however, all the serenity in the contemplation of death that the reading of the Scriptures and the Apostolic Fathers throughout the day had induced in Fray Juan suddenly
disappeared and gave way to revulsion, to an immense resentment
against circumstance, to a rebellion against the caprices of destiny.

It happened that the cupola was above the refectory, and that on
this account the bell rope hung down among the pots and pans. The
darkened eyes of the friar now rested on this rope, and a wild passion
possessed him. He rushed to the rope and leaned upon it with all
his might. The bell began pealing, and in the silence of the night the
friar thought its brazen voice must be rousing all Isfahan.

It was only a moment before the guard unsealed the gate and the
lieutenant hurried in demanding to know the meaning of the uproar
and why the prisoners had dared unseal the chapel. Fray Juan assured him that he had not tampered with the seals, and showed him
where the bell rope hung.

"Why should we not toll the bell for our dead?" Fray Juan demanded in turn. "Is that so barbarous as the head cutting that is
done among you for the martyrs?"

"I am not one to cut my head for the saints," replied Afsar Malek
scornfully, "and I assure you, my darvish, that I wept as much as a
man of my breed may at the sight of your young man impaled. He
died well, and had I had my way he would not have died at all but
would have been reserved for useful service to his Majesty, who needs
men of such stamp."

"And when will we be led out to make a spectacle at which you
may weep?" asked the friar with an asperity born of exhausted patience.

"When it pleases Abbas. No man can say more."

"Then take me to the Shah, that I may plead our case and demand
his verdict," cried the friar vehemently.

"That also is beyond my power," replied Afsar Malek, "for Abbas
has gone to Kandahar, to take up his quarrel with the Afghans."

VI

Abbas had indeed gone off to Kandahar, which his forces were besieging, and there were no further persecutions of the Christians; but neither was the guard removed from the convent of the Carmelites nor was any sign given of the Shah's intentions in regard to them.

And so began the long confinement. It could hardly be called an imprisonment, for confinement was of the tradition of the Discalced. With Balthazar and Dimas, at least, the course of events simply returned them to the contemplative life to which they had dedicated themselves in taking their monastic vows. They continued as before to observe the canonical hours, to celebrate Mass, to spend hours in meditation and in intercession for an errant, sinful humanity.

But with Fray Juan the restriction did not sit so easily. He had spent four years, off and on, in Russian prisons, but he had spent more years in court, the caravanserai, and the dusty streets of the city; it was difficult for him to adjust again to this hobbled life. He rejoiced that Balthazar and Dimas could keep the observances with such zeal and with such unconcern over their eventual fate: but for himself, if these were to be his last days, or his last weeks, or his last months, he must spend them in testimony, he must burn himself out, like a candle, in illuminating the darkness. It was for this, he now recognized clearly, that he had been called, that his temperament had been organized by nature from his birth—to preach the Gospel.

But his exaltation passed and a sense of horror returned as there arose before the friar's eyes the vision of Javan, and Abdallah Massih and his family, and Zamdar, and it seemed to him that their hands were lifted upward—was it in supplication, or imprecation?—and he asked himself again the question that tormented his soul: Had he baptized them in the name of the Father and of the Son and of the Holy Spirit, or in the name of Juan Thaddeus, and in the name of Thaddeus' pride, Thaddeus' ambition? When he appeared before the throne of God, would they stand there accusing him of having led them astray?

Fray Juan continued to ring the bell at the canonical hours; Afsar Malek permitted him to do so, finding no reason to forbid it, since his instructions had been only to seal the chapel and to deny the friars the use of their cells.

The lieutenant, in order to make sure that the friars were not circumventing the terms of their imprisonment, had investigated the observance, and finding it of curious interest, had remained. He tried to follow the ceremony, and not knowing the Christian forms of respect awkwardly bowed his head when the friars did, and presently he was kneeling when they knelt; but making the sign of the cross he found too complicated.

The ceremony seemed to illuminate for the lieutenant certain questions about the friars' mode of life that had puzzled him ever since the time he had escorted Fray Juan to the Shah's camp at Souj Boulak. Afsar Malek soon became a regular attendant at the observances. The lieutenant had the grizzled, forbidding expression of the veteran campaigner to whom the only reality is blood and death. His face was pock-marked, and a long yellow scar, gotten from a scimitar blow in battle with the Turks, ran from cheek to cheek beneath the nose. Afsar Malek was fairly young—in his late twenties—and far less cynical, far more simple, than he appeared.

Fray Juan had no sooner established his right to ring the bells and to hold the observances than he asked Afsar Malek whether his orders included a prohibition against receiving visitors.

"For," as the friar pointed out, "except for those confined in dungeons, it is the common rule that prisoners in cells or in camps may receive visitors from among their relatives and friends."

Afsar Malek was puzzled, and said he would have to consult his superiors. He consulted his superiors, who in turn consulted someone in court, and the reply came down that the friars were not to be denied visitors.

This news somehow spread, and the observances of the Carmelites began to attract such an attendance that at times the refectory was overfilled, and as warmer weather came services were occasionally held in the garden. Proof to the friar that the Holy Spirit was somehow at work came with the profession of faith of three men, who were baptized on the 24th of June, the Birthday of St. John the Baptist. One of these men was the lieutenant Afsar Malek himself.

In October Abbas returned to Isfahan from his Afghan campaign, and some days later Fray Juan was brought in custody to the Ali Gapou.

There the friar was held waiting in an antechamber for the better part of the morning while other, more important state business was transacted and couriers came and went. Finally he was escorted back to his house. Several times during the course of a fortnight the friar was summoned to court in this fashion. Eventually Abbas had him brought into his presence.

Abbas sat on the new ceremonial throne which he had had constructed for his solemn durbars—an elevated platform supported by six legs, with a railing and a high headboard at the back, the whole formed of ivory and gold with much inlay of precious and semi-precious stones and all made in the style set by the Moghul shahs at Agra and Lahore. Abbas sat in the middle of the throne, his feet tucked under him, one arm resting on a bolster thickly embroidered with pearls, his face a mask of ill concealed hostility, as if to emphasize further the gulf that he had placed between himself and the friar. Attending the hearing was a delegation of over a hundred of the leading mullahs, mujtahids, and ulemas, whose oversize turbans made a mass of mingled green and white and black along the wall. Nearer at hand were the Shah's principal officials and advisers, among them the Sirdar Allah Verdi Khan, his expression only slightly less hostile, it seemed to Fray Juan, than that of the Shah, but more self-possessed, more detached, as though the object of his hatred were not really worthy of his attention.

At least that was what Fray Juan read in the sirdar's expression, though it to seemed to him now, as it had often occurred to him, that the sirdar's face was a mask to hide a deeper feeling of hostility that existed within him—but toward what formidable antagonist the friar could not guess.

Abbas spoke to the friar in a remote tone:

"Out of my former regard and affection for you I have saved you unharmed this long from the just recompense of your evil, that I might hear from your own lips what excuse you have to offer for your betrayal of my trust."

He paused, apparently waiting for the friar to fall upon his face before him, as was the way of supplicants for Imperial clemency; but Fray Juan remained standing and silent, his eyes fixed upon the Shah.

"You may speak," said Abbas irritably.

"To what effect, your Majesty?" asked Fray Juan. "It is the custom in our Christian lands to tell the accused of what crimes he is charged, but to this moment I have been kept in ignorance."

"It is the custom, you say?" asked Abbas, showing interest, his curiosity overcoming momentarily his anger.

"It is also the custom and the rule that judges shall withhold judgment until they have heard the defense of the accused, neither pronouncing judgment nor making judgment in their minds," Fray Juan added.

Abbas scowled.

"These are words uttered only to delay," he said sourly. "The facts are well known, and it is effrontery to demand their reiteration. Is it not enough to wean my subjects from their proper faith, and to turn their allegiance from their lawful sovereign to your Roman Pope, but you must make my subjects the couriers for your treasonable correspondence with my enemies? And now you beg that I withhold judgment, as if I have not already exercised my clemency and saved your neck from the bowstring these nine months past. What have you to say?"

He seemed again to await the friar's response; but before Fray Juan could open his lips he was again speaking, and Fray Juan began to suspect that Abbas was not really convinced of what he was saying, and was working himself into a fury, either to satisfy some inner compulsion or to make a show before the assembled mullahs.

"How dare you go about preaching in my dominions, offering deliverance and salvation in the name of your religion, when you have not received my permission?" he demanded. "What reward is this for all the favors I have shown you since you have been within my borders —regarding you as a friend, holding you to my bosom as one cherished, seating you by my side as an equal, listening to your sermons and divagations, and commanding my court to attend your words? By what sorcery, by the aid of what jinni, have you succeeded so in deceiving me, in foisting yourself upon my court, laving me with your flattery?"

Abbas grew more and more impassioned. He continued excoriating the friar in increasingly violent language, at times half rising from his seat and gesticulating vehemently, until it seemed that he was in a state of possession. Finally, his hands trembling and his face livid, he concluded with, "What have you to say on your behalf?"

So much had been said, so much of mingled truth and falsehood, that Fray Juan did not know how to reply. If Abbas had been acting at first, Fray Juan was not so sure now. Abbas was in the state of intoxication that could become either maudlin or violent. Under the circumstances, Fray Juan concluded that the only policy was that of boldness.

"Your Majesty's strictures deserve no answer," he said firmly, "for your Majesty is aware of my calling as a Christian priest. I did not surrender my priesthood upon entering your Majesty's court. Further, I could not be faithful to your Majesty were I faithless to my calling. If I have done wrong by calling men to my Christian faith, by what right have you forcibly apostatized so many Christian Armenians whose freedom to worship according to their belief you promised to protect? Furthermore, I solemnly advise your Majesty that so long as I remain in your realm, with tongue in my head, I shall continue to proclaim this Christian faith to which I adhere."

A murmur of consternation filled the chamber, proceeding from the side where the mullahs were gathered. As for Abbas, the friar's outspokenness, which at other times he had accepted with respect or amusement or tolerance, now only intensified his hostility.

"You speak as one who lives in the past," he said bitterly. "By your treason you have lost all standing in my realm, and all the protection which you claim as an envoy of the Pope."

"What treason? I have committed no treason," said Fray Juan.

"How dare you stand before my face and deny your acts when you know that I have the evidence in your letters to the Portuguese governor?" exploded Abbas, again half rising from his seat as he shook his fist at the friar. He shouted for his keeper of the seal: "Assad Khan, fetch the letters!" The official must have anticipated this demand, for he opened his cloak, withdrew a silver letter tube that was thrust through his cummerbund, and presented it to the Shah. Abbas took out the letter and handed it to the friar. "Read that before this company and then tell me how you have dared to say such things against the man to whom you are indebted for hospitality these many years."

Fray Juan took the letter. It was the one he had written to Fray

Vincent commending to him the convert Abdallah Massih. He read it over quickly to familiarize himself with the contents, and then be-began a translation into Persian.

"To Father Vincent of St. Francis, Prior of the Convent of the Discalced Carmelites, Hormuz, greetings in the name of God our Father and the Lord Jesus Christ," he began, and as he went on he was aware of a disturbing silence throughout the chamber together with an irritated shifting of the Shah on his throne.

It was only a moment before Abbas cried out: "Liar, liar! Translate the letter as you have written it. Read to my court all the treason that boiled out of your heart in this letter."

"Your Majesty," protested Fray Juan quietly, "I am reading a correct Persian translation—so far as my knowledge of Persian permits—of what I have here written in Latin."

But Abbas was beside himself with rage.

"You lie to me! More, you insult me before my court by lying to me in their presence!" He spoke sharply to the saldan of the Qizil-bashies who commanded the palace guard. The saldan looked fright-ened, and his eyes turned to the sirdar Allah Verdi Khan, who com-manded all the Qizilbashies of the Empire.

The sirdar, who had been looking on with his usual enigmatic, unchanging expression, now stepped forward. He bowed obsequiously, and spoke to the Shah in a tone which an indulgent parent might use in rebuking a child, mingled with the slight impatience which a schoolmaster might show in correcting a favorite pupil.

"Your Majesty," he said, "this darvish has never been known to tell you other than the truth. And have you found in your realm any more honest? Why do you doubt his word now?"

The effect upon the Shah was immediate and magical. He subsided, as leaves in autumn settle when the wind dies; his expression grew sulky. He did not glance at his sirdar. There was a silence, and then the Shah muttered, "Continue your reading."

Fray Juan read on. When he had finished, Abbas sat for some time in silence. Finally he spoke:

"Since this is, as you say, the sum and substance of your communica-tion to those in Hormuz, and I find nothing treasonable in it, you are free to go, and I shall direct these men"—here he indicated with a gesture the congregation of the mullahs—"to molest you and your house no further."

After the audience, Fray Juan hoped to encounter the sirdar and express his gratitude for his intervention, but the sirdar had vanished and was nowhere to be found.

PART ELEVEN

The Final Decision

I

Fray Juan was walking along a quiet street leading from the Chahar Bagh to the Chandlers' Bazaar, where he was going to inspect a quantity of beeswax which was to be made into altar candles for the church. It was a day in mid-April; a brilliant sun shone in the clear sky and its rays were warm upon his back even as the air blowing down from the mountains was cool upon his cheek and invigorating to his spirit. From over the walls came the evocative fragrance of almond trees in blossom mingled with the slightly pungent odor of burning charcoal. The hum of traffic was subdued. It was a day for dozing along the sunlit wall, for reverie and reflection. The scene affected the friar with an acute nostalgia—and with a sense of desolation at the thought of leaving it. He yearned to grasp it all—the very atmosphere if he could—lest he lose it.

Life in Isfahan was quiet now. The recent persecution was only an unhappy memory. Daily the bells rang, daily the Eucharist was celebrated, daily the canonical hours were observed. The community now included a half dozen friars, and as many more lay brothers, adherents drawn from the Armenian community, while the Sunday Masses were attended by congregations numbering scores. Besides the convent there was now in nearby Julfa a community of Armenian nuns who looked to St. Teresa as their patron although they followed the strict and ancient rule of St. Basil for their government.

This was not all. There was now a convent in Shiraz, established there at the invitation of the viceroy of the south, Imam Quli Khan, as well as the older convent at Hormuz, now Persian territory, and a newly established residence at Basra, which had been taken from the Ottomans by the same redoubtable viceroy who had been responsible for the Persian successes at Hormuz. Imam Quli Khan, son of the late sirdar Allah Verdi Khan, had been showing an increasing interest in the Christians ever since the martyrdom of Abdallah Massih.

The work of the Carmelites in Persia appeared to be well founded and prospering. Fray Juan could consider his mission to have been divinely blessed. Carmelite convents had also been established in Goa, in Tatta, and in other parts of India, and Fray Juan had heard that a convent had also been founded in the New World, in a Spanish settlement known as Los Angeles. Not only could the friar consider his mission to have been blessed, but he could believe that the views that he had urged in the first instance, that the Carmelites undertake missionary work, had had Divine approbation.

Despite all these evidences of success Fray Juan was in low spirits as he walked along the quiet, sunlit street that April afternoon. Pessimism and dissatisfaction had been brought to a head by letters he had received from the General of the order authorizing him to return to Rome. A rule had been adopted by the order, since missionary activities had become so extensive, requiring missioners to celebrate Mass in Rome at intervals of not more than four years. Fray Juan had been absent from Rome now twenty-four years. The General's letters had said that the friar would no doubt be pleased at the opportunity for the rest and recuperation that the assignment in Rome would afford.

Despite this solicitude Fray Juan had put off replying to the instruction. He knew that he must go sooner or later, but he was not yet prepared to leave. Rather, the very thought of returning to Rome at this time filled him with dismay. Italy was foreign to him now, a distant and alien country. After twenty years in Persia, this land had become his home, and if it was not such a home as has its attic filled with mementoes and souvenirs, with books to be read again on some distant rainy day, with furniture too broken for use but too precious to be thrown away, yet it was a home no less encumbered—with memories and habits and usages, the encrustations of age that hold an old man from wandering as barnacles unfit a vessel for the open seas. Such things to be remembered there were as the massive ranges with their gaunt and brassy shoulders, and the tender green of the villages that was like a mold of moss upon their flanks, little things such as the Caucasian wild lily, or giant asphodel, that covered the plains in spring, the morning cry of the cucumber seller, and the smell of charcoal and spitted liver in the bazaars; there were the musical voices of children, and the song of the bulbul at night mingling with the rustle of water in the fountains; there was the sherbet seller with his goatskin bag, and the ferash with his lanterns. And there was the void in the friar's heart at the thought that when he returned to Rome, and retired to his cell, he would have no one to minister to and only his own soul to consider, and only memories for companionship.

These were all sensible elements in the friar's mood, but they were only surface elements. Beneath, deep within, like the tidal forces below the ocean's waves, moved the sense of failure in that to which his life had been dedicated. He thought of his failure in obtaining from the Shah the firman that had been the object of the papal mission, that would have established Christian missionary activities in Persia on a legal foundation and would have certified the rights of the Christian minorities of the realm. That would have been a diplomatic triumph had it been achieved, but in the long run was it so important? If a decree could be issued by one shah a later could annul it. The tenure of the establishment did not really depend upon decrees and titles and documents; the Church had expanded through the centuries in the face of such obstacles, and where it had relied upon the favor of princes rather than its own sustaining Gospel it had fallen into decay.

The important thing, Fray Juan recognized, was winning souls rather than obtaining firmans. He recalled the words of counsel given by the Pope in committing the Carmelites to their task in Persia. The Church, his Holiness had reminded them, was established in the hearts of men and not in land and edifices, the trappings of liturgy or the forms of organization. Fray Juan reflected on how great had been his failure therein. There had been a day when Abbas himself might have been redeemed. For a moment victory over the power of Satan had lain in the friar's hand. But victory had slipped through his fingers, and Satan was in full possession of Abbas's soul: the monarch had become an evil jinni overshadowing the land, malignant and unpredictable, defying the forces of light, spreading abroad a miasma of cruelty, lust, and madness.

Abbas no longer came to Isfahan. The aging monarch was building himself a second Isfahan at Ashraf, on the shores of the Caspian—a labyrinth of pleasure gardens and seaside pavilions, it was said, where, forswearing male companionship, he rioted in the attentions of two thousand concubines. He steadily succumbed to debility and, since the death of the Sirdar Allah Verdi Khan, had allowed the affairs of government to pass into the hands of subordinates. The latest news was that the Shah's health was failing rapidly.

If Fray Juan's relations with the Shah had been a failure, they had been even more a failure with the sirdar. Fray Juan realized now, too late, that the taciturn, steely-eyed Georgian had been a lost sheep which the friar had neglected to rescue from the wilderness of his loneliness. The last audience with the Shah, when the sirdar had so decisively come to his support, had been a revelation of the sirdar's feelings and of his need. Fray Juan had attempted to see the sirdar on several occasions to express his gratitude, but the sirdar had declined to see him, sending polite excuses through his officers that he was variously engaged. What unwritten, perhaps unintended, rebuke lay behind those excuses! Too late! Too late! they seemed to say. Too late indeed, for shortly afterward, one sultry night, the sirdar died.

Wherein lay his error? How precisely had he failed his apostleship? Fray Juan asked himself these questions again and again, and now, preoccupied with them as he walked along, he failed to observe that he had already entered the shadows of the bazaars and had passed the turning of the street of the chandlers and was now in the court given over to greengrocers. Habit had directed his footsteps here, for in this court was the shop of Jafar, the former convert and penitent. Jafar, who had by a dream been miraculously saved from martyrdom as he had earlier been delivered by a dream from his death by asthma, had then by a dream—in which he saw himself impaled before a shrieking mob in the plaza—quietly forsworn his Christian faith and ceased to come to church. Nevertheless, the grocer continued to make a great show of his Christian zeal whenever he saw the friar, and when it was to his advantage to claim the influence or protection or custom of the Carmelites he did not hesitate to do so.

"Ah, good morrow, Reverence," he exclaimed effusively. "How your coming warms my heart!" And, bowing, he set a bench for the friar while at the same time he called his apprentice to fetch a pot of coffee. He began to make inquiries about the convent, and apologized profusely that the pressure of work prevented his attending the observances as formerly. He had grown prosperous and employed several assistants; he was no longer the frail, emaciated creature who had first come to the friar, but was now rotund and well garbed and barbered. To put off his inquiries, Fray Juan asked him the news of the day.

Jafar was eager to show his intimacy with great affairs, and was equally glad to avoid any personal conversation. He began to tell what he knew.

"I was just speaking with my neighbor—he is Ismail Farshi, who deals in coffee, and who keeps much in touch with affairs of the world—of the news that has come from Sind. The Great Moghul Jehangir is dead and has been succeeded by his son Jehan. A pepper fleet has just been lost in a storm in the Laccadives and the price of spices is rising." He laid his finger to his nose as he reflected. "Now, what else was there?" he asked himself, and then excusing himself skipped away to consult his neighbor, the dealer in coffee. Fray Juan was too weary to move, too wearied with the sadness of his thoughts, with the disappointment of his hopes, capped by the change that had taken place in the formerly meek, diffident, appealing Jafar who had visited him in the night, deformed with asthma, ragged from poverty, but wide-eyed with the vision of Christ. Well, John of the Cross, that man of visions, had condemned visions as the illusions of Satan, and the Church regarded them with suspicion; but Fray Juan could not on that account deny baptism and the blessed hope of salvation to one who came to him on the strength of a vision he had seen. Let God decide whether the vision were false or not. But confident as he was of the correctness of his course, his confidence did not assuage his sadness, his sense of bereavement at the loss of an almost redeemed soul.

"Oh, yes," Jafar was saying, as he returned, "an ambassador from the English king has arrived in Isfahan to treat with the Shah on the silk trade—much, it seems, to the annoyance of the representatives of the English Company, who prefer it for themselves, and wish it not to pass to the English king as his monopoly."

Fray Juan was hardly listening. The apprentice had set before him a cup of coffee on a tray. Though it was Lent, the friar accepted it. He thanked the apprentice, murmured a prayer for his soul—as was his custom whenever he received anything of a Moslem—and put the cup to his lips. The liquid was scalding-hot; but it tasted good, and the friar drank. Blessed potion it was, he thought, and wondered if Europe would not be better off if it substituted such a drink for fermented spirits.

"And with the English ambassador," Jafar was saying, "is the other Englishman—the Shah's erstwhile ambassador."

Fray Juan suddenly choked on his coffee.

"Not Sherley Khan!"

"The same," squealed Jafar delightedly, noting the friar's interest.

Fray Juan wanted to ask whether Sir Robert was accompanied by his wife, but he dared not. He dared not acknowledge even to himself the profundity of the effect which the thought worked on him—the inner excitement, the lift to his spirit, the dissolution of his self-castigating pessimism. He was suddenly aware of how green and fresh was the spinach in the grocer's stalls, how red the pomegranates, and how plump and tender the strawberries; he finished off the coffee with a new appreciation of its flavor, and as he thanked Jafar and bade him good day he felt a new and sympathetic warmth toward the reverted convert, who, it seemed to him, had really had a difficult course in maintaining a religious belief at such variance from that so fanatically held by everyone around him.

Fray Juan had not been home an hour before Sir Robert and Lady Sherley arrived for confessions. These were heard by Fray Balthazar, and afterward the visitors waited on Fray Juan. Sir Robert was in ill health. He had risen at the friar's entrance, but he was unsteady on his feet; his eyes were sunken and he was trembling as he grasped the friar's hand. Fray Juan begged him to be seated, but the Englishman would not.

"The ambassador of his English Majesty, Sir Dodmore Cotton, in whose company we have traveled here, awaits me," he explained. "There is business that requires attention and as we wish to leave early tomorrow, I beg you to excuse me." He went on to say that he hoped, after the completion of his embassy, to return to Isfahan for retirement, for incessant travel had impaired his health.

"But meantime, Father," he added, "as my lady and I have recently celebrated the anniversary of the marriage which you solemnized, I ask you, have I not kept well this charge which you gave into my hand, despite the hardships to which I have subjected her in keeping her with me in all these lengthy travels?"

There was a glitter in the Englishman's eyes as he said this—a reflection no doubt of his ill health—and Fray Juan could not read precisely the meaning behind the words; there could have been a greater warmth, a deeper flow of affection toward both wife and priest; but then, the friar thought, the English were a difficult people for a Spaniard to understand, valuing reserve in the affections and reticence in their expression, placing stability above passion, and public above personal duty.

"Shamala looks as though she had never known illness nor fatigue," said the friar simply, using her maiden name in a kind of instinctive counterthrust against the Englishman's armor of formality. He spoke in truth, for it seemed to him that the passing years had made her only lovelier, more vibrant, more charged with the indefinable essence of womanhood. Though she was approaching forty, the only evidences of age were a minute, almost invisible, web of wrinkles about her eyes, and a delicately violet cast to the lids that the friar thought enriched rather than detracted from their beauty. She was dressed simply, in black, with a string of large pearls about her throat. The thought crossed the friar's mind that she seemed somewhat subdued in the presence of her husband, but he put the thought aside.

Sir Robert, despite his excuses of urgent business, did not leave at once.

"It has not been easy for Teresa," he said, meeting the friar halfway by calling his wife by the sacramental name she had adopted at her marriage. "We have had to leave our two sons in school in England—you have heard of this blessing of our union, no doubt—and to leave them behind has been a hardship for us both. Teresa is a devoted mother."

"And how are the boys?" asked Fray Juan eagerly. "And whom do they resemble?"

Shamala's eyes flashed in response, and her lips parted as she started to speak; but it was Sir Robert who answered.

"They are children that would delight you, Father," he said, and his eyes gathered a luster of paternal pride. "The eldest is six; he is named Thomas, after his paternal grandfather, the Sheriff of Sussex. The younger, two years his junior, is named Henry after his godfather, our English Prince of Wales. They remain in England, in the care of their grandfather, who finds in them his spit and image."

"They are being reared in our Catholic faith?" inquired the friar. Sir Robert hesitated.

"As Catholics, I would say," he equivocated, "though not as Catholics holding allegiance to his Holiness." At the friar's questioning look he went on to say: "You are not familiar with the violence of national attachments in England. Our family is close to the throne, as you can surmise from the fact of Prince Henry standing as our son's godfather, and the head of our house would under no circumstances tolerate the Roman rite in the christening of his grandsons. Our English theologians, moreover, assert that the English Church is rooted in an independent Apostolic Succession as ancient as that of the Roman.

"But be that as it may," he concluded, seeing the pain in the friar's face, and feeling that he was in water deeper than he could wade, "you may rest assured, Father, that our sons will be reared in due reverence toward God, and in knowledge of their duty to God and to man."

Fray Juan, despite his abhorrence of the Protestant heresy, recalled the charity of the Anglican cleric, the Reverend Mr. Cotmore, and tried to view this defection with understanding. He confined his response to a nod.

"We rejoice to find you well," Sir Robert said, "and to see the several houses you now have in this land. God has blessed your enterprise. But what of conditions—for we have heard little news? We learn that Abbas takes less interest in administration these days, and that he has divided the rule, so to speak. Who stands closest to the throne now that Allah Verdi Khan is gone?"

"The actual government is in the hands of two men," responded the friar, willing to divert the conversation. "In the south the undisputed power is in the old sirdar's son, Imam Quli Khan, whom you met in Shiraz. Happily, he has shown himself to be both a brave soldier and a wise administrator. Even more fortunate for us, he is favorably disposed toward the Christians. I cannot give you such good reports of the north. There, a rival of Imam Quli Khan, by name Mohammed Ali Baig, rules as viceroy from Kasvin, and being in closer proximity to the Shah he enjoys some advantage on that account."

"That explains much that has puzzled and troubled me," commented Sir Robert, showing weariness again. "It is this Mohammed Ali Baig who for a long time has been resentful of my good fortune and who on several occasions has tried to discredit me with the Shah. Now he seems to be in position to do so. This explains, no doubt, my recall."

"You have succeeded in inducing the English king to send an ambassador to the Shah," commented Fray Juan reassuringly. "To achieve more formal relations with the ruler whose forces were so instrumental in gaining him control of Hormuz Island has, I know, long been an object of Abbas's diplomacy. Surely for this success Abbas will be appreciative, and will reward you properly."

"Have you lived so long in Persia not to know how short is the memory of its ruler?" asked Sir Robert pessimistically, "And have you spent so many years in court not to know that the watchword of politics, Christian and pagan, is not charity but interest?"

"Come," protested the friar, even as he winced at the thought of how right the Englishman was, "you take too dark a view of things. You are tired, you are ill, but soon you will be better."

"Thank you for your consolations, Father, but you speak, I am afraid, without conviction. I may tell you, what no doubt you have already heard, that the governors of the India Company, English though they be, bitterly oppose Sir Dodmore's embassy. The main purpose of this embassy, as you may know, is to negotiate the monopoly of the silk trade for the benefit of the English crown, and this would undercut the position of the company. With such opposition Sir Dodmore's prospects are as bleak as my own."

Fray Juan's compassion went out to the Englishman as he thought of how bright hopes had faded, of how so many years had been wasted in unprofitable service. And then his eyes fell upon Shamala, and he thought of her devotion to her husband, keeping by his side in all his journeys even at the sacrifice of the companionship of her children:

it seemed to the friar that here was devotion matching that of Sir Robert's to his duty, that however bitter Sir Robert's disappointment here was sufficient balm and solace.

"You have not yet seen the Shah," Fray Juan urged, "and until you have I suggest that you do not think of the outcome. The results may be brighter than your hopes admit. In any case, continue to think upon those admirable precepts concerning duty which your father gave you, and to recall the many examples of fidelity to be found in Scripture."

"Your counsel cheers me beyond measure, Father, and I do thank you and ask your blessing," responded Sir Robert with lighter countenance, and there was an echoing look of appreciation in Shamala's eyes. The friar bestowed a blessing, and they left.

Seeing again Sir Robert and Shamala recalled to Fray Juan the instructions for his return to Rome over which he had been dallying. Suddenly there seemed no further reason for delay. The interview with Sir Robert and Shamala had strengthened his own purposes. Without making comparisons he could not but dwell with joy upon the recollection that the Sovereign he served was without fickleness or frailty—a *Father of lights, with whom is no variableness, neither shadow of turning.*

The following day Fray Juan went down to the Caravanserai of Shah Ismail to hire a mule and to engage company with one of the caravans that was traveling west toward Baghdad and Aleppo. A few days later he celebrated a farewell Mass with his companions and left Isfahan.

Fray Juan had not been a day on the road, however, before he had the uncomfortable sensation of having been too hasty, of having left something behind in his impatience to be off. He went through his haversack to see if he had mislaid any of the letters he was bearing or had conceivably forgotten his vial and chalice. Everything was in order, but the feeling persisted of having left something behind, of having omitted to perform some duty.

The caravan reached Sultanabad, on the way to Hamadan. The weather had grown warmer, and Fray Juan slept that night in the open with the camelteers among the tethered and kneeling camels. Sometime during the night he awoke in a sweat which was not from the weather. The feeling of some duty unperformed, some business to clear up, had become an oppressive premonition. The friar's thought turned upon the companions he had left behind, and upon the possibility of another persecution. He asked himself if this was the voice of God in his ear directing him to return to Isfahan or that of the Tempter luring him from obedience to his instructions. He committed the matter to God in prayer. . . .

Next morning Fray Juan awoke refreshed, his mind clear. He was certain that what he had heard in the night was the voice of God. He allowed the caravan to go on without him, while he turned his mule's head again toward Isfahan.

It was when he arrived at Khonsar that the friar heard the gossip in the caravanserai of the failure of the English embassy and the news of the serious illness of the two Englishmen. A few inquiries convinced him of his course of action, and that evening he joined a party of travelers leaving for Kasvin.

II

The embassy of the English ambassador Sir Dodmore Cotton had indeed proved as fruitless as had so many others. Abbas received the ambassador and Sir Robert Sherley in his new palace at Ashraf, some twenty miles down the coast from the older palace at Ferrahabad, and the company was treated to a magnificent *cheraghani*, or display of illumination, in the seemingly endless, flower-filled gardens lying between the sea and the hills. Abbas was abstractedly effusive in his attentions, but all attempts to bring him to discuss business were futile; the dull expression in his sunken eyes and flabby face became enlivened only by lewd conversation and lecherous exhibitions. He drank freely and in his cups drew Robert Sherley to him and whispered in his ear, "You look ill, my friend. Are you not well?"

Robert said that he had suffered a fever while in India, but that he had recovered except for a loss of weight and a want of his usual vigor.

The Shah glanced at Robert from the corner of his eye with a momentary return of his calculating shrewdness.

"I trust you have safely deposited with the Venetian or Florentine bankers the gains from your embassies," he remarked.

Robert turned the insinuation aside.

"I trust your Majesty does not think that I have gone on so many journeys in your Majesty's behalf simply for the benefit of Italian bankers."

"Then you have not been as shrewd as I always thought you," said Abbas with a sneer, "for you know that in this realm, when any of the court dies, the Shah may claim the escheat of land, movables, and slaves."

He allowed this to ferment, and then added slyly:

"And now may I ask, since you have not told me, how is my dear niece, the daughter of Sampsov Khan, the wife of my ambassador, the *Shahdokht* Shamala? From reports that reach me, she remains as charming, as firm of flesh, as inviting and delicious as when I first bestowed her upon you."

Robert's face purpled, but when he spoke his voice was controlled.

"It is true," he said, "that in every court of Europe the Lady Sherley subdued into reverent silence every tongue that would prate of her charms."

Abbas felt the rebuke and, turning away, had nothing more to say to his ambassador the rest of the evening. Robert understood that he had incurred the irrevocable displeasure of the monarch.

When Sir Dodmore Cotton, failing to obtain a second audience with the Shah, determined to return to England, Robert resolved to accompany him, to leave forever the service of the Shah to which he had given nearly thirty years of his life. Both men were bitterly disappointed with the unsavory end of their missions and physically exhausted with the ardor of the long journey, but Robert seemed the more so. By the time they reached Kasvin, he was very ill, running a high fever, and had to be put to bed. Sir Dodmore Cotton had also fallen ill and was likewise confined to his bed. They were lodged in separate houses which the viceroy of the north, Mohammed Ali Baig, put at their disposal.

These accommodations, while palaces by name, were but dilapidated houses tenanted by a crew of shiftless, quarrelsome servants and their families, relatives, and hangers-on; the rooms had been almost stripped of furnishings, the doors hung on rusted hinges, and in the garden the watercourses were broken and the verdure had turned brown and yellow. The heat was oppressive, and the flies made a continual buzzing in the rooms. The Shah's displeasure with Sir Robert was being manifested in many ways.

Robert lay on a pallet before a window overlooking the burned and desolate garden. Shamala remained at his side, driving away the flies, fanning his face, and keeping his forehead cool with damp cloths. At times, when necessity was upon him, Robert brusquely sent her away and called for his manservant, for he did not wish her to attend the repulsive and nauseating aspects of his sickness. There was no hope of recovery; Robert understood that very early.

During the night Robert's fever abated a little, and he could speak lucidly and calmly. He asked for Shamala, and when she answered he began to tell her of his conversation with the Shah.

"You have no desire, at this date, to be numbered among the Shah's household?" he asked.

Shamala shuddered.

"My husband," she replied, smoothing his coverlet, "soon we shall be far away from Abbas and all his ways. Would you relish a little lemon juice?"

Robert thought his wife sagacious, but it struck him now that she did not understand that they were about to be parted. He would have thought that she could read the signs of death more readily. Was it because she loved him that she could not see what was happening, or because she did not love him? He could not say. She remained, as she had always been for him, a complex and baffling personality, the secret key to which not even marriage had discovered.

But Sir Robert's life was not a mystery. It was a network of strong black and white threads in which his deeper yearnings had been snared and in which they had long since been obscured. As always, his duty now was clear to him, and it was upon that duty that he forced his attention through his pain.

"When I am gone—" he began, but Shamala put her fingers to his lips, smiling at him tenderly.

"Do not speak so, my husband," she whispered. "You will be well. Only keep up your courage."

Robert felt a constriction in his heart, recognizing qualities in his wife that he had never guessed at until now, and he was smitten with a pang of conscience. It occurred to him that for all his consecration to duty he might have neglected the chief duty of all, that toward his wife, and that either he should have cherished her more completely as his beloved or he should have renounced entirely the obligations of marriage.

But the time for such concern was past. His duty at the moment was clear enough. He had always provided for his wife's necessities; he had been a husband to her in the sense of one who provides and protects and conserves.

"When I am gone," he repeated firmly, "stay not for tears and lamentation, but go at once to the English ambassador, and put yourself under his protection, for the moment Abbas hears of my death you will be snatched off to his Haram: he still lusts for you, aged and impotent as he is. I have not left you penniless, though Abbas failed to discover where I hold my means. They are with the Roman bankers with whom we deal—you know the house. But for the moment you have only the jewels we wear. I was of course unable to obtain the moneys due me from the Shah. Guard the jewels carefully and go in haste to Sir Dodmore, for this Mohammed Ali Baig, once he learns that I am gone, will certainly attempt to abduct you and to seize the Shah's escheat. Would that I could get you away myself—"

Robert had half risen from his pallet as he spoke; his eyes were brilliant with pain, fever, and excitement. The effort was too much for him; he fell back exhausted.

Shamala wept and clung to his hand.

The man of duty and devotion asserted himself again.

"Do not weep," Robert whispered. "The bond that the friar sealed between us draws to its term. Our covenants have been duly kept, and we may part in peace with clean accounts and a clear conscience."

A cool breeze from the garden revived the sick man's strength, enough for him to continue speaking.

"I have not been such a husband as you have deserved or needed, Teresa, but I have been a husband, and this for myself I say, that I have not left you unprovided either with substance or offspring, and I have also done this for your soul's sake: I have kept you from the unholy grasp of that lecher Abbas."

Shamala had fallen on her knees beside the bed, and her head, with the rich walnut-colored hair loose, was pressed against the coverlet. Robert lay back, spent, but with frail fingers he stroked Shamala's hair.

"Is there not something I can do to relieve your suffering, my lord?" she asked.

"You have discharged every obligation of a wife," Robert answered. "You have been worthy of all I have been able to offer you. There is no need for tears, Teresa."

Shamala repeated her question, and after a moment Robert said: "I would that I were shriven."

But the friars were fifteen days or more distant, and in lieu of the sacrament Shamala held Robert's hands and caressed them. Her husband continued to stroke her hair until gradually his fingers grew slack, and then their movement ceased. A peculiar stillness possessed the bed; it was as though someone had quietly left the room. Shamala raised her head, and looked at her husband; the sight of the pale face, from which all life had departed, filled her with a faintness, and a sob escaped her. . . .

III

Robert Sherley had died toward nine o'clock in the night. The evening breeze had done little to relieve the sultriness of the torrid mid-July day. The buzzing of the bottle flies had ceased, but was replaced by the persistent hum of many mosquitoes, that in the silence of the night was like the sound emitted by the plucked strings of an overtaut sitar. The silence that surrounded the hum of the insects was in its own way as oppressive and as devouring as the heat; Shamala, sitting nerveless by the body of her husband, could feel herself being emptied of her soul, could feel her vitality slipping from her, evaporating into the night through her parched skin. Instinctively her ears strained for some familiar sound out of the stillness that would reassure her, that would speak to her of a world in which she still had a part, where there was a place for her to fill and things for her to do.

The night hung over the city, still and oppressive. A veil seemed to hide the stars, and the garden lay in obscurity. Some dread, it seemed, had silenced those little sounds that ordinarily punctuated the dark: the quick little hoofbeats of a donkey homeward driven, his master hurrying him along with the petulant, nasal grunts that were the language understood of donkeys and donkey drivers; the melancholy notes of a reed pipe played by a disconsolate lover behind a wall; the cries of the lantern bearers of some wealthy house as they escorted their lord through the streets from a late dinner. The absence of these familiar noises made the city seem sepulchral.

And then, like an answer to prayer, the sound of bells crept into the silence. Faint and silver-thin it was at first, but it slowly increased in volume and sonority as the lighter bells were joined by heavier; the sound came nearer, until the air was filled with music—an orchestra of bells, pealing and reverberating like a carillon in a great cathedral.

It was a camel caravan assembling in one of the caravanserais for the night journey upon the desert, and then filing slowly through the streets toward the city gate, and beyond, into the open desert, on the caravan tracks that led to the east toward some distant city—Meshed, Herat, Kabul, Samarkand? The sound of the bells now grew fainter, and at last came only as a whisper from across the wastes, but it was enough for Shamala. Her spirit was revived; her faculties assumed their dominion, and alertness governed her senses. What now invaded her consciousness was the thought that Robert had died unshriven, without benefit of the Church's comfort, and in a land in which, though he had served its monarch devotedly for thirty years, he had never felt at home. Upon these considerations Shamala made her decision: she would take the body to Europe for burial in consecrated ground.

Because of the heat it was necessary that the body be embalmed at once. Throwing a chuddar about her, and calling the servant to fetch a lantern, Shamala set out for the Place of the Washers of the Dead, in the Gabristan quarter of the city.

She had traversed the garden and was standing at the gate that opened onto the street before Robert's premonitions were recalled to her. Mohammed Ali Baig might have put the house under surveillance. But her hand was upon the latch; she must go and fetch the embalmers in any case.

As she feared, Shamala was met in the street by a sentry in the yellow livery of the viceroy. Respectfully he explained that he was under orders to allow no one to pass.

"It is because of the plague within," he said, in the manner of a man to whom this had been given him to say.

"There is no plague within," Shamala exclaimed impatiently, "but only one who was sick, and now is dead."

"That is news which his Lordship has expected and which I am bidden to send to him at once," said the sentry.

Shamala bit her tongue at her indiscretion, but it was too late to remedy the error.

"Now that you have the news, will you not let me pass to bear it to the English ambassador?"

"Nay, my orders remain. But abide you until the morning, and perhaps then it will be arranged."

Shamala studied the man by the light of her lantern. He appeared simple enough, and a trifle awed at being in conversation with a woman, and a lady of position besides. She thought he might be a pious person, and spoke to him on that basis.

"It is my husband whose body lies within," she said quietly. "I would see him buried in holy ground, but in this heat his flesh will soon be consumed if the body washers are not fetched at once. It is for that that I must go abroad."

"It may not be," said the sentry firmly, "but return you to your chambers and I will send at once to fetch the washers."

It was well enough, under the circumstances; but to ensure and hasten the deed Shamala drew a coin from the purse at her belt and pressed it into the sentry's hand. There were not many more coins left in the purse, but she could not qualify necessity, and must use her means as necessity demanded. An hour later the embalmers came and carried away the body, telling Shamala that she might send for it in a double fortnight.

There was nothing more to be done about that. As to Mohammed Ali Baig, Shamala thought she could only await developments. She returned to her chamber and lay down to rest, and, being physically and emotionally drained, was soon sunk in sleep.

It was toward mid-morning that Shamala received a visit from the viceroy. Mohammed Ali Baig was a handsome, full-chested man in his mid-forties, with flashing black eyes, plump, wheat-colored cheeks, and long, thin black mustaches. He was gorgeously appareled; his voice was deep and hearty; and he was effusive in his condolences; but when Shamala asked if she might not now be escorted to the English ambassador, he became evasive.

"His Excellency also suffers from the flux, and is too ill to recognize those about him," he said apologetically and in a tone of the deepest regret. "But I have dispatched a courier to his Majesty," he went on, "who has expressed his solicitude for your welfare, and no doubt so soon as I shall hear from the court you will be appointed means and escort as you require."

He surveyed Shamala discreetly from head to foot.

"It is not good to be a widow," he commented.

"I have had little time to consider that," replied Shamala shortly.

"His Majesty has grown old and enfeebled," continued Mohammed Ali Baig, "and it were better, I think, to be a widow than to re-enter his household where there are so many to beguile his hours."

"You have rightly spoken," responded Shamala, who had begun to wonder if there were advantage to her in what the viceroy was saying.

"But if Sherley *Hanim* were so disposed," insinuated the viceroy, "I would offer her a position far better than widowhood."

"And that would be?"

"As first lady in my household."

Shamala's eyes narrowed.

"Ah," he exclaimed, in sudden rapture, seeing in Shamala's expression what appeared to him to be a responsive interest, "had I believed but half the reports I have had concerning the beauty and charm of Shamala, Countess Sherley, niece of his Majesty Abbas! Ah, hanim, I will not only make you first in my household, but for your sake I would willingly send all others away and, like your late husband, acknowledge only you."

"But what of Abbas, to whom you have sent word in such haste?" murmured Shamala pensively.

"His Majesty is so much indebted to me that he will not hesitate to grant me such a boon."

"I am afraid you do not know his Majesty so well as I," ventured Shamala. "But let it be. Meantime, can you not grant me a little freedom of movement?"

The viceroy was abjectly apologetic.

"Ah, it pains me to the heart," he exclaimed with an expressive gesture, "not to be able to allow you your slightest whim. But in this I am under his Majesty's strict orders which I dare not neglect. Moreover, I am under the even more painful duty of taking an inventory of your possessions—or rather the property that appertained to Sherley Khan—to which, under the laws of the realm, his Majesty may assert a claim as remainder man. Will it suit your Ladyship's convenience to provide me with an accounting, say, this afternoon?"

"Do you not sorely press me, my lord, in my grief?" asked Shamala, bringing a handkerchief to her eyes and lowering her head.

"Ah, so I do, so I do. Forgive me, your Ladyship," replied the viceroy effusively. "Then let it be tomorrow. Tomorrow I shall return, and at that time you will show me the inventory."

While this exchange was going on, the viceroy's servants had been quietly taking possession of the premises. The viceroy had seated himself on an ottoman, as one who is master of the house. A eunuch had brought in coffee, but at Shamala's show of grief the viceroy had motioned him away. Mohammed Ali Baig now rose and begged leave to depart, bowing in what he conceived to be the European manner.

"My servants?" interrupted Shamala, for the first time noting the changes that had taken place.

"Sherley Khan engaged them in Hormuz, did he not? This altitude is much too rigorous for their health, and out of regard for their welfare I am sending them home," the viceroy stated, and added, "But you are excellently provided for, I assure you."

"The women's quarters are well guarded, I trust?" Shamala asked.

"Oh, indeed."

"Then you will discover later the results of your solicitude," said Shamala enigmatically.

"Oh, thank you, my lady, thank you. I shall attend you tomorrow."

The viceroy bowed himself out, unctuously smiling.

Alone again, withdrawn into the chamber where her husband had lain and which now gave off the odor of death, Shamala fell upon her knees and prayed. Prayer had long been a habit with her, ever since she had made her confirmation vows, but always it had had in it a large element of habit and ritual. She had made requests of God, but always with a certain willingness to see her requests denied. But now she desperately wanted something of God; she wanted to escape; and prayer seemed at the moment so ineffectual. There were no bells now to remind her of the solaces of the Church; there was only the oppressive heat and the persistent hum of the bottle flies.

Dusk came, and a servant entered with a platter of cold rice and a pot of coffee, but Shamala had no appetite, and when the servant withdrew she made a sort of bolt to the door by driving the blade of a ginjil into the jamb. She resumed her praying. The night closed in and the air grew a little cooler; the hum of the bottle flies once more gave way to the drone of mosquitoes. Shamala did not notice them. She had not ceased to pray, but she had grown listless; a fatigue possessed her mind that quieted her anxiety and stilled the fears that had held her captive since the interview with the viceroy.

Could it be an answer to prayer, or was it only an increeping mildness of the night, offering a refreshment upon the cheek, as when the air, after a long dry summer, grows damp with the promise of rain? Shamala felt a recovery of her strength, a restless vitality surging up within her, a clearing of her mind. She was aware of an intense need to be up off her knees, and about. Suddenly she could keep her thoughts on prayer no longer. She stood up, and instantly was in a fever of activity.

What was she doing? She hardly knew herself. But she was a Circassian, quick of mind and swift to act. Hastily she gathered up her more precious possessions. She worked in the dark, not bothering to light a lamp. By good fortune the jewels and the small sum in abbassis were in the travel chest where Robert had kept his confidential state papers and which never left his side. Shamala snatched these up and carefully wrapped them all in her purse of soft lambskin.

What next? Without conscious thought, but driven by the same insistent urge to be active, Shamala tore at the fastenings of her dress. Now she stood disrobed; and then, with terrible urgency but without conscious purpose she seized her husband's travel clothes from the wardrobe and dressed herself in them. It took only a moment for her to put on the loose-fitting trousers gathered at the waist and wrapped from the knees down with puttees, to draw on the cotton undershirt and shirt, and over them a sleeveless jacket of leather. She made a turban of her scarf and about her waist she fastened her husband's sword belt, with the rapier and its scabbard, and the scabbard of the ginjil that held the door bolted. Her own narrow poniard, which she always carried, she thrust within her shirt, against her breast. It was as though the blood of ancient Colchis had reasserted itself: she stood erect, alert, defiant—an Amazon warrior.

So dressed, Shamala opened the door and entered the garden. She did so cautiously, though fortunately there was little need for caution, as the garden was a private enclosure for the use of the women of the house. She scanned the garden walls with the restless alertness of the imprisoned, seeking some means of escape—an extended tree limb, or a gardener's ladder by which she might scale the wall.

It was in the course of this light-footed search that Shamala heard a scratching at the base of the wall, such as a dog might make with its claws. Instantly she was alert, her rapier drawn and her body poised. The wall was of the customary sun-dried brick plastered over with a mortar of clay and straw; it was not unusual for thieves to break into houses by burrowing through. It seemed unlikely, however, that thieves were at work now, with the sentries just beyond; it was more likely, in view of the viceroy's proposals, that Mohammed Ali Baig was attempting to defraud the Shah by an abduction. Let him come, Shamala thought grimly. Once before her Amazon blood had asserted itself in a moment of crisis: it was on her first journey with her husband; robbers had attacked the camp, had held Robert bound and had frightened off the servants but had ignored her, until she fell upon them furiously with a sword and pike; she slew two of them and drove the others into howling flight. She was ready for bloody battle now. She felt the edge of her blade with her thumb.

There was no moon now, but the radiance of many stars falling through the cloudless summer sky filled the garden with a mild pallor in which objects could be distinguished dimly. The murmur of the breeze among the trees was like the whispering of voices from the past, and out of the hollow night Shamala seemed to hear her name called: "Shamala," and again softly, insistently, "Shamala," in an accent that brought to her vision a gaunt, concerned face. . . .

The scratching at the wall was more pronounced; in the starlight Shamala could see specks breaking from the surface, and then a crumbling, and then a dark spot, like the spreading stain of water on a cloth. In a moment the hole was large enough for a man to crawl through, and as Shamala raised her rapier a head appeared, close-cropped like a workman's, and then shoulders, cloaked in a short-sleeved tunic, and then a body. The figure stood erect.

"Fray Juan!" Shamala's cry was out before the friar could clasp his hand over her mouth; and then she was in the protective circle of his arms, sobbing away the tensions of the last days.

IV

"I came in answer to prayer," Fray Juan whispered when Shamala had recovered herself. "Gather quickly what you need. I have horses ready and we must flee at once. The English ambassador has died also, and everything is in confusion."

"Then the same voice must have told me to expect you," said Shamala, "for as you see, I am ready." Indecision held her. "But I cannot go. Robert—I must attend to him. I must see him interred in consecrated ground. He lies now at the Place of the Washers."

"Rest your conscience," said the friar. "By God's sweet will that matter is in good hands—those of Kazim Sarkis, with whom I lodged last night. I was at the gate and saw Sir Robert's body being carried out, and to Sarkis have I entrusted the task of bringing it in due time to Isfahan—where by God's grace we shall ourselves arrive safely."

They left at once, creeping through the hole which the friar had burrowed in the wall. They hurried through the lanes and alleys until they came to where the friar had horses tethered, and at length they rode out through a breach in the ancient unused city walls into the open desert. It might be morning before Shamala's escape was discovered, but six hours was no great headway, excellent as were the mounts which Kazim Sarkis had provided. The viceroy might think, of course, that Shamala was hiding somewhere in the city, and lose time in making search, but he might also assume that she would flee toward the south, to the dominion of the rival viceroy Imam Quli Khan, of whom she could be sure of protection. Fray Juan had thought on that account that they should not strike directly south, but should take the road that led down to Baghdad through Hamadan.

For the five hours left of the night they groped their way, the friar and the princess, across the broken ground of the desert, keeping to the trail mainly by allowing the horses their heads, but holding them steadily to the southwest. Then the track began to drop sharply by rutted gullies and treacherous shale slopes to the narrow floor of a stream which, at this season, was hardly more than a trickle. Fray Juan guessed this to be the upper course of the Kara Su, which, flowing eastward, loses itself in the vast, empty, salt-encrusted flats known as the Salt Sea. If so, by following the course of the stream they would be moving in the general direction of Isfahan. It was hardly likely that they would be observed in these wastes, so far from the usual caravan trails. At the same time, the route would offer problems of forage and water for the horses.

The friar explained the choice, giving his views but consulting Shamala's. Shamala agreed with his opinion. Fray Juan warned her that it was a blind choice, that he knew practically nothing of the region, and that he was going by touch as the voice of God might lead them. Shamala assured him that it was enough for her.

Shamala's anxieties were quieted. It was comforting and reassuring to be escorted through this unfriendly land by one who so obviously was led by the hand of God in all that he did. As the night lengthened, Shamala gradually began to see the friar in another aspect. In the darkness, with her imagination aflame, she saw herself riding not beside a contemplative Carmelite of the Barefooted Congregation but companioned by a medieval Hospitaler who had ridden out to deliver a Christian maiden from the hands of the Saracen.

The fancy persisted as morning broke. The dawn was a surge of cherry-colored light that flowed toward them like a flood through the V of the gorge, and in this light the friar, who was riding ahead, appeared clothed in scarlet and gold—the very image of chivalry straight from the pages of Italian romance. He was in native dress, which he had put on as a precaution. He sat his saddle with singular ease, and it occurred to Shamala that his calling, before the Church laid hold upon him, might have been that of a caballero, a conquistador, or a master of many ranges and herds upon the New World pampas. Without his gaberdine the muscled strength of his frame was visible; fasting and meditation might have made it gaunt, but they had not deprived it of native grace and vigor. Against the sun Shamala could see the ripple of power along the shoulders and arms.

They rode for yet another hour, and then, with the sun well above the rim of the gorge and its rays beginning to beat upon the rocks, the friar reined up and turned in the saddle.

"We will rest now," he said. There was the familiar gentleness and concern in his voice, but to Shamala it seemed now surcharged with particularity, addressed to her and having qualities which only she would understand. "I have brought raisins and walnut meats and a little bread," he added. There was also a water bottle in the saddle-bag, and he gave her to drink. For the horses the friar had brought a bag of barley, but the water in the stream proved so brackish that the horses would not drink of it. This was a serious misfortune. With the increasing heat of day it was out of the question for the fugitives to push their thirsty mounts farther; the best they could do was to tether them in the shade of the canyon walls and to get as much rest themselves as they could.

Shamala fell asleep at once. The sky was gray when she awoke. It was late in the afternoon; Fray Juan was standing over her when she opened her eyes, and in his own eyes was the look of peculiar concern and tenderness which Shamala had discovered in his voice during the night. Suddenly she was acutely conscious that she was looking up at him not as to a friar but as to a man. There returned to her recollection the image of the lean-faced darvish of the Ardebil plain of so long ago whose burning eyes and solemn expression and whose curious conversation had stirred in her unrecognized hungers of both body and soul.

Fray Juan had long since satisfied the hungers of her soul. This he had done by his example of piety, by his instruction in the doctrines of his faith, and by receiving her into the Holy Catholic Church. In the relationship that had grown up between them, of penitent and priest, had flowed an increasingly rich and deep affection; but Shamala had learned to regard it as something that flowed through him rather than from him—as God's love, of which the friar in the sincerity and purity of his vocation was but the channel. But now she felt a compelling urge to another view of the relationship. Human necessity called for something to calm and dilute the flow of divine love, to make it bearable for human consolation, just as pure sunlight for human comfort must be sifted through a jalousie.

"Are you rested? Are you ready to travel?" the friar was asking. "I have found a spring—brackish but bearable—and have given the horses to drink."

"I am ready," exclaimed Shamala leaping up, a lilt in her voice that caused the friar to open his eyes in surprise and to remark upon her resiliency.

They mounted and rode again. The gorge opened and spread into a confusion of eroded red and yellow hills daubed with splotches of dirty vitriolic blue, naked of life or vegetation. Fray Juan reined up, his expression clouded. He studied the angle of the setting sun, and presently turned his horse's head to the right. There followed another night of seemingly endless riding under the canopy of stars, following the course of the earth's creases, the veining of prehistoric rains, the wrinkles of an aged and decaying land, but always bearing to the south and east, until the fagged horses could not be urged to so much as a trot.

Shamala's strength began at last to ebb and she felt her weariness weigh upon her. But she had no desire for rest. The figure before her on the horse reassured her like an image of fortitude and endurance, and she felt an odd contentment the like of which she could not recall in all her life. In her weariness, as she drowsed upon her horse, the pictures that flitted before her were light and airy—sunlight and such things as falling petals, a shower of gold and azure and willow-green and the pink of the ripe peach; there were pellucid depths in which seaweed waved, and a cobalt mist of morning in which the branches of the birch stirred quietly. There were faces too, but she did not dare look at them; she knew whose they were, and she was content that they remain simply disembodied faces in her dream. . . . Oh, if she could only go on forever, lost in such sweet repose!

They had finally emerged from the chaos of badlands, and the first pallor of the morning found them traveling across a verdured plateau with snow-rimmed ranges in the distance and a cooler atmosphere that enlivened the spirit for all the exhaustion of the body. There was the sound of running water that was like music at dusk, and the smell of damp earth, and in the violet mist appeared a ribbon of sparkling blue that marked a water channel for the irrigation of the fields. They reined up and allowed the horses to drink their fill, and Fray Juan refilled the water bottles. Out of the mist appeared an orchard and a grove of silver-stemmed poplars and, beyond, the coral-pink walls of a village. There were laborers already in the orchard; Fray Juan gave them a morning greeting, and one of them went to fetch the headman of the village. The katkhoda was a gray-bearded and kindly man; when Fray Juan explained their weariness he insisted upon their accepting his hospitality. His eyes were dim and he took Shamala for a youth. While one of his men stabled the horses he escorted the two travelers to an upper room of his house. Since they were still in Mohammed Ali Baig's territory and every discretion was necessary, Fray Juan did not protest.

Shamala slept on the pallet, having first removed her boots and her turban, and the friar made a pillow of his cloak on the floor in the corner. But he did not sleep. Instead, he knelt, reciting psalms and collects in a whisper.

This was not the only time the two slept in the same room during the two weeks before they reached Isfahan. They were in the caravanserai at Kashan one night when there was a commotion in the courtyard, accompanied by the rattle of arms and the hoarse cries of a sergeant. Fray Juan, instantly awake, crept into the gallery to hear the cause. The sergeant was giving a description of a fugitive he sought—a Firenghi lady, as he described her, who nevertheless spoke the language like a native; she would be accompanied by an attendant, likewise a Firenghi, but the attendant could not be described. The arbaab declared that he lodged no such persons, but finally, to quiet the uproar the man was making, told him to go look for himself. The sergeant began by sending his men to all the chambers on the ground floor. Fray Juan returned to Shamala.

"Dress at once, and come," he whispered urgently.

In a moment Shamala was with the friar on the gallery. There had been a moon, but it was down. The gallery roof was supported by poplar poles and the gallery itself was enclosed by a railing. By standing on the friar's shoulders Shamala was able to grasp the roof and draw herself up. Fray Juan returned to the chamber to take up his haversack containing the consecrated articles of his calling. When he came out, the sergeant's men had reached the gallery. Slipping in the shadow to the pillar the friar drew himself upon the railing and caught the ledge of the roof, but he was no longer a youth and for all his hard conditioning he had not the strength to mount. He lost his footing, and there was a clatter as the fragile railing shook. However, the noise went unnoticed: the sergeant's men were doing their work industriously, with such banging and shouting that they had started several mules to braying. Quickly unloosing her turban, Shamala looped the scarf under the friar's armpits and helped him to scramble to safety.

While the search went on below, the two sat huddled together on the roof of the gallery, until finally the sergeant gave up and went away with his men and quiet settled again over the caravanserai. But Shamala and the friar did not immediately return to their chamber. At first they were held by continued anxiety, but as the caravanserai slumbered this gave way to relief and Fray Juan recited softly a psalm of thanksgiving. Still they did not descend, held now by the balm and wonder of the summer night, by the air upon their cheeks, and by the stars overhead—the Swan swimming in the Milky Stream, the Scorpion crawling across the southern horizon, Arcturus gathered with his sons. To the accompaniment of the tinkling of camel bells in the courtyard, Fray Juan recited the majestic passage from Job beginning, *Canst thou bind the sweet influences of the Pleiades, or loose the bands of Orion?* But when he came to the verse, *Who hath put wisdom in the inward parts? or who hath given understanding to the heart?* he suddenly ceased speaking, as if caught by something in his throat, and Shamala understood then that his soul, like her own, was at that moment drawn by polarities.

The thought filled Shamala with new contentment, which persisted despite uneasy pains that shot through her from time to time at the realization that this strange journey and sweet companionship must soon end. They reached Gez, a short day's journey from Isfahan. This would be their last night on the road. That evening in the caravanserai, as they recited Complin before retiring, they read responsively the verses of the psalm:

Blessed is every one that feareth the Lord . . . happy shalt thou be, and it shall be well with thee.

Thy wife shall be as a fruitful vine by the sides of thine house: thy children like olive plants round about thy table.

Behold, that thus shall the man be blessed that feareth the Lord. . . .

As he read the verse Fray Juan's voice stumbled. Shamala waited in tremulous and secret joy while he gathered himself and continued; but she heard no more. Now she recognized more clearly than ever how throughout the years the friar had been the emotional fixity of her life, the continuing object of her interest and affection. Now she understood that this was to be so until the end of her days.

This was no romance in the Italian sense. Shamala's marriage with Robert, if not ideal, had not been without its moments of ecstasy. Shamala was too schooled as a Catholic to think of the friar apart from his calling. Yet she was aware of needs of his which the discipline of his order did not meet, which Holy Church had not supplied, which the sacraments themselves were not designed to satisfy.

That Fray Juan also understood this, Shamala was now certain. She felt, however, the necessity of bringing it to explicitness. Her heart was bursting with a thousand things she wanted to say to him by way of reassurance. As she lay awake on her pallet, watching the moonlight streaming through the window, she was aware that Fray Juan was also awake. He was on his knees in his corner of the room, with his hands clasped before him, but Shamala knew that he was not praying. She spoke to him.

"Juan?" She uttered the word softly, for the first time without the priestly prefix. She thought she saw him shiver.

He turned and faced her.

"Yes?"

Shamala experienced a kind of vertigo; she felt an urgency to speak to him as she thought: How precious he is to me! What can I offer him that he may know?

"When you return to Rome what will you do?" she found herself saying.

It was a moment before the friar answered, and when he spoke it was with the deliberateness of one speaking in an unfamiliar tongue, choosing his words as he speaks.

"I shall re-enter our monastery there," he said. "I shall resume there the life of a contemplative which I formerly followed."

"Will that be easy, after your years of activity?"

"Not easy, but with time I shall become accustomed to it." He hesitated and added: "And you? What will you do, Shamala?"

"I shall take Sir Robert's body to Italy for burial, if that is possible. I think he would wish it so. His Holiness signally honored him: he held the title, you know, of Count Palatine and Earl of the Lateran Palace."

"And then?" the friar asked.

"I will see my sons, and consult their necessities, and if their grand-father consents I shall bring them to Italy and settle there."

"To Italy?"

"Yes. . . . I find neither the English climate nor the English temperament congenial, nor do I feel at home in the Protestant atmosphere of England. I shall remain in Italy, where there are so many mementoes of the faith that has sustained me throughout the years—and of the—"

She stopped abruptly, caught up by what she found herself saying. But the wells of her soul had opened, and she could contain her feelings no longer.

"Oh, Juan," she cried, "it were as hopeless to stop the birds from singing or the flowers from budding as to stop my loving thoughts of you. Was it on the Ardebil plain that like an innocent Moses you struck the rock and opened the springs of my heart? Again you have done so, and what seemed to lie ahead as a wasteland of sterile memories has now become a vista of endless promise. Are you certain, Juan, of your calling as a contemplative? Had you entered the service of the State instead, what victories for the King of Heaven might have been yours!"

Shamala choked back further words and regarded the friar mutely. In the pallid light from the window she could see the line of his cheek, and the ripple of flesh as his jaws tightened.

"Only God knows," he said tonelessly. And then, more firmly, he added, "But as this is my calling, so it must remain."

Shamala expected no more, she asked no more, the flood diminished. But it continued to flow.

"Even as a friar," she said, testing her words, and speaking in a strained, almost inaudible voice, "your career in Rome need not be closed around by convent walls. Surely you will come into the sunshine a little?"

The friar was immobile; he took a long time to reply; Shamala thought she could see the glitter in his eyes.

"Perhaps," he said.

The friar roused himself.

"Shamala, dear heart," he said in a voice overflowing with tenderness, yet hollow and remote, "I dare not tell you—I dare not dwell upon it in thought—how you have been the explicit blessing and reward of my ministry. I am certain that I have learned more from you than I have ever taught you—that I have gained from you more solace than I have ever given. It is a mystery, and will remain a mystery, that in you I have seen and experienced the love of God; and I reverence you in that knowledge."

The friar seemed on the point of saying more; he had half risen from his kneeling posture, but suddenly he checked himself, and murmured a benediction.

Shamala waited, with beating heart and suspended breath, for him to continue, but he said no more, nor did she. Yet it was enough. Her secret contentment returned to her, and a sense of perfect reconciliation. . . .

The next afternoon they reached Isfahan. There the friar escorted the princess to the convent of the Armenian Daughters of Carmel. After giving the prioress explicit instructions to hold her concealed until the English Company could arrange for her passage to England, he bade Shamala farewell.

V

Despite the constant protection of the Church it was three years before Shamala succeeded in reaching Italy. For over a year the viceroy of the south, to placate the mullahs, refused her permission to leave Persia while she was compelled to stand trial on the charge of having apostatized from Islam; meanwhile she was forced to ward off marriage suits and even attempted abductions by several khans who found her desirable for one reason or another. Released at last, she set off for Europe with her husband's embalmed corpse. The Carmelites helped her as far as Baghdad, and the Capuchins in Baghdad assisted her to reach Aleppo. There she was detained on the charge that her passport was not in order and she was compelled to go to Constantinople. In that city the Augustinians gave her lodgings and exerted their influence to obtain her release; but it was nearly two years before this was accomplished. She arrived in Naples where the nuncio graciously arranged for her to journey northward in the company of the secretary of the Sacred Congregation for the Propagation of the Faith, who was returning to Rome after an extensive missionary journey.

Monsignor Ingoli was elderly, benign, and loquacious. Throughout the day, as the carriage swayed to the incline of the road and the dust seeped in through the windows, he relieved the tedium of the journey with talk about his work. The Sacred Congregation was an agency recently created by the Pope for the direction and co-ordination of the far-flung missionary enterprises of the Church. Emphasis was being put on missionary work these days, Monsignor explained, and he spoke enthusiastically about the new missionary foundations abroad in which the Holy See was interested, of the work being carried on in India by the Franciscans and the Jesuits, and by the Dominicans in the New World.

"During your sojourn in Persia, did you become acquainted with that estimable Carmelite, Father Juan Thaddeus of St. Elisaeus?" he inquired politely.

"It was he who baptized me into the Catholic faith," Shamala replied in a restrained tone. "For a long time he was my father confessor."

"Indeed!" exclaimed Monsignor warmly. "A most unusual man. A most unusual man," he repeated. "He arrived in Rome some three years ago and immediately took to his cell, hardly leaving it until recently. A strange asceticism for one who had lived so long in almost secular freedom of movement and dress and diet. He became almost Carthusian in the strictness of his confinement. For all my experience it was baffling to me."

He looked at Shamala inquiringly, as though he thought she might be able to shed some light upon this paradox.

"It is in character with Father Juan, and understandable to those who know him," she said. But as she offered no further explanation the secretary of the Sacred Congregation continued.

"Well, he sowed the Seed widely—and shrewdly," he remarked. "As you know, since the accession of Shah Safi, grandson of that notorious Shah Abbas who vexed the Christians, broad privileges have been conceded to the minorities, and missionary work has greatly expanded—so much so in fact that the Sacred Congregation recommended to his Holiness the appointment of a bishop over the Persian flock. The Bishop of Isfahan was the title which his Holiness conferred."

"That is good news indeed," commented Shamala.

"Yes, and Father Juan Thaddeus' experience and common sense will be invaluable."

"I beg your pardon?" Shamala exclaimed. "Father Juan—a bishop?"

"Yes, Bishop Thaddeus. Did I not tell you? An excellent appointment, for which I may claim some credit. For it required some exercise of the art of persuasion and negotiation to bring it about. The friar protested that the rule of his order and the vows he had taken forbade the acceptance of hieratical office. But those prohibitions had been waived by papal dispensation. And then, he said, he was but a simple religious, unfit for ecclesiastical responsibility and having neither the calling nor the manner to sit the episcopal throne and to deal with prelates and princes. Ha! A man who had lived for so many years among the splendors of an Oriental court! Such protests only revealed the profound humility of the friar."

"Are you unwell, my lady?" Shamala heard Monsignor exclaiming in her ear, and she heard him calling to the driver to stop the carriage. "It is only a little nausea," she protested faintly. Monsignor's servant fetched a casket of aromatics, but Shamala waved it aside. The opened door brought in a breath of air from the Italian countryside, and she begged that they drive on. She assured Monsignor that she was quite recovered; in any case she wished to reach Rome without delay. As they drove on, Monsignor resumed the thread of his narration.

"The appointment was confirmed, of course, for the Carmelite friar was the only man for the post. And Bishop Thaddeus has shown his grasp of practical as well as spiritual realities, for besides his miter and crozier he is carrying with him to Persia a printing press with Persian characters. It will be, I understand, the first printing press in that land, and should prove a powerful aid in spreading the Gospel."

"He has always been concerned with disseminating the Scriptures in the vernacular," said Shamala. "When will his consecration take place?"

"He has already been consecrated. It is now two months past since he left Rome to take up his duties."

"Two months past?"

"He went by way of Spain, expecting to take passage on one of the Portuguese fleet, that makes the winter route around the Cape."

"Yes, Spain is his native land," remarked Shamala mechanically. "No doubt he wished also to revisit the scenes of his youth which he had not seen since taking orders."

"Possibly," assented Monsignor, "but doubtful. The friar, as you are doubtless aware, was a person of few human attachments, one whose loyalty was to the Cross, whose interest was the spread of the Gospel, whose obedience was to the Church, and whose only love was for Our Lady."

He glanced at Shamala for confirmation, but Shamala only gazed at him mutely, and how she felt and what her expression told was a mystery that caused Monsignor to study her for a moment in perplexity, and then compassion, and then to turn his head away.

"Yonder is an excellent inn," he said after a moment. "It is a trifle early for stopping, but my lady appears fatigued, and unless your urgency to reach Rome is great, I suggest—"

"It is of no consequence," broke in Shamala apathetically. "Let us stop."

The morning after her arrival in Rome, Shamala had herself driven to the familiar district of Trastevere, across the Tiber, to the Church of Santa Maria della Scala, to make her confession and to commune, and afterward to speak to the pastor concerning permission to bury her husband in the consecrated ground of the church. A solemn Mass was being celebrated when she entered the sanctuary—a requiem Mass, she saw, for the furnishings of the altar and the vestments were black; but the collect had already been read and she did not hear for whom it was being sung.

She quietly approached the altar and knelt at the transept. As always, but particularly after a long journey, the Mass was a soothing balm, and filled her with a peace of soul that was like a spring welling up within her. She whispered a prayer for the unknown dead for whom intercession was now being offered. He must have been a person of some consequence, for the whole community was present, and the celebrant she recognized as the Father General of the Carmelite Congregation, none other than Father Paul Simon, the Carmelite prior of the little band that had gone to Persia a quarter-century before.

In the congregation were a number of high Church dignitaries, as was plain from the amount of crimson and ermine in evidence. The celebrant was reading the Epistle:

Brethren: We will not have you ignorant concerning them that are asleep, that you be not sorrowful, even as others who have no hope. For if we believe that Jesus died and rose again, even so them who have slept through Jesus will God bring with him. For this we say unto you in the word of the Lord, that we who are alive, who remain until the coming of the Lord, shall not prevent them who have slept. For the Lord himself shall come down from heaven, with commandment, and with the voice of an archangel, and with the trumpet of God; and the dead who are in Christ shall rise first. Then we who are alive, who are left, shall be taken up together with them in the clouds to meet Christ, into the air: and so shall we be always with the Lord. Wherefore, comfort ye one another with these words.

What precious comfort was in those words of the Apostle, Shamala thought, as she murmured the *Deo Gratias*. The assembled friars, sitting in the choir stalls, sang the Gradual, and the incense was blessed, after which the *Dies Irae* was sung. The Mass proceeded to its grand climax, the Consecration, and with the ringing of the bell a profound disturbance passed over Shamala, and it seemed to her that at that moment she was lifted up, as never before, in the mystic Sacrifice, close to the heart of God, to the mystery of all life, in which she found understanding of her own longings and the sources of the inner joy she had known, and the identification of herself with all the purity and love for which she had striven.

She moved to the altar, kneeled, and received the Host, while the celebrant recited over her head the comforting *Corpus Domini*.

The Father General had returned to the high altar to recite the post-Communion prayer for the departed:

"Grant, we pray, almighty God, that the soul of thy servant Joannes Thaddeus which has departed out of this world . . ."

It was much later that Shamala learned the circumstances—how Fray Juan, riding through the mountains of Catalonia on his way to Lisbon, was thrown from his mule, receiving head injuries from which he died the following day. At the moment all strength went out of her, and all the joy which the sacred Mass had conferred was dissolved. She could not subdue her weeping. She was aware that the

Mass had ended: the chanting of the assembled friars had diminished to a whisper; Shamala could hear the celebrant departing, accompanied by his deacon and the acolytes; the sacristan was extinguishing the candles on the high altar. Gradually the lights of the church were lowered, until the only illumination was that from the ruby lamps before the images and an aqueous gray that sifted through the clerestory windows. A single candle burned before the Tabernacle to signify the Divine Presence within.

Shamala lifted her head and gazed at the altar, and she observed, for the first time, the altarpiece high above the Tabernacle. An ordinary gilt sunburst it was, a cluster of diverging bars that caught and reflected the light from the candles below. It was much bedimmed by candle smoke. At the moment, however, perhaps the effect of her weeping, it seemed to Shamala to glow with an incandescence, and to be a nimbus through which the face of a saint shone, tender and compassionate and immaculate.

Glossary

ABBASSI	A gold coin struck by Shah Abbas
ALLAH HAZRAT	God's Presence (form of address to the Shah)
ARBAAB	Head man, proprietor
BEGUM	Lady, one of the four lawful wives of the Shah
CHARVADAR	A contractor of beasts and vehicles for hire, a muleteer
CHERAGH	A lamp or lantern
CHERAGHANI	A display of illumination by lanterns at a fête
DARUGHA	Magistrate
DEV	A malign supernatural spirit, demon
ESFAND	The last month in the Persian solar calendar, corresponding to February 21–March 21
FARSAKH	Measure of length, today approximately four miles; traditionally, an hour's journey by mule, the distance varying according to the terrain. The word is the modern equivalent of the *parasang* referred to by Herodotus and others.
FERASH	A keeper of the tents, corresponding to a janitor
FIRENGHI	A European (corruption of *Frank*)
FIRENGHISTAN	Europe
FIRMAN	Royal decree or writ
GABA	A long, tightly fitting outer coat with a flaring skirt, a redingote
GACH	Plaster lime
GINJIL	A Turkish or Caucasian dagger with a broad, curved blade
HANIM	(variant of *khanum*, feminine of *khan*) Madam. *Hanim* is a Turkish word, but in Shah Abbas's time Turkish was commonly spoken at court
HARAM	The women's quarters of the royal palace; also, a Mohammedan sacred place, forbidden to infidels. (Arabic, *forbidden*)

287

ILKHAN	A tribal ruler, a Mongol prince
IVAN	A vault open at one end. Ivans, a distinctive Persian development, were anciently employed as throne or audience chambers. Their modern descendants are found in the concert shells of parks and open-air theaters. The ivans at the Shrine of the Imam Reza in Meshed are gateways recessed within an ogive vault.
JINNI	(plural, *jinn*) One of a class of supernatural beings subject to magical control
KAFKAS	The Caucasus
KAISAR	Caesar, emperor
KALENTAR	Governor of a city or a sub-province
KASHA	(Syriac) A Christian preacher or religious teacher
KATKHODA	Headman of a village
KAVAH	Coffee, which was introduced into Europe from Persia, probably by the Sherley brothers. At first opposed as an infidel drink, it was sanctioned as a beverage by Clement VIII. It was grown in Yemen, Arabia. It is little used in modern Iran, where tea has supplanted coffee as the common beverage; but teahouses are still known as *kavah khanehs*.
KAVIR	The Salt Desert (properly *Dasht-i-Kavir*, Plains of Salt)
KEBAB	Meat roasted on a skewer
KHAN	A tribal ruler, also a title of rank
KHATCHATURAN	Armenian Epiphany celebration
KHODJA	(Turkish) A Moslem preacher or religious teacher, a mullah
KHWAJEH NAZAR	Title of the chief of the Armenian community at the time of Shah Abbas
KUCHEH	An alley
LUT	Desert
MAIDAN	A public square, plaza
MALEK	King
MASJID	Mosque
MAST	A milk ferment, yoghurt
MOHR	A pellet of earth used in Moslem ritualistic prayer
MOUFLON	Wild sheep
MUJTAHID	A Moslem ecclesiastical officer, chief of a mosque
NAFT	Naphtha

NAIB TOLLIEH	The chief administrator of the Shrine of the Imam Reza
NOO ROOZ	Persian New Year, corresponding to March 21st
OSTANDAR	Governor of a province
PEDAR	Father
QIZILBASHIE(S)	Literally Red Heads, from the red turbans they wore; the Imperial troops, as distinguished from the tribal levies
RUD	River
SALDAN	A military title corresponding to lieutenant or captain
SEYYID	A descendant of the Prophet Mohammed. As a mark of distinction they generally wear a green turban, or green cummerbund, green being their identifying color.
SHAH NAMEH	Chronicles of the Kings, title of Firdausi's epic poem
SHAHDOKHT	Princess, daughter of a shah
SHARIYA	Moslem religious law
SHERBET	Iced fruit drink
SIRDAR	Military title of general
SITAR	A three stringed lute. (Lit. "three strings." Probably the original from which *zither* and *guitar* are intermediately derived.)
TAKHTIRIVAN	A litter borne by two camels tandem
TAQIA	Doctrine of Shia Islam that justifies dissimulation for the faith or concealment of one's religious faith in case of necessity
TOMAN	A unit of monetary value
ULEMA	A body of scholars trained in Moslem religion and law; also, the body of Moslem tradition and law

√